The Same But Different

SERENA CLARKE

FREE
BIRD
BOOKS

Copyright © 2014 Serena Clarke
www.serenaclarke.com

The Same But Different
Free Bird Books
ISBN 978-0-473-28304-9

Cover design by Books Covered

For my sisters.
(I should tell you why more often.)

Praise for *The Same But Different*

"A beautiful story about one woman's adventure of a lifetime."
– Written Love

"You can't help but want to keep reading. It's not just romance literature, but also a story about sisterhood, loss and finding yourself. Extremely glad I found this book and *All Over The Place!*"
– Amazon reader

"Plenty of steamy tension...a recommended fun, feel-good story with some unexpected twists and surprises."
– WiLoveBooks

Praise for *All Over the Place*

"Filled with rich, deep emotion, engaging characters and dialogue, and plenty of intrigue that kept me turning the pages...Ms. Clarke is certainly an author to keep an eye out for!"
– Storm Goddess Book Reviews

"This book reminded me of a great chick-flick kind of movie, only in book form. And everyone knows the book is always better!"
– SMI Book Club

"One of the best, most romantic, awe-inspiring and awwwww-inspiring happily ever afters I've read in a long time. Brava, Serena Clarke! I plan to read more by you."
– Random Book Muses

Chapter One

A last wish is not to be argued with. Unless it comes from your mother, who's been driving you mad for years, and she only *thinks* she's dying.

Cady Morrow sighed, reaching across to adjust the pillows to a more comfortable angle. "You daft thing. You're not going anywhere." She smoothed a few stray hairs from her mother's flushed cheek, but she slapped Cady's hand away.

"Just promise me! It's important."

"Mum, don't be melodramatic. The last test results were pretty good, remember?" She pressed a glass of water into her mother's fragile hand, and she took a token sip. But she wasn't going to be diverted.

"Look, I'm the one in this damn body, and I know how I feel." She passed the water back. "Cady, just promise." Her pale blue eyes were vivid with determination in her thin face.

Cady gave in. "Okay. I promise."

Stubborn. That was Anne Morrow's defining characteristic. Or bloody-minded, more like. Luckily Cady had inherited her father's patience, or she might have cracked under the pressure of caring for her mum, charming and crabby in equal, unpredictable measure. Just the night before, she'd dreamed again about running away, joining the California flash mob she'd discovered on YouTube and was following on Twitter. A twenty-five-year-old runaway... bit tragic really. No surprise they didn't follow her back— between working at the bank and looking after her mum, there wasn't much worth tweeting about in *her* life.

Now her mother struggled to sit up. "This isn't what I wanted for you. I want you to get out and have some fun. Travel. Have some adventures. Find a gorgeous man."

Cady shrugged. "I'm okay, really." And as for men, her most recent experience hadn't inspired her to try again any time soon. Gorgeous or otherwise, she was in no hurry.

"I want you to be more than okay. And you will be, eventually." Anne sighed and leaned back on her pillows again. "There's something...important. I've been carrying it with me for years. I almost didn't tell you, but now I'm on my way out—"

"Mum! You're not on your way anywhere."

"Shh!" She shook her head. "Just listen! Now I'm on my way out, I have to tell you. But you're not to tell your father, or Shelby. One day she might need to know, of course. But not now. She's not ready."

"Well...okay." Cady felt her stomach tighten as she realized this must be something big after all. Keeping a secret from her father and sister was no small thing.

"Cady." Her mother's voice was steady now. "This will be a big promise to keep. But you're the one who can bear the weight. I think you should sit down."

She sat. And heard the news that turned her world on end.

★

Cady watched as her sister re-read the solicitor's letter, her forehead crinkling as she tried to make sense of the contents. There was a deep, settled kind of quiet in the wood-paneled solicitor's office. It wouldn't last. Cady knew what would happen as soon as Shelby had finished reading.

"What the hell is *this*?" Shelby stood up and waved the letter in the air, almost knocking over the standard lamp next to her chair. "Where did she get all this money?"

The solicitor, Mr. Palmer-Hatch, cleared his throat. "Miss Morrow," he began, looking anxious. "Anne—Mrs. Morrow—asked me, ¦as an executor of her will, to personally advise you both of this endowment. I myself know nothing about the origin of the money, only that it was to go to you in equal shares." He pushed his glasses back up the bridge of his nose and looked at Cady, clearly hoping she would deal with her twin sister.

They might be twins, but they couldn't be more different. She could only shrug apologetically. At times like these it was better to stand way back and let Shelby run her course, like a tornado.

"Can I read yours?" Cady grabbed the paper that Shelby was still waving around, and scanned it. Exactly the same as hers. She'd wondered if her mother might have decided to confess—but no. Cady was still the only one who knew the truth. Shelby snatched the letter back, and resumed questioning poor Mr. Palmer-Hatch, who had retreated behind his wide, leather-topped desk.

Cady could imagine all too well the hurricane-strength drama that Shelby would turn on when she finally found out that their dad—their sweet, steady, loving dad—was not their dad at all. After years of trying, and none of the babies they so desperately wanted, Anne had taken action. A liaison with a younger man, a visiting American, who would remain none the wiser. A necessary deception, in her mind. On the wrong side of forty for baby-making (though still ten years younger than her husband), she had no idea if it would work. But it had—twice as well as she'd hoped. And amongst the man's belongings, Anne had seen a photo of him with two young women, their arms flung around him. So Cady and Shelby were named after them—his beautiful sisters.

Shelby would be gale-force furious, Cady knew. She was still trying to process it herself, all the wrongs and rights. How could her mother have done it, and then kept it a secret? On the other hand, if she hadn't done it, neither of them would be here to get mad about it.

Anne had been right about one thing—she'd passed away the day after their talk. Cady had answered the phone at work to the news that blindsided her. She hadn't for a moment believed that her mother—feisty, determined, maddening—was really about to die, and the two shockwaves in two days left her reeling. She'd lost a father one day, her mother the next. Anne was free of her secret, and mercifully free of the illness that had progressively shrunk her life into a smaller and increasingly painful existence. But now Cady was the one carrying that secret, along with the grief of her losses. And somewhere out there, their biological father was going about his life, unaware that he had twin daughters.

She looked at the letter, with the astonishingly large figure right there in black and white. Or maybe he did know.

Maybe there was more to this secret than her mother had confessed.

★

Shelby had gone straight off from the solicitor's office in a rage. Cady figured she'd probably calm down a little once it sank in that the money was hers to spend however she wanted—wherever it came from.

Shelby's tastes ran to far finer things than she could fund with her admin job at an architectural firm, and her taste in men ran to a correspondingly higher income bracket. High drama was her way of dealing with everything that happened, good or bad. And while Shelby was grieving for their mum too, she was also dealing with the fact that they'd never seen eye to eye—and never properly made peace after Shelby flounced out of home in a teenage fit, and found her own place to live.

As for Cady, she'd spent years caring for their mum, and increasingly their dad too. Living at home, working in the bank, responsible and careful and...dull. Dull as the navy blue uniform she pulled on every morning to go to work. Dull as the dishwater she plunged her hands into every night, because her parents agreed a dishwasher was a waste of money. Now she squirted too much dishwashing liquid into the sink and watched as the bubbles rose up, each little curve reflecting rainbow colors under the kitchen light. Well, she wouldn't have done it any differently. And now certainly wasn't the time to falter.

Her dad came into the kitchen, struggling to carry a plate and manage his walking stick. She hurried to take the plate from him. "You shouldn't worry about that!"

He smiled at her, his face a soft map of smile and worry lines. "And neither should you. Come on, let's have a talk."

She turned off the water and followed him into the living room. He sank carefully into his chair, the new ergonomically correct one that had replaced his beloved easy chair when his arthritis got too bad. Cady sat opposite on the sofa. No one had yet sat in her mother's favorite chair, even when all the mourners had come back after the funeral, and there weren't enough seats for everyone.

She'd gone through the motions, organizing the funeral and doing what needed to be done. Shelby wept, her loss accentuated by regret as she counted all the ways she'd pushed her mother away. But as Cady hugged long-lost family members and old friends, receiving their heartfelt condolences, her own grief stuck in her throat.

"Poor Cady," she overheard a neighbor telling her mum's Aunt Netta in the kitchen. "She's being so stoic, isn't she?"

"She's strong, like her mother," Aunt Netta said. "But it'll hit her eventually."

Cady retreated back into the living room before they noticed her. Stoic? Stunned, more like. No one knew the secret she was trying to get to grips with, along with her mother's death. It felt like she didn't really know this woman she was mourning after all.

Now her father regarded her as they sat in the quiet

house. "This has been hard for all of us, hasn't it?"

She nodded, her eyes filling with tears. Between the two of them, their whole lives had revolved around her mum. Caring for her as she battled against the rare autoimmune illness that had taken too long to diagnose, and too short a time to defeat her. And all the while, her dad struggled against the arthritis that was spreading its gnarly grip through his body. In the second half of his seventies, she knew he was tired, but he'd never have admitted it while Anne needed looking after. His patience—the patience she'd thought she inherited from him—and his love had kept him going. Her heart ached every time she remembered what he didn't know.

"I've thought a lot about what I'd do, when this time came," he said. "And I've decided. I'm going to go into a retirement community."

"A home? Dad, you don't have to do that."

"I know I don't *have* to. But I'm going to. Remember my friend Bill, from Rotary? He seems very well set up in his apartment at Ingleside Heights. There's a swimming pool, and a library, and clubs to join and all sorts." He looked around the small living room. "Anne always wanted to stay in the house. But what would I do here without her?"

"I'll be here!" There was no way she'd leave the man who'd been her father in every way, if he needed her. The guilt of keeping the secret about her 'real' father was killing her, but how could she tell him? Even if she hadn't promised her mother, he'd had enough heartbreak.

"You're very welcome to stay in the house if you want to. If that's the case, we won't sell it. But...don't you think it's time you had that adventure? Take that bit of money Anne left you. Do it for her."

The money. She could only guess that it had come from their biological father. How else would their mother, who'd only ever done volunteer work, have independently come up with such a sum for each of them? One day, there would be money from Aunt Netta, but she'd outlived her niece. Shelby was trying to guess too, of course, and driving

Cady mad with questions. Neither of them had told their dad how much it was—they both felt too uncomfortable about it. And he hadn't asked, just said that Anne had had a savings account for each of them, right from when they were born. As far as he knew, she'd been putting some of the housekeeping money away every week. Nothing too unusual there, on the surface—except for the amount. Even the magic of compound interest surely couldn't explain that.

"What?" she joked now, feeling awkward that the money topic had come up. "Go, and give up my thrilling job at the bank?"

He laughed. "You should have given that up years ago. Or at least taken one of those promotions you were offered." At the sight of her shocked face, he said, "One of the Rotary fellows works there too. I know you turned down jobs that would have taken you to bigger things...away from here. After you and Jeremy broke up, we would have loved to see you have some fun."

"Oh, well..." Even newly single (which was actually for the best, once she found out how self-absorbed Jeremy really was) there was no way she could have taken any of those offers. Who would have looked after her parents? Shelby was utterly useless.

He pointed to her laptop, her portal to the world, sitting on the coffee table. "Go and live a little. I'll be fine."

If she opened it now, Twitter would spring back to the screen, a stream of other people's achievements and opinions and excitement. Maybe he was right, and her mother too. Maybe it was time to add some more-than-okay tweets of her own.

Chapter Two

The plane tilted as it circled for landing, and Cady caught a glimpse of a bridge below. Was it the right color to be the Golden Gate? She leaned across to see better out the window. Wodges of San Francisco's trademark fog clung to the hills, but the blue sky and blue ocean held a Californian promise of...something.

"Get off!" Shelby elbowed her in the ribs.

"Ow, that hurt!" She glared at her sister, now awake, her hair on end and her face crabby. "You had the window seat all the way across America. And you slept through most of it. I'm having a look."

"Whatever." Shelby rolled her eyes and made a great show of straightening the blanket over her knees.

Cady rolled her eyes in return, but she was more interested in the new territory outside the window than in re-traversing the old ground of their relationship. She was actually surprised that Shelby was here at all. After years of playing the role of wild child, she'd been suddenly circumspect when Cady said she was going to the States, and would Shelby like to come too?

"Oh, I don't know," she'd said. "I have things going on here. And is it a good idea, really? It's not your kind of thing, surely."

Straight away, Cady felt her blood pressure rise. "What's my kind of thing? Staying home like an old maid?"

"No, you'll probably get another boyfriend eventually, I suppose. And you're not old! I mean, we're the same age."

Cady waited for more, but that was it. "I have a life to live, the same as you." As she'd said it, she realized how true it was. "I thought you'd be up for an adventure. You love being the wild one."

Shelby shrugged, bypassing Cady's point. "I just think, well, are you sure? Have you really thought it through?"

Cady thought back to all the nights she'd sat in bed switching between YouTube, Twitter and Facebook, her little MacBook on her lap, but only after tucking her mother in, and with one ear on alert for any sounds from the bedroom. Now she gave her sister a sharp look. "I've had plenty of time to think about it. As you know. Or *would* know, if you'd been there."

Shelby ignored the jibe. "Well, yes, but...what about Dad?"

Now they were getting to the truth of it. She'd always avoided responsibility, relying on Cady to be the sensible sister. She obviously didn't want to take anything on now, either.

"Let me get this straight. I've been here for years and years, looking after Mum, while you've played around town. And now she's gone." She pressed her fingers to her eyes. "Dad's got a plan, and so have I. What about you?"

"I have all *kinds* of things happening here." She looked sideways, avoiding her sister's eye. "I can't up and leave right now."

Cady snorted. So much for the wild child. "Here's a chance to go and *do* something, and not only do *you* not want to go, you don't want *me* to go either. I don't know why I even asked you."

The thump, rattle and roll of landing brought her back to now. She'd given up her job—no great sacrifice, although they'd told her to come back any time—and the sum of her old life was packed into her dad's storage shed at Ingleside Heights. Now, there were things to do. Shelby was here, for better or worse, and there was only the two of them—sisters, come what may. She'd had a dad pulled out from under her feet, but there was no doubting her twinness with Shelby. Whatever this California adventure might bring, they'd be doing it together. However much they might drive each other mental.

They edged their way off the plane and cleared customs, a tedious procedure of scanning and scrutiny that made them both feel guilty even though they had nothing to hide. Finally out in the arrivals hall, they watched other passengers being enveloped in hugs. Joyful welcomes from families, friends and lovers played out in English, Spanish, and languages Cady couldn't identify. The two of them stood for a moment and watched a mother tearfully embrace her newly arrived daughter. They looked at each other, both thinking the same thing—they'd never have a reunion like it again. They both knew well enough, from different angles, how difficult and obstinate their mother was. But she'd loved them with the same determination—even if Shelby, too much her mother's daughter, had cut and run. It was unbelievable that such a force of nature could be gone.

Then Cady hitched her bag on her shoulder and set her suitcase on its wheels. That force of nature wouldn't want to see her fall into a slump now. "Come on," she said, and gave Shelby a nudge. "Let's find a taxi. San Francisco awaits, and we need flowers in our hair. Let's go."

★

The taxi driver gave them a wink as he dropped them off outside their bed and breakfast on Valencia. "Double trouble in the Mission."

They'd heard that one before. Shelby gave a 'pfft' and shook her hair, ignoring him to study the neighborhood. Cady made a quick calculation—how much should you tip a cab driver?—and pressed some notes into his hand. By the look on his face when he saw the amount, she knew she'd paid too much. Damn. Well, she'd call it good karma. They weren't in Haight-Ashbury, but good vibes wouldn't go astray.

As the cab pulled away she looked at Shelby standing on the pavement in the sunshine, her hair flowing down her back. A bit of paisley and a headband and she'd be right at home in 1960s San Francisco.

Of course whatever Shelby suited, Cady did too. The two of them had never felt the need to purposefully have wildly different hairstyles or clothes, maybe because they were such polar opposites in personality that no one would mistake one for the other, no matter how similar they looked. They weren't identical twins, but to look at them, they could have been. Perfectly run-of-the-mill long, straight, light brown hair, or honey chestnut, as Shelby preferred to call it. Blue eyes. Straight nose. Peachy English rose complexion. Pretty good cheekbones. It was all there, twice over. But somehow Shelby carried it off with an extra dash of panache (and now with her new going-on-holiday fake tan). When they went out together, they always attracted attention, but it was Shelby who held that attention, and turned it into an opportunity.

To be honest, Cady had come to prefer it that way, especially after her split with Jeremy. She'd had things to do anyway—apparently she couldn't juggle a man and a social life with looking after her mum. But now...well, this was her new start. There was still no hurry, of course. But who knew what the new Cady might do?

"It's not very hilly," Shelby said. Her tone implied that her sister had chosen the least satisfactory spot in all San Francisco.

Cady looked at the colorful buildings, the vivid street art, and the eclectic characters walking and cycling along the tree-lined street. Über-hip tattooed customers emerged from a thrift store opposite, while on their side of the road a pavement stall sold vinyl records and ragged band posters. If she had to change anything, she'd only replace the trees with palms, to fit the sunny day. Other than that, it was just perfect. She shrugged and pointed to the surrounding hills. "I think we'll have plenty of chances to do some hill-climbing."

They turned to their home for the next few nights, a big Victorian bay-fronted house tucked between two others painted in ice-cream parlor colors. It looked every inch the San Francisco native.

"I need a lie-down," Shelby sighed as they went up the steps.

"You just lay down for about six hours," Cady retorted. "But actually…it would be good to have a rest before dinner. And we can see if there are any Flashpoint updates."

They did have a plan, and it all revolved around Flashpoint. Cady had stumbled across them on YouTube one particularly sleepless night, when Anne was struggling with the side effects of a new treatment. They were a flash mob movement based loosely in San Francisco, led by Kyle Baxter, a social media savvy, charismatic hipster. And, apparently, a slick ladies man. Well, that was his reputation. Cady couldn't see it herself, online. But, give him the benefit of the doubt—maybe the whole hipster thing didn't translate so well to her pebble-dashed London suburb. Charisma was most powerful in person, after all. She'd wait and see.

And he obviously had *something* going on. From their city base, parked in random spots around the Mission district, Kyle and the select few Flashpointers in his inner circle travelled the Bay Area in a stonkingly ostentatious rock star bus. With their Facebook likes growing by the hour, and thousands of Twitter followers, Flashpoint could rally hundreds of participants for a flash mob at short notice. Cady could see that it would be thousands before long.

And the fun of it! It was more than a cheesy dance routine in a shopping mall. Cady had watched them all on YouTube. Completely filling the curves of Lombard Street with color-coordinated flash-mobsters. A jaunty, clattering musical tribute in Chinatown, played entirely on hundreds of pairs of chopsticks. Surrounding the towering column of the Dewey Memorial in Union Square with concentric circles of chanting dancers.

Some of it did verge more on 'mobster' than 'flash'—in the eyes of the authorities, at least. The choreographed bike riding stunt on the Golden Gate bridge cycle lane had gotten them in trouble, when half the city's bicycle messengers showed up unexpectedly, turning it into a melee. But it also brought publicity—the best reward of all for a budding social media phenomenon.

If Kyle was thinking all that up, Cady was willing to overlook the scraggly moustache-less goatee (shudder), the over-gelled quiff, and even the fur vest (faux, she assumed) that he seemed to be constantly wearing. Now she was finally going to join in on one of the flash mobs. And Shelby too, who had put her usual eye-rolling on hold to concede that it was actually pretty cool.

The message had been going out online—a rendezvous at noon the next day in Dolores Park, the center of Mission hipsterism. There was an mp3 file to download, which would guide them through the event, and everyone was asked to wear either black or white. Shelby had baggsed black, of course, so Cady was left to wear what she thought was a very unflattering all-white ensemble. Well, it would be worth it. They had ninety days before their visas expired and they were on a plane home. She intended to make the most of every one of them.

She knew Anne would want her to. She'd kept her mother's secret, despite a thousand questions and endless speculation from Shelby in the weeks since they read their letters. As the days went by, the deception weighed more and more heavily, but the image of her mother, thin and determined in her bed as she extracted Cady's promise, made her hold her tongue. For how long, she didn't know. Didn't Shelby have a right to know, as much as she did?

As they went up the foot-worn steps of their guesthouse, the front door was flung open and a motherly figure came out to greet them. Motherly with tattoos and a nose stud, that was.

"Look at you!" she exclaimed, holding out her hands in welcome. "I knew you were sisters, but you're peas in your own gorgeous pod!"

Shelby stopped in her tracks on the steps, but Cady, with her mother still in her mind, went straight into the waiting embrace. When she stepped back, she found Shelby alongside, waiting for her own hug. Maybe both of them were feeling their loss just as keenly.

"I'm Marian," said their host as she let Shelby go. "Come in, and be at home. While you're here, this is your home as much as it is mine." She gestured for them to come in, and they followed her along the hall and up the staircase, a gentle waft of fragrance—could it be patchouli?—leading them onwards. As she opened the door to their room, she paused, her grey pixie cut making Cady think of Judi Dench—if Judi Dench accessorized hers with a tattoo snaking down her neck and encircling her arm with flowers. She pointed to a door across the hall. "That's the bathroom. It's separate, but it's just for this room, so you're not sharing." She smiled. "When you're ready to head out, come find me downstairs. We'll get you officially signed in then, and I can give you some pointers on good places to eat around here."

"Thank you," they replied in unison.

She laughed. "You guys are too cute. Love that accent. Okay, see you in a while." And she left them to it.

Chapter Three

C ady woke up suddenly. Was that an earthquake?
Disoriented, she brushed the hair from her face and
squinted in the light coming from the window. No, it was a
truck going by, making the old wooden house vibrate. She
looked across at the other bed, where Shelby was curled up
fast asleep, her suitcase still standing unopened in the
middle of the floor. The long plane trip had obviously
caught up with them. How late was it? She checked her
watch, which she'd changed to local time when they
landed. Six thirty. As if in protest, her stomach gave a loud
growl. If it was six thirty here, it was...something, at home.
Whatever, it was ages since she'd eaten. She grabbed up her
toilet bag and headed for the bathroom. San Francisco was
out there, and she wanted to be out there too.

An hour later, they were sitting at a long table in the
café Marian had recommended. Around them, an
assortment of self-assured customers laughed and ate
organic food and sipped coffee in mismatched cups and
saucers.

"Probably skinny-soy-decaf-vanilla-macchiato-lattes,"
said Shelby over the top of her menu, making Cady laugh.

"I dare you to order one of those," she replied.

Their fellow diners, and the wait staff too, ranged from geeky cool to model-agency cool—even the grey-haired ones were more effortlessly camera-ready than Cady knew she could ever hope to be. They gave their order to the surprisingly friendly waiter, and swirled the ice in their diet Cokes while they waited for their food, talking about what might happen tomorrow.

When two guys came in and sat at the other end of their table, Shelby's eyes widened and she pointed behind her hand. "Babe alert," she mouthed, indicating the guy further along her bench.

Cady took a surreptitious look. Yep, he was Shelby's style all right. Tanned, with blond hair swept to one side, and sporting the kind of perma-stubble that takes careful maintenance. Just the right amount of smooth chest showed behind the unhemmed 'v' of his t-shirt. His tight grey cardigan was buttoned up, and Cady was pretty sure that his large, black-rimmed glasses were purely decorative.

Then she peeked at his companion, sitting further along the bench on her side of the table. Oh, mercy. She sucked in her breath, her heart doing a little hop in her chest. This one was more rugged, with dark hair, a strong profile, and a properly trimmed goatee (the only kind of beard Cady could tolerate). He was wearing a regular-issue black tee, just tight enough to set off his substantial build. No man-cardi coddled his broad shoulders. And there were no man accessories either, apart from several thin leather bracelets on the same wrist as his watch. But—he was sporting the kind of messy little ponytail that gave her the screaming heebie jeebies. Brad Pitt, Colin Farrell, David Beckham…there wasn't a man alive who could successfully pull off a ponytail, in her opinion. Mostly, 'shave and a haircut' was her rule of thumb, when it came to men. The more elaborate the hair (face and head), the more inflated the ego, in her experience. Jeremy had been conclusive proof of that, with his Beckham-ish obsession with styling and restyling.

She took another quick glance at the two of them. On her side of the table, ponytail guy reached out and picked up a menu, and she couldn't help appreciating the way his arm and shoulder muscles flexed, surely more than was strictly necessary. He said something to his friend and grinned, making a dimple flash in his cheek. The friend laughed heartily, adjusting his glasses and re-sweeping his fringe across to the side.

"Probably gay," she whispered back to Shelby, mostly to annoy her, and she pouted in exaggerated disappointment. Laughing, Cady distracted her by asking about the latest boyfriend she'd left behind in London, and she was soon recounting the disappointing last date they'd had. As she talked on, Cady nodded and made the right noises, trying not to take peeks at ponytail guy. He wasn't even her *type*, for goodness' sake.

When the guys had ordered, they handed their menus to the waiter, and the object of Shelby's admiration turned his attention their way.

"What are you lovely ladies doing in this neighborhood? Sounds like you're a way from home."

Shelby was instantly nonchalant. "Yeah," she said cooly. "London was getting kind of same-y."

He raised a well-groomed eyebrow. "London? There must be plenty to keep you busy there. Where do you live, like, in a manor house or something?"

Cady laughed. "Not many manor houses in Peckham Rye."

Ponytail guy turned to her and smiled, the dimple she'd seen on his left cheek now matched by one on the other side. His nose was a tiny bit crooked, as though it had been broken at some stage. "We have no idea where that is," he said. "With those accents you could tell us you lived in a castle, and we'd probably believe you."

"I'll try that next time." She smiled back, caught in his gaze. From this angle she couldn't see the ponytail— instead, she found herself transfixed by his eyes. They were a really remarkable light golden brown. Like a tiger... She worked to pull herself back into focus, also trying not to notice the way his t-shirt stretched across his broad chest. Or the surprising size of those tanned arms. Or the sharp angle of the clean-shaven part of his jaw, and the shadow where it met that tender spot right by his ear... She cleared her throat. God, what had she been going to say? She got herself together.

"This is actually the most middle-of-the-road accent there is. I'm Cady, by the way."

"Reid." He held out a large hand. "Pleased to meet you, m'lady."

Despite herself, she blushed and laughed. "Oh, stop." But she let him give her a firm handshake. His hand engulfed hers, warm and smooth, and his thumb pressed gently along the softest part of her hand. Her own thumb itched to slide across and play, but she settled for letting her fingers trail along his as she reluctantly let go. It was barely the tiniest hint of suggestion—she was pretty sure he wouldn't even notice—but after all her dull single months, post-Jeremy, it felt positively wanton. He smiled politely, obviously unaffected by the handshake. She didn't know whether to be disappointed or not.

Shelby and her benchmate Gavin shook on their introductions too, but then he lifted her hand to his lips in a knightly parody, making her giggle. "Your Highness."

"I could get used to that," she said, looking pleased.

"So if you're not here on royal duties, is it a holiday? Or business?" Reid asked.

Cady was kind of reluctant to tell all to a couple of guys they'd just met, even though they seemed okay. But when he regarded her with those eyes, she felt her reserve falter. "Well...holiday really. We're going to have a look around the West Coast. But tomorrow we're joining in with a big flash mob."

Gavin and Reid looked at each other. "Flashpoint," Gavin said.

"Yeah. She's on a mission." Despite her previous enthusiasm, Shelby's tone made it clear she was cooler than that. Just in case Gavin thought Flashpoint was not cool.

Reid looked at Gavin. "Didn't you go to school with him? What was he voted, like, most likely to succeed or something?"

"Nah, he was a real asshole. Pain-in-the-ass trust fund kid." He grinned, and the girls had no idea whether he meant it or not. "Most likely to talk people into doing crazy pointless shit."

"He knows what he's doing though." Reid looked thoughtful. "They've made a splash. Wasn't he trying to negotiate some big sponsorship deals?"

"Dude, you have a point. Being an asshole doesn't prevent you from being a success in this state."

"Yeah, it probably helps." They both laughed and took swigs of their beer.

Cady and Shelby looked at each other. Cady shrugged, trying not to feel disappointed after their thorough dissing of Kyle. Bill and Ted here might be right—but anyway, who cared what a couple of random guys off the street thought of Kyle? It wasn't like she had any special attachment to him. She was just here for the escape, and to join in on something fun and uplifting. God knows she needed it. If a complete dickhead was in charge, so what? He was making things happen.

Purposefully avoiding the unexpected distraction provided by one of those random guys, she looked at the whitewashed brick walls. They were covered with hand-written comments from customers, and doodles from the more artsy ones. She picked up one of the black marker pens sitting in a chipped mug on the table. "I have to do this. Shel?"

But Shelby was engrossed in a story Gavin had started telling, and waved her away.

Reid stood up. "I'll keep you company."

"Oh...okay."

They both edged out from between the long bench and the table, and he held out a hand for her to go first. They wound their way through the other tables and found a small free space on the wall. But standing in front of it, Cady was suddenly stumped.

"How stupid. I can't think what to write. Like when you unexpectedly have to write in a birthday card."

"May I?"

He reached out a hand, and she laid the pen in it. Of its own accord, her hand lingered a moment on his, and she could feel the warmth against her fingers. Then he closed his own fingers around the marker, almost capturing her hand in his before she pulled it back. He gave her a quizzical look, and she was suddenly self-conscious. Wake up, girl, she told herself. One dose of jetlag, and she was going hazy over the first American guy to come near. With the dreaded ponytail, no less, and, if he was here with Gavin, possibly already spoken for. More sleep was what she needed, obviously.

Then he leaned in close to the wall and started drawing. As she watched, captivated, he effortlessly drew a little castle with a moat and battlements. Out of a window gazed a girl with flowing hair and a dreamy expression. Underneath, he wrote in flowing script: *Lady Cady, Castle Middle-of-the-Road, Same-y Lane, London.*

Cady felt her insides tingle as she looked at the sweetly quirky illustration. She peeked sideways at him. "It's perfection. Thank you!"

"Hm. I should have put Shelby somewhere." He tucked a strand of dark hair behind his ear and tapped the marker pen against his chin, considering.

"Nah. She's such a pain in the arse."

He grinned. "I like it. Aah-s." With his cruisy, laid-back way of talking, he made it sound just right.

She laughed. "Oh, right, sorry. Ass." She worked to perfect it in an American accent. "Aaass."

"Aaah-s," he countered, a wicked challenge in his expression.

"Aaaassss."

A passing waiter gave them a curious look, and Cady suddenly realized she was standing in a public place, shooting a curse word back and forth. She blushed, but Reid was on a roll. "Aah-s," he whispered back.

"Seriously, stop!" she admonished him, shaking her head even as she laughed.

They both looked back at the table, where Shelby and Gavin were deep in conversation. Just then, Gavin stood up and flung his arms out to illustrate whatever story he was telling, then sat back down again.

"If she *is* a pain in the ass, they'll get along great—he's a complete doofus." Reid shook his head in mock exasperation, a smile softening the insult.

"They drive you mad, right? I say that in a loving way, of course." She smiled, and he returned it to her, the warmth in his golden eyes making her feel suddenly at home. "So you guys are..." She let the almost-question hang in the air.

He looked at her for a moment, then laughed. "You're kidding me."

She blushed, immediately realizing her wrong assumption. "Oh, God...sorry!"

"That's okay." He was unfazed. "He's not my type. At *all*."

And Reid was nothing like *her* type. Shave and a haircut, after all. But still, she found herself waiting to hear what he'd say next, wanting to stand just that little bit closer, tempted to let her gaze linger on those amused golden-brown eyes. Well, despite his straightness, this uncharacteristic attraction to a signed-up ponytail guy had to stop. She was blaming it on that jetlag. Sure, it was nice to know her man receptors hadn't completely seized up after her dull years—in fact, they were working at maximum with him around—but there was no point in getting any more hot and bothered on his account. Tomorrow they were doing the flash mob, and then the West Coast, and maybe beyond, was hers to explore. Even if it was with her pain-in-the-aaass sibling along for the ride.

"Come on, our food's there."

She looked over to see that all four of their meals had arrived at the same time, so they went back to the table and sat down. But before they had a chance to talk any more, two long-legged, sun-kissed girls arrived and greeted Gavin and Reid with loud exclamations and a great show of cheek-kissing. The girls stepped into the middle spots on the bench seats, giving Cady and Shelby narrow looks before turning their backs to drape themselves over the guys. The signal was clear—the California girls had ownership. Reid sent an apologetic look their way, and Cady smiled and gave a little 'that's okay' wave. She didn't have the legs, the tan or the inclination to take that on.

Shelby looked like a baby who'd had her candy snatched away, but Cady passed her the pink salt (Himalayan and kosher, according to the jar) and shook her head. "Just eat," she advised her sister.

Shelby frowned, but obeyed. The food was too good to let go cold, anyway, and they were properly hungry. If they both suddenly wished they'd ordered carb-free salads instead of open burgers—the new arrivals were very thin indeed—well, it was too late. Cady made a supreme effort, and avoided looking along the table until they stood up to leave. Then she glanced over, and caught Reid's eye. He smiled and mouthed *bye*. She did the same, taking one last look at his handsome face. That was a *very* nice distraction, on the first day of her new start.

As they left to walk back to the guesthouse, Shelby looked accusingly at Cady. "You were *so* wrong. Just because someone's a bit original in their style, and looks after themselves nicely, it doesn't mean they're gay, you know."

"I know that! Jeesh. Thanks for the lesson in political correctness." Looking at her sister's reproving face, she sighed. This could turn out to be a long and trying holiday. "Remind me again why I asked you to come with me?"

"Whatever." Shelby stuck out her tongue. She was obviously still peeved at losing out to a twosome even more terrible than herself.

"You and those California girls are made for each other." Cady tried not to think about one of those girls in particular, and what she might be doing later...

Then she stopped, mid-pavement. "Chris Hemsworth."

"Ooh, can you see him?" Shelby looked hopefully up and down the street. "What about him?"

Cady laughed. "The exception that proves the rule." Okay, there *was* one guy who could pull off the ponytail.

Maybe two, now.

And maybe the new Cady (whoever she was) would turn out to be the kind of girl who was susceptible to a ponytail, with a hint of rock god-ness, combined with artistic flair and mesmerizing honey-brown eyes. An interesting development. But she'd have to wait until the next ponytail guy came along to test that theory. For now, it was time to focus on her new, tweet-worthy start—starting tomorrow.

Chapter Four

Dolores Park was teeming with people by eleven thirty the following day. From their vantage point partway up the sloping hill, Cady and Shelby watched people of all shapes, sizes and shades—young and old, California sleek and lay-it-all-out large—mingle and talk and laugh as they waited for noon. Cady was heartened to see how many people had come for the white team, and by how many of them clearly hadn't wondered *Does my butt look big in this?* for even a moment.

She and Shelby had watched the instruction video for the day's flash mob on YouTube, and downloaded the mp3 file that would talk them through the routine. Watching footage of the other flash mobs had given them an idea of how big the event might be, but they were still unprepared for the sheer number of people and the electric atmosphere. Judging by the heavy greeny-sweet aroma wafting by every now and then, the 'atmosphere' was obviously being enhanced by some. It seemed wholly appropriate. They could see the Flashpoint bus down in the parking lot, looking just like it did on the website—a gigantic silver coach, both retro and space-age at the same time. It towered over the cars around it, proud and shining in the sun.

From where they stood, the view out over the city was spectacular, and Cady felt a thrill at finally being there. Their mum would have loved this. She made a note to send their dad a postcard at his new place. Maybe postcards were old school, but he'd like it. And it wasn't like he'd be on Facebook any time soon, after all.

She took out her phone. "Come on," she said to Shelby. "I need a photo of you with this view."

Shelby jutted one hip forward and put her hands on her waist, tipping her head sideways in an exaggerated supermodel pose. With strands of hair blowing across her face in the Pacific breeze, she actually could have been in an editorial shoot.

"Next stop *Vogue*," Cady laughed, as she took the photo.

Shelby came and looked at the screen. "Oh! That's a good one." Beyond her model self, and then the scattered crowd and assorted palm trees, the jumble of city buildings shone with possibility in the late July sun.

Cady nodded. "It's a great photo. And you look so much like Mum."

It was true. As well as the same features, which they all shared of course, she had the same determined look, the same set to her chin.

"I do." She frowned, thinking. "Where *did* that money come from? I've thought and thought about it. What do you think, really?"

Cady hesitated. "I don't know." Strictly speaking, it was true.

Then, to her relief, a voice came over the loudspeakers. "Hey everyone! Thanks for coming today." A cheer went up from the crowd, and when it died down, the voice continued. "Can everyone take their places now please, and don't forget to be a friend to those around you. Let's make some history!"

Cady felt a rush of excitement as they watched the crowd slowly begin to split into two blocks of color. "Shel, come on. It's starting." She started to head down the slope.

"Wait!" Shelby grabbed her arm. "Where will we find

each other again?"

She thought for a moment. New start, starting now...

"Meet me at the bus. I'm going to say hello to them afterwards."

"Really?" Shelby looked at her. "Who gave you a shot of courage?"

"Been breathing too deeply up here, maybe." Cady grinned. "Now go! Your people need you."

Shelby set off to the black-clothed half of the park, putting her earbuds in as she went, and Cady jogged down to the white half. There was a happy, inclusive vibe amongst her own white-clad people, and although she was alone she felt totally at ease. Up above, camera cranes were ready to film on each side of the park, and she spotted more guys with full-size video cameras on their shoulders. It was a proper production—maybe they could convince their dad to find his way to YouTube to watch it later.

At exactly noon, the flash mobsters all pressed play on their recorded instructions. The introductory music swelled in Cady's ears, atmospheric and uplifting, then a deep, resonant voice began to speak.

"Welcome to today's special flash mob event. We love that you came to share this unique experience. Please follow the instructions, and enjoy our time together as two sides become one. First, please shake hands with the people around you."

There was a lot of giggling and bashful faces, but everyone obligingly shook hands with their neighbors, as though they were in a strange and silent, but welcoming, outdoor church.

"That's great," the voice continued. "Now, on the count of three, please jump in the air five times."

At the countdown, everyone jumped—slightly out of sync and not especially gracefully, but with plenty of enthusiasm.

"Wonderful. Now, please spread your arms and spin around five times, then five times in the opposite direction. Take care not to collide with anyone."

Cady hadn't spun around like that in years, and it only

took a few rotations before she started to feel dizzy. But as she finished whirling around in the sun, surrounded by other laughing people whose heads were obviously also spinning, she thought that it was high time she pushed herself a little off center. Actually, that was the whole point of this trip.

The people who hadn't come for the flash mob—who were just enjoying a sunny afternoon in the park—looked perplexed at first. Some of them even looked worried at being surrounded by crowds of seemingly possessed people, all going through the silent motions of some unknown routine. But soon bystanders were getting out their phones and taking photos, laughing at the scene playing out in front of them.

"Excellent," intoned the voice in Cady's ears. "Now, please turn and face the other team, at the opposite end of the park." She turned and shaded her eyes, trying to spot Shelby amongst the black-clad crowd, but there was no chance at this distance.

The voice went on. "When I say go, we're going to walk toward the opposite team, stopping a few paces apart. But we're going to alternate between regular speed and slow motion, so listen carefully to my instructions. First, regular speed...and, go."

Everyone set off, with a sort of techno walking music soundtrack in their ears. But before they'd taken many steps, the voice came again. "Now, slow motion."

The techno music slowed to a distorted kind of caterwaul, still only audible to those listening with their headphones. The people who had been sunbathing or reading in the middle of the grass now found themselves surrounded by flash mobsters doing silly, exaggerated slow walks, inspired by the discordant music. Some got up in alarm and scuttled off, but others let it all flow around them, laughing at the surreal scene.

They went through more rounds of regular and slow walking, stopping when the front line of each group was an arm's length apart. Cady was in about three deep on her side, but she could see through to the happy, animated faces of the opposite team.

"Okay everyone, please take out both of your fabric pieces."

Cady reached into the little bag slung across her body and pulled out one black and one white square of fabric. She and Shelby had come equipped, as requested in the video. Now she went with her team as, following the voice's directions, the two sides flung themselves together. With the white team holding up white fabric, and the black team holding up black, the blending and mixing of the teams was sharply illustrated. As they then alternated holding up the black and white fabric pieces in time to the music, Cady knew that if it was this dramatic on the ground, the cameras above must be getting amazing footage.

"And two become one," the voice exclaimed. "Great job. Now, everyone crouch down—we're going to do a Mexican wave starting at the parking lot end, then back again. Are you crouching down? On three. One, two, three."

As the wave hit where she was crouching, Cady fell on her butt, then sprang back up, behind everyone else but laughing at the silliness of it. And when the wave passed back, she was ready, leaping up with her hands in the air like a crazed soccer fan.

Next, the voice asked them to get out their water guns. To the accompaniment of tinkly-strange piano music, they all squirted water into the air, and more than a few people squirted their neighbors, the temptation irresistible. At the same time, water shot up from several points around the edge of the park, and a cheer erupted as the flash mobsters found themselves in an unexpected shower. Cady looked up at the droplets catching the sun and making rainbows against the clear blue sky, and was taken back to her childhood, when playing under the sprinkler in the back yard provided endless joy and entertainment on a summer day. Mesmerized by the glint and glimmer above her, she felt the cool droplets land on her face, and thought of her mother. Wherever she was now, this was probably exactly the kind of thing she'd meant when she urged Cady to get out and have some adventures.

"Beautiful." The voice interrupted the music, and her thoughts. "Okay everyone, high fives all round. Try and high-five as many people as you can, including someone not wearing earplugs. Go!"

There was a triumphant atmosphere amongst the slightly soggy flash mobsters as everyone high-fived the people around them. Some did the whole double-high-five jump-in-the-air, but Cady settled for the regular version, even though by this point she'd lost pretty much all her reserve. She high-fived a few eager bystanders too, making them laugh. It struck her as remarkable how a few small things, done together, could create such a warm bond between strangers, if only for a while.

"Now it's time to finish our day's experience. Look up, everyone, and wave and shout goodbye as loudly as you can. Thank you again for coming...and goodbye!"

Earbuds stood no chance of blocking out the goodbyes bellowed out by everyone in the mob. Looking up, Cady could see the cameras panning across the crowd, and a teeny remote-controlled helicopter circled around, filming the joyful, swirling mass of waving flash mobsters.

"Goodbye," she shouted into the way-up-high. The blueness was nothing and everything, an endless somewhere that was the only place her mother seemed to fit now. They never had said a proper goodbye. She waved more urgently, straining her voice as she yelled louder and louder, along with everyone else. "Goodbye...*goodbye...goodbye.*" Goodbye.

★

As everyone milled about afterwards, Cady felt a sweet kind of melancholy. It had been as much fun as she'd imagined, and more moving than she expected. The lingering sweetness gave her a blissful feeling that any old-school California hippie would surely recognize.

A reporter approached her with a smile, a cameraman

behind him. "Hi, I'm from KPIW. That looked like fun."

"It was!" She ran her fingers through her damp hair, lifting it to cool herself down. "Such a brilliant day."

The reporter's face registered surprise at her accent. "Oh, where are you from?"

"London."

As she spoke, she spotted a familiar face in the crowd behind the reporter. Reid caught her eye and gave a teasing bow, a reference to their conversation the night before. Her heart jumped as he smiled at her. She took in his snug-fitting jeans, and the breadth of his shoulders in his black Alter Bridge t-shirt. Oh, my Lord. Danger, right there, of the most inviting kind. Second time around, his effect on her was no less. She itched to go over, but the reporter was asking her something.

"I'm sorry, what did you say?"

"I said, you've come a long way. Would you be happy to do a short interview?"

"Oh! Yes, I suppose so." She smoothed her hair as best she could and pushed her sunglasses up her nose, hyper-aware of Reid watching along with others in the crowd.

The reporter held up his microphone. "You've come all the way from England for this. Why did you want to take part today?"

"Well, I've been enjoying watching online for ages—I wanted to come and experience it for myself."

"But what's the point of it, really?"

She could see a challenge in the reporter's eye, but she was unfazed. She'd had enough time to think about this, back in her little London bedroom. "The point? Look at these people." She gestured around at the happy faces. "They came here just to do something together, something uplifting. Life's so full of difficulty and complication. Don't you think that the more we join together on the small things, the more connected we feel? And then maybe we'll be better at working together on the big things too."

A smattering of applause went around the listening crowd, and she saw Reid raise his hands to clap too. He gave her an affirming nod, and she smiled.

"Okay, well said." The reporter reached out and they shook hands. "Thanks very much." He turned to the cameraman. "Let's just do the outcue and get out of here."

Free to go, Cady looked back to where Reid had been standing a moment ago, but there was no sign of him. She scanned the crowd, walking back and forth a little, but finally had to admit defeat. He was nowhere to be seen, and she couldn't put off meeting Shelby any longer.

Flushed with enjoyment, the sun's heat, and the buzz of seeing him again, she made her way across to the bus. It was surrounded with fans—mostly women, which didn't surprise her—and she couldn't see if Shelby was there or not. Eventually she walked back and stood up on a park bench, to get a better view. Straight away she could see Shelby standing by the door of the bus, striking almost the same supermodel pose she'd used for the photo. And she was listening intently to a smallish, scraggly-bearded man wearing a fur vest.

Cady grinned. That was her sister all right—straight in there. Did Kyle Baxter stand a chance? Well, she might be a huge pain, but maybe Cady could take a leaf from her book. She jumped down from the bench. She hadn't come this far...

Elbowing her way through the gathered crowd, she made it to the bus and gave Shelby a poke in the back.

"Ow!" Shelby jumped, but quickly regained her poise. "Kyle, this is my sister Cady. Cady, Kyle."

Kyle's eyes widened as he took in the two of them standing together. "Holy shit," he said. "There are two of you?"

Sometimes Cady forgot what a novelty they were. And today, both with their hair loose and dressed in basically the same outfit of not-quite-short shorts, slim t-shirt, and sneakers, they looked exactly alike, just opposites on the color wheel.

Fake it 'til you make it. Cady took a breath. "I'm the bonus." She held out her hand and Kyle shook it, looking from one to the other. His quiff emerged from the front of a brown beanie, the fur was definitely faux, and the beard had seen better days. She supposed it was designed that way. All the same, there was something kind of compelling about him, she'd admit that. Maybe it was the baby blues. "Nice to meet you," she added.

"I think it's nicer for me," he said. "Thanks for coming."

"It was fun," Cady said. She decided to go straight in, a la Shelby. "What are you all doing now?"

"We usually help the hired hands with the cleanup. A few of the core team are still out on the field of play." He looked at the crowd milling hopefully around the bus. "And I'd better do some schmoozing with all these ladies." He took a step in their direction.

Shelby threaded her arm through Cady's, playing up their twin-ness, obviously hoping not to lose his interest. "Can we help with anything?" The jutting hip again.

He paused. For a moment he looked them up and down, weighing them up. "You're from England, right?"

"London," they replied in unison, making him laugh.

"Very entertaining. Want to hang around a while? You can make yourselves at home on the bus while we finish up, all right?"

Shelby looked like she would burst if she said anything, so Cady replied casually, "Thanks, that'd be great."

"Okay. Help yourselves to coffee, whatever." He pushed a button on a little remote, like for a car, and the bus door opened smoothly, sliding out and to the side with a quiet hiss. Then a small flight of steps emerged and settled themselves on the tarmac. "Just close the door behind you. See you soon."

They watched him step away and immediately get swallowed into a mass of enthusiastic fans. Then they turned to the doorway.

"I can't believe it was so easy," Shelby said.

"I'm starting to think we might be able to do all sorts of things if we work together," Cady replied.

They both looked up into the bus as though it was a portal to some other, magical world. Maybe it would be, Cady thought.

"Come on." She stepped onto the stairs. "Let's see what we've started."

They went up, and Shelby pushed a button just inside to close the door. It slid across and sealed them in with a gentle sigh, muffling the bustle and hum from the park. They were in.

"Wow." Cady looked around. The decor was like something from an interior design magazine, a cross between a luxury yacht and a private jet. They were standing in a sort of lounge, with cream leather seating along the windows and a wall of crystal-cut glass behind a very full drinks cabinet. Chrome fittings glinted in the light coming softly through the Persian blinds, and the plush carpet under their feet added to the hushed effect. It exuded class and glamour, an elegant cocoon to hide away in. She tried to picture Kyle in there, but it just didn't fit. "I wasn't expecting it to be like *this*."

"This smells like serious money." Shelby looked like a kid in a candy store. "It's *beautiful*." She sat gingerly on a leather armchair and swung it around a little, testing.

"And it's like the Tardis," Cady said. "I can't believe it's this big inside."

Beyond the lounge was a kitchen, with a dining table bigger than the one in their little kitchen at home. This was closer to a castle than their house would ever be. She peeked into the hallway further down, lined with cabin beds on both sides. They were curtained off, but one was slightly open, and she could see a TV screen above the bed. At the very back of the bus was what looked like a bathroom on each side.

"Look." She nudged Shelby, and pointed to where a stairwell rose up in the corner of the living area, leading to who knew what. "I'm dying to look up there."

They both peered up, but propriety stopped them from going any further.

"We're too British by half," Cady said. "We'll have to work on that."

"Yes, definitely," Shelby agreed. But neither of them went up.

Instead, they found the coffee machine and made themselves a cup each, lingering over their choice of Nespresso capsules. Shelby chose blue, while Cady chose a gold one for herself, and sighed as the aroma filled the air. They took their little cups back to the lounge, and sat down to enjoy, and wait.

"I saw him again," Cady said, as Shelby raised her cup to her lips.

She lowered it again without taking a sip, instantly curious. "Who? Chris Hemsworth?"

"Yes," she said, her tone making it clear she'd seen no such thing. "Yes, Chris Hemsworth."

"Okay, no need to be snarky." Shelby stuck out her tongue. "You mean Reid."

Lying in bed the night before, they'd talked and giggled in the dark, like when they were little girls sharing a bedroom. Shelby had been full of sighs and admiration for Gavin, and was satisfied when Cady said no, she liked Reid better.

"Where did you see him?" Shelby asked now. "Did you talk to him?"

"It was after everything finished. A TV reporter was asking me some questions and I could see him in the crowd, but then he disappeared." She smiled to herself, recalling the bow. "I don't know where he went."

But she'd left Shelby a step back in the conversation. "Wait. A TV reporter? You're going to be on TV?"

"I suppose so. Crazy, right?"

"Welcome to America, baby."

Cady laughed. "Everyone's on TV here, don't you know."

Then the door sighed open, and voices floated in from the parking lot. They looked at each other, the look on Shelby's face matching Cady's anticipation, and both stood up.

And found themselves looking at two golden California girls.

"Oh. My. God," the taller one said, crinkling her oddly small nose. Surgically enhanced, Cady guessed. "Look who's here." She put a hand on her hip, where it rested against smoothly burnished brown skin above her *very* short shorts.

"Oh my God," echoed the other.

"So matchy-matchy," sniffed the first.

Shelby stood up, her face pink. "I *beg* your freaking *pardon?*"

Cady was tempted to let her rip—Shelby at her raging best would give these two a run for their money. But they were here to make the most of it, not get in a cat-fight with the first girls they met. So she stepped forward, keeping it friendly.

"Hi. We're just visiting—on holiday—and Kyle invited us to hang out for a while."

It was immediately obvious that this was the wrong thing to say, as their expressions darkened even more. For a moment all four of them stood in silence, two sets of two looking at each other from their own sides.

Then the sound of footsteps came from the bus stairs, and as all four of them turned to see who it was, the California girls instantly put on their best faces.

"Hi guys," cooed the tall one.

Cady's face suddenly felt as hot as if she was back out in the high sun. Gavin was coming up the stairs, a different pair of glasses on today. And behind him, of course...was Reid.

Chapter Five

Kyle came up the bus stairs after Gavin and Reid, followed by a huge muscle-bound guy with a face that looked like it was thrown together with spare parts.

"Okay, all the team's here," Kyle said. "Looks like I need to do introductions."

"Some of us have already met," said Gavin, giving Shelby a wink.

Cady had quickly regrouped, and now looked across at Reid, teasing-accusing, an unspoken *why hadn't he said?* He grinned and shrugged, his expression mischievous, and gave a Gallic shrug that said, *just for the hell of it.* She shook her head in a silent mock rebuke, but while her outside was cool, her mind raced. He was one of them. They were on the bus together. He was so completely not the kind of guy who'd usually make her so swoony, and yet her body was buzzing, super-charged. She smoothed her hair, half expecting that it would be lifting and floating in his direction, the attraction irresistible.

"All right, just a round-up then," Kyle said. "Lovely Londoners, you know Gavin and Reid?" When they nodded, he slapped the arm of the colossus next to him. "But not Tino? He's our driver, and our lift-anything guy."

Tino gave a nod and a shy smile, his face lighting up into such sweetness that the girls were instantly won over.

"And this, of course, is Jennifer and Alison," Kyle finished. "Team, this is Shelby and Cady, visiting from across the pond."

While he looked pleased, Jennifer and Alison were transparently not. But when he turned to them, they both put on their good girl faces again. Alison's sweetest smile was for Kyle.

"Shelby and Cady," she repeated. "I'm waiting for you to break into a country and western number." She looked at Jennifer, and they both laughed.

If they'd known what a direct hit that was, they would have laughed even harder. Shelby had always complained about their names, saying she felt like they were some cheesy country music duo. It was just one of the many reasons she'd found to be mad at their mum. Now, of course, Cady knew where the names had come from, and it explained why they were so American. For all she knew, their aunts might actually *be* country singers. There was a lot she didn't know...yet.

Now Shelby looked from Gavin to Kyle, obviously weighing up. Cady knew that look. She was clearly going for getting even, not mad. It only took a second before her decision was made—Cady could see the moment when the determined light came on in her eyes, and she stepped toward Kyle. At the very same moment, Alison stepped forward too. The game was on.

Shelby laughed, purposefully taking the high ground. "You wouldn't want to hear my singing! But I do have *other* talents." She lay her fingertips on Kyle's arm, ever so briefly, and he laughed too. Round one, and Shelby had a point on the board.

"I bet you do," he said. "Well, great that you girls have been getting to know each other. I have to finish up here, and do an interview with a blogger. Let's meet at Sanctuary later, all right?"

"Sounds great," Alison said, taking the chance to tuck her arm through his. "It was lovely to meet you, Shelby-

and-Cady. Have a great holiday." The fake-sweet tone made Cady want to slap her, but Shelby just smiled.

"No, all of us," Kyle clarified, tapping Alison's hand pointedly. "It's easy to find, just on 16th, at the back of a bar called Diorama," he added, for the twins' benefit. "Eight o'clock."

Everyone nodded, some looking happier than others. "Don't forget we're hitting the road tomorrow night," he called back, as he and Tino went out.

"I think you have a fan," Gavin said to Shelby when he was gone.

She gave another tinkling laugh. "He's a bit of a star, isn't he? Good that he's got such a great team around him." She waved generously around, making sure to include Alison and Jennifer in her approval. They looked less than appreciative.

"Yeah, okay." Alison flicked her blonde hair back over her shoulder. "Come on Jen, let's go get a coffee at Tartine. We'll come back *later*."

"Okay, see you later then!" Shelby said brightly as they left.

On the way out, they stopped to give Gavin and Reid goodbye kisses on the cheek. Was it Cady's imagination, or was there a particular intensity to the kiss Jennifer gave Reid as she trailed out? He smiled at her, the same smile that Cady had seen the night before. Watching, she felt a little twist in her guts. They were walking into the middle of these people's lives, and she had no idea what was going on behind the scenes. The show was already underway, and she was only destined to be a bit player, so she'd better suck it up and make the most of it.

"Is it just me, or was there some serious atmosphere in here?" Gavin asked the room in general, when they were gone.

"That was kind of intense," Reid agreed.

Cady shook her head. Shelby had given a master-class in handling catty bitches, but she wanted to enjoy her night, not get caught up in drama. "No, it was fine."

Then she gave Reid a look. "Why did you—why did

you both—keep it a secret? You were part of this and you didn't even tell us."

Reid laughed. "I don't know. It was too easy...plus some girls get kind of crazy about Kyle."

"God knows why," Gavin muttered.

"Charisma isn't a muscle group, man," Reid told him. "You can't pump it up at the gym."

Gavin flexed a bicep at him. "Yeah, yeah. Tell that to these babies." He raised the other arm and gave them a gun show. After the colossus that was Tino, they paled in comparison.

"Shit, put it away dude." Reid shook his head, and turned back to them. "Anyway, sometimes if you mention you know Kyle, people sort of latch on. That's why the girls were so wary about you last night, and today. We've had some weird ones."

"And what about us?" Cady asked him. "Weird, or...?"

"Oh, completely. You're all weird over there, right? Plus, you talk funny. Must be the chill in your castles."

Cady laughed. "Stop being such an ass." She used her best American accent just for that one word. "In my realm, you'd be beheaded for that, and your head displayed on a spike outside my castle walls."

"Stop blowing smoke up my aah-s," he returned. "Your puny knights are no match for me and my henchman." He pointed at Gavin, who was looking perplexed.

Damn, that cheekiness was too, too good. "Now you're talking out of your aaass," she said. By this stage she was laughing too hard to think of another quip.

Shelby and Gavin were staring, incredulous. "What the hell?" Gavin said. He looked at Shelby. "I think we're missing something here."

"Nothing new there," Reid said, as Shelby shrugged. "Come on, man, we'd better help puny King Kyle get finished out there. Can't let Tino do all the work." He looked at the girls. "See you later then?"

"Yes," they answered in unison again, making the

guys laugh.

"Nice teamwork," Gavin said teasingly, as they all went out of the bus.

Shelby shot Cady a glare. Then she smiled at Gavin, slightly less tantalizing than before. She was saving those smiles for Kyle now, Cady knew. Whether they'd work was yet to be discovered.

★

"Why do you do that?" Shelby asked as they left Dolores Park, heading for the guesthouse.

"Do what?" Cady thought she was in trouble for her crazy back-and-forth with Reid. She still had a warm glow from it, despite the uncertain Jennifer factor. And despite the whole California dude thing he and Gavin had going on, and the beard, and the ponytail...yep, those poor neglected man receptors were screaming with the sudden Reid-induced overload. Well, things had changed lately. Clearly her taste in men was changing too.

Shelby gave her a shove. "Answer the same thing as me, at the same time. It pisses me off. And it makes us look silly."

Cady snorted. "*You* answer at the same time as *me*! You don't need any help looking silly, anyway."

"Oh, shut up." She was all over-charged. "And, those two girls bring me out in a rash. Talk about princesses."

Cady didn't like to say anything about Shelby's own princess tendencies. She suspected that 'takes one to know one' wouldn't go down well right now—but that probably made her sister more equipped than anyone to take the California girls on.

"They're obviously not keen to share any of the guys," Cady observed.

The competitive high made Shelby extra indignant. "They can't have them all!"

"But they were here first," Cady pointed out. "Sounds like you've decided you'd like one yourself."

A little smile. "Maybe."

"Not Gavin, though." She waited to see if Shelby would admit her Kyle plan.

"Um...no."

"I thought not. You've obviously set your sights higher. And you definitely got under Alison's skin."

She grinned. "It was too tempting to resist. Sometimes being bad is so damn good."

"I can see that. But they're leaving tomorrow, you heard that, right? And we're going off on our travels too, in a couple of days. LA, baby. Remember?"

"I know!" Shelby looked away, concentrating on the windows of the boutiques and coffee houses they were passing. She was thinking about something—and Cady was pretty sure she knew what it was. They knew each other too well.

"Shelby...are you thinking what I think you are?"

They stopped outside an ice-cream parlor. "Well, we could, couldn't we? If they asked us?"

Cady imagined being on a luxury bus—overnight—with Reid. Oh, mama. Then she imagined being trapped on a luxury bus with Alison and Jennifer. Hmm. Maybe not...

"Well, they're not going to ask us, so don't get your hopes up. Just enjoy the night, and don't get yourself into trouble. Or me." That might be asking too much, knowing Shelby, but she had to say it. If only because the inevitable 'I told you so' would be so much more satisfying.

A defiant look came back at her. "We'll see."

Chapter Six

At quarter past eight that night they were outside Diorama, showered, made up, and, in Shelby's case, over-perfumed. She'd taken an age to decide what to wear, finally settling on her tightest jeans, with a sparkly top and plenty of bracelets along her newly spray-tanned arms. Cady didn't have many going-out clothes, but she'd gone shopping before they left London. Dreamily imagining what San Francisco would be like, she'd fallen for a 60s-inspired peasant dress with a tiny floral pattern. Although it had three-quarter sleeves, the deep v-neck, fitted high waist and short hem meant there was nothing matronly about it, even with a cardigan over the top. When she bought the dress, she'd planned to wear it with tights, but now it was warm enough that she left her legs bare, just clad in her old brown cowboy boots. They weren't really tanned enough yet, but hey, who was looking anyway?

She wasn't going to say anything out loud—even in her own mind—about Reid maybe looking. There'd probably be enough conflict as Shelby trampled over what was obviously Alison's territory, without Cady starting a fruitless battle too. Maybe Reid and Jennifer weren't a couple at all, but Cady didn't want to get into one night of trouble over a guy, and ruin her long-awaited Flashpoint experience. Even if that guy set her dangerously, deliciously off-kilter. She was on new ground here, literally and figuratively, but she could embrace her new start without walking herself straight into difficulty.

"Come on," she said, as Shelby hesitated in the blue diamond-tiled entranceway, doing a final fluff of her hair. "This is your territory, remember."

Shelby had told her enough tales of London nightlife to fill a (pretty low-brow) book, and now she was ready to create some stories of her own. Low-brow or not, either way was fine at this point. Since meeting the Flashpointers, she'd started to think that 'fake it 'til you make it' might actually work. She'd been bottled up for so long, being the good daughter that they all relied on her to be (including Shelby, who counted on Cady to be there, so she didn't have to be). Now she was bursting for some living. She just had to cut herself loose, which was easier said than done after years of being dutiful and responsible. But the longer she was away from home, work and reality, the more unfettered she felt. Her teeny bedroom seemed unconnected to her now, like it was the set of a play she might have seen once upon a time. She could see herself sitting on the bed, pillows behind her back, laptop on her knees, listening for any sound from her mother's room as she watched clips of other people *living*, in other places.

Her mother hadn't specified what kind of fun she wanted her to have, and now she'd never be able to tell her about these adventures. There was no one to answer to or be responsible for. That reality was gone, which made her terribly sad—but it was kind of freeing, too. She took a breath and stepped through the door, pulling Shelby in with her.

Their eyes took a moment to adjust to the light as they went into the long, narrow bar. It wasn't crowded, but there were enough people to make the place hum. It glowed in the red lighting, and at the end of the room a screen played an old movie that Cady didn't recognize. She looked up at the stuffed animals on the wall. Was that one a rabbit...with antlers? She nudged Shelby—*what the?*—but she just laughed and shrugged, and pointed to the 'Sanctuary' sign at the far end of the bar.

Past the bathrooms, they found the secret bar, tucked at the end of the corridor like a hidden speakeasy. The whole team was there, already each in possession of a fabulous-looking cocktail.

"Hi," Cady said, as they all looked up. Shelby echoed the greeting, and there was a general 'hi' from the group. Alison and Jennifer looked less than pleased to see them, but the guys squashed up to make space in the booth.

"Choose your poison," said Gavin. "Kyle's buying— it's tradition."

They looked at the drinks list, a lineup of potent and exotic treats. Cady wished she'd had a decent dinner. Shelby had taken so long to get ready that they'd only had time to grab smothered fries from a food truck on the way there, and they hadn't had time to eat them all. She was so out of practice with drinking, just one of these delectable-sounding creations on a half-empty stomach would probably put her on her ear.

As they were considering their options, Reid leaned on the table. "Someone here is newly famous," he announced. As everyone wanted to know who, looking around at each other, he winked across at Cady.

Jennifer, sitting next to him, caught the wink instantly. "Is it you?" she asked Cady.

"Famous for two minutes, on KPIW," she clarified. "It was just a couple of questions. No big deal."

"You did great," Reid told her. "He wanted to catch you out, but you made us all look good. I had no idea we were doing something so noble." He raised his glass to her. "Lady Cady."

Cady felt herself flush pink, and noticed Jennifer do the same.

Kyle leaned back in his chair. "You're only here five minutes and you're doing PR for us. Nice."

"It wasn't anything, really. I don't even know if they'll use it."

"Alison will check," Reid said. "She's been keeping up with the traditional media stuff." Alison looked peeved, but nodded.

Kyle pointed to the bar. "Go get some drinks," he told Cady and Shelby. "Just put it on the tab. Order the Killer's Lullaby."

They looked at each other, wondering what the heck they'd be drinking, but obeyed. It turned out to be a concoction of strong gin and cider, as well as other ingredients Cady couldn't identify as the barman spun and tipped bottles in a Top Gun-worthy performance.

When they got back, each carrying a tall, dangerous-looking glass sprouting a sprig of mint, Kyle was frowning, reading something on his iPhone. "Shit."

Everyone turned to look at him. "What is it?" Reid asked.

"That blogger at SF-ly. He's done a total hatchet job."

Immediately everyone was on their iPhones, looking it up. Cady found the site and started reading, but Shelby sat on her hands. "What does it say?" she asked, leaning close.

"Just look it up on your phone too," Cady said.

She shook her head, looking embarrassed. "I don't want to. It's a Huawei."

Cady laughed and held her own iPhone so that Shelby could see the screen, and they read the blog post together. It was hilariously scathing, brilliantly written, and completely tore Kyle to pieces.

There was silence as everyone absorbed the eviscerating genius of San Francisco's most popular blogger. If it had been about anything else, Cady would have laughed, and admired the evil talent at work. But in this case...ouch.

Quietly, she signed into Twitter and searched the #Flashpointers hashtag. The blog post was being shared and commented on at a rate of knots, and as fast as she clicked, new tweets were popping up. *2 new tweets...5 new tweets...9 new tweets.* Some of them were supportive, telling the blogger not to take everything so seriously. But most of them were joining in the fun. They were on a roll, loving the thrill of tearing down something that only hours before had, by general agreement, qualified as 'cool'.

She caught Kyle's eye. "Look at Twitter."

Her tone made it clear that he wouldn't like what he saw. Especially the tweeters who were reveling in being snarky about him in particular, and the ones who'd taken it from snarky to cruel.

He immediately looked it up, and sat reading, his face growing darker and darker.

"For fuck's sake, don't these people have anything better to do on a Saturday night?" He rubbed his beard vigorously, making part of it stick out sideways, and despite the situation Cady had to try not to laugh. She knew he was the height of cool for a lot of people, but for anyone not on board with the hipster thing, he provided a *lot* of material for snarkiness.

Now he adjusted his vest and sat up straight, taking his drink in hand. "Screw them," he announced. "Twitter can do what it likes until we've had our drinks, all right? That was a fucking good day."

"Screw them," echoed Alison, and they all nodded and put their phones away.

"Let's get on to the next round," Kyle said. "Drink up."

So they did.

By the end of their second cocktail—this one involving mescal and white vermouth—Cady knew she definitely should have had dinner, but no one was ordering food. She whispered to Shelby that she was going to the bathroom, and got up, feeling less than a hundred percent composed.

Shelby was clearly feeling the lack of food too, as she wavered a little when she stood up. "I'll come with you."

In the ladies' room, Cady looked at herself in the mirror and sighed. "I really need to eat. What about you?"

"Pfft, nah." Shelby leaned over, letting her hair fall forward, then stood up and quickly flipped it back over, so that it fell lush around her shoulders. She wobbled a little as she checked the result in the mirror. Satisfied, she put on red lipstick, looking sideways at Cady in the mirror as she rolled her lips together. "Wouldn't hurt you to use a bit of this."

"Oh, shut up." But she smoothed on some lip gloss, and tousled her hair a little, squinting at her slightly blurry reflection. "I don't need lessons from you."

Shelby raised an eyebrow in her direction. "You could learn something from me, you know. You might not be single now if you followed my example a bit more."

"Your example? Oh, please. And he wasn't worth having anyway." It was true. Jeremy was no loss. His ego couldn't stand that he wasn't always at the top of Cady's list of priorities. She shook her head at Shelby. "I'm better off being single, than being stuck with a complete dickhead. That's something *you* obviously haven't learned yet."

Shelby turned to face her, hands on hips. "At least there are men out there who *want* to be with me."

Cady sucked in her breath. "If it wasn't for me, you wouldn't even be here. You'd still be in London, playing at being the wild one." She knew she should walk away now, but she kept going. The wind was in her sails, and the mescal was running hot in her veins. "You might be fooling everyone else, and yourself, but I know that wild and free schtick is an act. If you were really wild and free, you wouldn't need a man to hold your hand all the time."

That well-aimed arrow struck home, and Shelby's face grew red. "Yeah, whatever. I doubt you would have come here at all if I hadn't agreed to hold *your* hand. You'd still be living through your laptop. Sad."

She smirked, and Cady felt her temperature rise as anger grew in her chest, and years of resentment threatened to overflow.

"You little...I carried the whole show at home while you kept on being a teenager way past the point where it looked cool."

Shelby flinched, but regrouped. "You didn't want me to help! If I helped, you'd have to take off that cloak of martyrdom you're so attached to. Then you might have to actually go out and *live* your life."

"Like you, I suppose. You must have run out of fingers

and toes to count the men on."

"Well, why shouldn't I? I'd rather be out having fun than floating about at home like a tragic old spinster. You should have stuck to that. It suits you. You're not cut out to be anything more than a boring banker, like Dad."

By now the red mist was threatening, and Cady's head was pounding, a combination of cocktails and rage about to tip her over the edge. "He's not even our..." She stopped, realizing what she was about to say.

But Shelby was all over it. "Not even our what?"

Cady looked away, but her face obviously gave something away.

"Our *what?*" Shelby persisted.

"Nothing." She tried to push past and go back to the bar, but Shelby planted herself firmly in the way.

"You think you know me so well, but I know you too. I can see you're hiding something. And you're so boring you *never* have anything worth hiding. What is it?"

The thought *I'll show you* flashed through Cady's mind, and she snapped.

"He's not even our father, okay? Happy now?"

For a moment she basked in the power of the blow she dealt, as Shelby's face went from shock to pain to disbelief, and around again. Then she realized what she'd done. Broken her promise to her mother, and pulled the rug out from under Shelby's feet. Her sister may have rebelled against home and family, but at least it was something steady to rebel against. Now she was staring at the same empty space that Cady had been swimming in since Anne broke the news and promptly died. In her down moments Cady cursed her mother's flair for the dramatic, even in death.

Shelby was struggling to process the bombshell. "I don't believe you."

"Fine. Don't believe me." It was too late for regret now.

"Did Mum tell you?"

Cady nodded. "But you have to know the whole story. There's more to it than you think." She told Shelby what their mother had revealed. Even in the retelling it was bare bones, and she realized how little detail they had.

"I can't even...who is he? And how could you not have told me?" Shelby glared at her.

"Because she asked me not to." She remembered her mother's pale, determined face. She hadn't believed it could possibly be her dying wish—she was nowhere near dying, surely. But the shock of her death had made breaking the promise seem impossible, until now. She wished she could turn back just five minutes, and undo the revelation. "She made me promise."

"I don't give a shit. You should have told me!"

Cady pressed her hand to her forehead. "I wanted to. But she said it was her dying wish. I *promised* her."

Shelby shook her head. "This is bigger than that. Oh my God, I can't believe it. And he's American? We have to find him."

"I don't know if that's a good idea..."

Shelby snorted. "You obviously have no freaking clue what a good idea is. I want some answers."

"But Dad doesn't know about any of it."

Shelby paused. "Well, he should know. Mum lied to him our whole lives."

"*No*, Shelby. Think about what it would do to him. And Mum isn't here to explain, to talk it through."

"So we should continue the lie for her? I don't think so. Jesus, I'm so sick of you always being the admirable, reasonable one. You can do what you like. I'm finding my father."

"No, you're *not*. You're not doing this to Dad. It's not your decision to make."

"Watch me." She stepped out of Cady's way and went into a cubicle, slamming the door behind her.

At that moment, Jennifer came in. "You're taking forever." She hesitated when she saw Cady's flushed cheeks and brimming eyes. "We've ordered food...are you going to eat?"

"I'll eat," Shelby called from the cubicle, her voice full of a challenge even now.

Cady had been starving, but now her hunger was gone. "No. I can't...thanks." She slipped past Jennifer and went back to the table, pressing her hands to her cheeks in the hope of settling the rage-induced redness, and grabbed up her cardigan. "I have to...sorry..." She avoided everyone's eyes, especially Reid's, and turned to Kyle. "Thanks for tonight. I have to go."

Before he could say anything, she headed back through the main bar and out onto 16th Street. She allowed herself the luxury of one tear before she scrubbed the rest violently away. That little cow...yet again, she couldn't believe they shared the same DNA. She started down the sidewalk, then stopped, hesitating. The streets were full of people, but she had no idea whether it was safe to walk back to the guesthouse alone, especially with those two cocktails under her belt, blurring her usual sharpness. And she didn't want to go back without Shelby and face Marian, who'd seen them off with such enthusiasm, admiring their outfits and encouraging them to have a wonderful night.

It was all very well to pretend to be someone else, someone more confident and certain. Whoever you decide to be, your problems still drag around behind you. Served her right for dragging her sister along too. She shook her head. You might flatter yourself that you're different now, but some things remain the same. She pulled her cardigan tighter around herself in the evening coolness and set off, not quite sure where she was going apart from *away*.

Chapter Seven

S he'd only gone half a block when she heard a voice call
her name, and turned. Reid was coming after her. For a
moment her heart leapt as she saw the concern in his eyes,
his handsome face serious. But the thought of having to tell
the story—especially the part about how she'd kept a huge
secret and then whammed her sister with it—made her
plunk back down to earth.

"Hey, are you okay?" he asked as he caught up with
her. "Jennifer said—"

"I'm fine, thank you." She knew it was a glaringly
obvious lie. "I'm *fine*."

He looked skeptical. "Okay...so, where are you going
then?"

"Actually, I have no idea." She looked around at the
lively street. The night was getting later and rowdier, and
she stumbled as she was sideswiped by a guy dashing to
catch up with his clearly smashed friends. "Somewhere
quieter?"

He put an arm around her shoulders, gathering her into
shelter. "Come on then, Lady Cady. The bus is around the
corner."

She had no clue, really, whether she was any safer

being escorted 'around the corner' than running the gauntlet of Mission revelers back to the guesthouse. But she decided to trust her cocktail-compromised gut on this one. It felt good being tucked under his arm, and she'd been standing strong for so long, through so much, that it was a relief to lean in just this once.

At the bus, he pulled an electronic remote from his pocket and hit the button. "After you."

She went up into the lounge area and plopped down on the leather sofa, relieved to be off her gin-and-mescal feet. Reid sat in an armchair, leaning forward with his elbows on his knees, and regarded her steadily. "So…what's up?"

"Family drama." She waved a hand, dismissing the fuss. Maybe she'd get away with stopping there. "Seriously, you don't want to know all the tedious details."

"Yeah, but I do. And, you're in California now. Most people pay someone to listen to their problems. You're getting it for free." He pointed at himself with both hands, making her laugh.

"Cheap at half the price."

"Exactly." Then his face became more serious. "You were upset."

She snorted. "Mad, more like." She could feel the anger and frustration of their fight rising in her chest again. No one else made her as infuriated as that damn woman. Damn child, she should say.

"Spill, then. It'll do you good."

She sighed. "Okay." Maybe he was right. It couldn't hurt to let off some steam, and he looked genuinely sympathetic. Probably as instructed by Jennifer, but, oh well.

Starting from the beginning, she gave him the edited version. Her mother's illness, that crept up on them until investigations finally gave a name to the mysterious symptoms. The doctors had given her only a short time to live, saying the disease usually progressed rapidly as organ function deteriorated. True to character, Anne had refused to be dictated to, and fought back with enough determination to rival Muhammad Ali. But it wasn't long before Cady had to move back home and help her dad look after her. He was ten years older than Anne—he'd been fifty-one when the girls were born—and although his mind remained as sharp as ever, he struggled with the arthritis that was slowly, relentlessly twisting his joints. As a crisp thinker and precise operator, who liked to do things *just so*, the frustration must have been intense. But he never let Anne see him show any resentment about his own condition.

Then, after a moment's hesitation, she told Reid about her mother's last wish—the deathbed revelation and request that knocked Cady sideways even while she didn't believe for a moment that her mother was dying. Not yet. And then, the money, and the keeping of the secret, and how she finally slapped Shelby with it in the middle of their fight.

She skipped over Jeremy, and the breakup he blamed on her not having enough time for him. The real deal-breaker, that she knew but he'd never admit to, was that illness. Even in only their year-and-a-bit together, he'd seen her mother decline and fail. Of course he must have looked at Cady, and feared the same fate. In truth, she could hardly blame him for not wanting to sign up for that.

"And her illness—Wodarski-Ebner?" Reid carefully pronounced the name she wished she'd never heard. "It's a genetic thing?"

"Yes. I kind of try not to think about it." She pressed her fingers to her temple as though squashing the thought itself. "We both try not to think about it."

"Is there a test you can do?"

"There is, but we haven't done it..."

How could she explain why neither of them had taken the test? In this case, ignorance wasn't exactly bliss—but for them, so far, the lurking not-knowing was better than confirmation of their worst fears. And if one of them had the test, and it came back positive, that would surely increase the chance that the other would have it too. Even though they weren't identical, their genetic inheritance was the same. Years before, they'd made a pact, for better or worse—neither of them would be tested, and in the future, what would be, would be.

He let her answer hang in the air, unfinished. "I'm sorry."

"That's okay," she said. "We were lucky to have her as long as we did. The specialist said it usually starts much younger."

"And your dad?"

"He seems really happy in his 'retirement community'." She made air quotes. "We're not allowed to call it a home. He says that sounds like somewhere for old people, and he doesn't accept that seventy-six is old."

He laughed. "More power to him. But I meant your real dad."

"He *is* my real dad." She sighed. "He's always been our dad. I can't break his heart."

He looked sympathetic. "Life gets complicated."

"That's for sure." She made herself smile. "What about you? Is your life complicated?"

He shrugged. "Only as complicated as the next guy's."

She waited, but he just leaned back in the armchair, swinging it a little from side to side as he gave her a lazy smile.

"Well...how did you end up here, with this crowd?"

"I met Gavin at a Crusty Demons show. My friends had missed their flight to come see it with me, but I decided to go anyway. The ticket was expensive, couldn't waste it. And Gavin was there with a couple of his friends. I don't know, we got talking, and went drinking afterwards...and here I am."

"I have no idea what Crusty Demons is, but it sounds very Gavin."

"Freestyle motocross. Lunatic stunt biking kind of stuff."

"Boy stuff."

He grinned. "You got it."

"And you live in San Francisco?"

"I do." Nothing else was forthcoming.

"Um, and, are you working, or...?" Her voice faded out. This was starting to feel like she was putting him

54

through an interrogation, but he was so vague. It wasn't like she was just making conversation—she really wanted to know more about him. Maybe he wasn't the type to share personal details. Not that her questions were all that personal. But luckily, this question brought him to life.

"I do sand sculpture."

A laugh burst out before she could stop it. "Sorry. But…really? Sand sculpture?"

"Sure." He wasn't offended. "Like for special events, or photography, or promotions. I can even bring the sand to your house and create a sculpture for you there. People love it for theme parties. I'll show you."

He came and sat next to her, and took out his phone. "Here, have a look."

As she watched, he scrolled through photos of incredibly finely carved sculptures. Along with various company logos outside office buildings, there was a fierce dragon on the beach guarding a treasure chest of coins and jewels, an old-time sailing ship on swirly sand waves, and a magical castle in the grounds of a real Hollywood-style mansion.

"Wow. That's so California."

"Yeah." He put the phone away. "You know, it's a living."

She shook her head, impressed. "I wasn't expecting that at *all*. You're really clever."

"Thanks. What about you? What do you do?"

"Oh…" After that display of his amazing creativity, she felt like such a nana. "I worked in a bank. So boring."

Her embarrassment must have shown, because he said, "Well, looking after people's money is important. Lots of the really important stuff is kind of boring, from the outside, anyway."

"I suppose so. But it actually was *really* boring. I was only in a branch. But it served a purpose." Doing regular office hours suited her. If she'd taken any of the promotions, it would have meant longer hours, moving to a different branch in another part of London, or even a different city. She'd just needed something close by that she could balance with her commitments at home.

He was about to reply when they heard voices outside. Shelby and Kyle.

She looked at him, shaking her head. "I really can't face it," she whispered.

He put a finger to his lips and stood up, holding out his hand. She took it, and they did a cartoonish super-fast tiptoe down to the sleeping area, where he pulled back the curtain to one of the beds. As the bus door opened she dived in, and he followed, settling the curtain into place just as Kyle and Shelby came up the stairs.

The childish mischief of hiding, combined with getting the better of her sister, was a delightfully wicked feeling. In the gloom, every part of her was exquisitely aware of his nearness. She was so, so tempted to turn closer, pressing her body against the length of him, but she lay perfectly still on her back. Although she was hardly breathing in her effort to keep quiet, the warm smell of him filled her senses. He was so close, she could feel each breath he exhaled, gentle on her cheek.

"Hey, Reid, are you here man?" There was a pause as Kyle waited for any reply. Cady worked to squash the giggle that was threatening to come out. They heard him go up the inner stairs and call out again, then come back down. "Nah, not here. I thought they might be. We must've left the lights on."

"Well, I hope she'll be okay. She can be kind of dramatic."

In the darkened nook, Cady resisted the temptation to leap out and slap her sister. Hello, pot calling. And she seriously doubted Shelby would have come if Kyle hadn't suggested it. She gritted her teeth.

"If Reid's with her, he'll look after her. Come on, let's go."

"Okay."

She could picture Shelby shrugging: *whatever.* Then the lights went out and they heard the door sigh shut, leaving them in almost complete darkness. She breathed out into the silence, a huge release of tension and irritation and desire all in one. With no more need to hide, she expected him to get up…but he didn't move. In their little bed nest, a possibility seemed to hang in the air.

She laughed, a nervous reflex. "My God, we're so immature."

"Totally." In the dark, the teasing tone was oh-so-tempting. He shifted a little, and a chink of light came through a gap in the curtain, illuminating his face. His expression was the one that had hooked her the night before, in the café. Like he was a step back from it all, watching with easy-going amusement. Taking it all in, but not taking any of it seriously. Combined with the intelligence in those honey-brown eyes, the overall effect was enough to leave her weak. Lucky she was already lying down. She certainly forgave him the ponytail, the beard and the occasional dude-speak that seemed such a mismatch. All at once, she couldn't bear for him to be just a breath away. *New start, starting now…* She reached out a hand and lay it on the curve of his neck, just below his ear. The heat of his skin in that tender spot instantly warmed her fingers. Before she had time to doubt herself she rolled toward him, pressing her lips against his. This was no faking, but her real self, doing the only thing that came naturally in this moment.

But his whole body tensed—not in a good way. She pulled away and whipped her hand back, embarrassment slamming into her, and he rolled back and sat up, banging his head on the bed above as he swung his legs around to the floor. For a moment she thought he was going to say something, but when he pulled back the curtain, letting the light from the street wash over them, his face said it all.

"Oh, God." She put a hand over her eyes. "Let's pretend I didn't do that."

He gently took her hand away from her face. "Cady. It's just not a good idea."

She shook her head, mortified at how she'd misread the situation. It wasn't possibility that had been hanging in the air, but her own delusion. She wished she could blame the cocktails, but their effect had worn off.

"It's okay, you don't have to say anything." She struggled to get out past him, one boot getting caught between the mattress and the wooden edge of the bed. "Damn it!"

He held out a hand to help her, but she grabbed hold of the opposite bunk and unwedged her foot. "I'm okay." She stood up straight and smoothed her crinkled San Francisco dress. "I'd better go and find Shelby."

"I guess so."

She waited to see if he had anything else to say. He didn't. She cleared her throat. "Thanks for listening."

He nodded. "Any time."

"Next time I'll bring my check book," she joked awkwardly, as they got off the bus. But it was perfectly obvious that this first time would be the last time.

Reid helped her flag down a cab, and they said an uncomfortable goodbye.

"It was a pleasure to meet you, Lady Cady," he said.

"You too."

She didn't want to dwell on exactly how much she'd liked meeting him, and how the feeling was clearly not quite mutual. Maybe Shelby was right after all—she had some learning to do. Well, she was working on it. Lesson learned here: a bit of fun and banter is *not* the signal to throw yourself at someone. She got in and gave him a last wave. As the cab drove away, she couldn't resist a last peek. He was still standing, watching her go. She decided to claim it as a small consolation.

★

Back at the guesthouse, she snuck in without seeing Marian, and found Shelby in their room.

"Where *were* you? You can't just disappear into the night, in a strange city. What was I supposed to do? I had to get a taxi back here by myself."

For a moment there, she'd thought that Shelby might've been worried about *her*. Should have known better. "Can we just not talk about it, please?" She didn't want to relive her rejection. What she was about to do was chastening enough. She got herself ready for a big slice of humble pie. "There's something we do need to talk about, though."

Shelby looked wary. "I suppose so."

"I know that news was a shock. I felt the same when Mum told me. And maybe I should have told you before now."

"Huh. Do you *think*?"

Cady ignored the tone. "I don't know. But we have three months here, just for ourselves. The trip of a lifetime. We can't fall to pieces in the first forty-eight hours."

"That wasn't *my* fault," Shelby pointed out.

She let that slide. "The other thing is...don't tell Dad, *please*. Just let it be. I mean, don't you think he's been through enough lately?"

"Well..." She frowned. "I hadn't thought of it that way. I suppose you're right."

"Thank you," Cady said, with relief. "We really don't need to find our biological father. Let's just enjoy our holiday."

Shelby sighed. "I was really hoping they'd invite me on the bus. I mean us," she added hastily.

"Well, we were hardly a tempting prospect after that little drama." She sat down on the bed opposite her sister. "Will we be able to make this work? I mean, we kind of have to."

"Go hard or go home?"

"Pretty much. And I do *not* want to go home."

With their dad settled in at Ingleside Heights, the little house in Peckham Rye was empty, waiting for the estate agent to find a buyer. Her things were in storage, and someone else was wearing the mumsy blue uniform to her bank job every day. She'd have to go back home eventually, maybe even to the bank. These days a job was a job, and the manager had promised there'd be one there for her, if she wanted it. She didn't think she'd *want* it, but she might have to take it, and be grateful for it. She couldn't fritter away her mother's money, wherever it was from. She had to use it for something good—like this adventure, then maybe the deposit on a little flat when they got back. But she didn't want to go home until they'd made every one of these days count.

"Me neither," Shelby said emphatically. Her expression finally softened, and she threw a pillow across at Cady. "I hate you."

They were back on track—for now, anyway. The father question was settled, and they could get on with their trip.

Cady laughed. "I hate you too. And I'm sorry you didn't get your bus invitation."

And, just quietly, relieved. Okay, she'd been doing a pretty good job of faking her new-start boldness. But she wasn't keen to fake being okay with the big fat 'no thank you' she'd just got from Reid. After all her time as a house mouse, and the let-down of Jeremy, her first time back out at bat had been a fall-in-the-dirt strikeout.

Chapter Eight

T he next morning, Marian was waiting when they went down to breakfast.

"I saw you on the news last night," she told Cady. "Nice job."

"Thank you," she replied, blushing a little. "It was totally unexpected."

"Well, you did great," she said, laying a little hand-written card in front of each of them. "Okay, so this is our Sunday menu."

Inside a border of swirly flowers, bugs and stars was a list of three items—cornmeal blueberry pancakes, organic buckwheat granola, and breakfast burrito with free-range eggs.

"Ooh, a real California breakfast," Cady said, thinking how delicious it all sounded.

Marian chuckled. "Oh no, that's not on the menu. Not officially, anyway." The girls looked at her, puzzled, so she explained. "A California breakfast has nothing to do with granola. It's coffee and weed...you know, wake and bake."

"Oh!" they both said, laughing.

"Okay, that's good info to have," Cady added. Although after the night before, maybe she could have been tempted. "I suppose I'll just have the coffee part then. And the pancakes, please."

"Me too, thank you," Shelby said.

"You need to be well fed for your travels." Marian took back the beautiful little menus and gave them a smile. "Make sure to come stay here before you fly out."

Cady nodded. "We definitely will."

They were picking up a hire car today, and heading south. The plan was to make their way slowly down the coast as far as San Diego, through LA, doing side trips whenever something grabbed their attention. Then they'd fly across to Vegas and bus out to the Grand Canyon, before coming back to San Francisco in time for LitQuake (edifying) and the Castro Street Fair (entertaining). Then home, to whatever awaited there.

"You better. And no more fighting." Marian gave her a wink and left the room.

Cady looked at Shelby. "What did you tell her?"

"Everything." At Cady's expression, she said, "So what? She's not going to judge you."

"Judge *me*?" Cady took a breath. Let it go, let it go. To be fair, she'd told Reid the night before, so she could hardly criticize.

She got out the California map and lay it on the table, between a tiny vase of wildflowers and an old-school salt pig. "Okay then. How far shall we go today? San Jose? Santa Cruz?"

Happily distracted by the prospect of the adventure ahead, they settled on the day's plan as they ate their breakfast. Then they packed the last things in their bags, and hugged Marian goodbye.

"Drive safe," she told them.

"Cady's doing the driving," Shelby said. "She doesn't trust me."

Cady rolled her eyes and jerked her thumb at her sister. "Would you trust this?" she asked Marian.

She grinned and shook her head, the tattooed string of flowers twisting in bloom on her neck as she moved. "You might have to. Just be good to each other."

★

"Toyota Corolla?" Shelby had a mouth like a cat's bottom as she regarded the modest silver car. "I was hoping for a Chevy, at least."

Cady herself had imagined them cruising the interstate in a Thunderbird convertible. But the Corolla was affordable, and practical, especially in the July heat. "Thelma and Louise we ain't," she said. "Hurry up and get in."

Shelby sighed and got in the passenger side as Cady slammed the trunk shut. Then she got herself settled in the driver's seat. She didn't drive much in London, apart from taking her mum to doctor's appointments when she could get time off. She'd taken the train to and from work every day, joining the glum commuter crowds on British Rail. Now she adjusted the Corolla's mirror and scooted the seat forward. Everything was opposite, including the road itself. She grasped the steering wheel firmly.

"Say a prayer to Saint Christopher," she advised Shelby.

"Saint who?"

"Never mind." She indicated, looked over the wrong shoulder, then the right one, and pulled out into the traffic. They were on their way.

★

After three days in Santa Cruz, Cady thought she finally fully understood the whole California dreaming thing. The sun, the sandy beach and sparkly water, the sea lions, the boardwalk with its candy-colored amusement park rides...it was all perfection. Both of them were too chicken to go on the old wooden-framed Giant Dipper rollercoaster, and the various swirling, falling, and spinning thrill rides, but they looked out at all the fun from high up in their M&M-red gondola. They ate saltwater taffy and corndogs, but bypassed the deep-fried Oreos and other artery-busting treats. After a while, it was hard to even remember what her overcast corner of south London even looked like.

63

When they phoned to check in with their dad, it was like talking to someone in a whole other universe.

On the morning of their fourth day, she rolled herself over in the sun and looked at Shelby, baking lazily on the next towel in her black bikini. "Do you think we should start planning our next move?"

She opened one eye and peered at Cady, not lifting her head from where it rested on her arms. "Move?" She really couldn't have looked less like someone who wanted to move.

"To our next stop, maybe?"

"Oh..." She heaved herself up and flipped over, scattering sand on Cady's book. "Not yet, surely?" She stretched out her legs, all the better to get an even tan.

"No, I guess not yet."

It had been a blessedly peaceful few days. Shelby seemed pacified by the sun, slowed to a happy ease. There had been no mention of the secret, or of finding their dad, and Cady was relieved that she seemed to be coming to terms with it all. She turned back to her book, but was distracted by a pair of surfers making their muscled way down to the water, carrying retro wooden surfboards straight out of a Beach Boys movie. From behind her sunglasses, she watched as they passed by, tall, tanned, and clichéd in the very best way. Maybe it wouldn't hurt to stay a few days longer.

Inspired by the surfers, she decided to take a photo of the beach and post it on Twitter. She still had hardly any followers, but it was fun to finally have some interesting things to share. She lined up a shot of Shelby's pedicured toes in the foreground, with the baby-blue lifeguard tower in the background, looking like a landing pod on its steel legs. A lifeguard obligingly appeared at just the right moment, leaning on the metal railings. With model-worthy girls scattered around on the white sand, and surfers on the water, it could have been a scene from a Katy Perry video. She was pretty sure Shelby's bubblegum-pink polish was something Katy would go for.

"What are you doing?" Shelby complained, not bothering to open her eyes.

"Nothing."

Satisfied with the shot, she chose the 'Tweet' option. While she was there, she figured she'd just see what was happening with the Flashpointers. What she found made her heart sing...and sink. They were following her now! But the SF-ly led backlash was dragging on, with an op-ed in the San Francisco Chronicle expounding on the inevitable crash of fads that burn too bright, too fast. And it seemed like the turnout for the latest Flashinator event hadn't been good. In fact, it was pretty much a flop. She knew that they'd planned a mid-week flash mob to tie in with a wine tasting and music festival, taking advantage of the long summer evenings and the captive vacation-happy visitors. She tried to think what could have gone wrong. Maybe it was the wrong demographic. Maybe everyone was too drowsy with heat and Zinfandel. Or maybe it was just that the tide was turning, and their golden days were ending, partly thanks to SF-ly. She hoped not—but it happened all the time. What goes up, must come down.

They did leave Santa Cruz the next day, after all. And in the days that followed, as they made their way down the coast and inland, Cady thought about it a lot. It may have been a fad, but it was the fad of her heart. It had given her something to dream about through the dark times, and she didn't want to see it come to an inglorious end.

"What have you been thinking about so much?" Shelby asked one day, as they poked around in an antique store. This one was in a red barn behind someone's house, a picture-perfect little piece of Americana.

She picked up an old carpenter's plane and turned it over in her hands. The handle and knob were smooth with age and use, but the metal parts were still good. It had probably belonged to a family with a barn just like this. "I've been wondering if Flashpoint is going to fall to pieces now."

"That'd be a shame. I wonder what Kyle would do." She looked wistful at the thought of him. "But, you know, nothing lasts forever."

"I suppose not." She looked at the tool, still sturdy and useable. Then she sighed and put it back down on the display table, feeling flat. "Well, we'll see."

"Come on, let's go and eat," said Shelby. "Then we can decide what to do with our afternoon."

Before she'd finished her sentence, she was halfway out the door. Cady said a thank you to the sales assistant and followed her out. After their rocky start, the trip had been going surprisingly well. Shelby had come up with the idea of having a couple of hours to themselves every afternoon. That way, she said, they wouldn't get sick of each other. And, they could each do something they really wanted to. It was actually a great suggestion. Cady loved the antique stores and artists' studios that were tucked away in every little town they came to, and Shelby loved to browse the modern shops and boutiques. This way, they avoided any arguments about what to do, and had enough 'me' time to keep tension at bay. Sometimes Cady just walked around, soaking up the atmosphere and enjoying the sun. She was on holiday, after all.

After lunch that day, she found a quaint independent bookstore—kind of a rarity so far on their travels—and couldn't resist going in. It was good to support local booksellers, she'd heard, in the age of Amazon. She found the latest paperback from Kristan Higgins, ordered a coffee and a bagel from the tiny café counter at the back of the store, and settled in to read.

After an hour or so, and a second coffee, she decided to check in on the latest with the Flashpoint situation. She signed into Twitter and noticed that she had a direct message, for the first time ever. Curious, she clicked on the little envelope. It was from the Flashpoint account.

> *Hey Cady. How's it going? Guess you can see*
> *how it's going here—not best. Listen, I*
> *watched your interview. You made it all*
> *sound so simple and true. Yeah, noble even.*
> *Any ideas about what we should do next? K.*

Her heart skittered with excitement. Kyle was asking *her* what they should do? Well, as it happened, she did have some ideas. She typed a reply, making sure to keep her online cool.

> *Yes, been thinking about it actually. Have a*
> *few ideas. Happy to help if I can. Cady.*

After a minute she signed out, not wanting to be that sad person sitting there refreshing the screen, waiting for a reply. Then a text came from Shelby, asking where she was, so she texted back. Before Shelby arrived, she couldn't resist doing one more quick check—and there was a reply.

> *Come back? There's room on the bus. Bring*
> *that sister.*

She sat, grinning at her phone like an idiot. Uh, yes, she'd come back. Assuming Shelby wanted to. And she was pretty damn sure she'd want to.

Suddenly, though, she remembered the complicating factor—Reid. Could she handle the embarrassment of facing up to him again, knowing she was still nursing a mammoth crush—yes, she'd admit it—while he was most emphatically not? Well, of course she could. She'd handled tougher stuff than that. And this could be something amazing. She wasn't going to let a small (okay, *tall*, and dark and handsome) complication get in the way of being part of Flashpoint, if only for a little while.

There was a ring-a-ling as the door opened, triggering the old brass bell, and Shelby came in. She took one look at Cady's face and said, "What? What is it?"

"Come and see."

She held out the phone so that Shelby could read the messages, and laughed as her sister's face went pink and her eyes grew large.

"No! Really?"

"Yes, really." She laughed. "Does that mean you want to go, then?"

"*Hel-lo!* Yes, I want to go." She did a little happy dance right in the middle of the store, making the other customers stare. "Oh my God, I really hate you right now, Cady Morrow."

"I hate you too." She shook her head, laughing at her exuberant twin. "I hate you so much I got you back on that bus. Now let's get you out of here before someone calls the funny farm."

★

"How much of a trust fund do you think he has?" Shelby asked as they headed north again, air conditioning cranked up to high in the little silver car.

"I thought you would've found that out already," Cady replied. Shelby was usually quick to establish the financial credentials of any man that interested her. She liked to get as much info as possible, to see if a guy would be worth her while. Worth, as in *net* worth. "Didn't Reid say he had some sponsorship deals too?"

"He said he was negotiating." Shelby thought for a while. "That bus is expensive. And he's been funding the events. I guess the others are volunteers, maybe."

"Maybe." She wondered how Reid fit his sand sculpture work around the Flashpoint activities. Well, for better or worse, she'd have a chance now to find out—if he was along for the ride. "Do you think the evil twins will be there?"

"Twins more evil than us?" Shelby laughed.

"Actually I think you and Alison are the evil set," Cady said, earning a thump in the arm. "Ow! Don't injure the driver, or you'll never get there."

Shelby frowned. "I hope they're not staying on the bus."

"If they are, we'll have to cope. And you'll have to use your best behavior, seriously. I don't know how long we've got, so make the most of it."

She smiled to herself. If making the most of it meant being in Reid's company, she was willing to do what had to be done.

Chapter Nine

With only a few wrong turns, they found their way to the park on the outskirts of San Francisco where they'd arranged to meet the bus. As they arrived, Kyle came down the steps to meet them. He was wearing black, super-skinny skinny jeans, and the furry vest, as usual. The brisk wind blew the fur in different directions, but his quiff sat firm where it emerged from under his beanie. He scratched his raggedy beard as he approached, and Cady could see why he was such an easy target for the nay-sayers. But she noticed that Shelby looked slightly glazed as he approached—she, at least, felt the full effect of his charisma.

"Made it, huh?" He smiled at them both, but especially at Shelby, who seemed to have suddenly lost her usual bravado. She smiled and managed a small 'hi'.

Cady was intrigued by her sister's uncharacteristic flutteriness. She'd never have picked that someone like Kyle would hit Shelby's weak spot. "Made it, no trouble," she said. "Thanks for inviting us back."

"I'm interested to hear your suggestions," he said. "Come stash your bags on the bus, and we'll have a drink."

There was no one else on the bus, and Cady couldn't

tell who might be staying in the other curtained-off beds. They tucked their bags in the narrow closets between the bunks that Kyle gave them. "We'll have to take the rental car back tomorrow," Cady said as they went back into the lounge area. "We can't leave it here."

"No problem. Someone can pick you up from the yard."

He splashed drinks into glasses without asking what the girls would like, and handed them over, then checked a message on his phone. "Reid. He'll be here soon. Did you eat yet?"

They shook their heads, and he said, "We can go in Reid's car and meet up with the others in town for dinner."

Cady had been hungry, but with the prospect of seeing Reid her stomach suddenly got busy churning over her nerves. She took a swig of the drink, grimacing as the strength of it hit her tongue, but grateful for the hit.

Shelby had regrouped, and now stretched out her legs, crossing and uncrossing them in a leisurely way for Kyle's benefit as she toyed with her glass. "We haven't eaten for ages," she said. "Cady wouldn't stop, and we had an early lunch. I'm staaarving." She elongated the word, giving it implications beyond the usual meaning.

Cady defended herself. "I just wanted to get us here before it got too late."

"Mean big sister."

Shelby was this close to actually pouting. Kyle shook his head in mock sympathy, but Cady didn't bite. She was fighting the urge to try and peer out the window at every passing car. An old pick-up went by, then a people-mover full of kids, then a Prius...would he drive something green and eco-friendly, befitting his alternative-lifestyle job? She tried to keep one eye on the road without her distraction showing, but Kyle and Shelby were so caught up in their conversation, they probably wouldn't have noticed anyway. Shelby was over her initial coyness, and back in full flirtation mode.

"Okay," Kyle said eventually, looking at Cady. "Let's talk about these ideas of yours."

She dragged her gaze away from the window. "Shouldn't we wait until everyone's together?"

He shook his head. "No. I don't want any of them to think things are going badly."

"They must know it's not great though? They've been here, and they've all read the same stuff online."

"Yeah. But we don't all need to agonize over it. I just have to come up with a plan. You know, save the day."

"You've done such amazing things already, though." How could he be stuck now, after coming up with all those cool concepts she'd seen online?

"I know. But I've been dealing with some shit lately. Seems like the well is dry. Just at the moment, you know." He pulled off the beanie and scratched his head, strain showing on his face for the first time. "So, tell me these ideas of yours."

For a moment she saw behind his self-assurance, and she realized that he didn't want to lose face. He couldn't control everything in the online world, but as the leader of this little gang he needed to keep up the show. And she wanted this show to stay on the road—so if he needed to take her plan and make it his, she didn't care.

"I've been thinking about it a lot." She wanted to be diplomatic—she was afraid of offending him, or bruising his ego. She glanced at Shelby, still captivated by this oddly compelling man. If she lost their spot on the bus her sister really *would* hate her. Even more than for all the other reasons she'd apparently been stewing on for years, that burst out in their fight—plus the dad secret, of course. Also, if they weren't on the bus, Cady wouldn't see Reid again. Which, if she wanted to keep things simple, might be for the best.

But she pushed those thoughts aside, and launched in. "I'm wondering if the movement started to veer a little…commercial. I mean, it came across as really organic before. Even though I know every event took a heap of planning."

"Okay," he said, sounding wary. "Keep talking."

"It seems like…" She made sure to choose exactly the

71

right words. "It had that 'by the people, for the people' feeling about it. It was like a simple, honest connection—people were coming together to create something beautiful, just for the *goodness* of it. And the fun."

He leaned back in his chair, eyes narrowed, but listening. Cady ploughed on. "And maybe, if it seems too manufactured, it loses its authenticity."

"Yeah, but it's all manufactured," he pointed out. "Flash mobs don't just happen by themselves. And I can't totally rule out commercialism. If the movement loses credibility, and people stop coming, there's no way I'll get any sponsorship deals. And without them, I might not be able to keep this thing going."

This was a new factor. Shelby sent her a worried look. She'd never imagined money might be a problem, but it didn't seem appropriate to ask why.

"I have some money..." Shelby began uncertainly.

Kyle's attention snapped to her. "You do?"

"Shelby, no," Cady said firmly. "That's an inheritance. That's for your future." She knew she sounded lecturing, but too bad. This was serious stuff. Giving money away on a whim—on a crush—would rank as the topmost top of bad decisions made by her impulsive sister.

"Oh, yeah, yeah, of course," Kyle said hastily. "Your future."

Shelby shrugged. "I suppose. What's your bright idea then?" She looked at Cady as if waiting for her to pull a rabbit out of a hat.

"Okay. Commercial reality versus credibility. There must be a middle ground." Cady frowned. "Maybe now that the Flashpoint novelty has worn off, you need to find a new..." She struggled for the right word. "Um, paradigm?"

He laughed out loud, making her blush. "Paradigm? None of us are that high-brow."

"Trust you to fancify the whole thing," Shelby commented, rolling her eyes.

Her first instinct was to backpedal. "Well, I didn't mean..." Then she stopped. *Confidence, new Cady.* She looked at Kyle. "I meant that you can start again with a new approach. And I have an idea for how. A good idea."

He put his drink on the table and leaned forward. "Tell me."

★

By the time Reid arrived, Cady had shared her idea—and she knew their place on the bus was secure, for now anyway. Kyle loved it.

"I've got a plan," he told Reid the moment he stepped onto the bus. "And it's fucking good. We'll tell the others tonight."

"That's awesome, man," Reid clapped him on the back in true guy style. Then he looked at the girls, his eyes settling on Cady. "Hi, ladies. Welcome back."

Cady felt the heat in her face and knew she was blushing. Damn. "Hi," she replied, her voice casual. "Yep, you couldn't get rid of us after all."

"Looks like you got some holidaying in." He looked her up and down, just a little slower than necessary. "You're looking tan."

She wrapped her arms around herself, suddenly self-conscious. "We started with a few days on the beach at Santa Cruz."

"The water wasn't very warm though," Shelby complained.

Kyle shrugged. "That's the West Coast for you. We'll have to find you a swimming pool, so you can get your bikini back on."

He raised an eyebrow and she raised one back, playing with her hair as she replied. "You're on."

Reid was still looking at Cady, but she carefully made sure not to meet his eye. She'd leave the bikini banter to Shelby—the expert from way back. Banter hadn't done her any good lately. But as soon as he turned to go, leading the way out to the parking lot, she couldn't resist hanging back for a rear view. His shoulders were broad in his black t-shirt, and his long, strong back tapered down to... She

73

sighed and made herself look away. It was clearly going to be a struggle keeping her mind on things.

His eco-friendly car turned out to be an old Chevy Blazer—not what she'd expected. She leapt for the back seat, avoiding the possibility of embarrassing herself with distraction at close range. She could see Shelby was peeved—hoping for a cozy ride in the back with Kyle—but she accepted the offer of the front passenger seat with queenly grace.

From her seat in back, Cady had a clear view of Reid's profile as he drove. He laughed as Shelby said something funny, and appealing smile lines creased at the corner of his eye. A strand of dark hair had slipped out of his ponytail, and it tickled the line of his jaw above where goatee gave way to stubble. She remembered how it had felt to put her hand against just that spot, the darkness making her bold enough to press her lips against his. Her pulse increased just thinking about him lying near enough to touch, breathing him in, the possibility of where her hands might wander and what they might find. He turned and said something to Shelby, revealing white teeth made even more striking by the darkness of his surrounding beard. A dimple flashed as he grinned, and for a moment she let herself imagine a rerun of that night, as though her move was exactly the right one, instead of an embarrassing misstep...

Then she shook herself back into focus. Her new start was underway, and it didn't have to include a new man. In fact, better if it didn't. Three months was long enough to taste American life, and to make a difference with Flashpoint. And, maybe, to fall hard enough for someone that goodbye would be a painful wrench. Even more so if that person could wave you goodbye without a care. So, no more daydreaming. There were things to do, and she intended to do them so fully that she'd go home with no regrets—just a stack of great memories, and the satisfaction of having done amazing things. Oh, and a more interesting Twitter profile.

Chapter Ten

Kyle banged his glass on the wooden table, sloshing out a wave of whiskey. "Okay, people. Here's the plan."

They were at Sanctuary again, in what the girls now realized was their regular booth. Everyone quietened down and turned to him, waiting to hear something that would give their movement its mojo back. Cady hoped her idea—now Kyle's—would be enough.

"All right. There's a family in Rownville who already have two preschoolers—and now they're expecting triplets." He shuddered. "God help them."

"Five kids!" Alison looked pained by the very idea. "I can't even imagine having one at this point."

"I know, right?" Kyle agreed. "And, there are complications. The dad lost his job as a mechanic, and now the bank wants to foreclose on their mortgage."

A murmur of sympathy went round the table. Even though everyone there was single and childless, it didn't take a lot of imagination to see what a devastating situation that would be.

After seeing their story on the news, Cady hadn't been able to stop thinking about the Rownville family—the Isaacsons. There was something in the mother's expression, resignation mixed with determination, that stayed with her. Her belly was enormous already, although she was only halfway through her pregnancy. They were probably about the same age, and Cady couldn't imagine how she'd cope in the same circumstances. As her husband talked to the reporter, he looked like he was ready to break under the weight of his responsibilities, but he toughed out the interview. The international financial crisis might be officially over (or not—she couldn't keep up with all the differing opinions), but Cady knew that families all over America were still losing their homes. Here was one family they could help, at least.

"So," Kyle said, "I think we can do something. We need a new angle, and they need help. We're going to stage a flash mob right outside the bank, all right? We'll make it a fundraiser, and put pressure on the suits at the same time. Hopefully we'll raise enough cash to take the weight off financially for the Isaacsons, plus get them better terms with the bank."

"But why did they have more kids if they couldn't afford them?" Alison asked. "I mean, why have *three* more babies? They must have done IVF, to end up with three."

Jennifer nodded, a bobble-headed follower of her opinionated friend. Beside her, Cady felt Shelby about to say something—and she knew it wouldn't be in agreement. She elbowed her sharply in the ribs. That little feud had to be put to bed, unless they wanted their time on the bus to be a nightmare. Or cut short when they were kicked off for causing trouble. Alison had first dibs, after all.

"Nope, apparently not," Kyle said. "Just hit with crazy odds."

Alison shuddered. "Ugh. Frightening."

It was definitely a sobering thought for the free-and-easy Flashpoint gang. After some more discussion, it was agreed to go ahead and plan the event. There was a lot to be decided—what exactly would happen on the day, and how the money would be raised—but they all seemed to love the idea as much as Kyle had.

Cady smiled with satisfaction as they tossed ideas

around, excitement building. Across the table, Reid smiled at her too, and leaned forward. "Sounds like a hit—best idea Kyle's ever had," he said.

She nodded. "We can make it work, I'm sure." Kyle could take the credit. If it got Flashpoint back on track—and kept the Isaacsons in their own house—she'd go home happy.

★

After dinner that night, they all headed back to the bus. Cady was apprehensive, to say the least—about keeping a lid on Shelby's attitude around Alison, and keeping her own composure around Reid. Especially once she found out he'd be sleeping in the bed opposite hers. Kyle would be in his suite upstairs, of course. Both Cady and Shelby were dying to see what it looked like—especially Shelby, who was nurturing an ever-growing infatuation. But they'd be downstairs in cattle class, with Alison and Jennifer, Reid and Gavin. Tino lived nearby, so he said he'd join them early the next day, ready to head for Rownville and scope out the bank. It wasn't Ocean's Eleven—or any other number—but Cady still felt excited at the prospect, despite her nerves.

It was late by the time they got back, and she'd had enough drinks that she started to flag as the effects wore off. It had been a long day of driving, too. She decided to put off having a shower until the morning, and tuck herself into her little ship's bed. She wished everyone goodnight and scooted into one of the surprisingly spacious bathrooms at the back of the bus—like the kitchen, it was bigger than the one they had in Peckham Rye—and cleaned her teeth and put her pajamas on. Then she removed herself from temptation.

As she settled herself under the feather comforter, she could hear Reid's voice saying goodnight, and soon she recognized the sound of him getting into bed too. She rolled over, pulling the comforter up and squeezing her eyes shut.

Out of sight, out of mind was probably the best strategy when it came to that distraction across the corridor.

Out of sight was easy enough, but out of mind gave her trouble. She lay listening to the chat and clatter as the others bounced around, laughing and point-scoring. Shelby seemed to be behaving, luckily. The noise went on for what felt like an age, while she tried not to think about Reid lying in the bed opposite...

She must have finally drifted off to sleep, because she gasped with shock when she felt someone shake her awake. In her blurred, half-asleep state she struggled to remember where she was, feeling disoriented by the close walls and ceiling of the bunk bed. Then she rolled over and saw who had woken her, and everything came back.

"Shh." Reid had his finger against his lips, urging her to be quiet. There was only just enough light to tell it was him. His features were in shadow, but he gestured clearly for her to come with him.

She nodded, and he turned and disappeared, letting the curtain fall back. She got out of bed as quickly as she could, wondering what on earth was happening. He was already at the top of the bus stairs when she emerged, so she followed, trying to smooth her hair as she went. The dim night lighting in the lounge was enough to see by, and she made it down the steps on sleepy legs without falling flat on her face.

The cool air hit her as she stepped out of the bus, and goosebumps prickled on her skin. Even this close to the city, the stars were bright in the clear night sky. She shivered a little, suddenly acutely aware that she was wearing no more than little pajama shorts and a silky tank top. She crossed her arms, covering her breasts as her nipples inevitably reacted to the cold. Reid stood waiting for her at the bottom of the stairs, wearing navy cotton boxers and a t-shirt. She couldn't help wondering what effect the cold was having on a particular part of *his* body... A surreptitious peek gave nothing away in that department, but the sight of his long, tanned legs and strong thighs woke her up even more than the cold. He must wear shorts for all that sandcastle building.

"Come on," he whispered, and led her around the other side of the bus, away from the sleeping area. She trailed behind, wincing as loose stones stabbed the bottom of her bare feet, but unable to resist the view of muscular shoulders, and a perfectly formed butt clad loosely in really quite flimsy cotton.

They stopped on a narrow path between the bus and the grass, and he turned to her.

"That was your idea, wasn't it." It was a statement, not a question. "Something like that would never occur to Kyle."

She looked at him, letting her disbelief show. "You dragged me out of bed in the middle of the night to ask me that?"

"Sorry. But there's not much alone time with this crowd around."

Alone time with him was something she'd been planning to avoid. It was surreal to be standing with him in the parking lot, lit by only the moon and one distant street light. She suddenly had the urge to run across the grassy expanse of park, leaving footprints under the dewy moonlight. She leaned back against the bus, the chill of cold metal against her skin anchoring her in place and clearing her mind.

"I know it was your idea," he persevered. "You should get credit for it."

She shrugged. "It doesn't matter whose idea it is." She didn't know why he'd care about that anyway. "The main thing is to keep this movement on its feet, and help the Isaacsons. I can't imagine the shock of suddenly facing five kids under five."

She tightened her arms around her body, the night's chill starting to seep into her bones. The kid subject wasn't something she wanted to dwell on.

"Yeah, that would be a handful." He suddenly changed tack. "How many kids *do* you want?"

"What?" That was usually a question men went to great lengths to avoid. The randomness of it threw her off-guard. "I don't know...I'm not really planning on having kids." Just saying it out loud kick-started the ache that came with that probability, and she shivered.

"You're cold." He stepped closer, his pupils deepening his eyes to chocolate in the dark, his brows shadowing them further. Her back was freezing where she was pressed against the bus, but she could feel the warmth from his body in front, maybe an inch away. Any thoughts of running were replaced with an urge to step forward and meet that warmth with her own body. To slide her hands under his t-shirt and across his smooth back, run teasing fingers around the waistband of his boxers, and discover whether she could undo the cold's effect...

But he seemed unaware of where her wayward mind was going. "No kids?" he asked. "Why not?"

She sighed, back to reality. She didn't know for sure what the future would bring, but she wasn't going to hope and plan for something that could be so cruelly snatched away.

"You already know why. I do like kids, but I just couldn't give my children the burden of those wonky genes. I've seen what they did to my mum, remember?"

She'd told him more than she intended that night, after the epic Shelby fight. Maybe her over-sharing was what triggered her misjudgment. *I just can't,* he'd said. And done her a favor, really. She didn't know *why* he couldn't, and she wasn't going to ask—maybe the reason was Jennifer, maybe not. But anyway, if it was a letting-her-down-gently, she really didn't need to know why.

"About that night..." he began.

But she shook her head and stepped around him onto the damp grass, removing herself from any temptation, avoiding another strikeout.

"Let's not go there. I was just having an overwhelmed moment, you know, far from home, driven crazy by sister, too many cocktails, blah blah." It sounded believable enough. "And we have to work together on this event now."

Now it was his turn to fold his arms. "Blah blah, huh?

Okay. Come on then, we'd better get back inside." He waved for her to go ahead. "After you, Lady Cady."

Was the blah blah a bit much? Well, it was for the best. But walking ahead, she was suddenly self-conscious about her gait—like she'd forgotten which foot went where, and exactly how much hip-wiggling was her usual amount. Was he watching her the way she'd watched him, admiring his easy stride, his firm butt, and the darkness of his hair against his neck? She shook her own hair, so that it swished down her back. Let him look. No harm in looking, after all.

Back in the bus, they paused outside their beds. "Goodnight," she mouthed silently, and he did the same.

They both got into bed. She lay wide awake behind the curtain, waiting for her frozen toes to warm up, and going over the encounter in her mind. Her ears pricked at every little sound in the bus, trying to tell which might be him. If each of them reached out, they'd be able to touch hands across the space between their beds. She wondered what he was thinking, or if he was already asleep. Then there was the sound of movement, and her curtain was pulled back again. She raised herself up on one elbow, her heart beating a little faster.

"Don't let him take you over," he whispered, his voice serious.

She realized he meant Kyle. She was kind of flattered that he'd think to say that—even though it was totally unnecessary. Letting Kyle have one idea didn't constitute falling into a cultish thrall. But he waited until she nodded okay, then he let the curtain fall again, and was gone.

Her toes were still frozen, but one part of her at least was well-warmed by their encounter. She squished her thighs together and rolled over, pulling her legs up against her body. This was going to be some bus ride.

Chapter Eleven

The following week was a whirlwind of activity as they pulled together to make Cady's—now Kyle's—flash mob idea happen.

They were travelling the next day to Rownville, a sweet satellite town about an hour north of San Francisco. In the morning, Cady peeked out of bed, hoping to make a dash for the bathroom without bumping into Reid. But he was already up and gone, the curtain open and his bed neatly straightened. She resolved to keep her toilet bag in her bunk from now on, so she could do any emergency remedial work before facing everyone on the bus. Shelby's curtain above was still closed, which was no surprise. She'd never been a morning person. As Cady headed for the bathroom, the sound of gentle snoring drifted out from Alison's bunk. She laughed to herself, knowing Alison would hate that she was making such an unattractive sound. It was tempting to record it—maybe she'd suggest it to Shelby, and let her have the fun.

By the time she came back out of the bathroom, dressed and presentable, Reid and Gavin were joking around in the kitchen. Boxes of pastries sat on the table, along with cardboard trays of takeout coffee.

Reid gave her a wink. "Sleep well?"

She pulled a coffee from a tray. "Mostly," she replied, looking into one of the pastry boxes to avoid his grin. Damn, even first thing in the morning he was completely distracting. "You guys too lazy to make breakfast?"

"Yup," Gavin said, reaching over her to take the biggest pastry. "Just tell my man thank you. He paid."

She looked across at Reid. Leaning against the bench, long legs stretched out, he made the kitchen seem like it was built for munchkins. Her eyes wanted to travel up and down, up and down his body, but she made herself focus on his face. "Thank you."

"You're welcome, Lady Cady," he replied. "Can't have our foreign dignitaries going hungry."

Before she could reply, Kyle came into the kitchen, looking creased and ragged. "Morning."

"Morning," they all replied. Cady thought he looked like he hadn't slept at all. If he had slept, it had been with the beanie on his head. He looked terrible.

"Come with me," he told her, picking up a coffee and taking the tray with it. He grunted and batted it off, and it fell on the floor. "Come." Then he turned and went out.

After what Reid had said the night before, she felt self-conscious about following Kyle out. But she was her own person, and working closely with Kyle to make this happen for the Flashpointers—and for the Isaacsons—wasn't any kind of compromise. This new start had had its hiccups, but didn't any new thing? Until now she'd only really seen the charismatic Kyle, the hipster-cool face he turned to the world. But, hey, no one could keep that up 24/7. She went after him, grabbing a pastry to quiet her rumbling stomach.

He led her up to the second level. As they went, she glanced behind her to see if Shelby was up, but there was no sign of her. She'd be green with envy over this little excursion.

At the top of the stairs was a small hallway, with cupboards along one side. He opened a door in front of them, and they went through into his suite. It was as luxuriously appointed as the downstairs, with leather furniture, another bar, and cloud-soft grey carpet. The only difference was the state it was in.

He dodged across in front of her and pulled the en suite bathroom door closed. "Kind of a mess," he muttered.

As was the rest of the suite. Cady wriggled her bare toes in the plush luxury underfoot, but was careful not to step too quickly. God knows what she might stand on. This mess would be a credit to an entire rock band on the road, let alone one smallish hipster with a large ego.

"Have a seat," he said, sitting on the corner of his enormous bed. She spotted a space on the sofa next to the bar, and picked her way across, stepping over an empty Doritos bag, a sauce-smudged Taco Bell box, and, urk, a pair of black silk boxers. He didn't seem to care about the chaos, so she tried not to notice it. She wasn't his mother, after all. Thankfully.

He rubbed his glazed eyes, then flipped the lid off his coffee and took a huge gulp, obviously in need of something strong to sharpen himself up. Then he wiped his mouth with the back of his hand. Cady finished her pastry, waiting to hear what he'd got her up there for, and resisted the urge to tell him there was a little bit of foam on the corner of his topless beard.

"Listen," he said, coming right to the point. "We need this to be a success, all right? We need numbers on the day, and we need positive media coverage. If this goes well, my sponsorship negotiations will be back on track."

She thought for a moment. "If that's an important factor, we'll have to tread carefully with the bank. If we make them look bad, no big corporate will come near."

"Exactly." He nodded, satisfied. "I thought you'd get it."

She leaned back, trying to get her head around the delicacy of the situation. Something stuck into her spine, and she fished a half-empty bottle of Wild Turkey out from behind her and dropped it on top of a pile of clothes. "Okay, so...we need to set it up right. Make it possible for them to look like the good guys coming in to save the day, not the bad guys in sharp suits ruining the Isaacson's lives."

"And *this* is why I got you back," he said. "I was so right."

"Um...thank you."

He stood up, as though something was all decided. "So you're taking charge of this flash mob."

She looked up at him, nonplussed. "Me? But I've never organized anything like this before." And, she didn't add, wasn't *he* the one who should be in charge?

"You don't have to do all the work," he said. "But someone needs to keep the tone, manage the perceptions and the egos. I'm right about you."

He held out an arm, inviting her to leave. The conversation was over. It was settled—she was doing his job. For better or worse, Flashpoint's future hung not just on her idea, but on her own self. She hoped he *was* right about her.

★

On the way to Rownville, with the team together on the bus, Kyle announced what he had told Cady earlier—he was appointing her as official coordinator for the event. This set the cat amongst the pigeons—although actually, Cady felt more like the pigeon between two stalking cats. With no clue that it was all Cady's idea, Alison and Jennifer were obviously perplexed and pissed that this newcomer could walk in and take the coveted spot at Kyle's right hand. Reid and Shelby knew why, of course. Cady had sworn Shelby to secrecy at the beginning, and knew she'd be enjoying the other girls' annoyance.

Reid raised an eyebrow, but didn't say anything apart from congratulations. No one had noticed their midnight assignation, and neither of them mentioned it. It seemed to Cady like it could have been a dream, if it wasn't for the bits of grass in her bed that morning. There was something else she would rather have found in her bed. But even if the two of them were a happening thing—even if Reid hadn't said *I just can't,* and left it there—the bus was *not* the place.

Bunking down with one real twin, two evil twins (one of whom seemed particularly attached to Reid), and one cheery California doofus didn't exactly lend itself to romance. Time and a place, after all. Not that there would be either, it seemed.

As they drove, Cady put any lingering thoughts out of her head and got busy. She managed to contact the Isaacsons, and told the mum, Dayna, what Flashpoint was proposing. After she explained, there was a long silence on the line, and she wondered if they'd be turned down. But then there was a sudden shuddering intake of breath, and a sob, and she realized that Dayna had been silently crying on the other end of the phone.

"Yes!" she managed, in between sobs. "Oh my God, yes. Thank you!"

Full of relief, Cady laughed. "You're welcome. I just hope we can make a difference for you and your family."

"Brad!" she called out to her husband. "Brad, you're not going to believe this!" Then she addressed Cady again. "I can't tell you how much I appreciate it—how much we both needed some kind of miracle like this."

"I don't know if we can work a miracle for you," Cady had to warn her. "But we'll do our best to help. We'll come and see you soon, and fill you in on the plan."

Once she'd talked to Dayna, she realized how high the stakes really were. They were real people, a real family facing a life-changing crisis. Having promised to help, the Flashpointers had to come through, somehow. After that conversation, she felt like things had stepped up a notch, and the pressure was on. And as she told the others about it, she could see the same feeling reflected in all their faces.

In Rownville, they found a place to park the bus and did reconnaissance around town. Luckily, the Isaacson's bank was in a square that allowed plenty of room for the crowd they hoped would turn up on the day.

The plan was to use Iggy Pop's song 'Home' as the theme music—it was perfect for the occasion, talking about how everyone needs a home, and who's looking after you, and love of family, and ending up on the street. It was also simple, and ridiculously catchy. Cady had found a version online without the curse words, because this was a family event, after all.

The area outside the bank was more than big enough to chalk out the floor plan of a house. The plan was for the flash mob participants to stand along the outline, forming a house made of people. They were timing the event for sunset, so they could hold glow sticks lighting the outline. Any extra people—and they hoped there'd be a lot—would surround them. In the dusk there should be enough light to see everything that happened, made festive with the glow sticks. And anyone who didn't bring glow sticks could add sparkle in the dark with their phones.

They made contact with some local Flashpoint fans who were willing to help out however they could. There was talk about borrowing items of furniture for the day, so that their house made of people would have chairs, rugs, a table, and whatever other random household items they could get hold of. But then it occurred to Cady that maybe they could get a furniture store to donate some pieces, so she added that to her to-do list.

She also asked Shelby and Jennifer to choreograph simple but suitably Iggy-ish dance moves, and the two of them worked together surprisingly well. Once she was separated from Alison, Shelby reported, Jennifer was almost okay. In fact, she was even pretty nice. They came up with some great moves that could be done more or less on the spot, to hold the house outline, and spent an afternoon making a video to post on the Flashpoint YouTube channel. Judging by the giggling and fooling around that was going on every time Cady went to check on them, it promised to be very entertaining. Plus, their tiny outfits couldn't hurt, if they were hoping to attract plenty of guys to the event too...

Alison was charged with traditional media liaison, her usual job. She was definitely less inclined to warm to the twins, maintaining such a brittle veneer of faux friendliness that Cady was scared to go too close in case she smashed all over the floor. There didn't seem much point in trying to turn her around, so Cady just got on with the job. They started putting the word out on social media too, crossing their fingers that there'd be no snarky backlash this time.

The guys did their bit, racing here and there getting things organized and making contacts. If their version of making contacts included drinking quite a lot of beer with various locals, Cady figured it couldn't do any harm. And if Reid was out 'networking' with Gavin, and she was busy working, there would be mercifully few opportunities during the day to torture herself with sneak peeks and surreptitious admiration. When they all met up again in the evening, she sat herself firmly between two of the others—even if one of them had to be Alison—and resisted the damn-near-irresistible.

Chapter Twelve

C ady had arranged to go and see Dayna Isaacson on their second day in Rownville. Brad was out job-hunting, Dayna had said on the phone, but the boys would be glad of a new person to show off for. She was getting so big now that it was uncomfortable just getting around, and she was going out less and less. Cady wanted to take something for the kids, Max and Ty, so she asked what they were into.

"Oh, cars," Dayna sighed. "Cars, cars, and cars. I can't believe how much car info a four-year-old and a three-year old can memorize."

Cady laughed. "They must be very clever kids."

"Yeah, if only they were as clever at remembering their pleases and thank yous."

"I'm sure they're absolute angels," Cady said.

"Sure, when they're asleep," Dayna retorted, the standard parent joke. But then she added, "Actually, they are little cherubs. You know, sometimes I feel like they were just waiting for us to be ready for them to arrive. To give them a way to earth. And the same with these three. I can't imagine why they chose us...but everything will just have to be okay."

As she hung up, Cady let herself be envious just for a moment. She didn't think she'd ever be strong enough to cope with what Dayna was facing. Of course, there was a good chance she wouldn't ever find out how she'd cope with even one. The softness in Dayna's voice when she talked about her little ones, all five of them, and the simple way she knew their family was meant to be, brought on a pang of loss. She pushed it away, and resolved to do everything she could for this woman and her babies.

★

Although Kyle had decided that she and Alison should be the ones to visit Dayna and Brad, when the day came, Alison had a radio interview to do. It was actually a relief— Cady wasn't convinced that Alison was the most sympathetic of the team. But when Kyle chose Reid as the replacement, her relief turned on its head. She was sitting in the corner of the bus lounge, at the desk that served as the Flashpoint operations center. Turning in the chair, she blurted out, "Really?"

"Yes," he said. "You're my most level-headed two. I know you'll represent us well."

When Kyle went back upstairs, Reid came and leaned against the bar, next to where she was sitting. "You could have tried to look a bit less horrified."

"I'm not horrified," she replied, purposefully concentrating on the laptop screen while cursing herself for always being so transparent. "I'm just surprised. I thought he'd choose one of the other girls."

He grinned. "I know you've been avoiding me since I dragged you out in your PJs." He lowered his voice. "Your very small PJs."

The shock of his words hit her low in her belly, and she felt the heat rise in her face. Wow, that was out of the blue. She looked around, but they were alone. Sitting at the desk, she was right at the level of his belt buckle, the only point around his hips where his t-shirt was tucked into his jeans.

One of his hands was in his pocket, just the thumb out, pointing in the direction of...she swallowed. The heat suffused another part of her body, and she shifted in her chair.

"Just an observation," he added innocently, the expression on his face anything but innocent.

She stood up, trying to even the playing field. "Put your work face back on," she told him. Her voice came out more husky than she expected, and she cleared her throat. Now that she was standing, it took a huge effort to not step closer. As it was, her eyes kept dropping to his lips, but when she made herself look him in the eye instead, it was no better. He looked right back at her, and she could hardly look away. Her own lips parted of their own accord, like a character in a penny romance. Damn, didn't she have more strength than this?

At her words, he stood up straight too. "Sorry boss," he said, the hint of a smile playing on his lips as he looked down at her. "Couldn't resist that one." He was obviously pleased at the reaction he'd got.

"Well, you'll have to try harder." This was the first time they'd been alone together since their little interlude under the stars. She'd been faultlessly circumspect in company, but she was way too susceptible when faced with him one-on-one. "I'm avoiding you for a reason. You just can't, remember? So no teasing."

The gap between them was barely a breath wide. His smile broke free, the dimples a teasing flash in his cheeks. "Are you saying you want to, even if I can't?"

What kind of unfair question was that? A question from someone who wasn't going to go there, but wanted to know he could if he wanted to. Well, that was low. She wasn't going to dignify it with an answer. But actually, she knew she didn't have to say anything in reply—her face gave everything away.

"Oh no," she said. "You can't have your cake and eat it too. Or....not eat it, that is."

He raised an eyebrow, but she shook her head. "You know what I mean."

If she didn't like him this much, she'd be happy to play the game—no harm, no foul. But she'd already laid it out, and he'd said no, for whatever reason. She had no intention of letting him toy with her now, for his amusement, when she already felt so firmly on the back foot.

"What?" He feigned ignorance.

"Go," she said, finally tearing herself away and sitting back at the computer. "Go and do whatever you're supposed to be doing instead of bothering me. Just be back here in time to go and see the Isaacsons."

"Yes, m'lady," he said, unfazed. Then he gave a little bow, and was gone.

She collapsed back in the chair, letting it swing around. Half of her—the half with her brain—was properly mad. Seriously, it wasn't okay to mess with someone like that. But the hot and tingly half, that switched itself on whenever he came near, was singing with the thrill of being so near to him, and the suggestion behind his words. She wriggled in the chair and sat herself up straight. Not worth it, she told herself. Way too pleased with himself. Too hot for his own good. Too hot for *her* own good. And...too close for comfort.

★

When he came back later, she was ready for him—ready to resist any wickedness he'd send her way. But he was on his best behavior. She fought off the feeling of disappointment, and reminded her hot and tingly half that there had been no shift from *I just can't* to *I can*. Just because her traitorous mind (and other parts) had gone all the way from there to *oh baby fling me on the floor and make me cry for mercy*, didn't mean his had too. Or that it was a good idea.

They took a cab to the Isaacson's house, a simple but inviting two-story home on a small lot in a modest street. An American flag hung by the front door, and discarded sneakers littered the little porch. Someone had abandoned a creation of sticks tied together with loopy string, and a row of cars was carefully lined up along a windowsill, conveniently at kid level.

Cady grinned. "Boys live here."

"Makes me feel right at home," Reid said.

Dayna welcomed them warmly, and ushered them in, apologizing for the mess. There was no mess, of course— although the furniture had definitely seen better days, and the drapes were faded. When Cady sat down, the sofa springs collapsed into a sinkhole underneath her, and the arms were worn through. But the room was tidy and clean, even with two small boys on the loose, and books of all kinds filled the shelves in the corner.

After the introductions were done, Cady gave the boys their presents—an assortment of Hot Wheels cars each. They shouted with delight as they opened the packets, and Reid sat with them on the floor and made super-charged engine noises as they test drove each one. Then she gave Dayna the ultra-rich body wash and lotion she'd bought for her.

"Oh! You shouldn't have," she said, looking a bit teary. "Sorry, I'm a bit over-emotional these days. But you're already doing so much."

"Well, I hope we can do more," Cady said. "I should have asked, do you know what combination of boys and girls the triplets are?"

For a moment, Dayna looked downcast. "Two more boys," she said. "And one girl. Heaven help her." They looked at the two boys squealing and hollering as they wrestled Reid on the threadbare living room rug. It hadn't taken long to descend into a complete ruckus. "Can you imagine?"

"Not really," Cady had to admit.

Dayna laughed. "Neither can I. Sometimes it's terrifying."

Reid came up for air, lifting a small rosy-cheeked wrestler under each arm and depositing them on the sofa. "Time out!" he announced.

"No, no," they begged. "More!"

He looked at their flushed faces, and appeared to judge

them sufficiently over-hyped.

"If I wind you up any more, there's a serious risk you may suffer some kind of explosion." They looked equally horrified and fascinated by this idea. "And if that happens, it'll be extremely messy, and I really don't want to get in trouble with your mom. Why don't you show me some of your cars? Do you have any SUPERCARS?" He gave the last word all the oomph and pizazz of a NASCAR announcer.

It was exactly the right thing to say, and they leapt off the sofa and dragged him down the corridor. He went with good grace, not showing even a hint of reluctance.

"What's your favorite car?" Max asked as they went.

Dayna and Cady heard him reply, "You're kidding, right? Lamborghini, of course." There was a cheer and then a babble of little voices as they competed for his attention.

"Wow, he's great with them," Dayna said. "Are you guys...do you have any kids?"

"Oh no, no, we're just working together on the flash mob," Cady said hastily. "We don't have any kids. Together or apart."

"Well, you should think about it. He'd make one heck of a baby daddy. And I bet he'd make some *gorgeous* babies."

Cady cleared her throat. "Um, yes, I think he would too." Just not with her. She tried desperately not to think about the birds and the bees side of things, but Dayna was already there.

"Damn, that would be some fun baby-making," she sighed, rubbing her swollen belly wistfully. "Sorry," she added. "It's been a while. And I think it'll be a while yet. Five kids will be a mighty effective passion-killer. Not to mention having nowhere to fool around, anyway." She looked despondent again.

Cady was sorry for her change in mood, but grateful for the change of subject. "Well, that's where we come in," she said. "Not for the fooling around though!" she added, laughing. "Let's go over the plan. Hopefully this will keep a roof over your head, for whatever you get up to."

"Probably a lot of not sleeping, and a lot of not fooling around. But while we're not doing those things, we'll be eternally grateful."

Cady looked at the funny, honest, straight-talking, and enormously pregnant woman—someone she'd love to have as a friend in real life—and hoped like hell they could give her something to be grateful for.

Chapter Thirteen

O nce he'd handed over to Cady, Kyle started spending
even more time in his elevated, unkempt retreat. Cady
hadn't been up there again, but then she wasn't exactly
itching for a repeat visit. If anything, the memory of that
(possibly unsanitary) disaster area made her *feel* itchy. He
emerged a few times a day to check on progress, or to
announce he was going in search of food. There wasn't
usually much to be had on the bus, unless you counted
cheese puffs or Pop Tarts, or leftover fortune cookies. He
always insisted on going alone, and shut himself away
again when he returned.

Shelby was disappointed that he was so near, yet so
unattainable—but after her glimpse into his inner sanctum,
Cady thought that was probably a good thing. And she
hoped he was working on his part of the event organization
while he was up there.

But he did come out with them every night for
drinks—and when he was on form, he was the master of the
pep talk, the inspirational sound bite and the rallying cry.
When he was on a persuasive roll, she found herself
becoming quite captivated, along with Shelby and Alison
and the others. Now, she could totally see how he kept this

band of followers on board. And she started to understand what Reid had meant when he said, *Don't let him take you over.* If she was slightly more susceptible to his brand of charisma, perhaps there would be a risk. But she was just impervious enough.

She only wished she was equally impervious to Reid's charms. After their outing to see Dayna and the boys, her crush had kicked up a notch. A man who was good with kids held a certain attraction. Even as someone quite likely destined to be childless, she felt it. If kids—and dogs, apparently—liked someone, he must have a good heart. Good heart, good banter, good butt...oh, good Lord. What was the old saying—something about an idle mind being the devil's playground? Oh, so true in this case, she thought. It was a blessing there was so much to be done in preparation for the flash mob. The less time to think about him, the better.

"I wonder if we can push this Iggy Pop angle," she wondered aloud over dinner one night. They were having pizza 'at home' before they headed out to try another of the local bars. "He's so cool, I wonder what he'd think of it all."

There was general agreement around the bus. "Does anyone here know anyone who knows him?" Kyle asked. But no one did.

"I've been thinking, though," Gavin said, rolling his beer bottle between his hands. "I know someone whose girlfriend works for *E!* I wonder if they'd be interested in this."

"Gavin!" Alison despaired. "*Why* didn't you mention that sooner? I need every lead I can get."

"I don't know..." he shrugged, and ducked to avoid a pizza crust that came flying his way. "Sorry."

"Don't give me sorry," Alison snapped. "Give me a name!"

"Okay, okay. It's Fenella. But I'll get you a number too." He took a swig of his beer, unfazed.

Then Reid told them that he'd be leaving the bus in the morning, for a few days. "Sorry to leave you all in the lurch. I have to work."

"Pfft, call that work?" Gavin said. "I should send my niece to do it for you. She hasn't started kindergarten yet, she has plenty of time on her hands."

Reid punched him in the arm. "At least I have a job."

"Dude, watch the guns!" He rubbed his arm, feigning injury, and Reid rolled his eyes.

On the other side of the pizza box, Cady felt her heart drop. Yes, it was difficult being at such close quarters, but she had to admit—she didn't want him to go. Apart from the heady over-reaction he inspired in her, there was something else now. After their visit to see Dayna and the boys, she'd seen a side of him she hadn't expected. And she liked it. A lot.

There were only so many bars in Rownville, and that night they found themselves in one that was about as far as you could get from Sanctuary's urban hipness. It was a little bit country, and a little bit...more country. With its kitsch décor—including plenty of steer horns and random taxidermy—Cady thought it could have been plucked up from west Texas and deposited intact in northern California. Not that she'd been to west Texas, so she didn't really know. But to her mind, it only needed saddles instead of bar stools, and a mechanical bull, and the scene would be complete.

Reid came and stood next to her as she waited at the bar, watching Kyle swing Shelby around the dance floor to the world's cheesiest country song. Her sister—who would usually die rather than be seen doing something so clichéd—was clearly having the time of her life, pink-cheeked and laughing.

"I didn't think Kyle would like a place like this," Cady commented.

"That's the great thing about being a hipster," Reid said, his tone dry. "You can enjoy anything, so long as it's in an *ironic* way. Nothing compromises your own coolness."

"You don't count yourself as a hipster then?" Her tone was light and teasing, but underneath she was starting to feel decidedly flustered. And by underneath, she meant...well. There was nothing cool about the way her body reacted to this guy. She took a grateful sip of her newly arrived drink.

He gave a short laugh. "Uh, no. Not a hipster."

"What are you then? Tell me who the *real* Reid is."

She was joking, expecting a funny response, but his face clouded over. "I'd like to tell you. You, of all people."

There was an awkward silence while Cady looked for the right response to his sudden swerve. "Um...sorry. I was just kidding."

As quickly as the weight had descended, he seemed to shake it off. "Anyway, you're never going to get a guy to talk about that stuff," he said, exaggeratedly wagging a finger in her direction. "No deep and meaningful. It's a rule. It's in the manual."

This from the guy who shot straight to the 'how many kids' question? Okay then. But she took her cue and went back to levity. "What...the man manual?"

He laughed. "Yeah, that's the one. I shouldn't have told you about it though. That's actually one of the man manual rules."

"Damn, if I could only get my hands on a copy...maybe then I could figure you out."

"It's enough to know that I'm not a hipster," he said, bringing them neatly back to where they started.

"Well, I'm not really a hundred percent clear on what makes a hipster, exactly," she replied. "But you probably wouldn't have to grow that beard a lot more, you know. Let it bush out. Find a nice cardigan. Borrow a pair of Gavin's glasses."

He grimaced. "Yeah, no thanks. And anyway, Gavin doesn't qualify. No genuine hipster would care about their biceps the way that guy does."

He reached for the drink he'd ordered, thanking the barman. As he lifted the glass to his lips, she could see his own bicep flex below the short sleeve of his t-shirt. She itched to reach out and lay her palm on it, slip her hand up inside the cotton sleeve, pull him closer, and show how much she cared about a few of the other muscles that must be lurking under there. For a guy who made sandcastles for a living (if he made a living out of it), he seemed surprisingly well-built, and he didn't seem to work out the way Gavin did. Maybe it was a more strenuous occupation than she thought.

She pulled herself back to their conversation. "But just think, you could be cool too," she said, shaking her head sadly. "Such a waste."

He grinned. "I'll struggle on."

Something occurred to her. "Will you make it back in time for the flash mob?"

"I hope so. I want to see it."

She laughed. "Me too. I'm actually really excited about it. It's coming together so well."

"It totally is. You're good at this. Kyle was right to let you run your own idea. But if he was going to leave you to do all the work, he should've let you have all the credit too."

"It's not..." she started. Then she gave up—there was no point in arguing about it. "Just don't tell anyone, okay? I mean, it's not a big deal. And, it's not about credit. It's about making something amazing happen. I hope it'll be amazing, anyway."

He shook his head. "It's amazing that you let him get away with it."

"I'm not letting him *get away* with anything. I just think this is something worth doing, while I have the chance." She flicked her hair over her shoulder, like an irritated cat flicking its tail, and took another sip of her drink. He obviously had his own issues with Kyle, but whatever they were, they had nothing to do with her.

"Lady Cady. You flew in from across the ocean to save all of us."

Was he mocking her? She looked for sarcasm in his expression, but his gaze was open and direct as he considered her.

"If anything's amazing, it's you," he said quietly.

That small sentence hit her with a rush, and her breath

suddenly caught in her chest. That hot and tingly half of her claimed a little more heated territory. She allowed herself a swoony moment in the tiger warmth of his eyes, looking at her with appreciation. Admiration, even. But. She was getting to know his tricks. Somewhere between the flirting and the *I just can't* was the middle ground where she should safely stay. If she was the cake he wasn't going to eat (at this thought her internal temperature rose noticeably), well, she didn't have to lay herself on a plate for him. With that slightly confused metaphor in mind, she stood her middle ground.

"I *am* amazing." She made light of his comment, shrugging. "It's tough being the best twin." Then she jokingly echoed his earlier words, adding an exaggerated sigh. "I'll struggle on."

He was ready for more back-and-forth, she could tell. His eyes shone with the challenge of her teasing indifference, and he leaned closer. She blinked hard, trying to erase the idea of leaning in herself, and letting her lips meet his. That middle ground was slipping away under her feet. She could feel her eyelids grow heavy, the world slowing even as her pulse sped and raced. God, at this rate she might as well just cover herself in frosting and hand him a fork...

But right then, Jennifer came over and joined them. Cady snapped into reality, while Reid stood straight and took a step back, grabbing his glass and throwing back the rest of his drink. Jennifer gave Cady a wary look, but she found her feet on that middle ground, suddenly firm again, and smiled. Since they came back to the bus, she'd maintained her 'first do no harm' policy with Alison and Jennifer. Sure, they could be mighty pains in the butt (or aaass, as she'd say now, thanks to Reid), but this was their turf. And Jennifer had definitely turned out to be the lesser evil of the two. Even Shelby had softened toward her while they worked on the choreography, which spoke volumes.

At Cady's smile, Jennifer's face lost some of its hardness. "Hi," she said to them both. Then she smiled at Reid, sweet and clear. "I think you owe me a dance," she told him. "Remember?"

"I do," he said, turning to her. He held out his arm, and she threaded hers though. "Excuse us," he said to Cady, no trace of their almost-moment in his voice.

"Sure, yes," she said, keeping a neutral expression. Inside, though, she felt far from neutral. She wanted to do a Shelby—stake out her ground and compete for top spot with this man. But she stayed put, watching them go. Maybe their history included owing each other more than a dance. They joined Kyle and Shelby and the other dancers on the floor, and Reid practically scooped Jennifer up, making her laugh as they swung into some country and western move. For a tall, solidly built guy, who looked more like he'd be at home in a mosh pit than a country bar, he was really nimble on his feet. He laughed too as they did some kind of cheesy boot-scooting maneuver, and she had to admire his complete disregard for whether he looked 'cool'. She couldn't tell if it was ironic or not—but he seemed to be enjoying it very much. And Jennifer definitely was.

She couldn't watch any more. She finished the last of her drink and ordered another, then went to join Alison, Gavin and Tino at the table. The boys insisted that they *did not dance*, and Alison was clearly waiting for Kyle to finish dancing with Shelby. Looking at the two of them, it was obvious that she might have a long wait ahead. Cady had to appreciate the irony of the situation—finally, she and Alison had something in common.

Gavin and Tino were talking to each other about something to do with American ninja warriors, so she tried to spark up a conversation with Alison. "So, I never asked...where are you from?"

"Hidden Hills." At Cady's blank face, she clarified. "In LA. You know, by Calabasas."

"Oh, I've heard of that. The Kardashians, right?"

She rolled her eyes. "They're new. I grew up around there."

Cady knew she should be more impressed. "Well...that sounds nice."

"It is nice. Very nice." She sighed and looked out over the dance floor, maintaining her ice-queen demeanor.

Her posture really was very good, Cady had to give her that. She sat up straighter, pushing her shoulders back, and tried another topic. "How are things going, do you think? With our planning?"

Alison shrugged. "Pretty good."

Actually, Cady thought it was going great, and Reid's praise gave her proof. But she was having fun with this now—annoying Alison, while maintaining the friendly moral high ground, was a very satisfying pastime. And it couldn't hurt to massage that standoffish ego a little—she wanted her on board, after all. Especially as a potential source of info.

"You know more than me about how to organize things like this."

"Yes," Alison said darkly, not looking at her. "I do."

Cady pressed on. There was something she'd been wondering about. "So, in the previous flash mobs, was Kyle more...involved? You know, day to day."

Alison turned, suddenly fully into the conversation. "He was. He was right alongside us all the way." She frowned. "It's different this time. Like he's cutting himself off from us. Now that *you're* here." Along with her tone, her meaning was clear—Cady wasn't welcome.

It was tempting to enlighten her about whose idea this particular flash mob was, but Cady knew it wouldn't help. She opted for more massaging instead. "But really, I'm just coordinating. You guys are doing the important stuff."

"That's true." Alison's expression lost a little of its iciness.

"I suppose he has faith in everyone to get the job done. I mean, you've proved yourselves." She felt a bit bad about the fake appreciation, but she really wanted to know why Kyle, who had organized all those vibrant, whimsical flash mobs, was now shutting himself away so much. "Maybe now he knows he can step back a bit?"

Alison nodded, starting to thaw a bit more. "Maybe. But why would he *want* to? He used to love it all, and it was so much fun with him involved. He's so different these days. Not right this minute," she added. "But, generally."

Cady let the question hang in the air as they watched him playing up with the others on the dance floor. At times like this, he was irresistibly entertaining and funny. Maybe he just had an erratic personality, and the downs—made worse by the pressure he was under?—were nothing more than the flip side of the charisma rush. Or maybe his highs and lows were more chemically induced. Alison obviously didn't know any more than Cady, but at least things were a little less frosty between them now. High ground aside, that had to be a good thing.

Now, there was one other question on her mind...if she could just work out how to ask it right.

"Jennifer's having a good time," she observed, trying to ease into the topic.

"She loves dancing," Alison said.

"Well, she's good at it. Not like me." It was true. Anything more than the side-to-side shuffle and she was in two-left-feet territory. Not to mention, what the heck were you supposed to do with your arms? She just couldn't figure the whole thing out. "The guys are good too."

They watched as Reid dipped Jennifer backward. Her hair almost touched the floor and her foot came up in a graceful point as she arched back into his arm, trusting him to hold her. Then he pulled her back up and gave her a deft spin, which she finished with an elegant flourish. That was the last straw—Cady had to know.

"Are Jennifer and Reid...?" She tried to sound low key, letting the rest of the question ask itself.

But Alison wasn't buying the casual act. "Why?" she asked sharply, giving Cady a steely look. Ouch. The ice queen returneth. Damn, she really had to work harder at being sneaky. She'd never make a poker player (apart from the online version, maybe).

"They just, um...they seem so..."

"Perfect for each other? I know." Alison tilted her head, considering the two of them. "We all think so too. It'll happen, eventually." She looked pointedly at Cady.

"Anyway. People come and go, don't they? But some things are meant to be."

Cady felt slightly ill. They all thought so? She could hardly step on a whole bus-load of toes. On the other hand, it *hadn't* happened yet. But, on the other *other* hand, Alison was right (if transparently bitchy). Yes, people come and go, and soon Cady would be gone, and Jennifer would still be here. So, no contest really. She had to give that point, grudgingly, to the ice queen. She guessed Alison was heartily looking forward to Shelby being gone too.

The four dancers eventually returned to the table after a couple more songs, glowing and cheerful with their ironic-or-genuine country buzz on. Alison quickly scooted over and made space for Kyle, but Shelby bumped him further along with her hip. "Make room," she told him, and he obliged, much to Alison's annoyance. Reid ended up at the far end of the long table from Cady, opposite Jennifer, leaning back and letting his long legs stretch out to the side.

Kyle banged his fist on the table. "Refreshment!" he announced. "We must have refreshment."

For tonight at least, Kyle was his charismatic, engaging self. And for a while longer, she and Shelby were still here, so the original bus girls would just have to deal with it. But Cady would leave Jennifer to her prior claim on Reid. Even if he was a disgraceful flirt, and she was hopelessly weak in the face of it.

Travel, her mum had said. Have some adventures. Find a gorgeous man. Yes, here were all three. But Cady's new start was also a new start for Dayna and her family, and that was the most important thing right now. That, and keeping Flashpoint on the road. Men, and whether to play their games, were just a distraction at this point. So it was a good thing he was going back to work.

She looked along the table to where he lounged, easy as you please, one hand along the back of the booth, the other resting low on his flat stomach. If that was her hand...she tore her eyes away. Yes, the going back to work was a good thing. It was.

★

True to his word, Gavin got the number for Fenella at *E!*, and Alison made contact with her the next morning. She said she couldn't guarantee anything, but she loved the idea, and promised to bring it up at the day's planning meeting. The five-under-five concept was a daunting reality for the Isaacsons—but it was also proving to be a great pitch for the media and the public.

Sure enough, a text arrived later that day—one of the *E!* reporters Fenella knew was going to a red carpet fundraiser, and Iggy Pop would be there. If there was a chance, the reporter would ask him what he thought. But *only* if there was a chance. She made it clear that it was no sure thing.

That night, they all gathered (minus Reid) in front of the enormous drop-down screen in the bus lounge, and waited through endless chat and trivia for the fundraiser report. After reality stars and celebrity babies, fashion faux pas and gossip, the story finally began. There was Iggy, blue eyes brilliant and tan glowing as usual, but sporting a crisp white shirt and dinner jacket instead of his famous bare-chested look.

"Almost didn't recognize him," commented Gavin, but the others shushed him.

The reporter looked quite excited about being close to such a legend. "Iggy, you look great, very dapper!"

He mumbled something that sounded like agreement, obviously unimpressed by her gushing. She persevered, asking him about his involvement in the charity du jour, and he patiently answered her stock-standard questions. By now it was obvious that the interview wasn't going well, so she regrouped.

"Okay, sounds great! Now, have you heard about this flash mob movement in northern California—Flashpoint?—who're using your song 'Home' in an upcoming event?"

"Yeah, I've heard about that," he replied.

The Flashpointers in question held their collective

breath as the reporter continued on.

"For our viewers who might not know about this, they're raising money for a family who are facing losing their house, and are expecting triplets—triplets!—which would give them five children under five! They're hoping for a huge turnout for their flash mob this weekend in Rownville. What do you think about it all, Iggy?"

"I think that's gotta be a good thing," he said, starting to walk away. "The guys better go shirtless."

He gave her a wink and was gone, leaving her giggling.

"Well, there you have it. Ladies, if you're keen to see a mob of shirtless men this weekend—and all in a good cause—head up to Rownville and get in on the action. I'm kinda tempted myself, I have to say." She laughed. "Back to you, Chuck."

They cut back to the studio, where Chuck was joking about making extra trips to the gym, then the next story was underway.

On the bus, everyone looked at each other, loving the moment. "Did that really happen?" Shelby asked.

Kyle stood up. "Yes. Goddamn, that was *crazy*. Come on, get off your asses. We've gotta be all over that. Go share it. Alison, throw something up on Twitter and Facebook, and anywhere else we need to be. Good job, girl."

Alison glowed. Minus the scowl, she was transformed, and Cady wished she'd show them that face every day. The team leapt up, going for laptops and phones, ready to spread the word about this latest development.

In less than a week, the buzz had grown beyond what Cady had dared to hope for—she couldn't believe what they were creating. Her idea, born on the Santa Cruz sand, had become something b-i-g. And so far, the online reaction was positive.

There was something else she was really hoping would pan out, too. The lyrics for 'Home' mentioned a Jeep, which had given her an idea. Here, surely, was a chance for some feel-good publicity for the car company. She wasn't sure if the whole thing was too counter-culture for them—

some of the previous flash mobs had kind of pushed the envelope, after all. Just like with the bank, it would have to be carefully pitched to get them on board, but oh, she'd love to see the Isaacsons driving those kids around in a shiny new Jeep. She'd made that her own secret project, while Kyle had promised to negotiate with the bank. She hoped he knew what he was doing.

Chapter Fourteen

When the 'Home' day dawned, Cady was ready. She was too nervous to eat breakfast, but she was ready.

It was a perfect California day, just a few puffs of cloud in the sky. If it held out until evening, it would definitely be warm enough for any shirtless guys who might turn up. And she hoped they would. Not for the shirtlessness itself (although the girls agreed that a few buff flash mobsters would be very nice, thank you), but for the extra newsworthiness it would bring. It would be a gift for a bored field reporter looking for a way to liven up their footage.

Before everything got underway, she sat on the bus steps in the sunshine and called her dad in London. He was happy to hear about their adventures, and assured her that he was fine, but she thought he sounded tired. He'd been through a lot—losing his wife, selling his house, and getting settled into a whole new life—so she supposed it was only to be expected, but she hated hearing him sound so flat. Along with the guilt of keeping the father secret, the guilt of leaving him alone washed over her anew. But he wouldn't listen to any apologies from her about not being there. He made her promise to keep having fun, and to look after her sister. The first was no problem, the second…well, she'd do her best. As they said their goodbyes, she told him she loved him, and promised to call again soon. He said he loved her too, and sent his love to Shelby as well, and she felt a little better as she hung up.

Then she checked her messages, and the Flashpoint Facebook and Twitter accounts (all good comments so far), while watching Gavin start the day with a few bicep curls, press-ups, and pull-ups on the branch of a nearby tree. He was a personal trainer in real life, he'd told her, but he was taking a break for the summer to hang out with the Flashpointers. He wasn't worried about getting more clients when he went back to work. In this country, he said, there was a steady supply of flabby people waiting for his help. Hearing that, she wasn't sure how diplomatic his training approach would be.

"I'm getting out of shape," he puffed to Cady now. "Too much…drinking. I blame Reid. Should never have…let him…join up." He dropped from the branch and stood with hands on hips, catching his breath.

Tino stopped on his way to unload some equipment from the storage area at the back of the bus. With his huge barrel chest and powerful shoulders clad in a sleeveless t-shirt, he looked like a pro wrestler who'd wandered off from Monday Night Raw.

"It's kind of touching how you refuse to give up hope," he told Gavin.

"We're not all blessed by the gods like you, brother," he replied amicably. "Some of us have to work to look as good as this."

"As good as what?" Tino laughed as he walked away.

Gavin flicked his hair back across and pressed his arm to his sweaty forehead. "Don't want to let the side down," he told Cady.

She smiled. "You'll do us proud."

It actually seemed like the whole team would do them proud. Between them, they'd pulled together to organize everything to the nth degree. The only thing Cady didn't have under total control was Kyle's bank negotiations. He'd assured her the night before that everything was taken care of, but wouldn't give her any details. She could only hope he'd come through.

Luckily, Rownville's city council, recognizing a PR opportunity, had given them permission to use the square. During the day, they finalized all the last details, chalked out the house outline, and made sure everything was set up.

By late afternoon, clusters of people were gathering, with more arriving by the minute. Cady had found a couple of local bands who were keen to perform for free, and the first started playing on the small stage set up on one side of the square. With the music, the food stalls, and the relaxed crowd, the whole thing had a cool festival vibe. Along with the flash mob participants, the media contingent was growing, and Cady could see TV crews interviewing visitors—particularly the shirtless ones. She was tickled to see how many of the guys had taken Iggy's suggestion to heart, and gone bare-chested. And it was obvious that the female contingent appreciated it very much too—there were more than a few sparks flying around the square.

Once Kyle was satisfied that everything was in place, he set to work schmoozing. He looked super-charged as he worked the crowd, charming the girls and buddying around with the guys, shirtless and otherwise. His scruffy charisma was turned up to full, bordering on frenetic, but he had everyone there completely won over.

He pulled Cady into an interview with a news crew that had come up from San Francisco. "This is our secret weapon," he told the reporter. "She's imported from the UK. Highest quality."

Cady felt the heat of a blush in her cheeks, and for a moment it seemed like he was going to give her the credit that Reid was so hung up on. But then he started talking again, the moment passed, and she stood on the sidelines of the interview until it was over. Well, that was fine with her. She spotted an excited-looking Dayna and Brad, and went over to say hello. *This* was what it was all about.

Soon the sun was fading, and the square was full. With start time approaching, Kyle stood at the microphone at the top of the bank steps, the Flashpointers around him. While they waited, Cady took in the scene in front of her, imprinting it on her memory. The colorful bunting hanging in the trees behind the food stalls, the crowd dancing to the band, the last rays of the sun glancing golden off the windows of the buildings around the square. At the far end, cars slowed as they passed, people peering out to see what was happening. A big screen showed images from the Flashpoint camera crew, reflecting the good time back to the crowd. A little crispness was just creeping into the warm daytime air, laced with the aroma of burritos and burgers. She was suddenly acutely aware that she'd be back in London before she knew it, just regular old Cady again. Lady Cady, the Flashpointers, and all of this would be just a memory. She wanted to make sure she'd remember every detail of the time when she was different.

The only thing missing was Reid. He'd texted earlier to say he'd be back in time, but there was no sign of him, and she couldn't help feeling disappointed. She didn't want credit from Kyle, or anyone else—regardless of credit, she'd always know this was her achievement. So why did she want Reid to see it so badly? She shouldn't need his admiration, shouldn't want to see that appreciation in his eyes again. All the same, she scanned the crowd, hoping to see him threading his way through, toward the steps. As the light faded into evening, it was getting harder to make out who was who—but none of them were him.

Then the band wrapped up their last song, and Kyle began to speak. At his first words, every face in the crowd turned to him.

"*Look* at you all," he said, nodding with approval.

That was all it took to get the entire gathering—already warmed up by the band—cheering and whooping. Kyle grinned, adjusting his beanie as he bathed in the reaction. He was in his element.

"This is why we're here," he said, extending his arms to take them all in. "It's about people, isn't it? In the end, that's what everything's about."

The renewed hollering from the crowd showed that

they agreed. Cady had to laugh. She had the feeling they'd agree with pretty much anything he said at this point. Although it was exactly what she'd thought earlier herself.

"And also, *this* is why we're here." He put out a hand to Dayna, and she and Brad came to the front with him. Her belly was enormous, and she had the classic pregnant stance, legs slightly apart and leaning back a little. When the crowd cheered for her, it seemed like the wave of sound and love almost tipped her off balance. She grabbed onto Brad's arm, her face a picture of pleasure and disbelief. Brad just beamed, the smile on his face and the shine in his eyes showing how incredible the moment was for them both.

Kyle pointed to Dayna's belly. "Can you believe there are *three* new people in there, waiting to join us in the world?" he asked the flash mobsters. "Let's make sure their place in the world will be an awesome one."

The cheer that went up made it obvious that everyone was totally with him. He stood for a moment, nodding and soaking up the vibe. Then he grabbed the wireless microphone from its stand, stepped forward, and held it out to let the crowd hear itself through the speakers. They cheered and hooted even louder, loving the rock star move.

"Okay, if you're confirmed as part of the house, grab a spot. Everyone else, give them a little room. Let's do this!" As he raised his hands, the audience applauded wildly, and he laughed with satisfaction.

Cady and the others headed down the steps to help get the flash mobsters in the right place, some along the outlines of the house, then a space, and the rest surrounding them. As the driving beat of 'Home' began to flood the square at full volume, she felt a huge rush of adrenaline go through her. Almost every single person in the crowd snapped glow sticks and held one in each hand as they started the dance routine. Those who didn't have a glow stick held up their glowing phones. Cady caught sight of Shelby across the square, and mouthed a *Wow!* as the mob started moving to the dance steps she and Jennifer had come up with. Shelby nodded back, her face glowing with enjoyment at seeing her routine come to life. And also at being sandwiched between two shirtless flash mobsters whose chiseled torsos put the 'ab' in ab-tastic. She pointed to each side, mouthing *O.M.G!* back to Cady, who laughed and shook her head. That was a happy twin.

The glow sticks shone in the dimming half-light, a multicolored sprinkling of magic across the crowd. They moved as one to the steps, and if the occasional person was slightly ahead or behind, it didn't matter. Iggy's languorous voice punched into the air, the insistent guitar and drum rhythm charging everyone up as they went through the routine. The feeling was incredible. Cady could hardly take in that this was her idea, come to life. It felt totally surreal.

Someone had found Dayna a chair, and she and Brad watched from the top of the steps with huge smiles on their faces. Then, as Iggy and the electric guitar brought the song to a crescendo, Kyle took her and Brad down to the house of people. With the last riff reverberating in the air, they stood at the 'front door'—made of Dayna's mother and sister holding hands with Max and Ty.

Ty's little voice rang out in the sudden quiet. "Hi, Mommy!"

Everyone laughed as his sweet face filled the big screen, and Dayna bent to kiss him, and then Max. "Hi guys," she said.

Kyle gave a nod, and the front door family swung around to let Dayna and Brad go in. The people lining the hallway lifted their glow sticks to make a luminous guard of honor. With a cameraman in front, the two of them walked through the house, their smiles broadcast on the big screen for everyone to see. When they reached the 'living room', they found big tarps covering a bumpy collection of large items. All at once, the people making the house sat down, followed by the entire square-full of people. Dayna and Brad looked around, bemused.

"Thank you mobsters," Kyle said into the microphone. "You *killed* it!" He grinned and nodded as more cheers rippled though the square. "Okay, our official math brainiacs are doing the counting, and soon we'll be able to tell you exactly how much money we've raised for this amazing family. In the meantime, I think someone here could do with a seat."

Tino and Gavin came forward and pulled the tarps away, revealing an entire living room's worth of brand new furniture, laid out just like the real thing with rugs and cushions, a lamp, and even a TV.

"This is for you—thanks to the generous people at Rownville Furniture Emporium," Kyle told them.

From where Cady was standing by the steps, she could see the moment when it sank in, and Dayna instantly burst into tears.

"Thank you," she managed. "Thank you! Oh, I'm sorry, it's the hormones..." She wiped her eyes as the tears continued to flow.

"Thank you," Brad echoed. "Very much." He helped Dayna lower herself onto the sofa, and Max and Ty came scampering over and jumped up next to her.

Kyle nodded. "In a few minutes we'll have the final fundraising results. And flash mobsters, hang around for another special announcement soon. Eat, drink, enjoy the music—don't go away yet."

With that, the second band cranked up the volume, and the crowd were back on their feet, ready to move again. The glow sticks bobbed in the dark with the dancers, and the atmosphere was rocking. Somewhere in the middle of it all, Dayna and Brad sat in their soon-to-be real lounge with Max and Ty, waiting to hear what was coming next. From the number of people there, Cady suspected they'd have a good fundraising total. But had Kyle made anything happen with the bank? Maybe she should have done that part herself too, or insisted on being involved...

Then, through the swirl of the crowd, she heard someone calling her name.

"Cady. Hey, Lady Cady."

As he came closer, the jolt of her reaction was like seeing him for the first time all over again. While he'd been away, she'd tried to keep her mind in the safe middle ground, and not let it wander off to that Reid place, full of delicious, dangerous thoughts. But as he came closer, she remembered anew. Eyes that looked at her with amusement, but gave nothing away. The strong, jeans-clad thighs below the low-slung belt, and the broad chest in his usual black band t-shirt. The dimples that flashed in his cheeks above the goatee and even—okay, yes—the ponytail (heaven help her). And to top it off, the sharp mind and repartee that kept her on her toes, but also put her in most danger of tipping straight off those toes and onto her back. Not that *that* was an option, as they'd established already.

Now, in the half-dark, they stood an arm's length from each other, happy flash mobsters milling about on all sides. She fought the urge to fling herself at him, pressing her toes into the ground to hold herself in place. Did they both recognize something unspoken in the look that continued between them? Maybe it was just her. The pause drew out longer, as each waited to see what the other would do. Where were they at? Were they people who hugged hello after an absence, or just said hi? Maybe they were in the kiss-on-the-cheek place, but the seeming weight of the moment held her back from taking a step forward. It couldn't have been as long as it felt, but finally she snapped herself into words.

"I thought you weren't going to make it," she said, trying to sound brusque instead of relieved. It wasn't like she'd spent half the flash mob looking over her shoulder, trying to spot him amongst the crowd. Nope, it wasn't like that at all.

He smiled. "Sorry. The job took longer than I expected. Then when I got here, there was nowhere to leave the car." He waved around at the festive crowd still scattered with shirtless men, the TV cameras, the kids perching in the trees around the square to get a better view of the band. "Look at this. I had to park halfway back to San Francisco, and run to get here before it was all over."

If he had run, he'd done it without breaking a sweat. "Sure, swan in at the last minute, just in time for all the glory." Okay, that was better. Jokey was good. She had this.

"Well, yeah. Clever, right? I'm smarter than all of you put together." He grinned, then his face became more serious. "But this is incredible. Credit to you—you pulled it off."

"I did have help...but thanks." Maybe she didn't want credit from anyone else—but from him, it did count for something after all. She knew she was beaming like a fool at his praise. Plus, she was amped up on flash mob adrenaline and the pleasure of seeing him again. There was no fighting it.

"And there's a little surprise coming for them too," she added. "But we'll have to wait and see how much money we raised. All of this is for nothing if Dayna and Brad can't keep their house."

Then she saw Kyle waving to her from the steps of the bank. Damn. "I'd better go, sorry. See you after?"

He nodded. "Go. Enjoy. I'll be here."

She started toward the steps, noticing that as well as the Jeep representative she'd been dealing with, Kyle was standing with two other men in expensive-looking suits. She hoped they were from the bank. As she was about to go up and find out, someone grabbed her arm, stopping her in her tracks, and she turned around to see Shelby.

"I have something to tell you," she said, holding up her phone, obviously too excited to worry about the Huawei factor for once. "I just heard."

"Heard what?" Cady asked, one eye on the steps, where the suits were looking impatient. When Kyle gestured for her to hurry up, she broke away from her sister.

"Shel, I have to go," she said. "Tell me later."

"But this is important," Shelby insisted.

"Later!" she called back over her shoulder. "I promise."

Whatever it was, it would have to wait. The end result of her bright idea, and her work—all of their work—was here. Now, it was time to find out whether the Isaacsons would have something more than a roomful of new furniture to be grateful for.

Chapter Fifteen

High on anticipation, Cady said hello to the Jeep PR guy and the suits, and stood next to Kyle at the top of the steps as he took the microphone again. In front of him, the flash mobsters were a twinkly-colorful sea of glow sticks and cell phone lights. The band finished up, and the crowd turned to see what would come next.

"Sit down, guys," Kyle urged, and they obligingly sat, looking like a bunch of latter-day hippies. Cady noticed now that amongst the shirtless men was a good scattering of women wearing bikini tops, unfazed by the cooling night air.

"You were *amazing*," Kyle said, making them cheer and applaud, the lights bobbing in the dark. "Because of you, this growing family has a second chance." He gestured to Dayna and Brad, still sitting with their boys, their living room an island in the ocean of flash mobsters. They both still looked completely overcome.

He continued, his voice somehow capturing a tone somewhere between evangelist and slacker. The crowd loved it. "Thank you, Isaacsons, for giving us the chance to do something worthwhile here tonight."

Dayna managed a tiny wave, then locked her fingers

under her belly again. Her face glowed with emotion and excitement.

Now Kyle gestured to the men in suits, and they came forward. "And huge thanks to the representatives from West Interstate Bank. They've counted your donations tonight, and the total is a mind-blowing thirty-eight..." He checked a piece of paper in his hand. "Thirty-*nine* thousand, eight hundred and fifty three dollars."

As the crowd cheered, and Dayna clapped her hands to her cheeks in surprise and delight, he nodded. "Yeah." Then he added, "But there's more."

He passed the microphone to one of the bankers, who looked nervous but determined.

"West Interstate Bank makes our customers a priority," he began. The crowd's reaction to this little number, straight from the songbook, was predictable, but Kyle put up a hand and the jeers died down.

"Banks don't *want* to see people lose their homes," he said, looking increasingly hot under his stiff collar. "We're pleased to say that West Interstate Bank will match your donations, dollar for dollar. Dayna and Brad, this will not only halt the foreclosure, but will give you a major step forward in paying off your mortgage."

At this, Dayna broke down and cried again. Brad put his arm around her shoulder and whispered something in her ear. She nodded, and clutched her boys close as Brad made his way to the stage, picking his way through until he got to the steps. Then he took them three at a time and grabbed the banker's hand, shaking it vigorously. Over the noise of the crowd, Cady couldn't hear his voice, but it was clear that he was saying thank you over and again.

Kyle took the microphone back. "There's one more thing," he told the crowd. "You'll like this too." Then he passed the microphone over to the Jeep guy.

In contrast to the bankers, he had his jacket unbuttoned and his shirt was open, tie-less. Cady could hardly wait for him to make his announcement.

"Awesome!" he exclaimed, waving enthusiastically. "All right! Woo!" He was obviously going to make the most of his time center stage. "The team at Jeep thought this extraordinary event was something special. We know it can be hard to keep a big family on the road. But you know, like Iggy says, you can make it in a Jeep."

He grinned at the crowd. If they were cheering more for Iggy than for him, he didn't care. He had their attention.

"So Jeep would like to offer the Isaacsons a brand new, seven-seat, new generation, Jeep Waggoneer." He grinned and held up some car keys, playing it up for the crowd. Then he passed them to Brad, and pumped his hand in an enthusiastic handshake. Brad shook his head, speechless, and looked from the keys to Dayna, still sitting in the center of the square.

Cady looked too. Dayna's mouth was a little 'o' of amazement, matched by her surprised, rounded eyes. Cady laughed. It had been so hard keeping that secret, but it was worth the effort to see their reactions now.

"Also…" Jeep man turned back to the crowd, pausing for effect.

There was more? Cady had no idea what might be coming next—she'd only talked about the car with him. She held her breath.

"We know this family needs security, going forward," he said. "So Brad, your local Jeep dealership would like to offer you a full-time position in their service department. I hear you're more than qualified." He thrust the microphone under Brad's nose.

By this stage Brad had both hands on his head, as though it was going to fly off. He looked completely floored—which was kind of how Cady felt too. In a *very* good way.

"I am qualified," he said. "Thank you." He shook his head again, looking around at the scene in front of him. Then he took the microphone and addressed the crowd.

"This is completely unbelievable. Just a week ago we were facing disaster. *Financial* disaster, that is—because these babies are God's blessing on us."

He held out his hands to Dayna, and the audience cheered again as she cradled her very pregnant belly. The relief in her face was clear. Watching, Cady's heart felt huge in her chest as she realized that the Flashpointers had done it. They'd turned everything around.

"We can't say enough how thankful we are to West Interstate Bank and Jeep for changing the destiny of this family," Brad continued. He rubbed the top of his head and puffed out a long breath, obviously working to keep it together. "And thank you Kyle and Cady, and everyone with Flashpoint, for making this happen. You came into our lives and changed *everything*. And to all of you, who came tonight—we'll never forget your kindness, and we'll make sure to pay it forward every chance we get. Thank you so much."

By the time he finished this heartfelt speech, just about everyone's eyes were glistening. Then he handed the microphone to Kyle and charged back down the steps. The sitting audience shuffled apart to let him through, and Dayna stood to meet him. He caught her up in a huge bear hug—slightly sideways, to allow for the waiting triplets— and Max and Ty grabbed on to their parents' legs, joining in.

Cady wiped her eyes as whooping and cheering rang around the square. Oh, you'd have to have a heart of stone not to cry at that. To one side, she could see where the Flashpoint team had gathered together, and Reid looked up and caught her eye. She couldn't hear him, but his lips formed one word: *Amazing*. She nodded back, *I know!* When she and Reid had gone together to meet Dayna for the first time, they'd had no idea what they were about to create. They smiled at each other, a thread of connection over the heads of the rag-tag crowd.

Then everyone got to their feet, the band started playing again, the mood lightened, and the square was in party mode once more.

What a night. Kyle had come through, doing his part with the bank. Cady could hardly believe that he'd managed to get them on board in such a big way, working mostly from inside his garbage tip of a suite. And her first foray into corporate schmoozing had paid off big time too.

She was pretty sure there'd be no online griping about this. She defied *anyone* to be snarky about what they'd achieved tonight.

After doing a few media interviews, Kyle took Cady with him down the steps, where the flash mobsters swarmed him like ants on honey. He nodded to everyone as they went through, high-fiving, low-fiving, and accepting slaps on the back. But he didn't stop until they came to where the Flashpointers were waiting. He put his arm around Shelby's shoulder, making her glow with pride and delight. Then Alison sidled in, and he put an arm around her too. Shelby didn't seem to mind too much—it was that kind of a feel-good night.

"Good job, London," he told her. "You and your sister, and everyone. There's more work to do, but after that...shit, we've got some *celebrating* to do."

Chapter Sixteen

It was a painfully slow start on the bus the next morning. As Cady woke up, she realized it wasn't going to be good. Rolling over in bed, she was sure she felt her brain clunk against the inside of her skull. Ugh, she must have knocked something loose, or dissolved some brain connections with that merry mixture of celebration drinks. She scrunched her eyes shut again and gritted her teeth, bracing herself for the misery that would be getting up. If she didn't need to use the bathroom, she wouldn't be going anywhere at all.

She pulled the red bunk curtain back just a twitch and peered out, squinting in the morning light. It was quiet, apart from sleeping sounds coming from the other beds. She could hear whiskey-induced snoring coming from Gavin's nook further along, but nothing from Reid's opposite. Even in her drink-damaged state, she registered that as a point in his favor. Then, with the coast clear, she grabbed her toilet bag and made a delicate dash for the bathroom, trying to keep her head steady as she went. It didn't work, but she made it in and closed the door without anyone seeing her.

Showered and dressed, she felt fresher and slightly less like death. And the memory of what they'd achieved the night before made her much more cheerful in her hangover. What a night! She even hummed a little as she made coffee and opened the bus windows to let fresh air in. Outside, she could see a few girls hanging around, in hope of meeting Kyle probably. She checked her watch and laughed. Eight forty-five for everyone else was Kyle's middle of the night. The girls would have a long wait this morning.

With the smell of coffee in the air, and a couple of Excedrin working their magic, she sat down at the kitchen table to wait for the others to emerge. Images from the night before floated back into her mind—including a dance with Reid. It was just one amongst many people she'd danced with, but those were the few minutes that burned strongest in her memory. She wouldn't admit that she was sitting exactly at this (hopefully) flattering angle now, with her hair arranged *just so*, in the hope that Reid would be the first person up.

But...he was. He came into the kitchen in his boxers and t-shirt, running his fingers through his mussed-up hair. Her heart flippity-flipped. Oh, help. Even morning-bleary and rumpled, he was ridiculously hot. Actually, rephrase that. *Especially* morning-bleary and rumpled, he was ridiculously hot. While she'd raced for the shower to get herself scrubbed and polished, he obviously didn't mind being seen fresh from bed. And she didn't mind either. In fact, the first thing her mind did was imagine taking him straight *back* to bed.

"Morning, Lady Cady." He took juice from the fridge and poured himself a glass. "How'd you sleep?"

"Good, I guess. Not long enough, though." She pointed at her head. "Repercussions."

He laughed. "It was a good night."

"It was."

It had been a *great* night. In the flush of success, any Flashpoint rivalries were forgotten while they celebrated. The story made the late news—shirtless men featuring heavily—and the reaction on Twitter had been all positive, knock on wood. In Rownville last night, it seemed like every bar in town was full of happy flash mobsters, all eager

124

to clap Kyle on the back, or shake his hand, or buy him a drink. After a couple of stops, they ended up at the world's cheesiest country bar again, where the dance floor was full, the music was loud and the drinks flowed freely.

And between dances with the other Flashpoint guys, and a few other random flash mobsters, Cady had danced with Reid. It was only the same kind of dance as with any of the others, nothing more than a token nod to 'proper' dance moves. But when she reached up and put her hand on his shoulder, and his hand slipped around to cradle the small of her back, she could hardly breathe. In the days he'd been away, she'd tried not to think about him—but that attraction had been quietly percolating, keeping warm for his return. Now all he had to do was touch her and she was lost, or maybe found. He took her other hand in his, and pulled her against him. Her body was melty with his closeness, every limb heavy with the slow desire that washed through her. She let herself meld against him, not caring for once if he knew exactly what effect he was having.

Until that moment, she hadn't realized the pressure she'd been carrying, getting ready for her flash mob. Now it was over, and being gathered in close to him triggered such a feeling of relief that she let go all her reservations. For now, for tonight, she was going to forget about that boring, safe middle ground and wade into this delicious sensation. They'd never talked about her attempted kiss (she still squirmed just thinking about it), but whatever made him turn her down wasn't enough to stop his teasing. Maybe she should be annoyed, but oh, it was too good to stop.

Now, with the other revelers crowded on all sides, he moved her around the dance floor. As a slow, seductive country duet played, the singers urging each other to *give in to me*, she did just that and looked right at him, willingly drowning in the steady honey-brown gaze he returned. He smiled at her, and she felt all the heat in her body concentrate in one slow, insistent burn at her center. He leaned down to whisper in her ear, and there was honey in his voice too as he told her what an amazing job she'd done, and how she was as smart as she was beautiful. If he hadn't been holding her firmly she might have slithered to the ground, her legs wobbly with the directness of his words and his breath against her ear. When the song ended and Alison broke in to have the next turn, she was almost thankful to step back and find her feet. Her reaction was so intense that she knew she'd crossed from a manageable (if distracting) crush into a whole other level of compulsion. Damn, that was the last thing she needed. And...it was *exactly* what she needed. And wanted.

As he and Alison started to dance, she turned and squeezed through the crowd, back to sit with Gavin and Tino at the table. She took a sip of her drink and pressed her hands to her hot cheeks. One dance would have to be enough. Anything more, and she'd be dragging him off the dance floor and into the corner, pressing him against the wall, and claiming what he hinted at but wouldn't deliver.

Now he was looking at her closely in the morning light, reading her mind it seemed. "Shame we only had one dance, though. You were feeling it." He grinned, a knowing look in his eye.

She instantly felt her cheeks flare, matched by a sudden rush of heat between her legs. Oh God, after last night her body had really stepped it up a notch. She searched about for some snappy retort, but drew a blank. He was no help at all, regarding her with an amused expression, making her even more flustered.

At that moment Shelby came in, her hair still damp from the shower. She had her determined face on. Straight away, Cady knew that last night's news—whatever it was— was on the agenda this morning. She was half relieved to have the moment interrupted, half sorry to not be alone with him still.

"Hi, Reid." Shelby was unmoved by Reid's attractions. He was a bit player, after all, and she liked to be where the real action was. She turned to Cady. "Can we go somewhere and talk? I have something to tell you, remember?"

She hadn't mentioned it again the night before, instead flinging herself into the celebrations along with everyone else. But something was obviously up. Cady glanced at Reid. She hated to leave that rugged piece of morning glory, mid-tease, even though he was the cause of her heady discomfort. Discomfort of the best kind. But she knew Shelby wouldn't be put off any longer, plus she was curious to know what was going on. She hoped it was something good, but needing to be alone for the talk was an ominous sign. With her unpredictable sister, you could never be sure what was coming next.

"Okay," she said, purposefully pulling herself back together, but hyper-aware of Reid still leaning against the counter. "Let's go to that café with the amazing pastries. I'm starving."

"Me too," Shelby said.

"Can we bring something back for you?" Cady felt like she ought to offer. As usual, there wasn't much on the bus that constituted a decent breakfast.

"No, that's okay, thanks." He gave her a grin. "Gavin will need feeding soon. We'll find something."

"Okay then. See you later?"

"I'll be here."

As they left, she wondered what later might bring. Was he still holding to the *I just can't*, or was he changing his mind? A shiver went through her as she remembered the feeling of his hot breath in her hair, his low voice murmuring sweet compliments. She sighed. She was absolutely useless around him. She'd have to get herself back on a more even keel if they were going to stay on the bus.

As she followed Shelby down the steps, she realized they had no idea what would happen now the flash mob was over. Maybe Kyle didn't need them any more, and they'd have to go. Maybe they *should* go, anyway, and continue the trip they'd planned. They needed to decide what they both wanted to do, and it was better if she didn't count Reid as a factor in the decision. He wasn't going to help her make any sensible decisions. Insensible decisions, more like. And...after years of being the sensible, responsible one—okay, the boring one—she was learning how appealing insensible could be.

★

The retro-styled café was only a short walk from the bus, and had quickly become a Flashpoint favorite. They'd all gotten addicted to the treats laid out row by delicious row in the glass cabinets. Gavin grumbled about getting as flabby as his clients, but it never took much arm-twisting to get him along too.

But this morning it was just Cady and Shelby, and a scattering of other customers reading newspapers and iPads. They got settled, Cady with a huge brown sugar and walnut brioche, and Shelby with an enormous buttermilk berry scone. In contrast to the oversized food, their coffees were small—but supercharged. They agreed that all of it was completely necessary, and deserved, after the night before.

Cady stirred a sugar into her coffee. "So, I'm sorry I couldn't stop and listen last night. What was it about?"

"Well..." Shelby paused. "I have something to tell you."

Her sister's face was a mixture of guilt and triumph, and Cady's stomach lurched. What had she been up to? That face didn't bode well. "What have you done?" she asked warily.

"I found him."

Him? Cady had the feeling she knew already, but she asked anyway. "Who?"

"Our father. I *found* him." She looked exhilarated but nervous, obviously realizing she might be in trouble.

"But how did you even...?"

"Well, it wasn't me who found him, exactly. We have all that money from Mum, so I paid for a private investigator. It seemed an appropriate way to spend it." She smiled, satisfied at the neatness of it.

Cady frowned. "You promised you'd leave it alone."

"I said I wouldn't tell Dad. I never said I wouldn't look for our real father." She looked smug at this loophole.

Cady resisted the urge to shake the smug right out of her. Now it was obvious why she'd suggested their 'me time' afternoons while they were on the road—she'd been using them to work with the private investigator.

"That's what you were doing on those afternoons. Not shopping."

Shelby just shrugged. "I needed to get it underway quickly, so there was time to find something out before our visas expired. I never thought it would happen this fast."

"Damn, Shelby, you should have talked to me about it. This doesn't just affect you, you know."

"Yeah, right." Shelby gave her an arch look. "Like you talked to me about that teeny tiny bit of info Mum gave *you*."

Touché. She was right. "Okay, fair enough."

"*Thank* you." She paused. "So…will you come with me?"

Cady already knew she would. When he was just the idea of a father, out there somewhere-or-other, it was easy to dismiss the idea of meeting him. Now that he was found and real, she couldn't resist the chance to see him. God knows what would come of it. Maybe he'd be less than pleased to see them. Maybe he was completely horrible, and they'd hate him. Maybe he had a family, a wife who knew nothing, and their appearance would be a disaster. Maybe they had brothers and sisters. The maybes and implications and possibilities tumbled around in her mind, but she focused on the first, most basic fact.

"What's his name?"

Shelby smiled. "It's a good one. Lawson Holt. He should be in a John Wayne movie."

"Wow, definitely. As the sheriff." It was a great name, supremely American. It brought to mind a handsome, upright man, squinting into the sun as he scanned the range for trouble. Cady wondered if he could possibly live up to a name like that. "And where is he?"

"This is the amazing part. He's not far from here, in the Sacramento Valley. He's a farmer—a nut producer."

Cady laughed, despite herself. "Well, he produced you, so that makes sense."

"Ha ha, very funny." Shelby rolled her eyes. "He

grows almonds. Apparently it's a big crop around here. The company's called Santa Almendra."

"Pretty name," Cady commented.

"Yeah. So, are you coming with me, or not?" Her gaze was fixed on Cady, waiting. "Because I'll go without you if I have to." Her voice rose as she emphasized her determination.

"Yeah, okay, calm down. I'm coming. But, does he know we're here? Does he even know about us at all?"

"I'm pretty sure he knows about us. The investigator has a colleague in London who went to see Aunt Netta, and she had some info."

Aunt Netta was one of that great breed of British eccentrics, moneyed but living in shabby grandeur, childless but always with several mismatched dogs. She was loud-voiced and plainspoken, with a dress sense that defied description, and had been coloring her hair purple long before Kelly Osborne made it a thing. When the girls were born, the family lived around the corner from Aunt Netta in Broadstairs, a picture-book seaside town on England's south-east coast. But when their dad got a job in London, they had to leave behind the sandy beach and sea air, barefoot afternoons paddling in the foamy water, and impromptu summer fish-and-chip dinners surrounded by marauding seagulls. And Aunt Netta of course, who came to visit them in London over the years whenever she could. She'd been a godsend at the funeral, organizing food and cups of tea, and fending off well-wishers when she could see that the girls had had their fill of sympathy.

When they were small, going back to Broadstairs and Aunt Netta was always the best fun they could imagine. As teenagers, though, they sighed and reluctantly got in the back of the car, complaining about how they'd miss this party or that movie with their friends (although the secret supply of Pimm's and lemonade from Aunt Netta helped a little). Cady remembered her mum and Aunt Netta sitting up late into the night talking, their voices a murmur lulling the girls to sleep. They were so close, their relationship was more like sisters than aunt and niece. Sisters who got along, that is, not the squabbly, scratchy kind of sisterhood that Cady and Shelby had as chalk-and-cheese twins.

Later, as an adult, Cady came full circle, longing for sand between her toes and salty air in her lungs as she trudged around grimy old London. Shelby's mention of Aunt Netta took her straight back to all those childhood memories.

"Why did he go and see her?"

"Because she and Mum were so close around the time we were born. I was sure she'd know *something*. And...she did."

Cady realized she was holding her breath. "What? What did she know?"

"Well." Shelby paused, building the drama. "When Mum and Dad hadn't been able to get pregnant for so long, Aunt Netta could see that it was putting a huge strain on their marriage. And apparently all Mum's friends in Broadstairs were getting pregnant one after the other. So Aunt Netta offered her the use of her apartment in London, just to get away every now and then."

"I didn't know she had an apartment in town."

"In Bayswater. She inherited it, apparently. Anyway, you can guess what happened."

Cady looked at her sister. "Lawson Holt."

She nodded. "The American."

"And then?"

"I don't know any more. Only that Aunt Netta said she was sure the money must have come from him. Apparently Mum didn't tell him she was pregnant until he'd gone back to the States."

"So he knew about us all along."

"Yes."

"And Aunt Netta knew, but she kept the secret too."

"Yes."

"Wow."

There was silence as they both pondered this. Their mother had an affair. They'd already had to wrangle with that concept—but how could they be angry about it, when it was the only reason they were here at all? Cady wondered if her mother had fallen in love with him, or if it was strictly business in her mind—baby business. How had she felt, knowing her deception as she told her husband she was pregnant after all, and saw the joy in his face? And now, there was something new. Their birth father had sent money, but never come to see them. Had he wanted to? Had their mother wanted him to? Was the money his way of paying her off, or an arrangement they'd come to? Cady's head spun with questions, including how the private investigator convinced Aunt Netta to talk about something she'd kept secret all this time.

"How did the private investigator get Aunt Netta to reveal all that?"

Shelby shook her head. "I don't know—Pimm's?"

They both had to laugh. Aunt Netta's Pimm's had been their first, secret introduction to alcohol. Their mother never knew that while she and her aunt were sitting in the drawing room chatting in front of the fire, and her husband was in bed snoring, her daughters were sipping Pimm's and lemonade in their attic bedroom, giggling and shushing each other.

"I haven't had a Pimm's for ages," Cady said wistfully. "But Shel, I've been thinking. Why didn't they have IVF?"

"I don't know. Maybe it was too expensive for them then. Or maybe it was something to do with the Wodarski-Ebner."

"But that didn't appear until much later." The ever-present shadow of that illness was something they'd learned to live with, but they never, never stopped to dwell on it. "Anyway, back to Sheriff Lawson Holt, of Santa Almendra." She moved the conversation on.

"So...we're going then?" Shelby's voice was uncharacteristically tentative, and Cady realized that, for once, her sister needed her along. And this was definitely something they should do together.

"Yes," she replied. "But listen, don't go with high expectations. We don't know what his circumstances are."

"I *know*. I have thought of that. But I need to find out some things. Like, if he knew about us, why did he never come and see us? He sent all that money—but money doesn't count for everything. How could he have stayed away all this time?"

Those were things Cady wanted to know too. "I suppose he had his reasons. Just don't go in guns blazing, okay? And whatever happens, don't take it too personally."

"Personally?" Shelby retorted. "It *is* personal. How much more personal can you get?"

"I know, I know. Just...look after yourself. We might be in for a disappointment."

"I can handle disappointment. It's the not knowing I can't live with."

Cady nodded. "It looks like we're going to know soon enough."

Chapter Seventeen

This time Cady did a bit better with the rental car, choosing a Chrysler for their trip to Santa Almendra. It still wasn't the movie-worthy vehicle Shelby longed for, but it was American at least. She nodded her grudging approval as they loaded their bags the next day. They'd agreed to go straight away—once they knew where their father was, it seemed impossible to put off going to see him. The pull of curiosity, and family, was too strong.

It felt strange to be leaving the bus, though. They'd only been official Flashpointers for about a week, but the intensity of the experience made it seem longer. Living at close quarters and working on a huge project brought them all closer together, whether they liked it or not. Some of it, she'd liked *very* much. (A bit too much.) Some of it, not so much...although even the evil California twins weren't all bad, in the end.

Kyle had told them to come back whenever they wanted. After the triumph of the 'Home' flash mob he felt confident that the movement was back on track, and they were going ahead with planning the next event. But the twins' bus beds were there for as long as they were in the country, he promised. This open invitation made Cady feel a bit better as they did the rounds of saying goodbye, everyone wishing them luck. Gavin, Tino, Jennifer, and even Alison received hugs. Kyle too, who tipped Shelby back and gave her a resounding kiss on the mouth, making her blush scarlet. It was overdone enough to look like a joke in front of everyone, but Cady knew the effect it would have on her sister. While Cady had seen enough to shatter any illusions (not that she'd had any to start with), Shelby was still crushing hard on their chaotic, charismatic leader.

When Cady came to Reid, who was standing next to Jennifer, she hesitated. Self-conscious, she had a ridiculous should-I-shouldn't-I moment. After all the heat between them, would a hug be loaded with implications? But to not hug him was just silly—everyone else was, after all. Her thoughts swirled in her head and her feelings in her chest, in barely the time it took to draw a deep breath in front of him. And once she went in for the hug, oh, she so badly wanted him to hold her tighter, show that he was reluctant to let her go, and let her leave. But she wasn't going to be the one to cling on in front of everyone else, and he was giving nothing away. Of course, maybe there was nothing *to* give away. With that thought, she abruptly let go and stepped back, feeling like her cheeks must be as hot as every square inch of the rest of her. He released her all too easily, seeming unbothered at their parting. No grand kiss for her, nothing to take away, no encouragement to think that all the teasing had been based in anything real.

"Goodbye everyone," she said, her voice on the squeaky side of unsteady. "Thanks again."

Then she hightailed it to the car before she could make a fool of herself, the sound of their goodbyes in her ears. Shelby followed, dragging her feet. Although she was desperate to meet their father, it was clearly a wrench to leave the object of her affection. She leaned out the open window, waving, probably planning how soon she could come back for another of those kisses.

As Cady pulled out of the parking space, she tried not to look back. Maybe just *one* peek in the rear mirror... She saw that Alison had tucked her arm into Kyle's, and

Jennifer into Reid's. With the others, they turned and started to walk back to the bus. Everything was slotting smoothly back into the shape it had been before. The way, of course, it was supposed to be.

Shelby saw it too. "Shit." That seemed to say it all. She turned and slumped in her seat, then started crankily fiddling with the stereo. "Screw this stupid country music."

Cady sighed. Well, onwards. New start, phase two, was underway. And who knew what lay ahead, for good or bad. So far, this new start had been way more adventurous than she could have imagined.

They'd had a long debate about whether to phone their father first, to say who they were and that they wanted to come and see him. Cady thought they should ring so they didn't spring it on him—landing him with a shock might not be the best start. Maybe they should give him time to get used to the idea before they met in person. But Shelby wanted to go in cold. If they gave him time to get used to the idea, she said, he might decide he didn't want to meet them at all. And she was determined to meet him, come hell or high water. In the end, Cady agreed. He was going to get a surprise either way. Might as well get it over with in one hit.

But before they left the bus, she'd phoned the Santa Almendra head office to check that he wasn't away. She introduced herself as a reporter from a fictional British farming newspaper, planning to write a series of articles on California's biggest crops. When his secretary confirmed that he was in the office for the next two weeks, Cady promised to call back to schedule an interview time. She only felt slightly guilty. There would be an interview of sorts, after all...just not about almond production.

It was a picture perfect August day as they drove through the Sacramento Valley toward Santa Almendra. The radio had reported forest fires in other parts of the state, but here the land lay peaceful in a summery haze. It was drier and dustier than Cady had imagined in her California dreaming, in the days when the big wide world was no bigger than the thirteen or so inches of her laptop screen. Reality had come with a few jolts, but being out in it made her feel like she was really breathing for the first time in forever. She rolled down the window, intending to symbolically breathe in the warm California air. But at interstate speed the roar of the wind was way too powerful, so she closed the window, sealing them back in their air-conditioned cocoon, feeling silly. So much for symbolism...but anyway, she definitely wasn't sealing herself in anywhere, any more. Her mum would approve of that.

She wondered if Anne would also approve of today's expedition. Well, whether she'd approve or not, once they had the information about Lawson Holt, they *had* to do something. And anyway, Anne's disapproval was usually reason enough for Shelby to specifically go ahead and do something.

It was strange to imagine meeting this man, the man their mother had chosen to be their biological father. Again, she wondered if Anne had had feelings for him, or if she'd been utterly pragmatic about the whole thing. On the face of it, her choice was sensible: a young, healthy guy, who'd be leaving the country. If it had gotten complicated—if feelings had crept into her carefully measured calculation—it didn't seem like she'd let that change things.

Cady thought of their father, loving and constant through it all. She hoped, more than anything, that none of this would touch him. Her mother loved him, she knew that much. By keeping the secret to the very end, she must have felt she was protecting him from a painful truth. Was it right for the girls to continue keeping the secret? Cady was still wrestling with that particular question. For now, this trip would bring them the answers to some others.

Now, her sister was unusually quiet in the passenger seat. "Are you okay?" Cady asked.

She fiddled with her phone, zooming in and out of the map on screen. "Yeah...I'm nervous," she admitted.

"Me too. But we'll be okay. We're not doing this alone." She smiled. "There are *some* advantages to having an annoying twin, you know."

"Pfft. This must be the only one," Shelby replied. Cady poked her tongue out, and Shelby grinned and sat up straighter, regaining a little of her zing. She pushed her sunglasses up her nose and pointed ahead. "Take the next right."

Cady made the turn, onto a road lined with oak trees. "You know, this is the most time we've spent together in years," she said to Shelby.

"Yeah, I know. Apparently we couldn't keep avoiding each other."

Her voice was deadly serious, but when Cady glanced sideways she could see the hint of a smile hovering on her lips. Shelby caught her eye and they smiled at each other.

"Sisters," Cady said, shaking her head. "Can't live with 'em..."

"Can't stand their taste in music," Shelby finished for her, pointing at the stereo.

"How can you not like Ryan Adams? Just wait for once. I love this song." It was plaintive and languorous and sexy...and today it made her desperately want to turn the car around and drive straight back to Reid.

Shelby sighed but gave in, muttering about harmonicas, and they drove on until the song was finished. Then Cady hit the CD button, and Kings of Leon replaced Ryan Adams' dreamy voice.

"Better," Shelby said, satisfied.

"Anything to keep you happy."

"Damn right."

They laughed. At least it was nice to have this time together, Cady thought. They should have made more effort before now, instead of letting old resentments and disagreements keep them apart. It was painful to realize that it took their mother's death to finally bring them back together. The thought of her mum brought on a pang deep in Cady's chest, but she squashed the feeling down. There hadn't been a time she'd wanted to let it out before now. And this wasn't the time either. With Shelby less prickly, Cady took the chance to distract herself from serious thoughts.

"So," she said. "Still Kyle, huh?"

Shelby blushed. "Shit, is it so obvious?"

"Maybe just to me. I know you too well." She'd thought Shelby might be put off by Kyle's increasingly unsociable habits, but his reclusiveness had only whetted her appetite, it seemed. And she hadn't mentioned the feral den that was his upstairs suite, thinking Shelby would probably talk her way up there eventually. But even he must have realized that disaster area wouldn't impress a girl. In any case, he seemed happy to string Shelby willingly along...not unlike Cady herself and another Flashpointer, come to think of it.

Now Shelby made the obvious comeback. "You know *me* too well? What about Reid, then?"

Cady adjusted her sunglasses. She'd been trying not to think about him, for a while at least. But the image of Jennifer slipping her arm through his, claiming him back as they walked away, kept popping into her head. She shrugged. "What about him?"

"I think he got the better of you. Miss Sensible had her head turned. I've never seen you so fluttery."

"Fluttery! I was not."

Shelby wagged a finger in her direction. "You can't fool me."

She sighed. "Yeah, okay. I just couldn't help it."

"You and me both."

"Men." Cady shook her head.

"Mmm, *men*," Shelby said with exaggerated relish, making Cady laugh. Then she leaned forward. "Left up here. Look."

As the road sign announcing Santa Almendra loomed ahead, the atmosphere in the car suddenly veered into more serious territory. Cady felt her nerves come flooding back, and Shelby clutched her stomach.

"Oh, man," she muttered, and Cady nodded in sympathetic silence.

The Holt farm shared its name with the local town, not much more than a village. Cady slowed the Chrysler, and they circled the pocket-handkerchief park in the center of town. There was neatly clipped grass, a band rotunda, and the Stars and Stripes flying proud on a tall flagpole. Along the main street was a little café, a barber shop, an ice cream parlor, a hardware store, and a beauty parlor, but none of the big-box retailers that seemed to be everywhere else they went. It reminded Cady of something, somewhere she must have been before...

"Stars Hollow," she said aloud, suddenly remembering.

"What?" Shelby started to check her phone again. "No, we're definitely in Santa Almendra."

Cady shook her head. "No, you know, the Gilmore Girls. Lorelai and Rory. This reminds me of their town, Stars Hollow."

"Oh, okay. I can see that. It's pretty."

It was delightful. And in the blink of an eye it was finished, as they completed their circuit, passed out the other side of town, and headed up a two-lane road toward Santa Almendra farm.

"This is it," Shelby said after a few minutes. "There, on the left."

Cady turned the car up a long, straight driveway, flanked with trees on each side. Greenish fruit hung thickly amongst long, slim leaves, weighing down their elegant branches. Although the fruit looked like apricots, or small peaches, she guessed there must be almonds inside. As they drew closer to the end of the driveway, her heart was racing, and her stomach felt twisted with anxiety. Looking at Shelby, her face pale and set, she guessed she was feeling the same.

They came to a wide turning circle, with a simple fountain in the middle of a grassy mound. A sign showed that the office was to their right. To the left, the driveway continued around the corner, behind more trees and buildings. Maybe the house was around there. She found a space in the parking area, and they sat for a moment. It was very quiet, which didn't help her nerves.

"Are you ready?" she asked her sister.

"I don't know." She held her seatbelt as if for comfort, making no move to undo it.

"Well, I am. Come on, let's get this done." She pushed her sunglasses up onto her head and started to open the car door, but Shelby lingered.

"Wait. Are you still the newspaper reporter, or are you going to be you?"

Good question. She paused to think for a moment, her hand on the door lever. "I'm me," she answered. "We are who we are now. Even though it turned out we don't really know who we are after all."

Shelby looked annoyed at these verbal gymnastics. "What?"

"Come on," Cady encouraged her. "We'll ask at the office."

They were just starting to head in that direction when they heard footsteps on the fine white gravel behind them. They both turned to see a tall, upright man walking toward them. His long legs were encased in dark blue jeans, his shirt was startling white in the sun, and his face was shaded by a brown cowboy hat. Cady took in the large buckle on his belt, the well-made boots, and the beautiful cut of his unfussy clothes. He gave them a smile as he came nearer, his expression relaxed. The grey in his hair only made the vivid blue of his eyes seem even brighter. Here was a man who projected confidence in himself, and in his world.

"Good afternoon," he said. "Can I help you ladies?"

They both knew it must be him. Wow, Cady thought, she chose well. She wouldn't have blamed her mother if she'd fallen for him just a little bit. Glancing at Shelby, who'd taken off her sunglasses as if to see him better, she could tell she was thinking the same thing. The words 'silver' and 'fox' were surely in both their minds.

"Um..." Cady began. "I think so."

If he noticed her sudden incompetence, he politely eased her through the moment. "Would you like to come along to the office? It's hot in the sun."

She pulled herself together. "Thank you, but we're not really here on business."

"Oh?" He waited to see what she would say next. In the pause that followed, he looked from one of them to the other. Did he seem to be looking with a sudden intensity, as though he was trying to place them? Wondering if he knew them from somewhere? Recognizing something familiar in the sweep of their cheekbones, or the set of their noses, or the blue of their eyes, a paler reflection of his own? Maybe it was her imagination. All the ways Cady had rehearsed this conversation suddenly went out of her head, and she had to just leap in, her heart pounding.

"We've come from England to ask you about Anne." She held her breath, waiting for some definite flash of recognition on his face. But there was nothing. Surely he couldn't have *forgotten*.

He maintained a polite expression. "I'm sorry...Anne?"

Shelby couldn't help herself. "Anne Morrow! You *know*."

"Anne Morrow?" Now he started to look uncomfortable, but probably not because he'd suddenly been presented with two unexpected daughters and was avoiding the truth. More like he'd been waylaid on a driveway by two increasingly rude strangers. He was either pretending, or...they had the wrong person entirely.

"I'm sorry," Cady said hastily, taking Shelby's arm and drawing her back. "We just assumed that you were the person we're looking for. Are you Lawson Holt?"

"Yes, I am." He held out his hand. "Pleasure to meet you."

Cady knew that probably wasn't true, so far—and he might not feel that way after what they had to say either. But she put her hand out in return. Her fingers were engulfed in a leathery handshake that proved he must work his land as hard as anyone on his staff. "I'm Cady," she replied.

"And I'm Shelby."

Right then, they saw the reaction they'd expected when they asked about Anne. Shock flashed across his face—but only for a moment. He composed himself so quickly that they had no clue what he could be thinking.

"Would you like to come to the house?" he suggested. "Seems like we might have some things to talk about."

Chapter Eighteen

They sat on the wide porch at the front of the house, sipping sparkly peach tea with ice, and eating vanilla cookies. The elderly lady who brought them out patted each of the girls firmly on the hand, her eyes shining and her lips pressed together as if to contain some emotion fizzing inside.

"Thank you," they both said, as she set out the refreshments.

"Elva, this is Cady and Shelby," Lawson Holt said.

"Yes," Elva said, looking fit to burst. "Yes. Hello, girls. Welcome!"

"Hello," they replied together.

"Oh!" Elva pressed her hands to her cheeks and shook her head, a joyous expression of satisfied disbelief animating her soft features. Then she grabbed the sides of her apron and bustled back inside, all in a flap.

Once she was gone, there was an awkward silence. Cady looked around at the beautiful sweepy trees, the simple but manicured garden beds, and the white pea gravel path leading to the comfortably shady porch. There was no evidence of children anywhere, no bikes leaning against the steps, or abandoned shoes by the door, or footballs on the grass. They'd come straight onto the porch, so there'd been no chance to nosy in the house. She checked his left hand. No ring. Surely he couldn't be single.

She didn't know how she'd expected to feel in this moment. An instant bond, their blood link making everything click into place? Angry, like Shelby, about the years of deception? Overcome with emotion at meeting him? Now that they were sitting together, she was surprised to actually feel a sort of detached calm. The man in front of them was just a man. An impressive kind of man, who happened to be their father. But she was relieved to find herself quite steady.

Now, like Shelby, she badly wanted to know more. With their mother gone, he was the only one who could tell them what had really happened. Everyone knew what needed to be discussed, but now that the moment was here, Cady found herself unsure where to start. She searched around for the right words. *So, you slept with our mother* was a bit blunt. Shelby was no help, looking nervous and tongue-tied.

In the end, he did it for them.

"Well, I know why you're here," he said. "I've waited a long time to see you."

Shelby looked skeptical. "You have?"

He smiled. "If twenty-five years counts as a long time."

Cady could see where Shelby was going next. "So you knew about us," she said accusingly. "All that time, and you never came to see us."

Her tone was bitter, but he took it on the chin. "I promised your mother that I—"

"Yeah, Cady made her a promise too," Shelby interrupted, her voice creeping upwards. "But, here we are."

He looked at Cady, but she just shook her head. That was a whole other Shelby grievance they didn't need to go into. They'd only been here five minutes, and already her sister was losing her balance. Although now she was starting to feel a bit edgy herself.

He cleared his throat. "There's obviously a lot we have to

say to each other. Do you want to have this conversation?"

Shelby sniffed, obviously overwhelmed now that he was in front of them, but Cady nodded.

"Yes," she said. "We need to. We only just found out about you. And…our mum has died."

He sat back suddenly, as if someone had socked him in the chest. Cady had never seen someone so tan actually go pale, but he did. He rubbed his temple, obviously processing the news.

"My God." He shook his head, a million miles away, then seemed to remember them again. "I'm so sorry for your loss. She was amazing. But you don't need me to tell you that."

"Thank you," Cady said. "It's been a…difficult time."

"How did it happen? If you don't mind me asking."

This was something Cady didn't want to discuss at all. "It was an autoimmune thing," she said. She could see he wanted to ask more, but her tone was so final it gave him no encouragement. Luckily, Shelby piped up.

"Didn't you know who we were, when you saw us?" she asked suddenly. "Didn't you recognize us?"

"I thought I did," he said. "But I didn't believe it could be you. I never expected to meet you at all, let alone find you on my driveway, out of the blue."

Shelby looked satisfied. "I thought you'd just know it was us, somehow, even though you've never seen us before."

Of course, Cady had secretly hoped the same thing.

"Well, I…" He stood up suddenly. "There's something I should show you. I'll be right back." He went in through the open French doors, letting the filmy curtains fall closed behind him. They peered after him, but couldn't see anything inside.

Cady sighed and leaned back against the pillows in the deep wicker loveseat. "What do you think?" she whispered. "So far."

"I don't know." Shelby frowned. She looked at his cowboy hat, sitting on the wide arm of his chair. "He seems okay, don't you think? But I'm not keeping my cool. I knew exactly all the things I was going to say, and now I'm just coming unglued."

"Well, it's not like we're here to talk about the weather. If it gets messy, it gets messy. Then we just jump in the car and go." She returned Shelby's relieved smile. "But he seems nice enough. Maybe."

"I suppose so." She nibbled around the edge of her cookie, her expression tense.

Before long he came out carrying a small leather-bound album, and sat back in the seat opposite. "This was in my study. I thought you might like to see it." He held it out, and Cady took it.

"What is it?" she asked.

"It's all I've had."

She gave him a quizzical look, but he waved a hand toward the album. "Open it."

Shelby came and sat in the loveseat too, and leaned over her shoulder. "Yes, open it."

She turned the first page. And the next, and the next. It was them. Page after page of Cady and Shelby, each page revealing two girls a year older, posing with a spectacular birthday cake.

"She sent me a photo every year," he said.

Their mother's birthday cakes had made them the envy of their friends: castles and princesses, butterflies, a paddock with ponies, a mermaid, a unicorn with a rainbow mane and tail... After hours of painstaking effort, Anne would take a photo of them with the cake, then stand back and watch as her work was chopped up and eaten in minutes. It was only as a grown-up that Cady realized what a huge undertaking each cake must have been, especially in later years when her health started to fail.

"Wow. So this is how you knew it was us." No family magic after all. She turned the pages slowly, Shelby looking on. It was surreal to see their lives documented year by year. All that time, they'd had no idea that someone far away was receiving a copy of the cake photo, holding onto this slender thread of connection. Someone connected to them in a way they never could have guessed.

The last cake—a masterful confection, exquisitely detailed in gothic red and black flowers—was for their seventeenth birthday, just before Shelby left home. In the photo she looked sullen behind the overdone teenage eyeliner, obviously there under sufferance and utterly unimpressed.

"I can't believe how different we look," Cady said. "That wasn't even ten years ago. This was the last cake, remember?"

"Guilt cake." Twenty-five-year-old Shelby shook her head, her expression reflecting her seventeen-year-old self. "All those years, lying. How could she do it?"

"I liked the cakes," Cady said.

"Well...I liked them too. But still!"

Cady closed the album and put it on the low table in front of them.

"The cakes were like her thing," she told him. "Her trademark. We never realized they were for your benefit."

"No. They were for you," he said emphatically. "Give her more credit than that."

The girls looked at each other. They remembered how much their mum loved revealing the cake each year, seeing their surprised faces, and knew he was right. But now that they were questioning even simple things like birthday cakes, it was like their whole lives were built on very shaky ground. How many of the other things they'd taken for granted were not exactly what they thought?

Now he had a question for them. "You called her Anne. Was that a nickname?"

"No. That's her name." Shelby stopped, corrected herself. "*Was* her name."

"Oh." He let it float.

"Why?" Cady asked.

"Well...she told me her name was Adrienne. That's why I was thrown when you asked about Anne."

The girls looked at each other. Adrienne. Was that who their mother saw herself as—or dreamed she might be—in her imagination? It was hard to reconcile the glamorous-sounding Adrienne with Anne's ordinary, everyday life in Broadstairs, then in Peckham Rye.

"She always said she hated how boring her name was," Cady said. "I guess she took the chance to be someone more exotic."

He looked awkward. "I'm sorry about all this. It can't be easy for you, having your world completely shaken up."

"Thanks." Cady looked at him, this father who wasn't her father. She hesitated. "Speaking of names—I don't know what to call you," she said.

"Everyone calls me Holt. My father was always Lawson, so I started out being 'Little Holt' around the farm. But, you know...I grew."

Holt. That was impersonal enough to sit comfortably with Cady. Then she registered that he'd said his father 'was' Lawson. "Your father has passed away?"

"Yes, and my mother. It's okay," he added, seeing their faces. "It was a long time ago now."

Cady thought of his sisters, the other Cady and Shelby in the photo, who they were named for. "So it's just you and your sisters now?"

"My sisters? No, I was an only child. Naughty. Spoiled rotten." He shook his head as if regretting the wildness of his younger self. "I could have done with sisters to keep me in line."

Shelby looked at Cady, her eyebrows raised. Cady shrugged a little, perplexed. She was sure of it: Anne had definitely said she named them after his sisters. Could she have remembered wrong, in her exhaustion and illness?

Before they had a chance to ask him anything more, he spoke. "Maybe the best thing is for me to just tell you my side of the story. If you want to hear it."

Cady nodded. "I want to."

"Me too," Shelby said.

"Okay." He took a breath, then let it out again, as if in preparation to relive the past. "I met Adrienne—Anne—in London. I'd had some...difficulties, here at home. I was young, but not young enough to excuse how immature I'd been. That's a whole other story, but believe me, I'd had the spoiled stuffing knocked out of me. Which was a good thing."

"What did you do?" Shelby had to ask.

"Nothing criminal, don't worry. But I left my growing up a bit late."

"How old were you then?" Cady asked.

"Twenty-four. When I met your mom, I knew she was older, but I didn't ask how much. She was just a woman who seemed to have it together, who knew who she was."

That was ironic, for a woman pretending to be someone else entirely. Cady held her tongue, waiting for the next part of the story, but Shelby rolled her eyes. "Pfft. Mrs. Robinson."

"No." He shook his head at her words. "Not like Mrs. Robinson, at all. She was a breath of fresh air. Straightforward. Funny. Honest."

"Honest!" Shelby exclaimed. "Hardly."

He acknowledged her comment with a small smile. "Yeah. But it was like...I don't know. Like she was really *living*, determined to make the days count. I liked her very much."

There was one thing in particular that Cady really wanted to ask. "Did you know she was married?"

"No." He was emphatic. "I didn't."

"Wasn't she wearing a ring?" Shelby asked. "You must have known something."

"No, I didn't," he said again. "Look, I'm sorry. I know this is upsetting for you. But if she'd told me she was married, I would have backed off."

Shelby persisted. "Well, wouldn't there have been a mark on her finger where her wedding ring usually was?"

"She actually wore rings on almost all her fingers, so..."

Wow. She'd thought of everything. Cady marveled at the amount of planning Anne had put into her baby-making project. She'd obviously organized it meticulously—and her secret had held until she gave it away herself.

"And what happened?" she asked. "Did you see her many times? I mean, we don't want the details, of course," she added hurriedly.

"No, of course." He looked embarrassed that they

were even indirectly referring to him sleeping with their mother. "I was in London for about a month. My father had suggested some time away might be a good idea. I had a room at a hotel on Queensway. I remember being impressed by how royal that sounded."

"Americans," Shelby snorted.

"Right." He smiled, not offended. "Anyway, on the second Saturday I saw Anne eating alone at a restaurant. I was alone too, so after she finished her meal I introduced myself. She said the girlfriend she was supposed to meet had missed the train to London. We went for drinks, and then…"

Cady held up a hand. "Aaand that's where we let the curtain drop."

He nodded. "She came back the next weekend, and then the weekend after that. After that I had to go home. Dad wanted me to buckle down and work here. I didn't want to say goodbye to her, but she let me go so easily. I tried to make her promise to come and see me. I offered to pay for her flights. But she wouldn't make any plans, wouldn't say any of the things I wanted to hear. It was only afterwards that I realized why." He looked genuinely unhappy, as though the retelling brought back the pain. "I couldn't believe it when I got her letter."

"She told you everything?" Cady asked.

"Yes. And she was crystal clear—she wanted her husband and her family. If I had any feelings for her, I had to respect that. I knew I couldn't wreck her life. So I kept myself busy. The business needed me, and I'd let that slip for long enough as it was. Somehow, I've been busy for twenty-five years."

There was silence, the girls taking in everything he'd told them. Cady realized she felt a bit sorry for him. They'd been so busy imagining him as a kind of villain, it hadn't occurred to them that he might have suffered collateral damage from their mother's scheme. She had to ask one more thing—the thing she'd been wondering for weeks, but never intended to bring up. Hearing him talk, though, and seeing his obvious emotion, she suddenly had to know.

"Was it love?"

He smiled. "There's a question spoken by someone who still believes in love." Then he paused, looking out over the lawn to the almond trees row on row, their leaves glossy green in the sun. "Love in three weekends? Sure, I fell in love with what I knew of her, and who knows what would've happened if things were different. But they weren't. She didn't love me, I know that much. But I wanted to do the right thing."

"And the money...?" That had to be acknowledged, if it was from him.

"She didn't want it, but in the end she agreed. A little each week, into a bank account, for your futures. The account was under the name A. Morrow, so I never knew she wasn't really Adrienne. And all our communication was in writing, via her lawyer. I had no idea where she was. I was tempted to find her, but what good would that have done any of us? I think I did the right thing, just sending the money."

"Thank you for that," Cady said, remembering her manners. She nudged Shelby.

"Yes, thank you," she said.

"That's okay," he said. "It's only what any of my children would get."

"And...do you have any children?" Cady asked, although she thought she knew the answer already. She'd been half hoping for more siblings, and half nervous at the prospect. Shelby was work enough—but maybe brothers or sisters would lessen the intensity of their twin-ness. On the other hand, they might only complicate things more.

"Any *other* children," her sister corrected her.

He smiled. "No. Never was blessed. Never found the right lady, in fact."

"Really?" Shelby said. "That's hard to believe."

It was. He was so handsome, and tall, and obviously financially successful, he seemed to be a great catch.

"There must have been someone," she pressed.

"Shel, leave it," Cady told her, as he looked uncomfortable.

But then he smiled. "That's okay. Let's just say I haven't been great at making things work. Now—would you like to see some of Santa Almendra?"

Chapter Nineteen

They drove for what seemed like miles in Holt's truck, a huge Dodge Ram. It was a real boy's toy, pimped out with just enough extras to show how much the owner loved it, but the dirt on the paintwork proved that it was more than a showpiece—it was a working vehicle too. They set out onto the farm, all three of them sitting up front on the kind of bench seat the girls never saw in England. Holt wore his cowboy hat and leaned his elbow out the window as he steered one-handed. The girls had their sunglasses on, their eyes still not used to the bright California sun, but he just squinted a little under the brim of his hat.

"These acres around the house make up the main farm," he explained, as they left an access road and made their way between rows of trees. "But we have holdings in other parts of the valley too, and further afield. Santa Almendra is the biggest almond producer in the state."

Shelby poked Cady in the side, her eyes big. The extent of his empire was impressive. And the idea that all of this was his, and they were his only children—his only family—obviously wasn't lost on her sister. But Cady shook her head. They hadn't come to dig for gold. Just for the truth.

"Santa Almendra." She tried out the words, rolling

them on her tongue the way he did. "What does it mean?"

He laughed. "Well, literally it means 'Saint Almond'. Sounds silly in English, I know. But when my grandfather—your great-grandfather—first came here from back east, he was getting to be an old man. He'd made and lost a decent kind of fortune already, and he told my dad that almonds were going to save them. He noticed that everything in California was saint this and saint that, so he called his new farm Santa Almendra. It started out as a joke, but it stuck."

"It sounds beautiful, to someone who doesn't speak Spanish," Cady commented.

"Well, it's a beautiful place," he said, effortlessly navigating the big truck along a narrow, climbing track. "And if you decide to stay awhile, you'll probably pick up some Spanish."

Stay awhile? Cady looked at Shelby, but she was one step ahead.

"Is that an invitation?" she asked their newfound father, direct as usual. "I suppose you have plenty of room for guests."

Before he could reply, Cady spoke up. Partly she felt the need to cover for her sister's boldness, but also, she wasn't convinced that staying at the farm was a good idea. It had been a pretty intense afternoon so far—forcing the getting-to-know-you might be a bit much.

"No, no," she said, giving Shelby a surreptitious look. "If we stay in California, he means. Tonight we can stay in town before we go back to San Francisco. We've been hanging out with a flash mob, and they're planning an event, so there's quite a lot to do," she explained, trying to give him an easy out.

She knew full well that the Flashpointers didn't need them, and weren't expecting them back any time soon—if at all. Yes, they'd found him, and found out some of the things they needed to know. There was more to come, of course. But they should probably give themselves, and him, some space. All three of them had a lot to think about.

"You're welcome to stay," he said. "It's just me, so

there are plenty of spare rooms in the house. Elva comes in every day except Sunday and Monday. Although I sometimes see her sneak in on those days too." He stopped the truck on a bare outcrop, overlooking the valley.

"Come on," he said, opening his door. "This is my favorite place on the farm."

They got out and stood in the sun, taking in the view. Below, orderly rows of almond trees stretched out into the distance, their green contrasting with the brilliant blue of the summer sky. Off to the side they could see the white plantation-style house, separated from the company buildings by more trees and the expanse of lawn. It was a scene of calm and plenty, a million miles from the hectic, flung-together city that was home for them. What if they'd grown up here, Cady wondered, instead of in London? A sunshiny, wholesome setting like this must make a totally different kind of person than the concrete and relentless— albeit historically rich—environment of London. Would she be less straight-laced, more ready to leap into things? Who would she be, if she was California Cady?

Which reminded her—there was still the question of the California Cady and Shelby. If they weren't his sisters, who were they? She resolved to ask him as soon as the time was right.

Shelby was captivated by the scene spread before them. "This is all yours." She couldn't hide the 'wow' in her voice.

"Yes." He smiled. "But I have a *lot* of help. If you do want to stay for a while, I'll show you. We're getting ready for harvest soon. It was my dad's favorite time of year."

Shelby pointed. "Your house is so pretty."

From here it looked like a dollhouse, waiting for a child to come and open the front and bring it to life with imaginary games. It seemed a shame that there were no children there. Cady's doubts about staying were toppled by what he said next.

"My parents always imagined that house full of grandchildren, but they both died without that wish coming true. You girls didn't make it in time to meet them—but you're meant to be here."

"Well…" Cady said.

And at the exact same moment, Shelby said, "We'll stay, thank you."

He nodded. "Elva will be glad. She's the only person who knows about you, now that my parents are gone."

"I thought she was strangely excited to see us," Cady said.

"Yeah. I had to tell *someone* else. You two are too big a secret not to share. And she's a vault. She wouldn't tell a soul."

"Wait," Shelby said, ready to be offended. "Why do you have to keep us a secret?"

"I don't have to, now," he said. "Before, I was a secret to you, so it was better to have it both ways. Now we can just be us."

For a moment, Cady felt a rush of happiness as warming as the sun on her back. But then she remembered the one person who was still in the dark about this secret— their dad. And then she felt sick. How did he fit into all of this? Once it was Shelby who wanted to tell him the truth, and Cady who held back. But now that they'd crossed the line and met their biological father, she didn't know if she should, or could, keep the secret any more. Now, the weight of it had increased hundred-fold. And the guilt was a creeping growth, poking its fingers into the doubting corners of her mind. She stood on the dusty ground, next to one father, and her stomach churned on behalf of another.

But Shelby was smiling. "Being us sounds good to me."

It did sound good, to Cady too. But what sounds good doesn't always turn out to be for the best, she knew. And a half-uncovered secret this big was a creature with a life of its own. Holt had said he wanted to do the right thing by them, and she wanted to do the right thing by her family too. She just had to figure out what that was.

Chapter Twenty

The porch at Santa Almendra was a sanctuary. Inside, the house was delightful—stuffed comfortably full of the collected furniture and belongings of a family that had lived there for many years, and done well. The rooms were quiet and welcoming, and the air-conditioning was an escape from the heat. But on the shady porch, the sweet breeze freshened the air, and the sounds of summer hummed around them. They ate dinner there that night, talking cautiously, feeling their way around what this new family connection meant. Beautiful though it was, inside the house was firmly Holt's territory. The porch felt like neutral ground, a kind of safe zone where they could begin to figure out who they were together.

Elva fussed around, bringing citronella candles and refilling their glasses.

"Eat with us," Holt urged her, but she shook her head.

"No, no," she said. "You need this time together. The girls and I will get to know each other soon enough."

As the three of them talked, it slowly started to feel more comfortable. But it was a strange situation, flung together, all the weight of their unshared history stilting their interactions. Cady knew that trying to force an artificial intimacy was never going to work. Still, the talk gradually became less stilted, the silences less awkward, and by the time they said goodnight, it didn't feel completely unnatural for him to give each of them a kiss on the cheek. But there was a long way to go.

The next day, he took them on a tour of the orchards and explained the yearly cycles of pollination and harvest. How the trucks would come, loaded with hives of bees to work their intuitive magic. The way the fruit developed, slowly ripening and splitting until it was ready for harvest. And how the machines would then drive down the rows, shaking the trees and letting the fruit fall to the ground to dry before it was collected. As he talked, it was easy to tell the pride he took in the work they were doing, and in the end product.

And to every person they met, in the orchard, the machinery sheds and the offices, he said the same thing: "These are my daughters, Cady and Shelby, from England."

And to every set of astonished raised eyebrows, he gave the same simple response: "I know. A good surprise."

Cady could only imagine the swirl of gossip and conjecture they must have been leaving in their wake. But when put on the spot, everyone took Holt's cue, welcoming them warmly and matter-of-factly. Hearing him say their names, she wondered again about where their mum had got them from. She couldn't imagine Anne getting muddled about something as big as that. But with no sisters, the origin of their names was a mystery. If they weren't his sisters, who were the women in the photo? Cady wanted to ask Holt, but the right moment hadn't seemed to present itself—yet.

At one point Holt took a phone call, walking away as he talked. They could see him nodding, his face serious.

"We need to go out to the edge of this orchard block," he told them when he came back, indicating that they should get in the Dodge again. After a few minutes' drive, they stopped in a field near the road. A man raised his hand in greeting, but his face was serious. Behind him, every tree in the first row had been hacked into. It looked like an ax murderer (or several) had gone mad, leaving great gashes and wounds in the beautiful trees, and dismembered branches on the ground.

Cady looked at Holt. "What happened here?"

His lips were a thin line. "Eco-protestors, making a point."

He got out of the truck and the girls followed, silently taking in the scene. It was upsetting to see the slashed trunks and chopped-off branches of the damaged trees, and their pitiful state was a painful contrast to the others still standing strong and lush.

Holt shook the man's hand, and surveyed the damage. "I heard there were plantings further south being attacked in the last few months," he said.

"Yeah. Looks like it's our turn all of a sudden. We'll up security, but there's only so much we can do, with so much ground to cover." The man looked at the girls. "New assistants?"

Holt laughed. "Maybe." He made the introductions. The man—his general manager—looked surprised, but took his cue from Holt and moved on to the problem at hand.

He pointed to an 'e' carved into a circle on one of the trunks. "Earth Stand. Environmental activists," he added for the girls' benefit. "They go for direct action, which usually equates to nothing more than eco-terrorism."

"Ecotage, they call it," Holt said. "Eco sabotage. This is small potatoes for them, but it could lead to more."

"Why would they do this?" Cady asked him, gesturing to the ruined trees.

He sighed. "Their line is that this kind of farming is environmentally unfriendly."

She looked around. Under the trees, in every field they'd visited, the ground was bare earth. She remembered his description of how they harvested the crop, letting the fruit dry on the ground. There was obviously nothing natural about the scorched-earth surface. "Is it?"

He'd obviously dealt with the question before. "Any food crop that's produced in large volumes becomes a monoculture. We have a lot of people to feed in this country, and almonds are a huge contributor to the Californian economy. We do our best, but there have to be compromises. Their kind of extremist propaganda and vandalism isn't helpful."

"Oh." She nodded, but in her mind she wondered how many chemicals were needed to maintain the pristine orchards around them. It was a complicated issue, but she could see how some people felt so passionate about protecting the earth.

The men continued their discussion, and Cady went over to Shelby, who had wandered back and was leaning against the truck. "Some people are assholes," she said pithily, waving at the damage.

"I guess," Cady replied. It seemed like one of those situations where the middle ground was no longer viable— no going back from production on a huge scale. Maybe there were ways to lessen the impact, but this kind of protest didn't seem like the best solution. God, the world was full of things that could be done better, but if she lay awake worrying about them all, she'd go mad. She tucked the problem away in the back of her mind, along with the Pacific trash vortex, global warming, and the Middle East situation. Sometimes it was enough work just figuring out how to be better herself.

★

The next morning, Holt said he had to go to one of the other farms. There had been vandalism to the plantings there, too. They were welcome to come, he said, but it would be a long drive, and he'd only be checking the damage and having a meeting, then turning around and driving back. Wouldn't they prefer to stay home and relax?

Cady was still looking for a chance to ask about their names, but he was clearly steering them in the direction of staying, and a long hot day of driving didn't sound all that appealing. Well, it could wait a few more hours, until he got home. They agreed that they'd stay at Santa Almendra for some quality porch time.

After he left, they settled in for a morning of reading, eating chocolate chunk oatmeal cookies, and drinking Elva's secret recipe pink lemonade. (Not so secret, she admitted—she got it from Martha Stewart. *Before* she went to jail, she hastened to add.) Every now and then Shelby would set down her magazine and sigh, looking wistfully out into the valley, no doubt with Kyle on her mind. Cady felt sympathetic—she was thinking about a particular Flashpointer herself, too.

After a while, a small woman on a huge grey horse appeared from around the side of the house. She rode Western style, her legs straight and relaxed in the intricately detailed saddle, the reins loose against the horse's sleek neck. She wore a cream cowboy hat, large sunglasses, and camel-colored boots under her slim-fitting jeans. Although she was middle-aged, she had a youthful trimness and vigor about her, and she looked utterly at home on horseback.

"Good morning," she called up to them. The horse blew out a long fluttery snort and danced a little, but its rider sat easy.

"Hi," Cady called back, and Shelby echoed with a 'hello'. Cady admired the figure she cut on the horse, so at ease. Neither of them had ever ridden, apart from donkey rides on Broadstairs beach when they were kids. Looking now at the animal in front of her, she felt a long-forgotten pang of the pony love she had as a child.

"What a beautiful horse," she said. He—or she—was like a picture-book horse, the kind of noble beauty that would feature on a calendar, or sit in porcelain on a little girl's windowsill.

"Thanks." The woman slapped the horse's neck, and he shook his head, his mane flying and bridle jingling. "This is Rambler. He's kinda naughty sometimes, but he's so gorgeous, you've gotta love him."

Cady laughed. "I can believe that. I'm Cady, by the way."

"I'm Shelby," Shelby added.

"I know," said their visitor. "Word's out."

"That was fast," Shelby said.

The woman smiled. "Actually, I have a source on the inside." Seeing their curious faces, she added, "Elva called me."

The way Elva had been so thrilled with their arrival, Cady wasn't surprised to hear she'd been spreading the news. They waited for the visitor to introduce herself in return, but she didn't seem in any hurry. Rambler shifted his weight, let out a deep sigh, and let his eyes droop shut in the sun.

"Um...do you live near here?" Cady asked, looking for any connection.

"Yes, not far from here, just on the edge of town. Close enough to ride over. We're practically neighbors." She paused. "I'm Bee. That's what they call me, anyway."

"Hi," they both said, and she smiled.

Then Shelby looked at her more closely, a sudden sharpness in her expression. "What's your real name?" she asked, straight out.

The woman adjusted her cowboy hat, as though readying herself for something. Then she regarded them directly, meaning in her gaze.

"My real name is Shelby."

Cady heard her sister's sharp intake of breath, but her eyes were fixed on the woman on horseback. Here was the other Shelby. She was real. And if *she* was real, where was the other Cady? And why hadn't Holt mentioned them, their namesakes? These women who weren't his sisters, as Anne had believed. Had he told her that—had he lied to her, for some reason? Or had she just assumed? Cady had planned to ask him, when she could...but here was the answer, right in front of them.

"Please come up," Cady said. "Have a drink with us. I think we have a few questions for you. If you don't mind."

Bee nodded. "That's why I came," she said. She dismounted, landing lightly on the ground, and let one of the horse's reins fall to the ground. He dropped his head and got busy nibbling the sweet lawn grass. Then Bee put a foot on the bottom porch step, and the girls watched as another piece of their story headed up the stairs toward them.

Chapter Twenty-One

E lva came out onto the porch, carrying a tray with another tall glass. "I thought I heard a familiar voice," she said. "Hello, Bee."

"Morning, Elva," she replied. For a moment the two women looked at each other, an unspoken conversation seeming to travel between them. Then Bee said, "I'm going to have a chat with the girls."

"Uh-huh." There was understanding in Elva's tone.

"Yes." Bee took the glass she held out. "Thank you."

"You're very welcome. I'll leave you to it." She went back inside, quietly but firmly pulling the French doors closed behind her.

Cady leaned across and filled Bee's glass with pink lemonade, letting a few ice cubes tumble in too. She offered the plate of cookies, but Bee shook her head. Then, with the niceties taken care of, she asked the obvious question.

"So, if you're Shelby, I suppose there really is another Cady, too?"

Bee nodded. "There is."

She didn't offer anything more, so Cady continued. "Our mum thought Cady and Shelby were Holt's sisters. She saw a photo of him with two women, and that was what he told her."

"Ah." Bee looked awkward. "I didn't know that. No, we weren't sisters. Not his sisters, and not each other's, either."

"So you were…" Shelby let it hang in the air.

"We were friends, at one time. But later, we were more than friends. And then, afterwards, none of us were friends."

The girls looked at her as they tried to make sense of this cryptic timeline.

"You were more than friends," Cady said slowly. "Do you mean that you were, um…involved? All three of you?"

"We were. Not all at the same time though. I mean, not at *exactly* the same time. In the same bed." She took a sip of the lemonade, a blush showing beneath her tan. "I haven't talked about this with anyone for a hundred years."

"Okay, wait," Shelby sat forward, poised on the very edge of her seat. "What you mean is, we're named after a *threesome*?"

"Well, you don't have to put it like that, exactly."

Shelby stood up. "Oh my holy God, that's so beyond…" She paced the porch, fired with indignant energy. "How could he let her name us after his *lovers*?"

"But that's why I came to see you as soon as I could," Bee said. "When Elva called to say you'd arrived out of the blue, and what your names were, I knew you'd find out sooner or later, if you didn't already know. I had the feeling Holt might not volunteer it, and I wanted you to hear the story from one of us, not out there on the grapevine."

"No wonder everyone looked so gobsmacked yesterday when he introduced us," Cady said. "Or do they not know the history there?"

"No, everyone knows," Bee said. "Unfortunately." She looked sideways out across the lawn, where Rambler was happily grazing, oblivious to the human drama going on. "It doesn't really reflect that well on any of us."

"What happened?" Cady asked.

"Pah, I don't want to know," Shelby said, still riled up.

"Shel, sit down," Cady told her sister. "We need to know."

Shelby sat, grudgingly, and Cady looked at Bee. She ran her hands through her hair, the blonde gently fading into grey, and began.

"Well. We were young. We'd grown up together. At high school, Holt was always 'the man'—the girls loved him, and he was sporty so the guys respected him. I mean, there were always a few people ready to tear him down because of his money. But he was charming and wild and always ready for a good time."

Cady looked at Shelby. "Apples and trees...sounds like someone I know."

Shelby rolled her eyes. "Whatever."

"Almonds and trees, I guess," Cady corrected herself.

Bee smiled. "Shelby, you could do worse than have his personality. He's a lot of fun, when he wants to be, and he has a good heart."

Shelby harrumphed, unconvinced, so Bee continued with the story.

"Anyway, his father expected him to go to college, then step right into the company. He worked him crazy hard all through high school—grooming him for the business, I guess. And he did go to the college Lawson chose for him, and did really great. He got top marks. But by the time he finished, and came back here, he was like a bomb waiting to go off. Lawson installed him in the business, but he only lasted a couple of months. One night, he turned up at my house, saying he was leaving for San Francisco. And I packed a bag, and went with him." She smiled at the memory, but her eyes were sad. "I would have gone to the moon for that man. Half the girls in town would have. Most of them, probably."

"Were you guys a couple then?" Cady asked.

"Kind of. We dated in high school, on and off. But we both went to college in different places, and in the summers we both worked. And when he came home, he did nothing but work at Santa Almendra. We still had a connection, I guess."

"What about the other Cady?"

"Right. Well, when Holt and I got to the city, we took

a room up in The Haight. It seemed like the rebellious thing to do, even though we were, like, fifteen years too late for the summer of love. There were still plenty of drugs around, of course, just fewer of the good vibes. Cady was already there, working as a waitress. She'd left town the minute school finished. She was always...on the periphery, you could say. Smart, but not in sync with the world somehow. I always liked her, though."

Cady had wondered what her namesake was like. She knew it was pure romanticism to imagine they might be the same in some way, connected across an ocean not just by their names and their link to Holt, but by being kindred spirits too. But Bee's description of the other Cady resonated—*not in sync with the world, somehow.* Where was she now?

Bee continued. "We all worked any jobs we could get, waiting tables, whatever. Holt was done with big business, he said. After a while Cady took a room on the same floor in the house we were sharing. It was more like a closet really, with a bed squeezed in. We slipped into trying various...things. The drug scene in the eighties was more hard-core than in the hippie era. And Cady had always adored Holt from afar. I mean, who could blame her? So when they started hooking up too..." She paused. "At the time, I was cool with it, I thought. It was just the scene. Everything took on its own momentum, somehow, and I was so stuck on him, I didn't question it. I've had plenty of time to question things since then..." Her voice faded.

By now the girls were hanging on her every word. "What happened next?" Shelby asked.

"Cady got pregnant. It was a massive wake-up call. Massive."

"Wow," Cady said. She and Shelby looked at each other. They were clearly thinking the same thing. All the scary school lectures they'd had about sexual health and alarming infections, infestations and viruses had scarred them for life, it felt like. Not to mention the huge responsibility of a baby. Ironically, now Cady's considerations included how life might have to be *without* a baby.

167

"Didn't you use protection?" Shelby blurted out, not bothering to pretty up the question.

Bee took it in her stride. "We did. We were as scared of AIDS as everyone else, and other stuff. I guess there must have been one time when they...you know, we weren't always completely clear-headed."

"And the baby?" Cady asked, remembering how Holt had told them he didn't have any other children.

Bee looked grim. "I got a call from Holt one day at work. I remember standing in the kitchen with the chefs shouting and cursing as usual, listening to him tell me that Cady had lost the baby. God knows it wasn't really a surprise, we'd been taking all kinds of drugs up 'til then. But there were a thousand thoughts and emotions going through my head."

Cady struggled to think of something to say. "I'm sorry."

Bee shook her head. "Oh, don't be sorry for *me*. I was selfish enough to feel relieved, along with everything else. But I should have taken better care of her. I knew she was more fragile than me, from the start."

"Was she okay?" Cady asked.

"She was pretty run down, I guess. None of us had been eating right, and the drugs... Anyway, she got an infection, and she ended up staying in the hospital for a couple of weeks. Emotionally, she wasn't okay, not really." She frowned, her face showing the weight of what they'd all gone through. "When she was well enough, she came home to Santa Almendra. Holt and I came back after that too, but she wouldn't talk about it, and she wouldn't see us. He and I could hardly look at each other, either. And that was that. We don't really talk, even now, but Elva told me he was away for the day, so..."

There was silence on the porch as the girls got to grips with everything she'd told them. It was a million miles from the beautiful, carefree sisters they'd expected to hear about, and hopefully meet. All these years later, and the repercussions of their youthful rebellion and misjudgments were still weighing her down.

"Where is she?" Cady asked. "The other Cady."

"She's around. After a while she did meet someone else, from out of town, but that marriage ended. I don't know all the details. But now, it's better to leave her alone. She wouldn't thank you for bringing it up, believe me. She never did come quite right afterwards."

That made sense. But Cady still wanted to see her. She felt huge sympathy for the unusual, damaged girl who'd gone through so much—now a middle-aged woman, but with the same heart, surely.

Shelby had a question. "How did Holt feel about all of it?"

"Terrible, of course, like me. Probably worse, because he'd come from such high expectations. He had to deal with his parents, who were old-school, straight as an arrow. They had no idea what was going on in San Francisco. It just about killed his mom. Mine wasn't exactly thrilled either." She paused, the emotion of the memories playing out on her face. "And you know…even if he wasn't exactly ready for fatherhood, that was his baby too."

"He should have kept it in his pants," Shelby retorted, making Cady burst out with shocked laughter.

"Shelby!" she said, trying to stifle her inappropriate laughing. Only her sister would leap in with such a blunt comment.

But Bee shrugged, a rueful smile on her face too. "That's okay. I could have said no. But we were so crazy about him, and Cady was determined. I mean, even now, he's hot, if you ask me. He has some kind of Clooney-ish cowboy thing going on, right?"

"Classic silver fox," Cady said, and Shelby had to agree.

"I can see him in you both," Bee said. "Something around the eyes, and the mouth too. And all this time, after Cady lost the baby, we thought he'd never had children—until you showed up. So really, he's lucky." She smiled fully at them, clearly pleased by what she considered his good fortune. "What happens now?"

Cady and Shelby looked at each other. Neither of them

had any idea.

"I don't know," Cady said. "We're just taking it day by day at the moment. I suppose we'll talk to him when he comes home."

Bee stood up. "Well, okay. I guess I'll leave you to chew on all that. I'm sorry to throw such startling info at you."

"No, thanks for coming. It can't have been easy."

"Yes, thank you." Shelby had regained her manners.

"That's okay," Bee said, putting her hat back on. "It was so nice to meet you. I'll see you again, I hope."

She went down the steps and clicked a couple of times to Rambler, who trotted obligingly over and waited for her to gather up the reins. With an easy movement, she swung herself into the saddle. Then she looked back up at them.

"It was such a long time ago. We were young, and we were making a point. You know—being our own people, not playing by their rules. Whoever 'they' were. I know it didn't end well, especially for Cady, but in the moment, we were living exactly as we wanted to. So please—don't think badly of him."

Without seeming to move, she turned Rambler, and he almost immediately broke into a canter. Cady raised her hand goodbye, impressed, but they were already heading around the corner of the house.

She turned to Shelby. "She still loves him."

Shelby nodded. "Yep. You can see it a mile away."

"Do you think he knows?"

"I doubt it. But I hardly think he deserves it. Doesn't it bother you that we're named after that set-up?" She shuddered dramatically. "I need a shower."

Cady frowned. "I don't know. You heard what she said. They were all just doing their thing."

"Yeah, I know who was doing his *thing*." Shelby scrunched up her nose.

"Settle, petal," Cady told her. "It's not like you've lived a blemish-free life so far."

"Compared to that I have!"

"Well, there's still time." She gave her sister a poke in

the middle, and had her hand slapped away. She laughed. "Two words: Kyle Baxter."

Shelby glared at her. "I don't believe in sharing."

"I guess you never know what you might do, until you're in the moment." She thought of Reid. So easily, he'd cut through her orderly row of what-ifs and better-nots, leaving her burning up for him. Despite the teasing, he was the one holding back, when it came to it. If he'd only pushed a little more, her last reserve would've fallen around her feet. As would other things...like the lacy briefs she made sure to wear every day he was around, just as a precaution. It wasn't like they'd be getting an outing—or an offing, more accurately.

Who knew? If it came to it, in a certain time and place, would she do the same as the other Cady and Shelby? The new Cady was—or was supposed to be—way more bold than the home version. Except, like her sister, she did *not* feel inclined to share this man. She'd left him with Jennifer, and there he'd have to stay.

In the meantime, there was another man's story to figure out.

Chapter Twenty-Two

B y the time Holt came home that evening, Shelby was ready for a confrontation. Cady had tried to damp down her outrage, but as usual, Shelby on a roll was unstoppable. She had no interest in thinking about it from both sides, or remembering it was a long time ago, or giving him a chance to sit down before she charged. And the truth was, Cady wanted to know all the same things Shelby did. So when he got out of the truck and came across the lawn, Shelby was waiting on the porch, and Cady stood back to let her fire away.

He paused by a pile of drying poop that Rambler had left behind. None of them had noticed it while they were talking that afternoon, but now he stopped and tipped his hat back, obviously wondering who had deposited it there.

"Bee came to see us today," Shelby said from the top of the porch steps.

He looked up, surprised, and possibly nervous too. "Really? I haven't seen her for...a long time."

Shelby nodded. "She told us about everything that happened in San Francisco. With you and her and the other Cady."

Now he went from surprised-nervous to taken aback.

"Everything?"

"Yes. Unless there's something you'd like to add?" She sounded like a parent confronting a teenager sneaking home after curfew.

"No, I doubt that."

He came up the steps and spun his hat onto a chair, then ran his fingers through his salt-and-pepper hair. Cady wasn't surprised that Bee was still harboring feelings for him. He had a presence that demanded attention, an effortless charisma that must have carried him through life with a definite advantage. Clooney-ish, maybe. Attractive, definitely. Trustworthy? Yet to be proven.

"We have a few questions," she said, stating the obvious. "You can probably imagine."

"I can," he said. He sat down, looking remarkably fresh after the day's travelling. He was probably used to it, Cady thought.

Shelby plunged in, her voice already half an octave higher. "You told Mum they were your sisters in the photo. How could you let her name us after your ménage à trois? It's so...gross."

He folded his arms against her onslaught and pressed his lips together. "First of all, it wasn't that." He ignored her huff of disagreement. "And I didn't know what she'd named you until it was too late. I couldn't write back and say, you need to change your babies' names, and here's why."

Cady spoke up. "Why did you tell her they were your sisters in the first place?"

He sighed and leaned forward, his arms on his knees. "She asked me out of the blue, and it was the first thing that came into my head. Stupid, I know. But she was adamant she'd never visit, so I thought I was safe. And honestly, I just wanted to keep her good opinion of me. Confessing the truth about them would *not* have helped."

"That's true," Shelby said. "But it doesn't justify the lie."

"Mind you, that's a small thing compared to the lie Mum was telling," Cady pointed out to her. "He had no idea what the real deal was."

He shrugged. "I found that out soon enough."

"No, the *real* real deal," Shelby said.

"Real real deal? What do you mean?"

There was a pause while the girls realized that he might not know the full story behind Anne's London trips after all. "Oh, you must be joking," Shelby said to the universe in general.

"We assumed you knew," Cady said. He'd found out she was married, but did he have no clue that Anne went to London with baby-making on her mind?

Sure enough, his face showed that he had no idea what she meant. "Knew what?"

"Oh…" This wasn't good. He might not have been so warmly welcoming if he'd known they were no accident. That he'd fallen into a sweet trap, and been in the dark ever since. "So she didn't tell you the full story, after all."

"There's more? You'd better tell me now."

So she did. Their parents' struggle to conceive, Aunt Netta's offer of the apartment, and Anne's plan, that had been a secret (except to Aunt Netta) until she confessed to Cady before her death.

"Goddamn." He rubbed the top of his head, ruffling his hair, and blew out a long breath. It seemed like he was working to contain his emotions. "Hell. She seemed so…*good*. And straightforward. And she only saw the best in me. She was like redemption, after everything that had happened in San Francisco. At the time, I felt like I needed her more than she needed me."

"That's ironic," Cady commented.

"Yeah," he said. "Karma's a bitch."

"Thanks a lot!" Shelby said.

He smiled at her now, apparently entertained rather than annoyed by her outspokenness. "You know what I mean. I'm glad to have you two, you know that. Why do you think I took you around and introduced you to everyone?"

She visibly softened at his words. "I know."

"You girls don't have to answer for your conception.

But hell, all this time..." he shook his head, still working to realign the new truth in his head.

"I suppose we're equal now, in the surprise stakes," Shelby said.

"I think you dropped the bigger bombshell, actually," he replied.

For a few minutes they sat in silence on the porch, the light gentling into evening. It was so peaceful, looking out on the rows of trees and the distant hills. From here, it was hard to envisage London or San Francisco, and the dramas that could play out in those hectic places. Cady tried to imagine how it must have been for Holt and Cady and Shelby, to come back after their heady months of cosmopolitan life. Was quiet country living a balm after their torrid adventures, or did they feel the slow, crushing weight of small town claustrophobia? No wonder Holt took a few weeks out, on the other side of the Atlantic. They would have come back to face not just their parents, but the opinion and speculation of everyone in town.

Then something occurred to her.

"Everyone must be wondering why we have the other Cady and Shelby's names," she said, "coming out of the blue from England."

"Ah, let them wonder," Holt replied. "They'll all talk amongst themselves anyway. It's what they do." For a moment the bitterness came through in his voice, then he shook it off. "Don't we have enough to think about, getting to know each other?"

But Shelby wasn't quite on board yet, still hanging onto questions from the past. "Would you have sent the money if you knew Mum had set you up?"

"We can't deal in hypotheticals," he said, with a shrug. "I hope I would have. She never asked for it. But it was one right thing I could do."

Oh Mum, Cady thought. I wish I could ask you more. Why did you tell him about us at all, when you could have kept your secret closer? Did you secretly hope he'd contribute money for his babies? Or did you think it was the one right thing you should do, too? Since her mum's death,

Cady had felt stuck in shock. How did you grieve for someone when everything you knew of them was snatched away, as well as the person themselves? She sighed, suddenly so tired. What would Anne say, if she was here now?

"She must have wanted us to meet you," she said aloud, as the thought occurred to her. "Otherwise she would never have told me what she did. And she was so insistent that I should get out and have an adventure. Maybe this was what she meant all along."

He nodded. "Maybe. And whether you were an accident or not, you're here. We all have secrets. Your beginning is different from what I thought, but it's turning out okay. Don't you think?"

Shelby agreed, her face reflecting the change of heart that was taking place. His youthful wildness was a few degrees beyond Shelby's, but Cady could see how alike they were. Ironically, Cady herself was less like her 'real' father and more like the dad they grew up with, even though she hadn't inherited his temperament via her genes. Now, even while Holt was getting his head around their non-accidental origins, and Shelby was ready to forgive him the stupid lie that gave them their names, Cady had a remaining reservation. Yes, it had turned out okay for him, she thought. For their own dad, their everyday dad who'd worked so hard for them, and loved their mother through a lifetime's deception, it might not turn out so great. But she wasn't unmoved by Holt's sentiment. He may have been a player, but he was all right. She felt sorry that he was alone, after all this time. He didn't have to be held eternally accountable for his wild youth—which wasn't really all *that* wild, compared to some. Not everyone was as dull as she was, after all.

He stood up. "Come on then. I'll get cleaned up, then we can go out for dinner. My treat, for my girls."

Cady realized she was hungry. "That'd be nice," she said. Sometimes, in a mixed-up world, it was good to focus on something simple.

Chapter Twenty-Three

They spent the next few days getting to know Holt and Santa Almendra better. They went out around the orchards with him again, listening in while he and his staff considered the need for a new well, debated whether crop receipts would be up on the previous year, and checked hull split on the ripening fruit. He lent them a farm pickup and a map, and they explored some of the back roads and beauty spots around the farm, going cross-country to secret places only the locals knew about.

Seeing the Santa Almendra sign on so many almond plantings around the area made them realize just how much land he must have. And that was only in *this* part of the county, Shelby pointed out. Maybe it was no wonder he'd never had time to find a partner.

"It's hard being alone," she said dramatically. Then she sighed, obviously thinking again about her own tragic lack of Kyle. Cady maintained a sympathetic expression.

When they were alone, they also talked about Bee and the other Cady. Bee had been firm that the other Cady wouldn't want to see them, but they were both so curious. She must be around here still—it couldn't be that hard to find her. Surely there wouldn't be any harm in it, Shelby said. She was probably still misunderstood, like in high school. Cady wasn't sure, but having met one of the original Cady and Shelby, she felt compelled to meet the other half too, despite what Bee had said about her emotional state.

They spent a lot of time with Elva, and she seemed to enjoy their company as much as they enjoyed hers. She loved to talk about what Holt was like as a kid, and she was full of stories about the local personalities. But when they asked her about the original Cady, she clammed up.

"Now," she said, "that's not something we should talk about. People deserve privacy in their troubles. Poor little Cady, it's just not right." Then she tutted and left the room, obviously emotional, leaving them looking at each other. So they had to settle for that.

They didn't hear anything from the Flashpointers, and Cady forced herself to not text anyone. Move on, she told herself. There are more ponytailed fish in the sea, if that's what you're into now. Although she had the feeling Reid was the exception that proved the rule.

Meanwhile, Shelby was so busy wallowing around in the loss of Kyle, and so determined that he'd thrown himself straight into a torrid affair with Alison, that she refused to contact him too. Cady suspected, sadly, that he probably wasn't thinking about much beyond himself and his empire. She kept her Reid pangs to herself. What a pair we make, she thought. Five minutes in the country and both obsessed. There must be something dodgy in the cheese puffs.

She did keep an eye on Twitter and Facebook though, and it was obvious that another flash mob was being planned. The details were still under wraps, but it would all go down in San Francisco itself the following weekend. She was excited to see what they'd do to build on the Rownville success. And, yes, a little disappointed that Kyle hadn't asked her to come and help. He'd still had his moments of irresistible Kyle-ness, but with his reclusive behavior, she hoped he wasn't slowly losing his grip on things. Alison's comments at the country bar that night, about his retreat from the team, backed up her own observations. Maybe it was just the flip-side of genius, maybe he was self-medicating up there in his retreat, or maybe behind the sporadic charisma he was just a prize ass, like the SF-ly blogger had asserted.

Whatever. The truth was, she'd secretly hoped that they'd fall apart without her. Nothing catastrophic, of course. Just enough to realize that they needed her. But, sadly, it seemed she wasn't indispensible.

And if Reid realized that he needed her after all, too...well, she was a big believer in second chances. She couldn't stop herself from checking her phone, in case a text had arrived without her noticing. It was all she could do not to go around with it tucked into the top of her bra, so she'd be sure to hear it. But there was nothing. Every now and then she took the phone out and opened the messages, her fingers aching to text him. But she couldn't formulate quite the right wording, the right combination of levity, detachment, and encouragement without giving anything away. It was hair-tearingly frustrating, and it made her feel like she was fourteen again. Were people even texting when she was fourteen? It seemed a hundred years ago, in the days when her mother was still hanging in there, and her father was still her father. She put the phone away again, nothing achieved but a new level of annoyance with herself.

One night though, she sat up suddenly in bed, fuddled and groggy, but sure she'd heard a new text arriving. Shelby was in her own room at the other end of the hallway, and Holt was in the other wing, so it could only be her phone. She felt around for where she'd tucked it under her pillow, and as her hand touched it, the second notification whistled clearly. She pulled the phone out, wincing at the glare of light in her eyes.

> *You up? Should be leaving you to your new*
> *start, but wondering how you are. Missing the*
> *flash madness?*

She grinned. Now she was glad she hadn't caved and texted him first. Not that she was playing games, she told herself. Nope, no, not at all. But hey, it was okay to be gratified that she was on his mind too, wasn't it?

She lay back on the pillow, thinking about what to reply. And thinking about him. All the hot-and-tinglyness came flooding back as she lay in the big bed, moonlight streaming in the windows. She let her mind wander, lingering over the memory of his golden-brown eyes, the unexpectedly acceptable ponytail, the teasing smile that could turn her lust-blurry in an instant. And the little things—the leather strings around his wrist, the slight kink in his nose, the way that old Foo Fighters t-shirt had lifted when he reached up to help maneuver the camera crane, revealing a flat stomach with just a tiny sprinkled trail of dark hair leading downwards...

Oh, this wasn't helping. What to write? She tossed on the bed, then threw back the comforter and top sheet so that the night air could cool her body. She was wearing the same little pajamas as that night outside the bus, when he'd stood so close, wearing his flimsy boxers, making her want to run her hands over the smooth warmth of his skin. And although she was over-hot, her nipples were doing exactly the same as they'd done then in the chill night air. She pressed a hand low on her belly and tried to focus. He was miles away, but she was as susceptible as ever. It was terrible. But, oh hell, it was *so good*.

She started to type.

> *Was tucked up but awake now! All good*
> *thanks. Found him. Been nice though a few*
> *surprises (long story). How's everyone?*

There were other things she wanted to say, but she settled for the oblique reference to bed. His reply came quickly.

> *Okay, a few new faces. Kyle camped out*
> *upstairs mostly, throws out instructions for*
> *next event. Jen & Alison trying to make sense*
> *of it all. Need you! ;-)*

She was torn between high and low. 'Need you' was good. Exactly what she hoped for. Well, minus the wink that made it a joke. But 'a few new faces'? Maybe their beds wouldn't be there for them after all, even if they did go back. And with Jennifer (she felt a pang at the familiar 'Jen') and Alison in action, they obviously weren't needed. Well, what had she thought? They'd got along brilliantly without her, until Kyle lost his nerve over the SF-ly debacle. They'd be fine now. Who did she think she was?

She hesitated, tapping her fingers on the screen as she considered her reply. He'd cracked open the door, but she wasn't going to leap into text flirting, much as she wanted to, unless he did first. So she kept it light, and threw the ball back in his court.

Hope it goes well. Haven't decided our next
step. Free as birds still. :-)

The message went off with a little whoosh, and she waited. In the milky light, the room had a vintage look about it, like she was halfway into a black and white movie. The bed was enormous and the sheets were crisp and heavy, not like the budget linen she slept in at home. Well, in the place that *was* home. Her dad had texted to say they'd had an offer on the house, and a sale was imminent. From here on, home was wherever she decided it would be.

She rolled over, scissoring her legs on the Egyptian cotton, and thought what a waste it was to be alone in such luxury. The phone was silent. Maybe she'd been too non-committal in that last message. Damn, she should have asked him a direct question. (Are you and Jennifer an official item now? for example.) Man-texting was a whole other art, she knew. Nuance and etiquette wasn't even on their radar, half the time. She let her eyes close again as sleep came creeping near. Would he even reply? She let out a long breath. The bed really was unbelievably comfortable...

Suddenly a tune broke into her almost-slumber and she felt around for her phone. It was him.

"Hi." She played it casual.

"I was trying to think what to text back, and then I thought, this is ridiculous, she's already awake."

His voice was late-night husky, snapping her right back to the heightened sensation of being with him in person. The familiar buzz started up in her stomach, the matching hum between her legs. But she was determined to keep her cool, even while her heart was flip-flopping.

"Who is this?" she said jokingly.

He laughed. "Just a humble commoner, Lady Cady."

She laughed too. "Humble?"

"Sure. Compared to some."

"Like who? Kanye?"

"Ouch. You slight me."

She laughed again. "You're tough."

"I am."

There was a pause, and the silence at her end merged with the silence at his. She wondered where he was. "Are you on the bus?"

"No, it's been kind of weird there. Some new characters around. Kind of shady. Kyle traded down when you left."

She glowed at the implied compliment. "That doesn't sound so great. Is everything okay?"

"Yeah, I think so. Hopefully things will have settled in time for the next flash mob. I'm at my mom and dad's. How's your family reunion going?"

It felt like such a long story, she hardly had the energy. "Pretty good. It's been interesting. I think he's an okay guy. Shelby and I have both been going back and forth, bit of an emotional rollercoaster. Every time you learn something new, it changes your perspective a little." She changed the subject. "But you never told me about your parents. Where do they live?"

"Out at Mill Valley, north of the city."

"I haven't heard of it."

"It's pretty nice. They're outdoorsy, so they like walking the trails, that kind of thing. They have a place with a guest house at the bottom of the garden, so that's what I use. From the bed I can look out the window right into the woods."

"Are you in bed?" In her own ears, her voice sounded suggestive.

"I am."

She cleared her throat. "Me too."

"Ah," he said, a warmth of meaning sliding into his voice. "Tell me then, what do *you* see out your window?"

The bed was set against the wall between two long windows, so she couldn't see outside. "This side of the house overlooks part of the orchards. But I can't see out the window from here, unless I get up."

"Hmm. Well, what do you see inside?" he said, his voice slowing.

She felt her pulse speed up a little. "I see...an antique wardrobe with velvet tassels on the handles. Um, and a chaise longue." She stumbled over the pronunciation, hyper-aware of the sexiness in the phrase, but carried on. "And a big French dresser with an orchid plant." Oh hell, now everything in the room seemed vaguely erotic. She realized her breathing had gotten shallower. "And when I look up, I see a canopy over the bed."

"Sounds nice." There was a pause, and then he said, "And when you look down?"

"Down?" For a second she thought he was asking about the carpet. "Just a kind of neutral cut pile, I suppose." Nothing erotic there.

"Not the flooring," he said.

"Oh..." Could he really mean...? She swallowed. Were they going in that direction? Any sleepiness was long gone now, and her senses were humming. "I see white Egyptian cotton sheets. I had to push the blankets off, it's hot here."

"Is it?" he said.

"Yes," she said, letting the meaning slide into her voice too. "It is."

"Huh." There was a pause. "So what else do you see?"

"I see...me." She'd never done this before, but if it was game on, she'd give it a go. Let new Cady have a run at things for a change.

"Tell me more."

"I see…my bare legs stretched out in front of me." She stopped, holding back, leaving him to ask again.

"What else?"

Her tongue slid out to moisten her lips. "I see pajama shorts. And a silky camisole top. You know what they look like."

"Oh, I remember," he said. "I remember that night."

It gave her a thrill to know she'd had an effect on him that night too. With the sound of his voice on the line, she held the image of him in her imagination. The way he'd looked down at her, his eyes dark, while she stood with the cold metal of the bus at her back and the hot attraction of his body tempting her in front.

"Do you have anything else to tell me?" he said now.

"Do you want me to tell you something else?" she asked, teasing, loving the feeling of power that was growing in her mind along with the arousal in her body. Oh, the old Cady would never have done this. She never had a chance, poor thing.

"Tell me how you feel," he said, his voice low.

"Feel, or *feel?*" she asked, deliberately obtuse, wanting him to feel as frustrated as she had in so many moments since they'd met. She had no idea why he was suddenly laying this on the line, but right now she didn't care. All she knew was what she wanted, wanted, wanted. She still couldn't have it—have him—alone in this room. But letting her desire loose, the unraveling of everything she'd held back, was its own pleasure.

He laughed softly. "Either one. Or both. Or all, if there are more."

"Hmmmm." She drew it out, the charge in her body growing as she thought about exactly how she was feeling. "I feel…compelled. Wanting." She slipped her hand under the camisole top, onto her belly, letting her fingers run across to her waist and then up to the valley between her breasts.

"And?" he asked, his tone gravelly.

184

With his voice in her ear, every inch of her skin was craving touch. As her fingertips travelled her body, she imagined they were his, and that all she had to do was reach up and he'd be there. With her eyes closed, the illusion was almost believable. As her hand moved down again, the pounding in her heart was matched by an insistent pulse between her legs, and her hips lifted of their own accord. This new, apparently shameless, version of herself had utterly possessed the old Cady, just as he had utterly occupied her mind. She took a shaky breath in, and the sound was loud enough that she knew he'd hear it. "And...I feel...heated. On the verge."

She was aware that his breathing had changed too, and she held her own breath for a moment, to hear him better. "More," he said, and in that one word, the intensity of his desire was obvious.

She pressed the phone harder against her ear, wanting to hear every nuance of his reaction. Any hesitancy she'd felt, any reservations, were completely gone. "I feel...abandoned."

There was silence. She strained to hear, but he was gone. Abandoned, for real. Then she realized, with a sudden thud back to earth—she'd cut him off. She made a sound halfway between laughter and frustration, the ridiculousness of it too much to bear after the heights of her desperate need. This never happened in the movies.

She called him back, and he answered immediately. "Oh-my-God-sorry," she said in a rush. "I was trying to hold my phone, and my finger must have hit 'end' by mistake."

"I thought you were putting a stop to it," he said. "I thought it must have gone too far."

Even though she felt a bit bashful, now that the heat of the moment had passed, there was nothing in her that regretted it. "Oh, it had definitely gone too far," she said, the old casual teasing back in her tone. "I was too far gone to stop it."

"Me too," he admitted, and her heart gave a jump. He really wanted her. It wasn't a one-sided infatuation.

Although, that was no guarantee that his physical wanting equaled her increasingly heartfelt attachment.

"But I don't know why you were even telling me those things," he continued now, echoing her teasing manner. "It's not very ladylike, Lady Cady."

"You never know what ladies do behind closed doors," she murmured back.

He laughed, a wickedly appreciative sound, making it clear that 'behind closed doors' was a place they could easily go. They may have had their moment cut short, but there was no mistaking the extra heat between them now. They'd crossed a line, acknowledging the insistent tug of wanting. She wondered what would happen next. Would they even see each other again? She'd been missing him, keeping the longing to herself (unlike Shelby, who pined extravagantly for Kyle), but she'd been held back in her mind by the thought of Jennifer. Yes, she was trying to be a bolder, more worldly Cady now. And she couldn't think badly of Bee and the other Cady for their triple entanglement with Holt. But she still couldn't go where another woman already had a claim. She had to ask him, straight out.

"Can I ask you something?" she began.

"Yes," he said, and that one word was rich with the weight of suggestion. For a moment she almost asked him what he was wearing, her mind struck with the image of him lying back on white sheets, shirtless, tanned and firmly muscled. Oh, and with just a sprinkling of dark chest hair. She'd never seen him shirtless, unfortunately, but she was blessed with a good imagination.

However, the Jennifer question was still there, and she needed to know. She gathered herself and took a breath to ask, but suddenly there was a turn-around in his manner. "Shit, I have to go," he said abruptly. It sounded like he was getting up. "Sorry, but I really have to go now."

What on earth? "Okay, well…"

"Sorry."

And he was gone.

"Whoa," she said aloud to the screen. "Okay."

Phonus interruptus, times two. What a night. What would make him race off like that? Was it something she said? She reached down and pulled the top sheet over herself, and then the comforter, covering her body. Deprived hardly began to express how she felt, but she wasn't tempted to let her fingers go exploring again. That, inconveniently, was something she wanted *him* to do.

Chapter Twenty-Four

The next morning, Cady's night of abandon seemed like a dream. It was only by looking at the call log that she really believed what they'd done. But the pleasure of knowing that he lusted for her too was dulled by the abrupt end to their conversation. She hoped he was okay, of course. But his sudden exit—and no explanation this morning—left a sting. The ball was definitely in his court now.

She and Shelby decided to go into Santa Almendra for brunch, to decide what to do next. They'd been at Santa Almendra for a while, and Holt had a business trip coming up, so it felt like time to move on. A planning session over plenty of coffee suited Cady—she didn't want to keep going over and over the previous night's events, good, bad and erotic. Despite it all, the erotic part kept returning to her mind, giving her little zings of pleasure. This new Cady was someone she wouldn't mind being more often, given the chance. Given the chance with Reid, that is. She sighed, and told Shelby she'd get the car keys.

Holt had left early to visit one of the other farms, and Elva was away visiting her sister in Sacramento, so there was no one to invite with them. They took the little rental car, not in need of a four-wheel drive for this outing, and found a coffee shop opposite the park.

"How are you feeling now, about everything?" Cady asked as she stirred sugar into her coffee. Asking Shelby about herself usually provided plenty of distraction.

"Pretty okay, actually. I'm getting the hang of having him for a dad. But I've been thinking a lot about Mum."

"That's no surprise. I have too."

They sat quietly for a moment. "You never even stopped to catch your breath after she died," Shelby said, out of the blue.

Cady bristled, instantly feeling defensive. "There were things to do! And Dad didn't need me falling to bits."

"It wasn't a criticism. I'm amazed at how strong you were—are. I just don't know how you keep it up."

"Oh." Cady deflated again, letting go all the justifications she had ready. A compliment from Shelby? That was something. "I don't know. I think maybe it hasn't sunk in yet. Such a lot has happened all at once."

Shelby nodded. "When we get home, we need to go to Broadstairs and talk to Aunt Netta. I want to know exactly what Mum told her, hear it from her directly."

"That's a good idea," Cady said. "Did the private investigator tell her who'd hired him? Do you think she knows that we know?"

"Yes, she does. She actually passed on a message through him, to say we should visit her. And I'd like to talk to her in person."

"Me too. I mean, it's not like we can ask Dad for more info."

Shelby looked sideways at her. "Not yet."

"What do you mean, not yet? Don't you dare do anything or say anything without talking to me first. We agreed to leave Dad out of it, remember?" They'd been calling him once a week, as promised, and it had been really hard not to give anything away since they found Holt.

"Okay, okay." Shelby held her hands out, palms down, placating. "But we can go and see Aunt Netta, right?"

When Cady nodded, she paused, something else obviously on her mind. "There's actually somewhere else I want to go, too. Sooner than that, though."

"Where?" Cady asked.

Shelby shuffled in her seat, concentrating on unwinding her savory brioche into a long strip as she answered. "It's not so much where, as who."

"Oh...I know. Kyle." She looked at her sister. Shelby's overt Kyle withdrawal had been painful for both of them. When Shelby fixated on something, she was like a very annoying dog with a bone. But Cady hadn't admitted that she was feeling much the same, about someone else.

Shelby nodded. "I don't even know if he gives a rats about me. I bet Alison swooped in the minute we left. But I just want to see him again. Is that crazy?"

"Yes." She thought of all the reasons why Kyle wasn't a good idea for Shelby. But who was she to comment? Once someone gets under your skin, into your bloodstream, not seeing them is like not breathing. "But crazy is a flexible adjective. Some people are worth crazy."

Shelby grinned, but Cady wasn't done. "I don't know if *he's* worth it, mind you," she added, giving her sister a mischievous look.

She stuck out her tongue, back to brash. "Ah, you don't know how to live. You should try a bit of crazy some time. It'd do you good. Can't live like a nun your whole life."

"Maybe," Cady replied, giving nothing away. She smiled to herself, Reid's throaty *more* echoing in her head. But Shelby kept talking, caught up in her own dilemma.

"The thing is, we've already booked that luxury star tour in LA, and our flights from San Diego to Vegas."

"That's true," Cady said. "And we've already lost a couple of weeks of our visa."

"Lost?"

"No, not lost, I suppose. Used. But we only have these three months. We had so many things planned, it was already going to be a challenge to fit them in. If we don't keep going, we'll find our time's up, and we might never have another chance to do all these things."

Even as she listened to herself talking, Cady knew she wasn't really convincing either of them. Vegas would always be there, you could see more of the stars on *E!* than by standing at their real-life front gates, and anyway, neither of them believed they'd never be back. But they might never have another chance to take this ride all the way with Flashpoint.

"I don't think the Flashpointers really need us, though," she said. "Alison and Jennifer are helping Kyle, apparently."

"Apparently?" Shelby leapt onto that instantly. "According to who?"

Oops. She felt her cheeks flush hot. Caught. "Um...I talked to Reid last night."

She could see Shelby's mind working, thinking about what they'd done the night before. "Last night? When?"

"After we went to bed."

Shelby's eyes grew knowing. "Ohhh. I see." She smirked. "I seeee." She stretched the word into a brazen innuendo.

"No, no," Cady said, knowing her scarlet cheeks would undo her denial. "He just texted, then he phoned..."

"Oh. My. God. You had phone sex."

"What? No!"

"You did. Look at your face! You *so* did."

"Not really. Just sort of...phone fooling around. But then he had to go."

"Oh, I bet he did," Shelby crowed. "Not such a nun after all, huh?"

Cady had to grin now. "Nope."

"Not just me who's the crazy one."

"No." She had to laugh. "But listen. That doesn't change anything. We still have miles to cover and a canyon to see and more corndogs to eat. We should concentrate on that."

Shelby sighed. "I suppose so." Then she brightened. "We can catch up with them when we get back to San Francisco for LitQuake and the fair. We'll have time then."

191

"Yes, we will. That's a good idea."

As much as she was mollifying Shelby, it made her feel better too. As time passed without a text from Reid, she was starting to feel sorry she'd let herself get so caught up in the moment. Once again, she felt like the cake he didn't want to have *or* eat. It seemed more like he wanted to just lick the frosting off, and put her back in the box. She had no intention of racing back to the bus after that. But...she still couldn't bear to completely rule out the possibility of seeing him again.

"So when shall we leave?" Shelby said. "Tomorrow?"

Cady nodded. "Okay, tomorrow. Eyes on the prize. Like Mum said, fun, travel, adventure." She left off the last one: find a gorgeous man. "There are plenty of men in London anyway." She was telling herself as much as Shelby.

★

After breakfast, they went into the pharmacy to get some antihistamines for Shelby, who'd been sneezing a lot since they arrived. The pharmacist was an older man, who smiled at them with interest as they came in.

"Morning, girls," he called cheerily.

"Good morning," they both replied, accidentally doing their twin chorus again. Shelby frowned at Cady, but she ignored it.

"Oh, my," he said. "I love your accents. English, right?"

"Yes," Cady said. "We're just visiting."

Realization dawned in his eyes. "Wait just a second. You're Holt's girls."

"Yes," Shelby said.

He came out from behind the counter and shook their hands in turn, shaking his head and clucking. "Oh, good heavens. Heavens above. I heard you were here, and I could hardly believe it. I'm Roger."

"Did you know about us?" Cady asked, taking his

outstretched hand and receiving a shake that practically made her teeth rattle.

"Well, no, no one did! That's why I could hardly believe it. Why no one could. And your names, well, that was the kicker."

They looked at each other. Here was a possible source of info. Cady decided to try her luck.

"Gosh, it must have been a real surprise," she said. "You know, we've met Shelby's namesake, Bee, but we haven't met the other Cady yet."

"Oh." He sucked air through his teeth. "That's Mrs. Greenwood. Poor Cady Greenwood." He shook his head, relishing the mournfulness. "*Such* a shame. All that drama, then when she finally found a husband, he up and left again before long. You know, she hardly leaves her house these days. Not that she was ever very..." He searched around for the right word. "*Sociable.*" His voice was low and he nodded conspiratorially, as though they knew just what he meant.

Cady felt sure that if she lived here, she'd be filling any sensitive prescriptions in another town. However, his loose lips might be just what they needed.

"That *is* a shame," she said. "She must get out sometimes, though?"

"Well, she does go to the library every day about this time," he said. "I guess she lives in those books instead of in the real world. One book, every day. Bernice in the library told me they had to start requesting books from other branches for her."

"She needs a Kindle," Shelby commented.

His eyes widened. "Well, that's just what I said. But, you know, I don't think she's very...savvy."

The girls nodded in pretend understanding, but Cady's mind was racing. Every day about this time. They'd better move. She nudged Shelby, who jumped.

"Ow! Oh, right. Could I please have some antihistamines? I've been sneezing such a lot since we got here."

"Oh, yes." He swung into action, leading her to the counter as he talked. "The privet is flowering right now, terrible stuff, it might be that..."

While he ran through the multitude of remedies, Cady peered out the window, half hoping to see someone going down the street with a book under her arm. Finally, Shelby came back with a brown paper bag.

"I had no idea that would be so involved," she whispered. "Benadryl, Clara-something, something-or-other else starting with 'Z'. Seriously, T.M.I. Just give me the drugs."

"Yeah, okay," Cady said. "Come *on*." She hustled her sister out the door, remembering to wave and call out thanks as they left. Roger waved back enthusiastically, a happy helper in more ways than he knew.

They'd already noticed the library on their drive into town, so Cady turned in that direction the moment they were out the door.

"I suppose we're going to the library then," Shelby said redundantly.

"You suppose right." She kept walking.

"You should have just asked him where she lives. He'd probably give us her blood type if we asked."

"Pharmacists don't know people's blood types," Cady said, her sudden purpose making her persnickety. But she stored Shelby's idea away. If they didn't find her, maybe they *could* ask him where she lived. He might be happy to help just that little bit more.

The library was probably the most beautiful building in town, a white columned edifice from days past that would be perfectly at home on a Universal Studios lot. She could imagine the town's founding fathers proudly opening the doors for the first time, full of hope and ceremony. They went up the steps and through the heavy swinging doors. Inside was the kind of old-time hush that libraries used to have, before they livelied up with internet access and book clubs and interactive story times for kids. The way she liked them, in other words.

They scanned the shelves, looking—hopefully in an unsuspicious way—for someone who might be Cady Greenwood.

Shelby picked up a book as a decoy. "You cover non-fiction, I'll do periodicals," she said, her voice full of muted drama worthy of a detective show.

"I'm guessing fiction," Cady said. "One book a day, to take you out of your real life? Only novels work that kind of magic."

Shelby shrugged. "I can't remember the last time I read a novel."

On this weekday morning the library was almost empty, making Cady feel screamingly obvious as an out-of-towner. Shelby followed her to the fiction shelves, near the back of the library—and there, between R and T, was someone who could easily be the other Cady.

She was about the right age, and she looked—although Cady hesitated to think it, given the bad rap she'd had from everyone—kind of eccentric. Hard-core boots (Doc Martens?) peeped out from under her flowing skirt, and she wore a long wraparound top with crocheted ties that went around and around her body. Over that was the kind of multi-pocketed vest that a fisherman would wear. The pockets were bulging, which probably explained why she didn't have a bag with her. Her greying hair was pulled back into a ponytail, and she had tucked a flower into the hair tie. She was, in short, unusual.

"You ask her," Shelby whispered, giving Cady a surreptitious push.

"Okay, okay," she whispered back.

Now that the moment was upon her, she wondered what the heck she'd been thinking. What connection could she find with this person? And what purpose would it serve to bring everything up again, especially if she was as fragile as Bee had said?

She didn't look especially fragile though. She was tall and slender, willowy even. But although she was thin, there was nothing wispy about her. She radiated a dogged strength, her individuality and her bearing like a kind of armor. In a way, she reminded Cady of Aunt Netta—wearing, and probably doing, whatever she saw fit. Faced with this character, Cady started to think that it wasn't too late to change their minds...

But she looked up from the book she was holding, and saw them. Then they could see how beautiful—no, striking—she still was. Her grey eyes narrowed as she took them in, so obviously hovering. There was nothing to do but jump in.

"Excuse me," Cady said. "I'm sorry to bother you, but are you Cady Greenwood?"

The suspicion in the woman's expression deepened. "For my sins," she said shortly. "And you are?"

"Well..." She hesitated. "I'm Cady, and this is my sister Shelby."

Cady Greenwood took a step backward, her hand going to her throat. "Is this a joke? Did someone put you up to this?"

Cady could have kicked herself for not being more delicate about it. "No," she said. "I'm sorry. I should explain."

But her no-BS demeanor was already back. "You should," she said in a firm but still library-appropriate voice. "I'm waiting. Go ahead."

Chapter Twenty-Five

S tanding between the shelves, in the gentle bookish hush, Cady didn't know where to start.

"Well, um, Mrs. Greenwood..." she began.

"You can call me Mrs. G, like everyone else," she interrupted. "I don't need reminding of that good-for-nothing sluggard. Now, come on—who are you exactly, and why are you here, stalking me in the library?"

Cady faltered. Why were they here, exactly? How could she explain it to this woman, when she wasn't sure herself? The romanticized notion of some intangible connection between the two of them seemed ridiculous now. Well, it was too late to back out. She kept it straightforward.

"We came to see Lawson Holt. He's our father." She figured it was okay to tell people herself, given how free he'd been about telling everyone.

Mrs. G's eyes widened. "Are you telling me Holt has *children*? And he named you after me and Shelby? Jesus."

Cady hesitated. "Well...it wasn't quite like that. But we only just found out he's our father. We were born in London. There was sort of a misunderstanding."

"Pah, that'd be right. Lawson Holt is hardly father material."

"Look, would you like to go and have a cup of coffee or something?" Cady suggested. Standing in the library really didn't seem to be the right place for this conversation. There was no one else here apart from an elderly man reading a newspaper in the corner, his nose practically touching the page as he took in the day's news. She doubted he'd be able to see them from there, let alone hear what they were saying, but still.

But Mrs. G shook her head. "No, I wouldn't like to have a cup of coffee. Lawson Holt has nothing to do with me now, so I have no idea why you're here."

"We're here because Bee told us you were in San Francisco too," Cady said. "And because...I don't know. I wanted to meet the other Cady." She shrugged, feeling sheepish.

"Well, you met her. But San Francisco? I'm willing to bet you didn't get the true story on *that*."

"The true story?" Shelby echoed.

"I think we'd better sit down." Mrs. G pointed at some child-sized seats shaped like hands, and they each perched in an upturned palm, with fingers at their backs. "Now, tell me what you heard. What Bee and Holt told you. Let's see how the story stacks up."

Shelby looked at Cady, obviously expecting her to do the talking. Nervously, she cleared her throat, then repeated the basics of what Bee had told them—the condensed version, minus her comments about the younger Cady's psychological state.

"I didn't lose the baby," Mrs. G said as soon as she was finished. "I hate that expression, as though you were just careless."

"You didn't?" Shelby said.

"No, I didn't. Do you really want to know what happened? Lawson Holt, hero of the county and beyond, is not the hero in this version of the story."

The girls looked at each other, no idea what to expect. "You'd better tell us, I guess," Cady said.

"Okay, then. He made me have an abortion. He took me to the clinic. Coercion, persuasion, manipulation, threatening...call it what you like. The end result was the same." She sat back, her head resting against the middle finger of her seat, and watched to see their reaction.

They were horrified.

"I can't believe it," Cady said. "How could anyone...I just can't believe it."

"Believe it, or don't believe it, I don't care," Mrs. G said. "I've spent my life in this godforsaken place with people thinking what they like about me. Whispering about me. First it was 'weird Cady' and 'crazy Cady'. And after San Francisco—after Lawson Holt—it was 'poor Cady'. I let everyone believe that lost baby story, because there was no point in taking on the mighty Holt family. And because I couldn't bear to think about what I'd given in and done. I was out of my depth, and I let him coerce me into it."

"I didn't mean I didn't believe *you*," Cady said hastily. "I meant that I just can't believe *it*. I mean, Bee said—"

Mrs. G snorted. "Of course she did. I bet she said all kinds of things." She shook her head, her lips pursed. "I was only in the way. There's no reasoning with her when it comes to Lawson Holt. She was always in love with him, even when we were at school. She probably still is. But sure, believe her, believe him. Even my own husband didn't believe me. Cady Greenwood is crazy, after all."

Listening to her talk, Cady thought she was hardly going to convince them otherwise. But still, there seemed a kernel of truth in what she said. Was Holt capable of such a thing? He'd said he had difficulties before he went to London—that his youth didn't excuse how immature he'd been. Could this be what he was referring to? Not just the wild times and the loss of the baby, but something darker.

Then Mrs. G stood up.

"I never had any more children," she said. "He doesn't deserve you."

The conversation was over. She turned and went out, leaving her library book lying on the floor, and the girls in shock.

★

On the drive back to the farm, they tried to get their heads around what Mrs. G had told them. Shelby was antsy in her seat, processing the drama out loud, as usual.

"What kind of person does that? How could he do that?"

Cady was trying to think rationally. He was sharp, single-minded, and tough enough to beat down his competitors and grow a huge business empire, but forcing someone to have an abortion was a whole other level of ruthless—especially when the baby was your own.

"Could she have it wrong, somehow?" Even as she said it, she knew she didn't think so. "Maybe she did lose the baby."

"Oh, come on." Shelby rolled her eyes. "I think a woman knows if something so brutal has happened to her. The other thing I can't believe is how she kept it secret the whole time."

"Why would she tell us now?"

"Maybe it was the shock of finding out Holt has kids after all. Seeing us must have been like a double slap in the face."

Cady blew out a long sigh. "We should never have gone to find her."

"But then we wouldn't know this."

Cady could only nod sadly. What's known can't be unknown. And she felt for Mrs. G, who'd carried it with her all these years.

As they went into the house, the phone was ringing.

"Holt residence," Shelby answered, as he'd encouraged them to do. It was their home too, he'd told them—of course they could answer the telephone.

"It's him," she mouthed to Cady, who raised her eyebrows. Shelby gestured her over, and they put their heads together so they could both listen. He wouldn't be back that night after all, he said. There had been more vandalism on the farms, so he was meeting with the local police to talk about how to prevent it. He'd be home tomorrow night.

"Okay," Shelby said aloud. "The only thing is, we

need to hit the road."

Cady looked at her, surprised. What was she doing? They hadn't discussed this. But she put a finger to her lips and shook her head.

"Oh..." he said. "You can't wait until I get back?"

"We'd better not. We have so many things booked in for our trip. But thank you so much for having us." Her voice was determinedly polite, not encouraging any questions.

"Well, okay...if you're sure." There was a silence, which was obviously Shelby's cue to say something more. But she didn't. "I hope we'll see you again before you go back to England," he added.

"Sure," she said. "That'd be lovely. Thank you for everything. Cady says thanks too."

She set the phone back on its charger. "I can't even look at you any more," she told the handpiece.

"What the heck?" Cady said. "Where did that spring from?"

"Well, do *you* want to stay now?"

She didn't need to answer. Shelby nodded. "Come on, let's get packed."

★

As they were loading their bags into the car, Bee arrived, on Rambler again.

"You're going?" she asked, looking surprised.

"Something...came up," Shelby said.

Bee looked from one of them to the other. "Oh, that's a shame. Well, I'm glad I caught you." Then she looked up at the house. "Is Holt here?"

"No, he's away until tomorrow," Cady said. "Did you want to see him?"

She tried to look noncommittal, patting Rambler's dappled neck. "Well, after we talked the other day, I thought maybe..." She let the sentence peter out.

The girls looked at each other. Before, they'd thought it

was so sweet that she still had feelings for him. After today's news, that potential love story seemed much less charming.

"We have to tell her," Shelby said.

"Tell me what?" Bee asked.

Shelby didn't mince her words. "About Mrs. G not really losing the baby. We saw her today."

Something flitted across Bee's face, and was gone. They saw it though, and Shelby was right on it.

"You knew already." It was a statement, not a question.

She flushed slightly under her hat. "She told me that story, yes. She and I only talked once after we all came back. But seriously, she just wasn't right in the head. Holt wouldn't do anything like that. He's not that kind of callous, like his father was."

There was silence. Rambler scratched a hoof in the gravel driveway, optimistically looking for something to nibble on. Cady could hear Mrs. G's words in her head: *There's no reasoning with her when it comes to Lawson Holt. She was always in love with him...*

"Okay, well, we have to go, anyway." Shelby shoved the last bag in and slammed the trunk shut. "It was very nice to meet you."

"It really was," Cady added, a note of apology in her voice.

"You too," Bee said. "I'm sorry you're going away with the wrong idea."

For the second time, she was asking them not to think badly of Holt. Cady wondered if she'd tell him about this conversation.

They said their goodbyes, and Cady turned the car down the long driveway. As they passed between the almond trees lining each side, the complicated history tumbled around in her head. Holt, Bee, Cady/Mrs. G, Anne and her alter-ego Adrienne... Truthfully, in that moment it was a huge relief to be driving away from Santa Almendra.

"I get it," Shelby said. "I don't blame her. She was

besotted enough to share him, even when she didn't want to. Of course she'd defend him. They might say Mrs. G is crazy, but love can make you the same way."

Cady could only smile. "That's what I hear. Got anyone in mind? A certain quiffed-up hipster?"

"You know me too well." Shelby put on her sunglasses and switched the stereo to a song that she approved of. "I need a little crazy myself."

Cady thought back to the late-night phone call. "Oh, God, me too." He might be maintaining radio silence, but she'd think about that later. Right now, she needed to step away from the claustrophobia of the past, look forward, and let new Cady have free rein again.

"So, where are we going?" Shelby asked.

They looked at each other and grinned, both knowing the answer. They had no idea if there was room for them on the bus any more—but for the chance of a little crazy, they were willing to find out.

Chapter Twenty-Six

O n the way back to San Francisco, Shelby texted Kyle. The next flash mob was taking place the following day, he said, so everyone was busy, but he'd love to see them.

"He'd love to see us!" she said triumphantly, waving the phone in Cady's direction. "Lucky I've been using that spray tan."

The closer they got to the city, the bigger the mob of butterflies in Cady's tummy became. It hadn't been twenty-four hours since her phone call with Reid. What would have happened if he hadn't hung up? Would they have carried on to the obvious, lusty conclusion of the conversation? She smiled to herself, the memory still fresh enough to give her a warm jolt every time it popped into her mind.

With everything up in the air, they returned the Chrysler to the hire company. It would be easy enough to hire another car when they set off again.

"But *I'm* choosing next time," Shelby said, as they wheeled their suitcases out of the office. "My car. A Mustang Shelby."

Cady smiled. "Sounds good to me. The coast road to

LA in a Mustang Shelby convertible?"

"Stop it, you're turning me on," she joked.

Cady looked up and down the road, and was relieved to see a yellow cab coming along. "Come on," she said. She held her arm out boldly and was pleased to see the cab pull over. "First we have some crazy to see to."

The cab dropped them near where the bus was parked in the streets behind 24th. Shelby stopped before they walked around the corner, putting on tinted lip gloss and fussing with her hair.

Cady hesitated, then caved in. "You'd better give me some of that," she said, holding out her hand for the gloss.

"I told you," Shelby said. "A bit of lippy doesn't hurt."

"Yeah, you told me a lot of things that night," Cady reminded her. "Let's not go there again."

She looked defensive. "I was right about some things."

"If you say so." She wasn't giving an inch on that one. Okay, maybe she had once been the boring spinster of Shelby's accusation. She'd been a homebody for a reason, and she wouldn't have done it any differently. But she was leaving that Cady behind—and she didn't need any lessons from Shelby to do it.

She passed the lip gloss back, then watched while her sister pinched her cheeks like a Jane Austen heroine, giving them a delicate blush.

"I could have given them a good slapping for you," she said.

Shelby stuck out her tongue. "Whatever."

"Any time, any place. I'm happy to help," she said, clapping her hands together so hard that Shelby jumped at the startling crack.

"Jeesh, that's random." She shook her head. "Come on, I want to get there *some* time today."

Cady sighed. Her sister really was supremely slappable. She adjusted her bag across her body, tipped her suitcase onto its wheels, and followed. Her stomach churned with nerves with every step closer they got. Would Reid be there? What would they say to each other? Maybe Jennifer would be there. After Alison's comments, implying it was only a matter of time for Jennifer and Reid, Cady was convinced they'd get together. Their telephone tryst either showed that she was wrong, or that he was happy to keep licking that frosting…

When they got to the bus, the door was open, so they knocked and went on up, heaving their suitcases behind them. Shelby called out hello as they went, imbued with confidence after Kyle's texts.

The bus lounge was full of people. Kyle took one look at Shelby and swept her up for a repeat of the farewell kiss he'd planted on her not that many days before. She surfaced pink and delighted, her carefully arranged hair in disarray, a smile illuminating her face.

"And they're back!" he announced, straightening his signature furry vest. Cady had to settle for a kiss on the cheek, which suited her just fine. She was on edge, waiting to see if Reid would emerge from the kitchen, or come up the stairs behind them as he'd done on their first bus day.

Alison looked across from her seat at the computer. "Hello," she conceded.

Well, it wasn't exactly warm, but it was better than the oh-my-God, matchy-matchy references from their first encounter.

"Hi," they both replied.

Cady glanced over to the corner of the lounge, where three unfamiliar men were sitting silently. Two of them had skinheads, and the other had dark dreadlocks. All three of them wore an expression befitting a villain in a Bourne film.

Before she could ask who they were, or introduce herself and Shelby, Jennifer and Gavin came out from the kitchen, and there were warmer hellos.

"Heard you ladies were coming," Gavin said. "Been living the high life on the estate, what ho."

Cady had to laugh. "What ho?"

"Santa Almendra. Pretty big deal." He waggled his eyebrows behind his square, black-rimmed glasses.

Kyle kept his arm around Shelby. "You come from good stock," he told her, with a wink.

"Mm." For a moment Shelby's face reflected her

distaste for Holt's not-so-good actions. But she let it go—she was obviously enjoying her spot too much to ruin it with any negative comments.

"Fell on your feet there," Alison commented.

"I suppose so," Cady said. The three scary stooges listening in the corner were making her uncomfortable. She glanced their way again. They were skinny, narrow-eyed characters, like a team of dangerously surly weasels.

"Oh right," Kyle said. "Cady and Shelby, this is Isaac, Dean and Brew."

Brew? Okay. "Hi," Cady said, echoed by Shelby.

In return, three staunch eyebrow flashes and lifted chins came back their way. "Hey," said the hairy one.

Cady had no idea which of them was which, but she gave a feeble wave and turned back to Kyle. "Thanks for having us back."

"That's okay," he replied. "Not sure about the bed situation, is the only thing…"

"Oh." Cady looked at the three guys in the corner. She didn't suppose they'd be giving up their beds any time soon.

Shelby was determinedly unfazed though, just happy to be back in Kyle's company. "We'll sort something out," she declared.

Kyle gave her a smile. "We will. Come on, London," he said. "Let's get reacquainted."

Shelby followed him upstairs, looking like all her Christmases had come at once. On the other hand, Alison's expression looked more suited to Halloween than Christmas. Cady could see why. Wow, he moved fast. Something to do with their unexpected lift in fortunes? She knew Shelby wouldn't be questioning his sudden turn-around though—she'd be throwing herself into it. Cady wondered what she'd make of the chaos that awaited her up there. Or maybe he'd tidied up. She doubted Shelby would be focusing on the décor, anyway.

She stood in the center of the lounge with two suitcases and her own shoulder bag. What now?

"Reid'll be back soon," Gavin said. "He's been at his mom and dad's. He was going to come in time for the flash mob tomorrow, but when I told him you two were on your way, he said he'd come back earlier."

Her stomach lurched. Steady, she told it. "Cool, it'd be cool to see him. I mean okay, great."

Gavin laughed. "Yeah, cool."

Jennifer smirked, and Alison rolled her eyes and turned back to the computer.

Oh, that was not cool. Way to not *keep* your cool. She wanted to kick her own arse. Or ass, as he'd say. She'd better keep it together more convincingly when he got here.

"I have to get on," Jennifer said. "There are still a few things to do before tomorrow."

"Yes," Alison said sharply. "Things that won't get done *in bed*."

Ouch. If that look shot actual daggers, Cady would be dead right now. For a second she felt like she should apologize, but the moment passed. She wasn't her sister's keeper. Heaven help any person who found themselves with that job. There were times when she felt responsible, sure—but Shelby would never let herself be 'kept' anyway.

"Come on," Gavin said to her now. "You probably need a drink after that drive. Cold or hot?"

"Cold, thanks." She definitely didn't need any extra hotness at this point. She shoved the suitcases into a corner and followed him into the kitchen, glad to get away from the intimidating gaze of the new trio.

They sat at the kitchen table and chatted. It was a relief to just shoot the breeze with Gavin, whose straightforward humor made him easy company. She wanted to ask about the new guys, but she didn't want them to hear. Later, maybe.

She was halfway through the Bud Gavin had given her when she heard someone else arrive. There was no way to prevent the hot flush that rushed to her cheeks as she turned in her chair and peeked through to the lounge, knowing who she'd see.

Reid was greeting Baldy, Baldy and Hairy with gusto, shaking their hands and giving each one a slap on the shoulder. The three of them had actually gotten up, even, and there was a round of vigorous man-slapping. They didn't seem like Reid's type, Cady thought, surprised at his enthusiasm. But then, let's face it, she didn't know him well enough to say what was his type.

She pressed her cold beer bottle hand on her cheek, hoping to cool it before he turned and saw her. There was nothing cool about the last time they talked. She had no idea what he'd say, if things would be different between them in person, or if the sudden hanging up was a sign of how it would be now.

But when he came into the kitchen and saw her, he grinned.

"Lady Cady," he said, with grandeur, then came over and pressed his lips to her cheek. He let the kiss last a little longer than necessary, and she felt herself breathing out, her eyes closing as she soaked in his closeness.

Then he stepped back and she pulled herself together, aware of Gavin watching them.

Reid looked around. "Where's your sister?"

She scrunched up her face. "Upstairs."

"Upstairs?" He looked at her, and she could see realization dawning as she nodded. "Oh. Upstaaairs."

She rolled her eyes. "Yup. Kyle was like a heat-seeking missile."

Gavin laughed. "That's exactly what he was like. Okay, I'd better get moving. I have a client who couldn't wait for the end of summer to see me." He looked at them. "If you stand still long enough you'll find yourselves with jobs."

"I'm happy to help," Cady said. "I don't want to be a freeloader." It felt wrong to not be involved. After Rownville, she felt a real—if unjustified—ownership in Flashpoint. Now, although she wouldn't admit it out loud, she was jealous of the others, working away.

"Nah, actually, we've got this," Gavin replied. "We've hardly had to do anything, really. Kyle says it's basically done."

"Oh. Well, okay then. If you're sure..."

He gave her a thumbs-up as he left the kitchen.

Then it was just the two of them. Reid leaned against the cabinets in the same place as that morning after the Rownville celebrations, when he'd been wearing only his boxers and t-shirt, and a bed-sexy morning vibe. She blinked firmly to try and erase the image. There was no way she'd be able to concentrate with that in her head, as well as the real, fully clothed, deal right in front of her.

"Come on," he said to her. "If they don't need us, let's take a walk."

"Okay." Suddenly she didn't mind so much that they didn't need her, if the compensation was time alone with him. What would he say—if anything—about the phone call? And what would *she* say, come to that?

They went out through the lounge, past the three new guys.

"Later," Reid told them, and they acknowledged him with various grunts. They didn't seem to be doing anything in particular, other than maintaining a hoodlum-ish aspect.

It was a relief to leave the strange atmosphere on the bus. As they walked down the street, she was acutely aware of him next to her—the occasional hints of his cologne, the way he walked, with easy, long strides. The space between them felt like it was humming with suppressed energy. Or maybe the way she felt inside was spilling into her aura, making it vibrate with Reid-ness.

"So, how are you?" His voice was relaxed. He was obviously not feeling as tightly wound as she was.

"I'm good, thanks. Yeah, good." She didn't add, I'm also ready to step right over, hustle you against a shop-front and disgrace myself in public. Oh, and what was that phone call all about? She cleared her throat. "Your mum and dad's place sounds nice. Did you have a good visit home?"

"I did, thanks."

She'd given him a sliver of an opening, but nothing more was forthcoming. Should she bring up the phone-sex-that-almost-was, or should she wait and see what he said? If he said anything at all. As she was tossing it up, they turned the corner, and she realized that they seemed to be going in a particular direction. "Where are we going?"

He stopped suddenly. "Here."

She looked up at the green canopy. "Dynamo Donut and Coffee," she read.

"Can't ever go wrong with donuts and coffee," he said. "I recommend the maple-glazed, apple bacon variety."

She looked at him. "The...really? That's an actual thing?"

"Sure."

She shook her head. "Seriously. Only in America." She paused. "I'll take one."

"You won't regret it," he promised.

"Hm, I'm not sure about that."

"I'll get a selection, just in case." They went up to the window and ordered donuts and coffee, and came away with a box full of sugary bliss.

"We'll never eat all those," she said.

"That's not the point."

She laughed. "Where shall we sit?"

"Ah," he said. "Come with me. Not far."

He set off down the street and she followed, intrigued. They crossed York Street, and a few doors further on he stopped by a green iron fence. "Here," he said.

She peered through the bars at the park, captivated. "Oh! How did you know about this?"

It was a magical place, a little gem in the middle of the city. Colorful murals enlivened the walls and the sides of neighboring buildings, and at the back of the park a spectacular mosaic-tiled snake slunk around, dipping in and out of the very ground. Its mirror-glass eyes reflected the light, and the rich colors of the cut tiles glowed in the sun. It sported fearsome white teeth and an air of exotic slithery danger.

"I have a friend who likes it here. But actually, I know all kinds of things." He winked.

"I bet."

"For example," he said, holding the gate open and following her in, "that...is Quetzalcoatl." He swept an arm out in front of him, following the line of the vividly colored snake.

211

"I'm sorry, quetz-a-wha?"

"Quetzalcoatl," he said, letting it trip off his tongue.

"Bless you," she said.

He laughed. "I give up."

They sat and watched the children race around, squealing and shouting as they clambered on the big snake's jeweled length. Where its tail curled around, jets of water shot out of the ground every now and then, and the kids danced under the sparkly droplets, loving the imaginary danger. Looking at them, she felt the familiar achy heart. She understood how Cady Greenwood might become bitter, having had and then lost her chance at motherhood. It was tough enough for this Cady, quietly getting to grips with maybe never being a mother herself.

"So, how was it? What was your father like?"

She turned her attention back to him, putting those thoughts out of her mind. He was holding out the donut box and waiting for her answer.

She took one of the maple-glazed, apple bacon extravaganzas. "He was...more complicated than we imagined." She chose her words carefully. There was no need to share the less-than-savory details, when she was still processing them herself. "But he was glad to see us. He doesn't have a family himself."

"Did he know about you?"

"He did." She took a bite of the donut. "Huh. Surprisingly good."

Somewhere along the way, she'd gotten comfortable in Reid's presence. It wasn't that she stopped noticing every aspect of him, or that her body had gone off high alert. But she'd relaxed into it. It felt good.

"Told you," he said. He reached out and gently brushed her chin with his thumb. "Powdered sugar."

Her heart practically stopped in her chest, but she took the chance for a comeback. "Thanks, Honey," she replied, making him grin.

"Handed you that one," he said.

She just nodded, her mouth full of donut again. Not graceful, but it was just too good to care. With the sun warming her hair, sweetness in her mouth and a hot guy beside her, it was easy to let everything troubling slip away. This counted as one of life's peak moments.

"Is that how they let you eat in the castle?" he asked. "Medieval style. Just need to give you a giant drumstick next."

She swallowed, and gave him a faux stern look. "You don't want to know what we do to traitorous subjects with drumsticks."

He laughed. "No, I probably don't. Consider me back in line." He paused, then abruptly switched tack. "So, last night."

Instantly she was back on alert, the easy comfort replaced with a hum of tension. "Last night," she echoed, wiping her sugary mouth.

"Yeah." He looked at her. Beneath the dark, straight brows, his tiger eyes were full of familiar mischief, his expression loaded. "Remember it?"

She took a sip of her coffee, looking away sideways. The heat from the sun was nothing on the burn that had sparked up in her body, and she shifted on the hard bench under his insistent, amused gaze. "Is this a suitable place to have this conversation?"

"No. Not at all." He was unabashed. "And if you need to ask that, I think you must remember."

"Oh, I remember. I remember you leaving me in the lurch." She tried to repeat her earlier teasing glare, but couldn't bring herself to meet his eyes now that they were on this topic. Being hung up on so abruptly, just as she'd let her inhibitions drop, leaving her exposed figuratively and nearly literally...that was pretty brutal.

"I'm sorry about that." He did sound sorry. "Something came up."

Strung tight with nerves and fraught attraction, she burst out laughing at his double entendre, almost snorting coffee out of her nose. Coughing and spluttering, she managed to look at him, and was satisfied to see his embarrassed expression.

"I bet it did," she said. Oh, that was too, too good.

He gave a rueful smile. "Go ahead, enjoy. I earned it."

"You did," she said, still giggling. "And I will."

After that, the tension was broken.

"I felt bad, but I just wasn't able to ring you back," he said. "I really am sorry."

She wanted to ask why, but he didn't offer a reason. Like so many other times, he gave only so much, and kept the rest back.

"That's why I came today," he added. "When Gav said you were both coming back. I figured I owed you more than a phone call or a text."

"Well. Thanks. I appreciate that." It would be even nicer if he added, *and I wanted to see you again.* Or if he told her *why* he hadn't been able to ring her back. But he didn't. It drove her mad, but that was him. She could fight it, or she could forgive him and slide a tiny bit closer, until her shoulder was just a millimeter, a nanometer, from his. She chose the second, and they sat in the sun, near and yet far, eating donuts and drinking coffee. It could be worse.

Chapter Twenty-Seven

B ack at the bus, the smell of pizza hit them as they went up the stairs.

"Pizza again?" Reid said, surveying the boxes balanced on knees and tables. Even though she'd had two and a half donuts, the cheesy-tomato aroma made Cady feel hungry.

"Help yourselves," Gavin said. "We got plenty."

Shelby was there, and she flashed Cady a grin. The rest of the regular crew was chowing down, but there was no sign of Kyle and the gruesome threesome.

As everyone ate, they talked about the next day's flash mob. Kyle had been in charge of the planning, they told the girls. It was designed to be a celebration of nature. It would start at noon, when the sun was highest and would flood the street with sunshine. This, Kyle had told them, was symbolic of the way that nature shines in every part of life. The music would be from the summer movement of Vivaldi's Four Seasons, and green helium balloons would be released at the end. Kyle had organized sponsorship, but it would be very in the background. The main thing, he'd said, was the celebration of nature's bounty and diversity.

"Well, that all sounds good," Cady said. She thought about the orchards at Santa Almendra, with their bountiful trees (the ones that were still standing, anyway). They were beautiful, and bountiful, although diversity didn't come into it.

"Why is it happening in the middle of a street, though?" Shelby asked. "If it's all about nature, shouldn't it be somewhere *natural* in the sun?"

"It's the contrast," Jennifer said. "Like, it's supposed to encourage people to think about nature, even though we have these urban lives."

"Hm. Okay, that makes sense."

"Is there something to watch on YouTube beforehand?" Cady asked.

Jennifer shook her head. "No, apparently there'll be instructions there. We've organized the sound system." She shrugged. "Kyle's been keeping this one close to his chest, for some reason, working with the sponsor. We've been spreading the word, but the only info is the theme of the event, and that people should wear white t-shirts."

"It feels weird to just be one of the participants this time," Shelby commented.

"It does," Cady agreed.

So Kyle had gone from involved in the beginning, to backed right off for Rownville, to backed off yet involved—and secretive—for this one. He was impossible to figure out. Cady wondered if Shelby might find out a bit more, now that she'd been granted access to the upper sanctum, and to the man himself. Well, they'd know everything tomorrow. If he'd found a sponsor, the money worries must be eased, this time round at least. She helped herself to a slice of Hawaiian, tangling the cheesy threads around her finger as she pulled it out of the box.

Just then, Kyle and the three weasels came down the stairs. They turned down the offer of pizza, armed themselves with beers, and crammed into the seats along the window. With not enough room for them all, one was forced to plop down on the floor. The others laughed and made obvious jokes about the cheap seats.

Reid turned in his chair, leaned forward on his knees, and joined their conversation, looking for all the world like they were best buddies. Cady suppressed the urge to screw up her nose, and turned to join the conversation the others were having. There were two halves to the bus now, and she knew which half she preferred.

When everyone had eaten their fill, Cady helped take the boxes into the kitchen. Shelby came too, and pulled her aside.

"I have to talk to you about something," she said in a quiet voice, her face aglow. "He wants me to stay with him tonight."

Cady looked out through the doorway at Kyle. He adjusted his beanie as he sat engrossed in conversation, talking nineteen to the dozen with Reid and the skinheads and...the other one. (She still hadn't figured out which one was which.) It was getting harder to see why Shelby was so caught up in him—he was so far from her usual well-groomed, slick, player type. But seeing how excited she was, it was hard to begrudge her this longed-for triumph. There was one thing Cady wasn't excited about, though.

"But there's no room on the bus for me," she said. "None of those new guys are budging."

"I know, I'm so sorry." She did look a bit regretful. "But I really, really, reaaaally want to stay." Even at such low volume, her voice burned with intensity.

"Shel. Seriously?" She tried to keep the whine out of her voice, but this sucked. Okay, all Shelby's fantasies were coming true, so yay for her. But what was the extra sister supposed to do?

Shelby gave her a look that combined desperation, determination and pleading. "Maybe Marian...?"

She sighed. If she ruined this for Shelby, she'd never hear the end of it. Like never, *ever*. And the rest of the trip wouldn't be worth doing with a mad, resentful Shelby as passenger. "Okay. No problem. But you *owe* me."

"I know, I know." She bobbed up and down, showing only a hint of the thrill she was obviously feeling. "Thank you."

"Meh," Cady said. "Off you go. And use some protection, for God's sake," she added in a whisper.

Shelby rolled her eyes. "Yes, Mum," she replied, turning to go. Then she stopped and turned back. For a second she looked at Cady, her eyes becoming misty, then she said, "I miss her. That lying, cheating, name-changing wench."

Cady nodded. "I know." She felt tears threaten in her own eyes too, so she took hold of Shelby and turned her around. "Go. I'll see you back here tomorrow."

★

With dinner finished, Cady felt like now was the moment to leave. She'd wait to phone Marian until she was off the bus. If there was no room at the inn, so to speak, she'd have to hunt around for somewhere else. But she didn't feel like doing that in front of everyone, and making a drama out of it. She'd handle it.

"Okay, that's me done," she said, slinging her bag across her chest and pulling her suitcase from the corner. "See you tomorrow, everyone."

There were general goodbyes, and then Gavin said, "But where are you going to stay?"

"I'll head to Marian's, where we stayed when we arrived," she said. "It's cool."

Reid looked up. "I'll go with you," he said.

"Good idea, man," Gavin said. "Have to keep our transatlantic VIPs safe."

He grinned at Cady, and she returned a grateful smile. In the newly altered atmosphere on the bus, his perpetual cheer and silly unnecessary glasses were a shining light.

Reid took her suitcase and held out an arm for her to go first, and she gave Shelby a last wave before she went out.

On the street, the evening air was still warm. While Reid leaned against the wall, looking for all the world like an extra in a Rolling Stone magazine photo shoot, she dialed Marian's number. After a quick explanation, Marian said yes, she could come as soon as she liked.

"Okay, I'm good," she told Reid. She double-checked the map on her phone. "I can walk, it's not far from here. You can get back to your conversation." She hoped the tone didn't reflect her distaste for the weasel gang, but she suspected it did, a bit.

"Are you kidding?" he said. "I'm not letting you go by yourself."

She thrilled a little at the determination in his voice. It was nice to have him looking out for her, even just for a few blocks of Mission streets.

He pulled out the long handle of her case and they set off. In the fading evening, lights from the shops and street lights threw travelling shadows across his face as they walked. The darkness of his beard and hair was matched by the darkness of his eyes in the half-light. He was such an unknown quantity. Why should she be surprised that he seemed so matey with Kyle's new friends? She didn't know what kind of friends he had himself. Apart from Gavin, who seemed worlds away from those three.

"The new guys are…interesting," she said, too curious to resist.

He made a non-committal sound. "They're okay."

"You seem to get on well with them."

He just shrugged. "I want the whole thing to be a good scene, you know."

She persisted, though she knew she probably shouldn't. "They don't seem to really, um, fit with the Flashpoint vibe."

"Well, it's not my bus," he said bluntly, looking fixedly along the street as they walked.

"But don't you think…"

He stopped in his tracks, his jaw set. "It doesn't *matter* what I think. It's not my bus."

She blinked at the harshness in his voice. "Okay, then."

They stood in the street for a few moments. What was going on there, to change the Flashpoint tone so radically in such a short time? The new arrivals seemed to have split the bus in two, with Kyle even more detached from the original team. After the joyous fun of Rownville, it was depressingly unpleasant. She felt a niggling worry about leaving Shelby there. At least Gavin was there too, and Tino and the girls.

But she didn't say any of that. She stood, waiting, and watched his shoulders relax as the unexpected anger left him. When he was fully back, she gave him a gentle shove. "Come on."

He flicked her a tight smile and tipped her suitcase back onto its wheels. Luckily it wasn't much further to Marian's, and they covered the distance in silence. Not awkward, but definitely cautious. She knocked on the door, and within a moment Marian flung it open.

"Hello, gorgeous girl," she said, pulling Cady in for a hug. "That wayward sister of yours, huh?" Then her eyes widened as she took in Reid standing behind Cady. "Oh, my. Hel-*lo* sugar."

He laughed, brought back to good humor by her admiration. "Hi."

"Nice work," she told Cady. "Very nice. Keeping up with Miss Shelby after all."

Cady blushed. "Oh, well, you know, it's..." Oh damn, she could hardly look at Reid, who was standing there with a grin on his infuriatingly handsome face.

"It is *indeed*," Marian said with relish, making Reid laugh again. She stood aside to let them go through. "Okay, come in, come in. You have the same room as before. Here's the key."

"Sorry again about the short notice," Cady said, taking it from her.

"Not at all. Glad to help. Nice to see you found yourself some *adventure*." She gave them an exaggerated wink. "Go settle in."

Reid picked up the suitcase and followed her up the stairs. She was all too aware of him a couple of steps behind her, and below her. She fought the urge to tug her blouse down, to cover more of her butt. She was sure these jeans had gotten tighter since their holiday started.

She scampered up the last couple of stairs and walked ever-so-slightly sideways as he came after her along the corridor. Then she pushed the key into the old lock and opened the door, and he set the suitcase on the floor in the middle of the room.

There was a pause then, as they looked at each other. With no more encouragement than his proximity, Cady felt herself begin to breathe more shallowly. Darn it, this was textbook cliché. She glanced over at the beds before she could stop herself, and his eyes followed hers.

"Which one is yours?" he asked, and her heart started to pound faster. Alone in a room, looking at beds, nowhere else to be...

"That one," she said, pointing to where she'd slept on their first San Francisco night. That one, her inner lusty devil echoed. *That one.* If she thought it enough times, maybe she could will him into thinking about her on it. *Them* on it. And then, heaven help her, she'd show him what he'd been making her think about since the first day they met.

He looked at the bed in question. "Okay," he said. Then he picked up her case and put it on the luggage rack on that side of the room.

"Oh," she said. That didn't work. "Thank you."

"You're welcome, Lady Cady." He gave a little bow, making her smile.

"Well, I don't know why I don't see more of that," she said, determined to keep on top of things from here on. "The service in this country really is terrible."

The expression in his eyes took on a new challenge, and his smile became teasing-crooked as he regarded her. "What kind of service are you missing?" he asked, his voice a tone lower than before.

Her breath caught in her throat. Maybe it had worked after all. She looked for a smart comeback, but his suggestive gaze was making her blurry in mind as well as body. She stood there staring at him, fully aware that her chest was rising and falling, and her lips had parted. Her tongue ran across her bottom lip, the moisture an echo of the dampness sneaking further below. She breathed in, out. In, out. Screw all this thinking and wondering. It had to be done. It *had* to. She stepped forward, pressing herself against him, threading her arms around his body. Under his t-shirt, his skin was warm and smooth, just as she'd imagined that night outside the bus. She let her fingers roam up his back, either side of his spine, then down again until they hit the top of his jeans. Then she slipped her fingertips just slightly under the waistband and pulled him against her.

He let out a breath, half sigh, half groan, and lowered his head. As she stood on tiptoe to meet his lips, her breasts grazed against his chest, and she felt him pressing hard and low against her. The rush of satisfaction she got from knowing she affected him, too, was matched by a rush of pure arousal that filled her head as much as her body. He grabbed her and pulled her even closer, his lips strong on hers, his tongue finding a willing reception as she opened her mouth, her heart, her self to him. But she wanted more, more. She widened her stance as they kissed, wobbling a little as she balanced higher on her toes, trying to stand high enough that he could press between her legs. He knew what she wanted. She felt him bend his knees slightly, just enough so that they connected, and she moaned as she felt the evidence of his desire closer against her. Their combined heat, separated by two infuriating layers of denim, zips getting in the way, felt to her like it must be raising the temperature in the room. The old joke about panty-melting suddenly seemed perfectly feasible. He ground harder against her, his arms hugging her closer and higher, their kiss deepening and redoubling in urgency, until finally they were forced to break for ragged, indrawn breaths.

He pressed his forehead against hers, holding her gaze. His eyes were heavy-lidded, darkened by widened pupils, and she knew she must look the same. Their deep, unsteady breathing was the only sound, his face the only thing she could see. A strand of his hair tickled her cheek. Or maybe it was her hair tickling his cheek. Right now, she felt so enmeshed with him that she hardly knew which way was up. She closed her eyes, not willing to do anything to break the moment.

"I have to go," he said.

She struggled up from the depths. "Go?" That one small word made no sense at all in her lust-hazy brain. "You can't stay?"

"I'm sorry," he said. "I just can't."

Ah. Those three small words did the trick. She was back to reality before he'd finished the apostrophe-t.

"O-*kay*," she said, taking a firm step backward. "Yep." She ran her fingers through her hair, working to bring her breathing back to normal.

"Don't be like that," he said.

"Like what? I totally understand. I remember." She kept her voice steady. "You told me already, so I shouldn't have...you know."

"No, you *don't* understand. It's..." He clenched his fists, frustration at something showing through. "Shit."

She might as well know, once and for all. "Is it Jennifer?"

"What? Jennifer? No."

"Oh. Alison said—"

He shook his head. "Alison says a lot of things."

"Oh," she repeated. "Okay."

Her doubt must have been obvious in her voice, because his expression darkened further. "Did you ever see me do anything to lead her on? Anything inappropriate?"

She thought for a moment. "No. But I think she's hoping—"

"No." He shook his head. "I don't think so. And she's a nice person, but even if you're right, I'm not going to feel obliged just because someone's *hoping*."

Whoa. Was he still talking about Jennifer, or about herself now? She straightened her blouse and stepped around him toward the door, determined to clamber back onto firm ground. "I won't keep you then."

"Don't talk to me in that extra-British voice," he said.

She blushed. "I'm not." She knew she was.

"You always sound more prim and posh when you're annoyed."

"I don't! Oh my God, you're making this worse. You were the one who said you had to go, remember?" She opened the door. "I'm all sorted here. Thanks for your help. I'll see you tomorrow."

He sighed, his dark eyes conflicted. "If I could tell you..."

This mystery was intriguing at first, making him fascinatingly enigmatic. But after two slap-downs—no, three, including on the phone—she had to call enough. She knew the saying. Fool me once, shame on you. Fool me twice, what the hell was I thinking? Or a version thereof.

"Well, you can't tell me, apparently. So forget about it."

Standing there with her hand on the door handle, a big part of her ached to know what was going on in his mind. But the rest of her wanted to get hold of him and shake him, slap him around the head, beat the living *I just can't* out of him...and make him stay. Yeah, that'd show him. Kind of.

"Take this." He pressed the door opener for the bus into her hand. "I don't need it tonight, but you might want it tomorrow."

She took it, and pointedly opened the door even further. He took the hint and went out. On the other side of the doorway he stopped for a minute, his hands tucked into his pockets. She averted her eyes, willing him to go before she threw herself at him again. The longer he stood there, tall, dark and insanely hot, the more her resolve weakened.

"Your sister should be careful." He paused. "In fact, it would be better if you both got out of here."

She swayed backward at his words, a sudden harsh ache in her chest. He couldn't make it any clearer, unless he literally gave her a stab in the heart. If there was some problem on the bus, he was welcome to tell her. But to go from practically mauling each other, to this cryptic but obvious backpedalling...well, she wasn't going to waste any more time being tempted to figure it out. To figure him out.

"Fine," she said. "I hear you loud and clear."

And she shut the door.

Chapter Twenty-Eight

C ady was used to sleepless nights. She'd had plenty of them with her mum, jumping up when she called out for help in the darkness. Or randomly getting up to check on her in the wee small hours, having jolted awake with a feeling of foreboding. But that night, after Reid left, was the kind of sleepless that sets upon you the minute you lay your head on the pillow.

It was only as she lay in the dark, staring at the ceiling, that she suddenly wondered what he meant about Shelby being careful. Then she started to feel sick, worrying about her there on the bus with the three weasels. With everyone else there too, it would be fine, of course. Wouldn't it? That same foreboding feeling crept over her, clammy and insistent. Then she was back to reliving the encounter with Reid, from the intoxicating bliss of their kiss, to the miserable ending, and back again.

By the time she fell properly asleep, it was well toward morning. Then, of course, she was so tired that she slept in, having forgotten to set the alarm on her phone. Marian had stayed away, maybe assuming that Cady still had company. Oh, how she wished she still had company. But not complicated, secretive Reid company. A Reid who would wake her with scattered kisses on the back of her neck, pull her close so that she could feel his morning desire against the curve of her bottom, reach around with searching fingers to rouse the warm, waiting spot between her legs, and...

She shook her head clear of that never-going-to-happen scenario, threw herself in and out of the shower, flung on a cotton sundress, and headed down, her suitcase banging behind her on the stairs. She breathlessly explained to Marian that she was late, and they sorted the bill in record time.

"No man?" she asked, looking surprised and disappointed. When Cady just shook her head firmly, she knew to say nothing more. "Okay. Do you want to leave your suitcase here?"

She thought for a second. "No, I'll take it, thanks though. I think we'll probably leave after the flash mob today. But we'll see you when we come back through."

If she had any say in it, they'd *definitely* be going today. Shelby would have to be dragged kicking and screaming, no doubt, but she wasn't shying away from conflict today. Tired and annoyed, without any posh accent, and with a don't-mess-with-me attitude—her sister would just have to suck it up.

She headed for the bus. They'd arranged to meet there, so Shelby might still be waiting. She'd drop her bag, and they could head for the flash mob together. There were ten minutes before it started, so she'd be late, but not by much.

But when she got there, the door was closed. She fished around in her bag for the door opener Reid had given her, and clunked her suitcase up the stairs. There was no one around. She rolled her eyes—of course Shelby wouldn't have waited for her.

She slid the case under the stairs in the corner of the lounge, and turned to go. Then she hesitated. Nobody was here. She looked up, straining her ears for any noise from above. Nothing.

Well. She could just have a little look. Only to make sure there was nothing untoward. For Shelby's sake, that was all.

She went back and pushed the button to close the bus door, then turned and quickly went up the stairs before she could second-guess herself. At the top she paused, listening for any sound from behind Kyle's closed door. Then she opened it and went in.

It was surprisingly neat. There were piles of mess shoved into a few corners, in a gesture of tidiness, and there were clothes scattered around, but it was a huge improvement on the last time she'd been up here. Shelby's suitcase was on the bed, along with her favorite silk nightie. Unless she started rifling in draws and closets (a step too far even in her curious mind), there was nothing alarming to be seen.

Just one more thing. She went toward the en suite bathroom, stepping on something by the bed. She lifted her foot, and had to smile when she saw a torn-open condom wrapper. That was good. Then, with guilty nerves rising further, she slid the bathroom door open.

Oh, hell. Not so good. On the cabinet lay a lighter, and a glass pipe, its spherical end milky white on the inside and darkened with heat on the outside. An empty plastic bag lay on the floor next to the shower door. It didn't take a genius to put two and two together. Even a tragic old spinster who'd been living under a cloak of **martyrdom would know what that was all about.**

She turned and left the room, her mind racing. Damn. Kyle and the weasels, she could see that. But Shelby? Did she have any idea? Down the stairs, out of the bus, and along the street, she turned it over and over in her head. Her sister loved to shock, and was proud of her wild persona. But for her, this was another level. Well, as far as Cady knew, it was. Then again, maybe she didn't know everything she thought she did.

Chapter Twenty-Nine

S he headed for the flash mob, clutching her bag against her as she half-walked, half-ran. Approaching the corner, she could hear the sweet notes of Vivaldi swelling above the noise of the crowd, just as she expected. What she hadn't expected was the harsh pitch of the noise: a rough, discordant hubbub, instead of a happy hum of voices, or whatever organized singing or chanting the flash mob might have involved. Jagged shouts and yells stabbed through the swoop and flow of the classical music. Without seeing a thing, she knew something had gone very wrong.

She came around the corner, only just stopping before she barreled into chaos. Instead of a coordinated flash mob expressing Zen-like appreciation of nature's wonders, there was complete disorder. The white t-shirted flash mob participants were matched in number by stridently shouting people dressed in black. Some of them were holding up long poles topped with a pitch-black cut-out of a bird, or a butterfly, or a bee, small creatures of the earth made dark and foreboding. They bobbed and turned above the heads of the crowd, seeming to reproach them.

Placards were being held up too. She read the messages on the nearest ones, trying to make sense of what was happening. *What price our purity?* said one. Others read *Eons in the making, gone in a flash*, and *TierraChem = TerrorChem*. With a shock, she remembered that TierraChem was the name of one of the world's biggest agricultural chemical companies—enemy number one in the eyes of staunch environmentalists and eco-activists. But what did that company, and the protestors, have to do with Flashpoint?

Then the music stopped abruptly, and a voice came over the loudspeakers.

"People, open your eyes! This event is nothing more than blatant hypocrisy. It's PR. It's manipulation masquerading as environmentalism. TierraChem are responsible for doing mind-boggling damage to our precious ecosystems, and yet you're here celebrating nature, sponsored by them. People, think harder! Paying lip service to our environment is not enough!"

A cheer went up, as Cady's heart sank. Kyle had organized sponsorship from an agrichemical company? Before Rownville, he'd admitted he needed funds to keep Flashpoint on the road—but was he desperate enough to take this kind of 'dirty' money? Surely, after their successful 'Home' flash mob, there would have been some other option for sponsorship. She looked around at the growing turmoil. What was he thinking? Especially here, in possibly the most avidly eco-aware state in the country. Having seen the trees at Santa Almendra, she knew how strongly some people felt about environmental issues.

She dived into the crowd, making her way to where the speakers were, assuming Kyle would be front and center. As she struggled through, she was jostled and bumped by the growing mob, and she started to feel afraid of what might happen next. Although they were a flash 'mob' movement, she'd had no idea how quickly a real mob could turn, or what that would look like. Now she was finding out.

There was no sign of Kyle. He'd assured the team that everything was under control. But now, with his judgment gone—and maybe she knew why—he obviously couldn't organize his way out of a paper bag.

Then she spotted Shelby in the mass of people. "Shelby!" she yelled. "Shel!"

Her sister turned at the sound of her name. "Where have you been?" she asked, as though the biggest issue was Cady's lateness, not the anarchy erupting around them.

Cady ignored the question. "What's going on? Where's Kyle? Where's everyone?"

Shelby shook her head. "He was here a minute ago, but now I don't know. The others must be here somewhere." She staggered a little as someone knocked her from behind. "Alison and Jennifer were looking after the balloons."

As if on cue, a flock of the green balloons floated past above them. They watched them sail away into the blue, up into the peaceful sky that contrasted so sharply with the turmoil below.

Shelby frowned. "Maybe not any more."

"Apparently not," Cady said. Well, now that she thought about it, helium balloons weren't environmentally friendly anyway.

Turning back to the street, they could suddenly see Gavin further along, talking to the people immediately around him, trying to settle them down. It wasn't working. They struggled over, ducking through protestors.

"Did you know about this?" Cady asked him, having to yell to make herself heard.

He shook his head, looking disgusted. "Nope. None of us knew who the sponsor was. He told us it was all under control." The irony of his words wasn't lost on any of them, as the increasingly out-of-control crowd grew around them.

"You girls get out of this," he added. "Just keep yourselves safe."

Cady nodded and grabbed Shelby, moving them away from the road, up onto the stairs in front of an office building. Holy hell. She'd been a bit late, but the event had only started about fifteen minutes ago. It was scary how fast something could go from warm fuzzies to aggressive rebellion.

"This is *insane*," she said to Shelby, waving her arm at

the growing melee. "This isn't what it should be about. Shel...we should leave." The image of the paraphernalia in Kyle's bathroom was still vivid in her head.

Shelby looked sharply at her. "Leave the bus?"

"Yes. I think we should go. Leave." She put aside thoughts of Reid. Oh, the flirting was too good, and he was so damn irresistible. And after that phone call, she'd thought maybe...maybe. Well, whatever she'd thought then, after last night, she was done. "We should go back to our holiday. There's so much to do. And we don't need this BS."

Shelby snorted, instantly inflamed by the suggestion. "BS? Tell the truth. You're just sulking because your crush didn't work out, and mine did. That was *obviously* never going to happen."

"It's not about that!"

Despite her denial, that one stung. Sisters knew exactly where to stick the pin. Cady had more to say, but on the other side of the road, some of the rioters had surrounded a car and were starting to rock it from side to side. She grabbed Shelby's arm and pulled her down the steps and further along the street, where they stopped outside a second-hand book store. A salesperson stepped out to see what was going on, then quickly went back in, closing the door firmly behind her and sliding the lock across.

"I'm not leaving," Shelby said.

"Shel, it's not a good idea to stay any more. Everything's changed so much, in such a short time." It killed her to know that her heart's project had gone so dramatically off course, but this wasn't what they signed up for. The little team was splintering—the regulars being kept in the dark, Reid all matey with the creepy weasel gang, and Kyle off on some trip that Cady didn't want to be part of. And that she didn't want her sister to be part of.

How had it all turned around so quickly? Flashpoint was becoming something else now, something altogether darker. For her, it was over, and she wanted them both safely out. And there was something else to think about— their visas. They couldn't afford to get caught up in anything dodgy. Being deported definitely wasn't one of the things on Cady's bucket list. She'd have to confront Shelby with her bathroom discovery. If she didn't know about it, she should, and if she did know...she needed a major, kick-in-the-pants wake-up call.

"Kyle's not good for you," she added. "You know what he's into, right? The drugs?"

"Yeah, I know now. But so what?" Shelby looked at her, petulant. "You're not my mother. Don't tell me what to do, like you know better. Like you always do."

Cady took a step back. "I don't always! But it's not about that anyway. It's about you being safe, and it's about this." She waved her arm at the chaos that was unfolding around them. The flash mob turned real mob was attracting overexcited opportunists. Taking the chance to join in the intoxicatingly bad fun, some kids were tagging a building with the jerky text of graffiti artists the world over. Someone smashed a beer bottle on the road, and a cheer went up. "This isn't what we came for."

But Shelby wasn't listening. "You were always their favorite. The smart one, the neat one, the responsible one...so freaking *good*." She spat the word out. "And the pretty one."

"The pretty one?" What the hell? She looked at her sister, years of competition and resentment now doing battle on her face. Her gorgeous face. "But *you're* the pretty one."

"No, I'm the one who works harder at it. Oh my God, I hate how this fucking fake tan smells." She jerked out her artificially brown arm, rigid with anger. "You just *are* prettier, and you don't even have to try."

This was getting mental. "Shel, what are you even talking about? It's not about trying—I have no clue what I'm doing most of the time!" Somehow, despite starting out with a very similar canvas, she just couldn't achieve the same end result as Shelby. She couldn't count the times she'd stood in front of the mirror despairing over her plain self, while her sister colored and tweaked and polished until she was magazine-cover glossy. "And anyway, it's not true.

Everyone knows you're the pretty one."

Shelby was about to reply when a teenager slammed into her from behind, almost knocking her off her feet. Cady steadied her and pulled her into the bookstore doorway, out of the way of the growing melee. The police would probably be here shortly.

"This is crazy—we shouldn't be having this conversation here."

"Right. Responsible as ever," Shelby said, stepping pointedly back out into the street, belligerent, daring Cady to bite. "Even when you broke free, you did it so...*uptight*. Plan this, schedule that, organize the other thing. Mum's gone, and you don't even seem to care. Just *live*, why don't you?"

Only a sister could be so ruthlessly dead-on. Those few words summed up everything Cady most wanted to change about herself. What she most disliked, what she most wanted to be different. But there was no way she'd show Shelby now what a direct hit it was.

"Whatever," she replied, borrowing from Shelby's who-gives-a-shit phrasebook, refusing to play the game. "Just go then."

But as Shelby started to do exactly that, something else occurred to Cady. "Wait," she called after her. "When did you decide I was the smart one? You're just as smart."

Shelby turned back and shook her head. "Not smart like you." She shrugged: *who cares?* "There was no point in trying to compete with that."

"Is that why you just gave up?" Cady remembered when it happened—when Shelby stopped caring about school, the approval of the grown-ups, the way they measured success. It was about the same time she discovered the power of her looks and the strength of her personality. "Why did we have to compete, anyway?"

Shelby ignored the question. "Look, you win, okay? You were their best daughter. Now Holt likes you better. I can live with that." Her face showed it was a lie, but she was toughing it out.

Cady shook her head. "But that's not true either! Holt

doesn't even know us. And Mum and Dad...just because I was there, it didn't make me the favorite. You *know* how much they wanted you around."

"I'm not going to feel guilty about that! And I'm not going to be where *you* think I should be *now*, either." Her voice rose higher as she spoke, and her cheeks reddened. "You leave if you want to. You were the star of the bus— that's fine. Kyle thinks you're smart, and he used your ideas. But he likes *me*. He said he *loves* me."

Cady's head was spinning with everything this argument was stirring up. And Kyle's sudden declaration of love rang major alarm bells. "Shel, stop, please. You need to—"

"No! There are other things you don't know. I can't even..." She pressed her hands to her face, closing her eyes for a moment.

"What other things? What?"

Shelby opened her eyes, and Cady could see that they were full of anguish. "I had the test, okay? For Wodarski-bloody-Ebner."

"But we agreed we wouldn't get tested!" Cady could feel panic pushing up from her guts at the prospect of facing that reality.

"I know, but that was just stupid."

Cady flinched at the words, but she knew it was true. Their avoidance strategy couldn't have lasted anyway— they'd both have to front up to it eventually. Her heart was racing. As sisters, whatever test result Shelby had got was quite likely to be hers, too.

"I had to know," Shelby continued. "I *had to*. And now I know." Her voice broke on the last word, making it obvious what the test result had been.

"Oh, shit. Oh, Shel, no." They looked at each other, the implications crowding in. "How long have you known?"

Shelby sucked in a long breath and looked up at the sky, battling the emotion. "About three years."

"Three years! Why didn't you tell me?"

"Did you really want to know? While you were in the

middle of looking after Mum?"

They both knew the answer to that. Cady searched for something positive to say. "You know, everyone's different. This doesn't mean you'll have the same outcome as her." She was telling herself, as much as Shelby.

"It does. You know it does. And until then, I'm going to live. Really *live*."

Cady thought of Kyle, the bus, the drugs, their visas, and pointed to the chaos on the road. "We can live, but we don't have to do it mixed up with all this. Come on, let's hit the road."

But Shelby wasn't having it. "Cady, you're such a fucking nana! I *know* what lies ahead for me. I've seen it. And you want me to play things safe? Be oh-so-good and careful?" She took a step back into the street. "Jesus, just let me have this *one* thing!" She spun around, her hair flying, and plunged into the crowd.

Cady's first instinct was to follow, but she held herself back. She needed a moment to absorb the impact of the shock. And anyway, it would be pointless trying to reason with Shelby now. Her funny, brash, glittery-confident sister had just let her cover slip. Or not so much let it slip, as ripped it off and thrown it on the ground. What Cady often envied—the determined wildness, the devil-may-care attitude, the bold personality—had obviously started as Shelby's way to paper over her insecurities. But they continued as a one-finger salute to the illness she could see waiting just over the horizon.

And maybe that illness was waiting for her, too. Her chest was a heavy wodge of anxiety, for what Shelby was facing, and for herself. More than Shelby, she had first-hand knowledge of the reality of Wodarski-Ebner, the slow, inexorable shutdown of a body turning on itself. She felt sick as this new truth settled around her, fogging her view of the future with dark uncertainty.

Well, she'd have to get a grip. This was no time to freak out. She looked around the street, where random kids were still racing to join the fun. Word must have got out. She took her phone from her bag, intending to check

Twitter, and see if the alert was being spread. But then, looking around at the turmoil, she decided she'd better wait until she was out of here. She slipped the phone into the pocket of her cotton dress, intending to grab Shelby on her way through and take her somewhere for a proper talk.

As she started down the street, she heard sirens approaching. She picked up her pace, holding the strap of her bag across her body. But as she got near the corner where she'd seen Shelby turn, a fight broke out in front of her, young guys pushing and shoving and giving each other lip. She backed off, looking for a way through. More of them were coming from every direction, their shouting and clamoring combining to make a constant kind of roar that seemed to bounce around between the buildings on each side of the street. Then there was a sickening smash, and she looked across to see the glass from a storefront window falling into the street. A teenager ran off, zigzagging wildly with a black bird on a pole that he'd managed to get a hold of.

Okay, now it was getting serious. She turned to run back in the direction she came from, but found herself facing a line of police in dark uniforms, their faces blank and grim behind their visors as they descended on the crowd. Oh, hell. If she was arrested, that was the end of her visa for sure. She made a split-second decision, and turned and ran toward the mass of rioters, forcing her way through the gaps in the churning crowd, letting the force of other people's lurching bodies propel her along. Something—an elbow? a fist?—hit her in the side of the face, but she ploughed on, her heart pounding, adrenaline keeping her moving.

As she struggled out the other side, holding her cheek, something caught her eye on the other side of the road. She could see Gavin off to the side, and then two of the three weasels, and Reid too, in the thick of a tussle on the sidewalk. As she watched, Reid grabbed hold of a kid who was flinging himself into battle—he must have been only a teenager, although he was enormous—and in one smooth move swung him around, his feet almost leaving the ground. Two thoughts flew into Cady's mind: *damn, he's crazily strong*—and then, *what the hell is he doing?* The kid hit the window behind him, and the sheet of glass cascaded down, showering the people nearby and scattering like uncut diamonds onto the sidewalk. Amazingly, the kid got up and ran off, seemingly unhurt.

She'd seen it in countless movies, but in real life the shock of it made her heart leap practically into her throat. Right then, she knew she didn't want Reid to see her. She turned and ran down the side street, not looking back, trying to process what she'd just seen. Who was this man, really? She knew almost nothing about him. Where he lived, his family, why he would give up so much of his time to hang around with Kyle the trust fund kid and his followers instead of working on his business. If that so-called business was a real thing at all. He had a bunch of pictures, but none of them had ever seen him in action.

Distracted, she stumbled as a trio of youths ran past her toward the rabble, one of them knocking her shoulder as she sped in the other direction. She grabbed at the nearest lamp-post and stopped herself, puffing. Back where the flash mob had fallen to pieces, half a block behind her, she could see the rioters running around, and hear the occasional smash. She couldn't see any of the team.

Or Shelby. She looked back up the street. Hadn't she come this way? There was no sign of her, but maybe she'd already gone back to the bus. She took one last look at the riot. Wait. There, in the middle of everything...was that her? Damn it, she couldn't leave her there. Shelby might be determined to *live*, but getting arrested and deported wasn't the way to do it. She adjusted the bag hanging across her body, and set off toward the chaos again.

Hitting the edge of the crowd, she could just see Shelby on the other side of the road, arguing with someone...Kyle. Of course. Behind her, kids in low-rise jeans and oversized t-shirts were jumping on top of a car as the driver sat helplessly inside with the windows rolled up, his hands over his ears. Another kid stood by, taking photos on his phone. Shelby shouted some last thing at Kyle, then turned to walk away, throwing her arms up. Cady strained to keep track of her as she disappeared into the throng.

"Shelby!" she yelled. "Shelbeeee!"

But there was no way Shelby could hear her. She tried to step back out of the way as a wave of young guys ran at her, some holding their hoodies to cover their faces. Forced to turn and run in the same direction, or be bowled over, she found herself right in front of a policeman. In other circumstances, she might have stopped to admire the figure he cut in his uniform, but faced with a long baton and a deadly serious expression, she knew she was in strife. This new start of hers was coming to a crashing halt, right here.

Chapter Thirty

S quished into a corner of the paddy wagon, Cady veered from nauseating fear of what the other hyped-up occupants might do, to stressing about where Shelby was now. Every time she thought about the Wodarski-Ebner, the acid panic rose in her chest again, so she pushed it out of her mind. She had enough to think about in the here and now.

The image of Reid flinging the guy into the window kept replaying in her head. How could it have come to this? The positive vibe they'd established with the Rownville flash mob was swept away. Okay, Kyle needed money—more than she realized, apparently. But choosing TierraChem as a sponsor, and presenting the event as a celebration of nature? That kind of blatant commercialism and sneaky manipulation bulldozed over the good they could be doing. They'd talked about commercial reality versus credibility—but that was what you called selling out.

At the police station, it took forever to process everyone who'd been arrested. They seemed to deal with the rowdiest ones first, so it was hours later by the time Cady had her turn at being booked. She was starving. They'd taken her bag, and it sat on the desk in front of the policewoman. Alongside was arranged her passport, makeup bag, and all the other things she had jammed in there. If she wasn't so scared right now, she'd be embarrassed about the amount of junk she carted around with her. No wonder she couldn't find her phone in there half the time.

Her phone. She felt in her pocket, but it was empty. Where was her phone? It must have fallen out of her pocket in the street. In all the confusion, she would never have noticed. Suddenly, she felt utterly adrift. She'd never learned the numbers of any of the Flashpointers, just entered them into the phone. And although she knew Shelby's English number, they'd both bought SIM cards with local numbers for their US trip. Shit. She tried to think. Okay, this was the age of connectedness, it wasn't a problem. First, buy a new phone. Then she could try and reach them via Twitter or Facebook...

"Okay. Cady Morrow," the policewoman began. "Arrested at flash mob riot."

"Yes, but I wasn't rioting. I was going to be part of the flash mob."

She sighed. "Miss Morrow. It's been a long night, and you don't want to know what I've already put up with from your friends."

Cady started to protest that they weren't her friends, that she was with the flash mob, not the rioters. But the policewoman raised her hand.

"If you were part of the flash mob, why weren't you wearing a white t-shirt like the rest of them? I'm advising you now that silence is your best course of action." She fixed Cady with a fearsome look. "Unless I'm asking you a *question*."

Cady nodded, cursing Reid again for keeping her up so late and making her so tired she forgot to wear the right outfit.

"I suggest you think very carefully about what you say to me from here on," she said, making a note on the paperwork. "You can discuss your defense with your lawyer, when you call them," she added.

Lawyer? She didn't have one of those…who could she call instead? Her first thought was to ring Shelby, but without her phone there was no way to reach her. Then it occurred to her that there was someone better equipped to help. Embarrassing as it was, she knew she had to phone Holt. His number would probably be listed. Well, he'd said he wanted to be a parent—nothing like diving in at the deep end.

As she listened to the policewoman read her rights—*the right to remain silent…anything you do say…if you cannot afford an attorney*—then had her fingerprints taken, and stood for mug shots, she felt encased in a bubble of unreality. It was surreal to go through the same procedures she'd seen on innumerable cop shows.

Then the policewoman showed her to a phone. When he answered, Holt sounded so pleased to hear from her that she hated to admit why she was calling, especially after they'd left in a rush, in a huff. There was more to talk about there. But, first things first. She gave him the bare details of what had just happened.

There was a long silence at the other end. Was he too mad at her? He may have had his own wild youth, but she had no idea how disapproving he'd be faced with this kind of situation. Maybe this was a line crossed, in his book.

"I'm not sure who else to ask for help," she said simply. "I've lost my phone, and all the contact numbers for the Flashpointers, and Shelby too."

"It's okay. I was just sending my attorney a message," he said. "We'll be there as soon as we can. Where *is* Shelby?"

"I don't know, and I can't call her without my phone. I'm worried about where she ended up."

Hopefully she was safely back at the bus, plumping up Kyle's ego and determinedly justifying everything in her own mind. The test result revelation made Cady look at her sister through a new lens. How had she coped all this time, carrying that knowledge? It hadn't seemed to make her more empathetic, just more determined to live on the edge. If she stopped to think of Cady, would she worry about where she was? Would she be calling the lost cellphone, wondering why there was no answer?

"I'll try and reach her," Holt said. "Just don't get in any more trouble until we get there."

★

A couple of very long hours later, a new police officer came and got her from the holding cell, where she'd been trying not to get to know any of her fellow occupants.

"Your lawyer is here," he said shortly, indicating that she should come out.

She followed him to a small room, feeling like an extra on *Law and Order*. He waved her in, and the door closed behind her. A man was waiting, his mouth a straight line as he stood behind the table with his hands on his briefcase, fingers spread. His sharp, dark suit and sleekly combed hair looked as perfect as if it was his first appointment of the morning, not a late-night emergency call-out.

"Thank you for coming," Cady said. It wasn't like any of this was her fault—she was only trying to get her stubborn-assed sister out of the trouble she was surely heading for. But she still felt shamefaced as the lawyer stepped forward and shook her hand.

"Preston Bridges," he said introducing himself. He had the direct gaze and bracing handshake of a man who made things happen. "I'll do what I can. Your father is waiting outside."

It was still jarring to hear him referred to as her father. "Thank you," she said again, grateful that someone was here to help.

"Don't thank me yet," he said brusquely. "You need to tell me what happened. Every detail."

Cady nodded. With this impressively efficient man on her side, she felt a tendril of hope begin to emerge. Maybe she wouldn't be flung into jail, only to emerge months later with an unwanted tattoo and a new, all-too-intimate understanding of 'sisterhood'. But what would happen?

Surely she'd be out of the country, at least. Could she hope for a voluntary exit, instead of an ignominious departure with a revoked visa? The thought of arriving back in London with her tail between her legs was too depressing.

She took a breath, and told him everything. He asked a few questions, and quizzed her particularly about Kyle. She gave him all the information she could, leaving out the meth pipe in the bathroom. She couldn't decide whether that detail would help or hinder things, so she skirted around it. It made her realize how little she knew about the enigmatic leader of their little band. She had no idea what he'd been like during the days they were away at Santa Almendra, but after today's flash mob disaster she suspected he must have gone seriously downhill, aided and abetted by the three weasels. And all the positive results from their Rownville event would now be overshadowed, probably erased, by today's drama. She was desperate to get online and see what was being reported and discussed, but she tried to focus on the questions Preston Bridges was firing at her.

After some time, he decided he'd heard enough. "Wait here," he told her. Then he left the room, leaving her sitting at the bare table with no idea what would happen next.

He was gone long enough for her butt to go numb in the hard chair. When he came back she stood up with relief, and hope, waiting to hear what he had to report. His face gave nothing away, but then a police officer followed him in.

"What's happening?" she asked.

"You're free to go," the police officer said. He handed over her bag, and she took it, resisting the urge to break out a little jig of relief right there in the sterile room. Taking her cue from the serious faces, she nodded somberly instead.

But when the police officer left, she turned to Preston Bridges.

"Oh my God, *thank* you," she said. She wanted to hug him, but the suit, combined with his upright bearing, deflected any kind of frivolity. She settled for another handshake, and he nodded, a glimmer of humor showing in his eyes.

"You're welcome," he replied, smiling at last. "Come on, your father's waiting."

She followed him to the building's main doors, where Holt was waiting, pacing. When he saw them he stopped and said a brusque hello, looking every inch the serious and disapproving father. The he looked at his lawyer. "Well?"

"The charges have been dropped," he said.

"Good. Thank you. I knew you could do it."

"Yes, thank you." Cady felt she could hardly say it enough times. "And thank you, too," she said, turning to Holt. "I really appreciate it. *Really*."

"You're welcome," he replied, a smile finally lightening his expression. "This man knows his stuff."

Preston took the praise as his due. "I do."

They went out of the building, emerging into a chilly night. Cady pulled her light denim jacket out of her canvas bag and put it on. She needed something warmer. And, more importantly, they needed to find Shelby.

Preston paused at the top of the steps. "Holt, I'll see you tomorrow."

"Yes. Thanks again," Holt told him, and they shook hands and clapped each other's shoulders.

"Any time," he replied. Then he looked at Cady, a little of his businesslike manner slipping now that the job was done. "Nice to meet Holt's daughter." He smiled, the older-than-his-years demeanor replaced by an appealing warmth. "Goodnight."

Holt's daughter. As she wished Preston goodnight, she thought about that whole world that she and Shelby could be part of, if Holt invited them in—and if they wanted to. But Mrs. G's story had changed everything in their minds. And the thought of her dad, at home in England unaware of all this, still made her feel awful. How had her mother carried the guilt all these years, without going crazy? Now Cady had inherited it, along with the money, and probably a genetic time bomb. Anne, or Adrienne, or whoever she was, had left her daughters with a bequest more complicated than cash.

Holt opened the door of his truck for her, and she

clambered in. As he started the engine, she shivered. Despite the jacket, she was cold in the summer dress and sneakers she'd put on that morning. Apart from the canvas bag she wore across her body, containing a few essentials, everything else was on the bus.

He turned up the heating. "The seat warmer should kick in soon."

"Thank you."

She rubbed her thighs vigorously, hoping to warm her hands and her legs at the same time. The last time they all saw each other, none of them had any idea the girls would be making an abrupt exit from Santa Almendra. The truth about the original Cady and Shelby had come as a shock, but part two of that shock—the abortion—had detonated like a depth charge under their fragile father-daughter relationship. It was probably better that they'd let it sink in away from the farm. But it had been an awkward departure.

"Um…about what happened. When we left…"

He took his foot off the gas, letting the truck idle in the empty street so that he could look right at her. "Bee told me why you left. It's not true, you know. I was a screw-up, but I wouldn't do anything like that."

Her face was obviously unconvinced, because he carried on.

"Look, you girls have had a lot to deal with lately, and that was just one more thing. But some things in life are way more complicated than anyone can know, looking from the outside." His voice was thoughtful. "Let's just cut each other some slack for now, and see what happens."

"Well…okay." She sighed, a long, weary breath that left her sagged in the seat. She was *so* tired. "I appreciate your help."

And the selfish truth was, she needed that help right now. She was exhausted, hungry, and lacking one sister. Figuring out the truths and untruths—whether Mrs. G's story was a revelation, or only an accusation—would have to wait. She just couldn't deal with everything at once.

"That's okay." He put the truck back in gear. "Family, right?"

245

She managed a smile. "Yeah. Did you talk to Shelby?"

"She wasn't answering her phone," he said. "Where do you think she might be?"

"I don't know really. Back at the bus, maybe." She looked around the night-time streets, with no idea where they were. "It was parked back near where we had the flash mob."

"That was no flash mob," he said dryly, indicating a left turn.

She sighed. "I know. It was a disaster."

"Plenty of time for post-mortems," he said. "Let's go find your sister."

They drove back to the street where the flash mob-turned-riot had happened. It was quiet now. One of the broken storefront windows was boarded up, and the other was being fixed by glass company workers. A security guard stood by their van, watching for trouble. Looking at the glass being replaced, Cady wondered where Reid was now. If he'd been arrested, they hadn't taken him to the same police station.

"That way, I think." She pointed down the side street she thought Shelby had turned down, before chaos broke out completely. "The bus should be around the corner at the end of this street."

But when they got there, there was no sign of the bus. "I'm sure this was it," she said. "That's the house we were parked in front of."

"They've probably moved it somewhere for the night," he suggested. "Any ideas?"

She nodded slowly. "Maybe."

First they went by Diorama, in case the team had retreated there for drinks. Cady was going to just run in, but Holt insisted on parking the truck and going too. He didn't want any more trouble at this time of night, he said. Given that it was pushing midnight, and the streets around the Mission were jumping with barflies and revelers, she was glad enough of the company. Cady asked at the little Sanctuary bar inside, but no one had seen Kyle or any of the Flashpointers.

"What went down today? That sounded major," the barman said. "Not cool."

Cady could only shrug and agree that it wasn't cool at all.

They drove up to the park near Tino's house, where they'd spent the first night on the bus, but it lay hushed in the moonlight and the parking lot was empty. As Holt drove, Cady used his phone to keep trying Shelby's number, but each time it rang out and went to answerphone.

"Is it okay if I check Twitter?" she asked Holt. When he nodded, she signed in and went to the Flashpoint profile page. Nothing. Suddenly it occurred to her that someone needed to tweet something about today's debacle. Damn. She should sign in as them and say…what? She probably had less clue than anyone what was going on. The internet could wait. She had bigger problems right now—like the whereabouts of her one and only, stubborn-assed sister.

Running out of ideas, she looked up the number and phoned Marian at the bed and breakfast. Maybe Shelby had gone there.

"I'm so sorry to wake you," she apologized. "I didn't want to get you out of bed, but I really need to ask you something."

"Oh, honey, you didn't get me out of bed," Marian said. "And I wasn't asleep." The murmur of a male voice in the background assured Cady of that.

"Oh no, sorry. I'm totally interrupting."

"No, it's fine. Your timing was just right." She laughed. "What's happening?"

Cady explained what had happened, and that she was looking for Shelby. Marian was serious then. "She didn't come here. I'm sorry I can't be any help. If you can't find her soon, you should call the police and the hospitals."

"I will." Cady tried not to let her mind go there. "Thanks so much, and sorry again."

They hung up, and Cady tried Shelby's number again. By now, she must have seen all the missed calls from Holt's number. But this time, it went straight to answerphone, giving Cady a jolt. Surely she wouldn't have switched it off in a huff. Had it run out of battery? Or maybe—best case scenario—she was calling Cady's lost phone at that very same moment. Now she was starting to seriously worry. Even Shelby—infuriatingly obstinate at the best of times—would realize that her sister would be worried. Wouldn't she?

"Now it's going straight to answerphone," she told Holt, as he waited patiently in the driver's seat. She leaned her head back against the Dodge's leather upholstery, letting out a shaky breath. She was so tired, but she had to find her pig-headed sister. Not to mention all her worldly goods—almost everything she had in this country was on that bus, wherever it was.

"It's getting late," Holt said. "I think we should go home. I can phone around some more when we get there."

"Home?" she said. The thought of leafy Santa Almendra—the big white house with its shady columned porch, the library lined to the ceiling with books, and her bed dressed with ridiculously high thread count linen—almost made her burst into tears. The idea that it might count as home, for her too, just about undid her. "I am a bit tired," she admitted, pressing her fingers against her burning eyes.

"I can see that," he said, restarting the engine. "It's been a big day. But everything will be okay."

She hoped he was right. Her head was swimming with Shelby's Wodarski-Ebner revelation, Kyle's illicit activities and badly judged flash mob, and Reid's hot-and-coldness and unexpected violence. She tried to keep her eyes open as they drove, scanning the streets in the unrealistic hope that she might spy the bus, or even Shelby herself. But they only made it as far as the outskirts of the city before she fell asleep.

Chapter Thirty-One

The next morning she woke suddenly from a deep, exhausted sleep, completely disoriented. Then the memory of the day before came slamming down into her brain, forcing the fog out. Straight away the sick feeling clutched at her stomach again. The flash mob, gone wrong. Reid, apparently gone to the other side. And most of all, Shelby—just gone. And tested positive, in the most negative of ways.

She leapt out of bed, the old John Deere t-shirt Holt had lent her almost an insult to the beautiful linen she'd slept in. She ran her fingers through her hair. Not much she could do about that, without any of her things. She cleaned her teeth with the wrapped toothbrush she found in the en suite bathroom, washed her face, and put on some of the tinted moisturizer she had in her bag. Then she pulled on yesterday's sundress, smoothed herself out as best she could, and went down to find Holt. Time for action.

He was in the big kitchen, eating breakfast at the long farmhouse-style table. Next to him was Preston Bridges, as sleek and well-combed in his suit as he'd been the night before.

"Good morning," she said to them both, wishing she

didn't look as much of a mess as she felt.

They both stood up, wishing her good morning too. "Would you like breakfast?" Holt asked, pouring her a coffee and setting it in front of an empty chair. "It's nothing fancy—Elva isn't coming in until this afternoon."

"Thank you," she said. "But, have you heard anything? I'm sorry, I shouldn't have slept so long."

The men looked at each other, and she felt a knot begin to form in her stomach.

"We haven't found Shelby," Holt said. "But the bus has been found." He paused. Preston pulled out the chair and made her sit down, only increasing her feeling of dread.

"What? Where is it?" Far from hunger now, her stomach did a one-eighty as fear set in.

"It was found in a parking lot, in a not very…desirable neighborhood. It was burned out. The police tell us they weren't able to retrieve anything from inside."

"Oh my God. And Shelby? All the others?" She braced herself for the worst, the very worst she could imagine, but had never even considered yesterday. The loss of all the things in her suitcase was nothing compared to the safety of Shelby, all the team…Reid. "Was anyone in the bus?"

"No." Holt shook his head, and a tiny bit of relief crept in. But she still didn't know what she needed to.

"Where are they, then?" she said to the universe at large.

Preston cleared his throat. "We don't know. Nothing has come up at the hospitals or police stations yet."

"Maybe they're just laying low," Cady suggested, hoping more than believing. She could see why Kyle might have extra reason for doing that.

"Maybe," Preston said, but his tone gave away that he was trying to be soothing. "We've reported her missing. Given the state of the bus, and yesterday's drama, the police are likely to get an investigation started at the earliest opportunity."

Well, this was no time for soothing, or waiting. Without anyone's numbers, she needed to get online and send direct messages via Twitter and Facebook. And she needed to be on the spot, on the streets, looking. She stood up again.

"I have to get back to the city." She looked down at her wrinkled dress. "Maybe I should borrow an iron."

"Bee's coming," Holt said. "If all your clothes are ruined in the bus, you'll need new things. She'll be here soon to take you into Santa Almendra for whatever you need."

"That's kind of her." Then she realized that Holt must have phoned her to arrange it. "And of you. I have my wallet, thank goodness."

"No, this is on me," Holt said, taking his own wallet out of his pocket. "Save your money for the big things."

She looked at the credit card he slid across the table. Yesterday, she'd felt reluctant to ask for his help, given how ambivalent she was about him after the disturbing revelation from Mrs. G. But there at the police station, she hadn't had a lot of choice. With Bee's contradiction, and then his denial last night, she'd been struggling to work out who she should believe about the abortion. Right now, though, that question wasn't the biggest issue. Finding her sister was. It over-rode everything else. But taking his money wasn't like accepting his help to find Shelby—who was his daughter, as well as her sister, after all.

She shook her head. "Thank you. But I have plenty already. Thanks to you."

"Just say yes," he said. "I haven't been able to do much for you over the years."

She hesitated, aware that Preston was watching. Arguing any further would be ungracious. Okay, the truth was she was turning him down because of the abortion— but that was a whole other thing to figure out. In the meantime, every minute they spent not looking for Shelby was another minute wasted. She gave in. "Well...that's very kind. Thank you."

He nodded. "Have some breakfast. We're going over to my office to make some phone calls. Once you've got what you need with Bee, the best thing you can do is stay here safely. We'll find her."

"We will," said Preston, his voice as authoritative as the pinstripes on his suit. "Leave it to us."

She had no intention of sitting here, miles away, while Shelby was somewhere out there in San Francisco. Last night, she was worried in a mid- to high-level way. In the back of her mind she knew that Shelby was feisty enough to handle herself in all kinds of situations. And after their argument, she might even be ignoring Cady's calls on purpose. But this morning, the news about the destroyed bus kicked her worry up to a new level of alarm. And what the hell was she going to tell their dad?

She reluctantly sat back down and took a croissant from the plate Holt held out. "Thank you," she said. But what she really meant was, *there's no way I'll be leaving it to you.*

They excused themselves, leaving her at the table. She forced herself to eat while she waited for Bee, but every mouthful seemed to have jagged edges as she swallowed. She slugged down some strong coffee. There was only one place she wanted to be—back in San Francisco, searching for Shelby herself. For all the times they'd argued, and fought, and wished the other would just get lost, they knew—didn't they?—that their twinny sisterness trumped everything else. Especially now they were facing a genetic fate they'd dreaded. It was hard enough to get her head around the world without her mother. The world without her exasperating, maddening, tiresomely contrary sister was unimaginable.

★

Bee arrived not long after, and found Cady waiting on the porch, antsy and unable to sit down. As they said hello, their previous uncomfortable goodbye seemed to be still echoing around them. Walking to the car, Cady had to say something.

"About Mrs. G…" she tentatively began.

"Let's not," Bee said. "Let's just concentrate on getting

252

you sorted, and your sister back." Her voice was definite, practical, but gentle.

"All right. Thank you so much for this. It'd be great to get it done as fast as we can—I just want to find her."

"I know. We all do. And if anyone can make it happen, it's Holt and Preston. They're a formidable team—and they won't let the police slack off."

Cady nodded. She didn't mention that she fully intended to scoot back to San Francisco herself as soon as she could. Although she was yet to figure out quite how she'd get there.

"I brought you a spare suitcase of mine—I figured you'll need one."

"Oh, thank you! That's really thoughtful."

Bee shrugged. "It's not fancy, but it'll get you through."

As they drove the short distance to town, Cady told Bee firsthand what had happened the day before. Even the edited version was enough to make her eyes widen. As Cady recounted the story, leaving out the condom wrapper and the meth pipe, she became even more sure Kyle would be staying out of view on purpose. Any police questioning might uncover things he'd rather keep hidden.

"What a disaster," Bee said. "But I'm *sure* we'll find her."

"I hope so." She sighed. "I need a phone too—mine's somewhere out in the streets. I suppose I can claim it on my insurance."

Bee nodded. "We can grab you a phone when we're at the pharmacy, keep you going in the meantime."

In Santa Almendra, Bee found a parking spot and they walked along to the pharmacy. As soon as they came through the door, the eager pharmacist was upon them.

"Hello again!" he welcomed Cady enthusiastically. "And hello, Bee. How are you? That rash clear away all right?"

"Hello, Roger," she said. "Yes, I'm fine now, thanks. Got tangled up in poison oak trying to catch one of the neighbor's horses," she explained for Cady's benefit.

Cady winced. "Ouch."

"A bit of hydrocortisone does wonders," Roger said confidingly.

Bee changed the subject. "Cady has just come in for a few things."

"No sister today?" He looked around as though expecting Shelby to pop out from behind a display rack.

"No, not today," Bee said firmly, dissuading him from any further questions.

"Oh, well..." He tried another tack, addressing Cady again. "Did you meet Mrs. G yet? She hasn't been well, you know. She's on her second round of antibiotics."

Cady and Bee looked at each other. "She seemed okay when we saw her in the library," Cady said.

"You did see her! That's good. Well, she must have had a relapse. I hear she's tucked up in bed."

A relapse. Cady sincerely hoped that didn't have anything to do with their encounter. If she was as fragile as people said, maybe that would have been enough to knock her sideways. She hadn't *seemed* like that kind of character—but then a few minutes wasn't enough to reveal the pressure points in a person's heart.

"Maybe you should go and visit her," he persisted.

"Maybe," Bee said abruptly. "Now, where would we find a mobile phone?"

As they emerged back into the street with Cady's supplies, Bee let out a muffled scream. "He is *so* insufferable! Goddamn busybody. He knows full well the story about me and Cady. Mrs. G, I mean. He just loves to stir things up."

"It's not very professional," Cady said. "What if you had something really personal wrong? Would he tell everyone that?"

"Probably not," she conceded. "Not if he wanted to stay in business. Come on, let's get you a few things to wear."

As she hurriedly tried on jeans and tops and dresses in the town's surprisingly good little boutique, Roger's words kept running through Cady's head. Maybe she *should* go and see Mrs. G. Not with Bee, obviously. But if she and Shelby had anything to do with this relapse, maybe they owed her a visit to smooth things over. When they found Shelby—she doggedly stuck to when, not if—they could go together. The first priority, though, was to find her, and make sure she was okay. If Preston Bridges was as good a detective as he was attorney—or if he knew the right people, as he said he did—hopefully it wouldn't take long. Meanwhile, she'd be out there doing her bit. And then, after she gave her sister a hug, she'd give her that major, kick-in-the-pants wake-up call she so richly deserved.

Chapter Thirty-Two

B ack at the house, Cady thanked Bee again for her help. Then she paused before she got out of the car. "Would you like to come in?" she asked.

Bee shook her head. "No, I don't think so. I'll leave you to it. You all need to concentrate on finding Shelby."

Last time they were here, Cady would have insisted. It was so tempting to try to re-engineer that thwarted love match. Now, though, she wouldn't push a sweet person like Bee together with Holt—not until she knew the truth about the baby. Okay, her view was slanted by the possibility that she wouldn't have children, which had increased with Shelby's test result. Soon, she'd have to face the test too. Despite her own situation, she understood how sometimes there were reasons why a woman would opt for a termination. But as far as she could see, there was *never* any reason for a man to make that decision on a woman's behalf, let alone force her into it. So she let Bee drive away, with a promise to keep her updated.

She came around the corner of the house, struggling with all her things. The suitcase wheels wouldn't run smoothly on the gravel path, so she turned and picked it up, cursing aloud as she juggled it and the phone with her shopping bags. Why hadn't she put everything into it? Damn it, she just wanted to get inside, get the phone charged up, and get back to the city. Somehow.

She was halfway up the wide porch steps before she noticed that someone was sitting in Holt's wicker chair—and it wasn't Holt.

He stood up. "Not very regal language, Lady Cady."

Her heart and her belly leapt in unison as the reality of him, here, washed over her. But just as quickly, images from the day before filled her head, doing battle with her delight. On the outside, he was just the same. The dark hair pulled back roughly, a strand or two always astray. The rock goatee, and another version of the black t-shirt, Kings of Leon this time. That very slight kink in his nose, adding character to an already compelling face. Tiger eyes under strong, straight brows. And, oh hell, there was her kryptonite—his direct, half-amused look that sparked an irresistible, spreading heat in her. Even as she knew she should fight it, she let it swell up, hot and heady. Like an addict, her body craved a taste of that reckless exhilaration.

But for all that, he was different now. She worked to force her body into line with her head. Whatever the susceptible, impressionable parts of her felt, her rational view of him was completely altered. Did he know she'd seen him in action at the flash mob? And had he forgotten their last encounter, before she closed the door in his face? It was a long moment before she replied, her voice wary.

"What are you doing here?"

"That's not exactly a royal welcome." He was unfazed, his tone dry.

She came up the rest of the steps and plunked her things down. "What do you expect? You wanted me to go. You *told* me to. After you totally felt me up."

He gave a laugh. "You felt *me* up, remember?"

She smarted at the sound of his laughter, but ignored his comment. "And then, I saw you rioting with the best of them at the flash mob. What the hell was that?" Was her voice getting posh? Well, too bad. There was another, more important question. "Anyway, none of that's important now. Have you seen Shelby?"

The humor went out of his expression, but he ignored her question about the flash mob. "No, but I think I can help you find her. That's why I'm here."

Something in his words sent up a warning flare. "Wait. How did you know she was missing?"

He looked sideways. "I called everyone afterwards, and the only other people I couldn't get a hold of were Kyle and Shelby."

Kyle too. That came as no surprise. His stupid decisions were responsible for the flash mob disaster—he'd better not be responsible for Shelby going missing too.

"Look, if you know where she is, just tell me," she said. "Holt has his lawyer onto it, and he said he'll be keeping on top of the police. Next stop is the British consulate. So if you have any information, you should just say so now."

"I can't do that."

She threw up her hands. "You can't, you just can't, whatever. This is *important*, Reid. Don't mess me around. I'm going back to the city to look for her myself." She bent to pick up her things, but he took a step forward.

"That's why I came. I hoped you might be here. I was trying to call you, too, but you didn't answer. I thought either something had gone wrong, or you were mad at me."

For a second she enjoyed the fact that he'd been worried about her...then she remembered all the ways she *was* mad at him. "I would have answered! Shelby's more important than *you*." She hoped it sounded as dismissive as she intended. "I lost my phone."

"Okay. Well, I can help. But it needs to be just between us."

"What do you know?" She looked at him. "You're tied up with the protestors, aren't you? You and bloody Curly, Curly and Moe Weasel."

A laugh burst out, but he tamped it down when he saw her face. He started to answer, then stopped, looking over her shoulder to the garden below.

Cady turned around, and saw a small figure in an

orange t-shirt, pink tutu and silver glitter sneakers coming across the grass toward the house. Her dark hair was caught up in a braided ponytail, and she carried a doll under her arm. She was maybe five or six years old, and she looked like the most charmingly colorful woodsprite Cady could imagine.

"Hi," said the little apparition, regarding her with big brown eyes. Brown eyes the color of caramel, or honey...

"Hello," Cady said, smiling, her anger extinguished by the little girl's arrival. Then she looked at Reid, her eyes questioning.

He nodded, knowing exactly what she was thinking. "Cady, may I introduce my daughter Lily. Lily, this is Cady."

"Dad!" Lily admonished him. "You forgot Violet."

"Sorry," he said. "Cady, this is Violet. Violet, please meet Cady."

Lily nodded, satisfied. She held out the doll, and Cady could see it was wearing a t-shirt that matched Lily's own, with a glitter star on the front.

"Hi, Violet," she said. "You girls look lovely today."

"Thanks," said Lily. "We were climbing the tree."

She pointed to the old oak at the bottom of the lawn. It had a ladder attached to the side and a rustic platform tree house in the lowest branches. From Holt's childhood, Cady guessed. Then she remembered something.

"Is this, by any chance, the friend who likes the park with Quetzalcoatl?"

He grinned. "It is, the very same."

Lily tipped her head to the side, regarding Cady carefully. "Your voice is different. You sound like a princess."

Cady laughed. "Thanks. I'm not though, sadly."

Reid came down the stairs and took Lily's hand. "Maybe just a little bit, right Lady Cady? Like you, Lily-Pilly."

Lily grinned, and Cady could see the same mischievous glow in each of their faces. Her heart pinged like mad seeing them there hand in hand, two sets of brown eyes, two matching smiles. Oh, danger, Will Robinson. This secret he'd been keeping was the very one that would hit right in the tendermost depths of her heart. She wondered why he hadn't mentioned Lily before, and where her mother was.

"So, what do you say?" he asked, going back to their conversation. "Do you want some help?"

If Cady had been surprised to see Reid, she was completely thrown by his daughter's appearance. "I do, but..." She looked at sweet Lily, hanging onto her dad's hand, Violet tucked under her other arm. Surely their mission wasn't one to take a little girl along on? But again, he knew what she meant.

"We can drop you with Nanny and Poppa, right Lily? Then Cady and I can go do our job."

"Will Nanny make pancakes?" Lily's face was hopeful. When Reid nodded yes, she pumped a small fist in triumph. "Yes! Aw-right!"

Her delight made them both smile. He caught Cady's eye, and for a moment they shared their pleasure in her excitement. Then she remembered, again, the situation she faced, and her smile faded. Bus burned out, sister gone, help offered by the flash mob rioter she just couldn't get a handle on. While father and daughter made a charming tableau, that didn't erase his potential dodgy dealings. There were plenty of shady guys wrapped around the fingers of their darling daughters.

He saw her expression change, and took the lead. "Come on," he said. "Let's hit the road. Your carriage awaits, in the parking lot." He gave Lily a wink, and she grinned.

Cady hesitated for a moment. "I need to charge this phone up."

"You can plug it in in my truck."

She nodded, decision made. "Okay. I'll just leave a note for Holt."

She headed inside, gathering her things from the porch on the way. Holt and Preston were obviously still over at the office. She felt a bit bad disappearing again, but she wasn't up for any discussion about why she should stay here. If Reid thought he knew where Shelby was, she was on board. She had to be. Okay, she didn't know which 'side' he might be on, but she'd take the risk. It might not be long before she wanted to throw her sister back out on the street, but for now, she wanted her safe—by fair means or foul.

As she threw the shopping bags into the suitcase, and wrote a quick note to Holt in the kitchen, she wondered about Reid. His actions at the flash mob may have veered into the 'foul' camp, but his appearance was still way, way on the fair side. Which was patently *un*-fair. Faced with him, she was all fluster and helpless sizzle, while he seemed to find it all too easy to step away. Well, back to faking her composure. Lucky she'd had plenty of practice.

Before she stepped back out onto the porch, she paused to peek out the window. Lily was pirouetting on the grass below, her braid flying, giving Violet a dizzying ride. Reid was watching them spin, an indulgent smile on his face. All this time, he'd never mentioned her to Cady—and obviously not to anyone on the bus, either. Why would he keep this little poppet a secret? He'd never given much away, even when she asked, but the last twenty-four hours had shown that she knew even less about him than she thought she did. One thing she did know, was that she was considerably more into him than he was into her. She only wished he didn't know it too.

Chapter Thirty-Three

A s they sped along, Lily kept up a stream of questions and commentary from her booster seat in the back. She was a lively conversationalist, to say the least, and Cady kept having to turn away to hide her laughter at the earnest comments. But eventually her eyelids started to droop, and she dropped off to sleep, Violet's hand clutched in hers.

"Tired," Cady commented, looking back at the sleeping cherub. She admired the thick, luxurious lashes resting on Lily's cheeks, still baby-plump. "How old is she?"

"Only five. She's exhausted. It's been a big few days."

She turned back to him. "What's she been doing?"

He was silent, his eyes steady on the road in front of them, and she figured he wasn't going to answer. But then he glanced over his shoulder at his daughter. "I have shared custody with her mother, Jody. I live in Mom and Dad's guest house so they can take care of her when I'm away for work, and her bedroom is in their house. They're like another set of parents for her. The night you and I...talked, she woke up with a fever and vomiting, so Mom came down to get me."

"Oh, no." Cady wasn't pleased to hear Lily had been sick, but she was relieved to know why he'd ended their heated phone call so suddenly. She looked back at the little girl, sleeping peacefully with her head resting against the curved side of the booster seat. "Poor little chicken. She seems okay now, though?"

"Yeah. They bounce back so fast. But I wanted to be there last night, in case she had a relapse. Sometimes they seem okay during the day, but go downhill again at night."

Cady listened to him talking like an old hand at parenting, amazed at this unexpected side of him— confident, thoughtful, and grown-up. She liked it. It shed new light on his ease with Dayna and Brad's boys, too. And maybe on his question about how many children she wanted, as they'd stood outside the bus in their pajamas that night. Then she thought back to the frustration of his sudden, post-kiss departure from Marian's guesthouse. "Why didn't you tell me that was the reason you had to leave?"

"I asked myself the same thing as I was driving home. You're the kind of person who would appreciate her."

She felt her cheeks warm at this compliment. His words were simple, but their implication was greater. Was this the beginning of him letting her into his real life?

"Anyway," he continued, "Jody came and got her early this morning, for her week. Then a while later I got a phone call, from a payphone on the road up north. She was planning to take her back to Canada, for good. But she had sudden second thoughts."

"Can she even do that? Take her to another country?"

"No. There are laws." He shook his head. "And the truth is, she doesn't really have the...temperament for parenthood."

His tone suggested that was a huge understatement, and she could only imagine what might have gone on up until then. "I'm sorry. Sometimes people don't turn out to be what you expected, or hoped." Jeremy, for one. Her mother. Holt. And Reid himself. She was learning that you could never predict what people might have in store.

He kept talking, apparently wanting to tell her more. "Yeah. It wasn't the best period in my life. I thought I'd found one thing, but it turned out to be something else. But I have Lily. She's my best thing. That makes it all worthwhile."

"Thank goodness she changed her mind. But then you had to drive all that way to get Lily."

"Not all that way." He shook his head firmly. "I'd go anywhere, any time, for her."

Damn. That was clumsily said. "Yes, I'm sure...of course you would." She cleared her throat. "I can't believe you never mentioned her."

"I have to keep some parts of my life separate."

This reminded Cady about the other unexpected side of him she'd seen the day before. "Like the part about being a rioting eco-activist?"

He kept his gaze fixed on the road, but she saw his jaw tense. "Yep."

She waited, but he didn't say anything else. "Come on, Reid. What's the story? My sister is gone. I'm involved in this now. Don't you think I deserve to know?"

Her voice was low, but insistent. She could hear the accusing tone, but she didn't care. He had his best thing, safely dreaming about pancakes in the back seat. It was a stretch to call Shelby her best thing, but she didn't have many things left, and Shelby was her nearest now, if not her dearest.

"I'm not going to explain myself to you."

So much for the beginning of something. She pressed her lips together, drawing on some of his restraint. If it wasn't for Lily dozing in the back seat, she'd up the volume a notch.

"Well, you bloody should. You were part of starting that mayhem, and look how it ended. You heard about the bus, right?"

"I did." He handed her his iPhone, ignoring the rest of her comment. "Here. Go online and register your phone. It should be charged up enough now."

"Fine," she muttered. They'd finish this conversation

later. For now, she focused on getting her phone set up and working. Samsung, not iPhone. Shelby would laugh at that.

By the time she figured it all out, they were through San Francisco and heading out the other side, toward the Golden Gate Bridge.

"Oh," she sighed, looking out and up at the iconic red spans as they drove onto the bridge. The sidewalk was dotted with cyclists and pedestrians, most draped with cameras. There was plenty of fog hanging around the bay, but the bridge itself was in sunshine. While Reid drove on, unmoved by what was everyday scenery for him, she craned her neck, taking in the view from every possible angle. But then she caught herself thinking how much Shelby would enjoy this too, and her pleasure was cut short. Well, when Shelby was back, they'd do all these things. When she was back.

She looked at Reid. Their brief moment of connection, thanks to Lily, had passed. The man of mystery was back in the driver's seat. Could he really find Shelby? And how?

He glanced over at her. "San Francisco's number one suicide spot."

She rolled her eyes. "Really? Did you have to?"

He shrugged, letting a sideways grin show on his face. "Real life."

Speaking of real life…something had occurred to her. "If you want to keep the parts of your life separate, why did you bring Lily to Santa Almendra today, instead of taking her home first?"

His face changed. If he wasn't so tan, she'd swear she could see him blush a little. He rubbed a hand across the back of his neck.

"I don't know, it's…I wanted you to meet her." He met her eye then, and even behind his sunglasses she could see an openness and vulnerability in his expression that she hadn't seen before. Then he returned his eyes to the road. But that one look was enough for her to understand the significance of him choosing to share Lily with her.

"Thank you," she said. That was enough, for now.

They travelled the rest of the way to his parents' house

in silence. There were a hundred things she wanted to know—the story about him and Jody, the reason why he kept Lily a secret, the truth about the three weasels and his involvement in the flash mob, and how he was going to help find Shelby. Some of it was none of her business, as much as she wanted it to be. But some of it she had a right to know. And once Lily was safely delivered home, she was going to find out.

★

With the new phone in action, she tried Shelby's number, which she'd copied down from Holt's phone. It went straight to answerphone again. There were endless comments and questions with the #Flashpointers hashtag on Twitter, but nothing from the account itself. Likewise on Facebook. She logged out of everything, frustrated. If he valued his organization and his followers, Kyle should be saying *something* about the debacle. Where was he?

Soon they pulled into the driveway of an unassuming-looking house at the top of a quiet, winding street. As Reid turned the engine off, Lily woke up.

"Dad, are we home?" Her cheeks were still flushed sleepy-pink, and her hair was mussed where she'd been resting her head against the seat. Cady reached back and picked Violet up from where she'd fallen on the floor, and returned her to Lily's lap. She was a little doll herself.

"Yeah, we're home." Reid's voice gave a hint of the relief he must have been feeling to have her back, instead of heading for the Canadian border.

In an instant, she was fully awake. "Can we have pancakes now?"

He laughed. "Probably. Come on then, Nanny and Poppa will be glad to see you."

Cady watched as he helped a wiggly Lily get out of her seat, and grabbed her suitcase from the trunk. Then they all went down a few steps and along the path that led to the front door. The house looked like it was from the sixties, but had been updated in an understated style, with low plantings along the path and front fence, and a single feature tree on each side of the lawn.

The front door opened and an older woman came out, her heart-shaped face matching Lily's in excitement. She flung her arms out and Lily went into them, full-tilt.

"Nanny, I'm back already!"

"I know! What a treat."

Lily held up her small matching friend. "Violet wants pancakes, you know." She looked long-suffering, as though Violet had been very trying with her demands.

Her Nanny laughed. "Well, if she uses her manners, that's definitely a possibility." She stood back up, smiling at Reid and Cady waiting on the path.

Reid took off his sunglasses. "Safely delivered." His look held all the things the grown-ups would have said to each other if Lily wasn't present.

"Thank goodness," his mother said. Then she held out a hand to Cady, smiling. "Hi. I'm Karen."

"I'm Cady. Nice to meet you."

"Oh! An accent. Very charming." She shot Reid a glance that Cady couldn't not see. "And how do you two know each other?"

Cady held her breath, waiting to see how he would introduce her. "Mom," he said. "Can we at least get her through the door?"

"That's okay," Cady said. "I'm kind of a hanger-on with Flashpoint."

"She adds a bit of class," Reid said. It seemed to Cady that his voice was only half-joking.

"You'll have your work cut out for you after yesterday's disaster." Karen gave her a wry smile. "Come in. I hope you like pancakes."

Lily ran ahead, yelling out for her Poppa. They followed her into an airy, tiled entranceway, then down a few stairs into a huge living room. It was decorated in pale neutrals, but the cushions, accessories and artwork were all in bright, uplifting colors. On the opposite side was an entire wall of windows, looking out onto a spectacular view of green, tree-clad hills. Behind its unassuming frontage, the house was a stunner.

"This is *so* beautiful," Cady said.

Karen glowed. "Thank you. It's been a labor of love, over many years." She adjusted a white potted orchid sitting on a low metal table, turning it just a smidge, then another, until she was satisfied.

"That's a gorgeous table," Cady said. It had a geometric lattice top that shone in the light, and delicate tapering legs with a fine grainy texture.

Karen smiled. "You have a good eye. That's my favorite piece of furniture. It's by a local artist. A one-off. Pewter, cast in sand down at Stinson Beach."

"Wow. Reid's sand sculpture, and this…there's a lot of art going on at the beach round here," Cady said. "Seems very Californian."

Karen and Reid smiled at each other.

"Yeah, we're just a bunch of hippies at heart," Karen said, laughing. "Would you like to see the rest of the house?"

Cady looked at Reid. "Do we have time?" She didn't want to be rude, but this wasn't getting them any closer to finding Shelby.

He nodded. "We do. Go on. You'll probably like it."

"Probably!" said his mother. "Cheeky. Never have boys," she added to Cady.

Cady was glad no reply seemed expected to that. Reid just laughed and made his excuses, saying he had some things to check, and Cady set off with Karen on the tour. The house stepped down in three levels, curving around the contour of the land. Each level looked out on a slightly different vista of hills, trees and valleys. As they went from room to room, Karen told her that the house had originally belonged to her parents.

"They bought it new," she said. "There are years of family history here. It felt strange doing some of the redecorating, as though I was painting over our own stories."

"But you've done a wonderful job." And she had—it

was elegant but still homely, the kind of place you could host a fabulous party, or just put your feet up and watch TV.

They went through the kitchen, where Lily was already supervising pancake making, and Karen introduced her to Paul, otherwise known as Poppa. He gave her a wave and a warm smile with his hello, then carried on stirring as per Lily's instructions.

When they came into the last room, on the last curve of the house, Cady gasped. From this angle, they had a view right to the water, with a glimpse of the city in the distance.

"This really is amazing."

"I know," Karen said. "You can see why we'll never leave."

"No, I wouldn't either."

They stood for a moment in comfortable silence, absorbed in the view. Then Karen said, "I'd better go and see if Paul needs rescuing from our mini Gordon Ramsay in there. Would you like to go get Reid? Lily will be mad if he doesn't eat pancakes with her."

Cady laughed. "Okay."

Karen went over and opened French doors on the other side of the room. "The cottage is at the end of the garden."

"Thanks. See you in a minute, then."

She nodded, and Cady stepped outside. She could see the cottage, tucked amongst trees where the garden angled into a point against the slope. It looked older than the house, a tiny inhabitant of the hills from another era. She crossed the grass, passing a trampoline, a playhouse, and a swing. Lily must have fun on her weeks here. She wondered again about Jody, and what the other weeks were like for Lily.

She came to the front of the cottage, where a well-established wisteria made a roof over a long wooden archway. It wasn't flowering at this time of year, but the leafy canopy formed a whispery green tunnel.

She knocked tentatively on the half-open door, and it

swung further open. "Hello?"

She could hear Reid's voice somewhere inside, so she stepped in. This little hideaway was decorated in a totally different style from the main house. The bottom halves of the walls were paneled in rich wood, and the top halves were painted warm red and hung with countless pictures. Lots of them looked like they could be art from a school-age Reid, and maybe a pre-school Lily. Mismatched sofas and chairs were gathered around a fireplace, instead of a television. Bookshelves took up the whole of the far wall, stuffed with hardbacks, paperbacks, magazines, and all manner of trinkets and mementos. There was no sea view, but to her left, large windows looked out to hills in the distance. It was the kind of place you could just sink into, and never leave. Cady wanted nothing more than to collapse onto a sofa, pull one of the throw rugs over her head, and not come out until everything was over. Until Shelby was safely found, and Flashpoint was back on track, and no one was sick, and she knew what the hell she was doing with her life.

She followed the sound of Reid's voice, and found him in a side room, on the phone. He was talking in the kind of blokey, abbreviated manner that guys use with each other when they're being extra manly. "Yep, sure...Damn, I know...yeah, true, true."

The room was obviously his. It was big enough to have an office space set up in one corner, where he stood by a computer. In the center of the room was a king-size bed, and at its foot a big picture window looked out over the garden. The garden he could see as he lay in that very same bed, talking to her late at night about...she felt a hot flush race to her cheeks. Oh, the things she'd almost said and done. The racy, uninhibited things, that only the new Cady would have done. Then again, maybe the old Cady would have too, under the intoxicating influence of Reid. And the truth was, she didn't know if she was pleased or sorry that she hadn't had the chance.

Right then, he saw her there, and raised one eyebrow, still listening on the phone.

"Pancakes," she mouthed, pointing in the direction of the house.

He nodded and held up one finger, so she made a relieved exit, pulling the door to behind her. For a moment she hovered in the main room, settling her imagination, not sure whether to wait or go back up. She had just decided to go, when he opened the door again.

"Sorry," he said, tucking the phone in his pocket. "Come in. I just had to make sure of our timing."

"That's okay." She followed him back in and waited while he shut down the computer, trying not to look at the bed and imagine him in it, doing whatever he was doing as she was on the other end of the line. Damn, why had she come in here?

Then she suddenly clicked that he hadn't been talking on his iPhone. "Your phone...you have two?"

"Sharp observation," he said, noncommittal.

"Why do you?"

"If we're going to do this, you have to let some things be." He paused. "Is Shelby the kind of person who can keep her cool, and use good judgment in a delicate situation?"

Cady thought about their last conversation, and all the times Shelby had blown her top over various upsets. She'd always been temperamental, but since the diagnosis Cady could see why she might tend to extra combustibility.

"I don't know," she said truthfully. "She had some bad news, and she's not feeling the greatest."

"What bad news?"

Did she want to go there? "She...I just found out she tested positive for Wodarski-Ebner."

"The disease your mom had? The autoimmune thing?"

"Mm." She looked away.

He stepped around into her line of sight, so that she couldn't avoid his words. "You think you'll have it too."

She'd always been good at putting on a brave face, but the truth was there to see underneath, if you cared to look.

"Yes. I mean, the odds are..." She swallowed, pressing her lips together to stop all the things swirling in her head from escaping. None of it was helpful right now. Or ever, really. "Look, I just want to find her. We should get on with it."

He reached out and took her hand. "Don't assume the worst until it's right there in front of you. Then you can smack it in the face."

She laughed, despite herself. "That's your best advice?"

"Yes." He grinned. "And you were supposed to bring your check book this time, remember?"

The reference to that night on the bus brought her up short. That embarrassing night, when she'd spilled her life story and he'd listened so patiently, and then she'd lurched at him in the dark, only to be turned down flat. *I just can't.* Because of her, or because of Jody, or Lily, or some other secret that he was inexplicably keeping? This lovely cottage, his delightful family, their gorgeous house, an innocuous-sounding career in sand sculpture...what needed to be kept secret out of all that? The jarring note was what she'd seen him do at the flash mob riot, and his mateyness with the three weasels. Some people lived other lives very efficiently, getting a thrill from walking on the dark side while others held the fort of children and responsibility. Maybe he was one of them. Maybe the teasing games he loved to play with her were just a part of that.

"Who are you, anyway?" she said abruptly. "Why all the secrecy?"

He kept hold of her hand. "I told you—if you want help, you need to let some things be. Do you trust me?"

She thought for a moment, her fingers warm in his grasp. The man she saw with Lily didn't seem like a game player. He seemed like someone steady and true. But the man she'd seen smashing a rioter into a storefront window was dodgy enough to be the fully certified fourth weasel. The one thing she knew was that she had to find Shelby, and she wasn't going to sit around waiting for the police if she could *do* something. She sighed. "I have to trust you. But why are you even helping me?"

He pulled her closer. "Does there have to be a why?" His voice was low, implication and possibility suddenly heavy in the air.

"Yes," she said, her heart starting to beat faster. "No." Oh hell, was this all it took? She felt like she was teetering next to the bed. If she leaned barely a degree or two to the side she'd tumble onto it, taking him with her and leaving the last of her British propriety in a heap on the floor. She cleared her throat. "Please, can we get going?"

"Yes. We have a pancake obligation to meet and a sister to find. Come on."

He let her go and stepped back so that she could go first, and she left the room, silently berating herself for getting lustfully sidetracked when she should only be thinking about finding Shelby. Shame on her, seriously. But she couldn't resist one last look over her shoulder at the bed. One thing definitely didn't need a why. Given the right time and place, she knew her answer would be a racy, uninhibited, no-reason-needed *yes*.

Chapter Thirty-Four

After a pancake stack each, Cady and Reid said goodbyes all round and headed back into the city. Lily had made Cady promise to come back and tell her all about 'Princess Catherine', who she was convinced must be a great friend. Cady didn't point out that Catherine was a duchess—like Lily, she imagined her as a princess anyway. Lily was less interested in Prince William, although she conceded that being able to fly a helicopter was pretty cool, if only to take his princess to the nearest American Girl doll store. She had her eye on a new outfit for Violet that she was sure Catherine would like too.

"She's such a poppet," Cady told Reid, as they drove down the hill away from the house.

"She knows what she likes," he said, smiling.

"That's a good thing. Strength of character."

"She likes *you*," he added.

She felt a rush of pleasure. That was quite the endorsement. "Well, the feeling is mutual."

"You both have good taste."

"That's a sweet thing to say."

"I'm a sweet guy, didn't my mom tell you?"

She snorted. "Okay, enough with the diversionary

tactics. Now you need to tell me what's happening."

"Okay. I'll tell you what I can." His tone made it obvious that she might not get every answer she wanted, but she launched in.

"Fine. First of all, what's the story with the weasels?"

He looked sideways at her. "You mean Isaac and co?"

"Yeah. The three new guys. Where did they pop up from?"

"Kyle."

She waited. "You don't know anything else about them?"

"I didn't say that." He checked the intersection and made a left turn.

"Okay." She sighed. "How about you just tell me what you already know you're going to, instead of me going through a hundred and one questions and getting blanked on a hundred of them?"

"Good thinking, 99." He shot her a grin.

"I like your casting. But if this was a spy story, I would have shot you by now. Kneecaps at least. Come on."

He laughed. "Okay." Then his tone changed to serious. "I think I know where Shelby is, and Kyle too. It's getting her out that'll be the tricky part."

"Why? Where are they?"

He paused. "Background first. Our Kyle is a real trust fund kid."

"I knew that. Trying to use the money to build his own thing. It's an unorthodox kind of thing, but he could make it something amazing if he does it right."

"Right. And word is, his dad got sick of the unorthodox place his funds were going. He's not on board with social media and online movements and power to the people. He's wanted Kyle to get a proper job for years. And before you came along, he gave Kyle an ultimatum."

"You mean, conform or...the money stops?"

He nodded.

"That makes sense. The sudden need for sponsorship. And..." She stopped.

"What?"

She sighed. "When Shelby and I came back, and we were talking to Kyle about ideas, he was suddenly super-interested in her when she mentioned the inheritance." She screwed up her nose. "I thought maybe I was imagining it, but..."

"But you weren't." He glanced across at her. "And those ideas? I know that 'Home' flash mob was your idea. Why did you let him take credit?"

This again? "Like I said already, it's not about me. Let it go." She looked pointedly out the window, watching San Francisco pass by, no clue where they were going. "Are we there yet?"

He ignored the question, tapping his fingers on the steering wheel as they waited at a red light. "Why are you so attached to them, anyway? There are plenty of off-beat, half-baked movements in California. Why Flashpoint?"

She really didn't want to recall the nights she'd spent sitting up in bed, looking at Flashpoint updates online while she listened for her mother's inevitable call. Dreaming of what she'd do if things were different. Imagining some other, sun-drenched, life. Well, she was here, but obviously it hadn't turned out quite the way she'd imagined. So she sidestepped the question.

"Half-baked? Jeez, disparaging much? You're one of them." Something sank in as she looked at him. "Or not."

He put his foot on the accelerator. "Listen. Here's what you need to know. Kyle needed money for Flashpoint, and he needed money to pay for his drug habit, which you might or might not know about. He got into deep water, and repercussions came calling, like he knew they would in the end. He'll be facing some hard questions about now."

So what she'd seen in Kyle's bathroom wasn't a one-off. "And what's the deal with you and the weasels?"

"Need to know basis," he replied curtly.

"Well, I *need to know* why they took Shelby too."

He relented a little. "The inheritance maybe, if they know about it. Or for extra leverage with Kyle. But that'd only work if he cares about her at all, not just her money."

"That seems kind of unlikely. Oh, shit. On top of everything, she'll be heartbroken."

There was silence as they let this fact settle. Then something occurred to Cady. "Where do the environmentalists fit in?"

"I don't know if they do. They were probably just the inevitable result of Kyle being an idiot, getting into bed with an agricultural chemical company. And it gave your weasels their chance to make a move, in the chaos."

"They're not my weasels, they're yours!" She'd cross the road to avoid those three. "What about the bus, then? Was that them, or the eco-protestors?"

He shrugged, turning into a side street. "I don't know. It could be either of them making a point. I'm sorry all your things are gone."

She shook her head. "That doesn't matter. Things can be replaced, people can't. What happens now?"

"I'm going to convince them to let her go—I hope." He pulled into a parking garage and stopped in a space near the exit. "I think I have enough cred with them."

The image of him flinging the rioter into the storefront window was still vivid in her mind. "Cred? It looked to me like you were fully one of them."

"I'm not." He undid his seatbelt and turned to face her, taking off his sunglasses. She did the same, and waited, but as usual he was giving nothing away.

"Well, it sure looked that way. It probably felt that way to the kid you tossed into the window, too."

"He was no kid."

He looked steadily at her, holding his ground. In the dusky light his eyes were dark, unreadable. She wanted to ask him more, but it was obviously pointless. She wanted to know a lot of things that he was wasn't telling, more than just the details of that day. And then, as they continued to look at each other, she wanted something else. To lean across and kiss him, hard and deep and determined, and force him out from behind that maddeningly impenetrable veneer. Instead, she steered herself back to the most important thing.

"Shelby, then?"

He looked at his watch. "Yeah. A couple of minutes. You stay here and just...be ready. Are you okay driving this?"

She snorted at the implication that she couldn't handle the truck. "Uh, yes." Then she picked up on the other implication—that she might be some kind of getaway driver.

"Is it dangerous? Do you think she's okay?" At this point she didn't give a rats whether Kyle was okay. And if Shelby wasn't, she'd be asking Reid to throw *him* through a window as well.

"I'm sure she's okay."

His tone sounded way too reassuring for Cady's liking, but she had to believe him. The alternative was unthinkable.

He opened the door. "I'll be back soon."

Cady nodded, suddenly feeling sick with nerves. She had no idea what he was walking into, and whether he'd come back with Shelby, or with news she didn't want to hear. Or whether he'd come back at all. He was halfway out the door, but she was seized with a sudden urge to pull him back in, just for a moment.

"Reid..." Her voice was an urgent, uncertain whisper.

He turned and slid back into the driver's seat. In the glow of the interior light, she knew her face showed everything she was feeling inside, the fear and worry and confusion. And the wanting, oh that persistent wanting, sharpened now by the unknown and the high stakes. Holding her gaze, he reached out and put his hand on the side of her neck, his fingers threaded in her hair. The way he looked at her, she knew he could see it all, and she didn't care. Right now, she *wanted* him to know that behind the teasing and flirting was something real. For her, anyway. He leaned closer, slowly, slowly, and she felt her lids grow heavy and her heart pound in her chest again. As his mouth met hers, her eyes closed, and the pent-up wanting of the past weeks surged through her body. In answer to some unspoken signal, their lips parted at the same time, and the first sensation of his tongue against hers set off a pulse of shock between her legs. With a small, urgent sound she pressed closer, wanting to feel more of him against her, frustrated by the arm rests between them. The answering intensity in his kiss sent her lust levels rising higher as she realized that he felt it too. Whether it was pure lust, or lust plus more, she hardly cared. Old Cady, new Cady...no version of herself would be insane enough to pass this up.

Then a car drove past, the roar of its souped-up engine sending a harsh vibration through her already humming body, and reality barged back into her head. Oh, God. How could she be thinking about anything other than Shelby right now? What kind of terrible sister was she, actually? She broke away, forcing herself back to clarity and sending a silent, guilty apology to her sister, wherever she was.

"Shelby," she told him.

He blinked, breathed out a long breath, ran his hand through his hair. She couldn't help feeling gratified that he seemed as overtaken as she was. She quietly stored away the triumph, hoping it wouldn't be short-lived.

He nodded. "I'll be back soon," he repeated, his voice a little husky.

Then he was gone.

Chapter Thirty-Five

The wait was torture. Cady sat in the driver's seat, poised for action, feeling like an extra in a heist movie. She adjusted the seat and the mirrors, started up the engine, then turned it off again. There was only so much getting ready to be done. She waited, alternately thinking about the kiss and trying to put it out of her mind, preparing herself for whatever was coming.

In the end, there was no dramatic scene, no racing away with squealing wheels, smashing through the parking barrier to escape. The two of them arrived back at the truck, walking quietly, and Cady jumped out to meet them.

In place of her glittery, mouthy sister was a different person. Through all her antics with unsuitable boyfriends, family fights, and their mum's death, she'd never appeared as devastated and hollow as this.

Cady wanted desperately to ask what had happened, but all she could say to Shelby was variations on *thank God you're safe* and *everything will be okay now*. She sincerely hoped the second one was true. She looked at Reid as they tucked Shelby's subdued figure into the back seat and closed the door, anxious to know what had gone down. But he shook his head, signaling that questions weren't a good idea.

"I think maybe we'd better go back to Santa Almendra," she said quietly. "Is that okay?"

She'd formed a vague plan to take Shelby to Marian's to regroup, rather than back up to Santa Almendra, then hit the road again. Her reasoning was that getting away from it all would be the best strategy. But it didn't seem like Shelby was in any state to travel, for now.

He nodded. "That's where we were going. She can rest before she talks to the police."

Ah. She'd forgotten what Reid had obviously remembered all along—the police would have to be involved. She hoped Shelby would cope with it all.

The drive back was agonizing. Shelby didn't say a word, just leaned her head against the car window, looking out blankly. There were no tears, but every now and then she pressed a hand to her eyes, as though she was determined to shut everything away, or out.

Faced with the reality of her sister's trauma, Cady didn't dwell on the kiss with Reid. And he was back in inscrutable mode...was that how short-lived the effects of their kiss would be? She sighed and concentrated on sending a text to Holt, asking if she could bring Shelby back. He replied straight away, saying of course yes, and wanting to know how Cady had found her. She looked at the screen, thinking.

"Wait, though," she whispered to Reid. "Didn't you say that if you helped, I had to keep it between us? What will I tell the police? And Holt, and everyone?"

He gave her a quick glance. "I'm not telling you to lie to anyone."

"What does that mean?" Bloody hell, what was she supposed to do? But he drove on, not saying anything more.

"Oh, never mind." She hesitated, then texted back.

> *Finally reached her on the phone this*
> *morning. In one piece but tired. Thanks*
> *again—be there soon.*

Thank goodness for texting obfuscation. His reply came back, just telling them to drive carefully—but she was sure there'd be more questions to answer eventually.

By the time they reached Santa Almendra, it was getting late. Reid took Cady's suitcase while she helped Shelby out of the car and around to the house. Holt, Preston Bridges and Elva came out, the men looking grim.

Elva came down the stairs and gathered Shelby in. "Oh, you poor girl. Come on, you're safely home now."

Cady let her take over, knowing Elva wouldn't be dissuaded anyway.

"I'm so tired," Shelby said in a small voice. At the same moment she wavered a little on her feet, and Elva put an arm more firmly around her waist.

"You need to rest. Let's get you upstairs. There are fresh sheets on the bed."

"I'll be up in a minute," Cady said, and Elva nodded. She watched them go, then turned to the men.

"Who's this?" Holt said, looking darkly at Reid.

"Sorry," Cady said. "I should have introduced you. This is Reid..." Well, how ridiculous. She had no idea what his last name was. She started again. "This is Reid, one of the Flashpointers. He took me to collect Shelby."

There was a round of handshakes then, as Holt and Preston introduced themselves, but the mood was anything but convivial.

"Collect her from where?" Preston asked, in full lawyer mode.

Cady hesitated, just for a nanosecond. "Well, she was with Kyle all along," she said, hoping she could carry off this casual not-quite-truth. Maybe it was better that she didn't know what had gone down—you can't lie about what you never knew.

"Where were they?" Holt asked.

"Um..." She looked at Reid. "I don't know. Somewhere in the city."

"The Tenderloin," Reid said.

Holt and Preston looked at each other. They were obviously less than impressed, poised to ask a bunch more questions. Even a San Francisco newbie like Cady knew the Tenderloin was a less than desirable location.

"I'm sorry, I really should go and be with Shelby," she said, acutely aware of her sister's distressed state. "Thank you so much for having us back again," she added to Holt, who nodded.

"The police will need to talk to her," Preston said. "And to you." He fixed Reid with a laser stare that made Cady nervous, but Reid seemed untroubled.

"Yes, of course," she said, jumping in hurriedly. "But for now Shelby needs some rest and care, and Reid needs to get back to his daughter."

The last thing she wanted was for him to go. Looking at him, the front seat kiss flooded her memory again, and she ached to know what he thought about it. And if he wanted to do it again. And again... But the longer he was here, the more questions would come his way. And right now, Shelby needed her more than Cady needed him.

Reid nodded. "I'll be in touch," he said, shaking hands with the men. Then he looked at Cady. "Take care of your sister."

His eyes communicated more than those few simple words, and her heart leapt. She drank in the silent meaning that seemed to be in his gaze. "I will. Thank you so much again."

There were a hundred and one other things she wanted to say before he left, but under the eagle eyes of Holt and Preston, she played it cool. She wanted to fling herself at him, press her body hard against him to see if she could reignite the car park spark. Instead, she ended up performing an awkward, one-armed half hug, clumsily pressing her cheek against his in an almost air-kiss, and finishing with a pat on the shoulder. She cringed inside at the ungainly maneuver, but made herself follow through with a cheerfully forced, "Drive carefully."

Yeah, that pretty much guaranteed no spark—and it probably didn't fool anyone either. She could feel the heat of a blush on her cheeks. Damn.

Reid just smiled. "Okay. Take care."

She watched him go down the porch steps and crunch along the white pea gravel path with his easy gait. Despite what he'd said about being in touch, with all his secrecy she knew it might be the last she saw of him. And if this was maybe her last look, she was going to make it a good one. He disappeared round the corner without a backward glance, and she closed her eyes for a moment, imprinting the image of his broad shoulders and jeans-clad behind on the inside of her eyelids. Then she excused herself to Holt and Preston and went upstairs, wondering what the hell she didn't know—and what she was never going to find out.

Chapter Thirty-Six

In the bedroom, she found Shelby sitting in a bedside chair while Elva fussed around, turning down the bed and closing the curtains. She dug in the little suitcase and gave Shelby the pajamas she'd bought with Bee only that morning. It seemed an age ago.

"I'll leave you to it," Elva said quietly. "Just let me know if you need anything." Her expression was full of sympathy, and Cady was grateful for her unquestioning, kind practicality.

"Thank you," she said, and Elva nodded as she closed the door behind her.

Shelby got changed slowly, her arms and legs seeming almost too heavy to lift as she pulled on the pajamas. Once she was tucked in, Cady sat next to her on the bed. She had to ask.

"Shel...what happened?"

Shelby sighed and closed her eyes. "Not now." She sounded exhausted.

"Okay." Whatever had happened, she'd find out soon enough—the main thing now was that Shelby was safe. But there'd come a time for questions, sooner rather than later.

"Holt and Preston say the police have to be involved,"

285

she added gently. "You'll need to tell them everything."

"No!" Her eyes flew open and a little of the old Shelby fire flared in her expression. "And you're not going to either."

Oh great, now she had two of them telling her she wasn't allowed to talk. But she definitely wasn't going to lie to the police on Kyle's behalf, and neither should Shelby.

"Why should you protect him now?" she exclaimed. "After what happened?"

"Does there have to be a why?" Shelby echoed Reid's words from earlier that day.

Cady looked at her sister, drawn and ragged, the quilt pulled up tight under her chin. They both knew there was a why, but now wasn't the time to push it. There was always a why, if you dug deep enough, even if your own was hidden under layers of justifications and excuses. She and Shelby were probably better at identifying each other's whys than at finding their own.

Shelby closed her eyes, just a breath away from falling asleep, and Cady sighed and straightened the bedding. In a moment, Shelby dropped off, finding the respite she obviously needed. Cady watched her for a couple of minutes, wondering what she'd been through. Thank God their mother wasn't here to see where her secret had taken them.

★

Downstairs, Holt was waiting for her. He suggested coffee, and she gratefully accepted. She collapsed at the long kitchen table, relief and tiredness suddenly overtaking her. She felt like retreating to bed herself.

"I seem to have magically disappearing and reappearing daughters," Holt commented, as he deftly worked the espresso machine.

Cady looked at his face, trying to tell if he was mad about it. They'd definitely brought a bit of drama into his life. Or *back* into it.

"I'm sorry," she said. "I think we've taken your hospitality for granted."

But he laughed and shook his head. "Isn't that what children are supposed to do? I'm just glad you're both here safely."

He put the coffee on the table in front of her, and she thanked him. "Has Preston gone?"

"He had to get back to his San Francisco office. He'll be back when we need him."

"Okay." She sipped the hot coffee, sincerely hoping they wouldn't need him. Not that he wasn't very nice, behind the lawyerly exterior. But the last thing she wanted was the kind of difficulty that required legal advice.

The next few days were quiet. Shelby stayed in bed, only getting up to eat or use the bathroom. It was shocking to Cady, to see her usually defiant, gutsy sister so withdrawn. She certainly didn't have the heart to administer that kick-in-the-pants wake-up call—Shelby's experience had already done that. What's more, she seemed to be continuing the job herself. One afternoon, Cady sat with her in the bedroom, reading a book from Holt's library and watching her drift in and out of sleep. She suddenly rolled over onto her back, and sighed loudly.

"I've always had piss-poor judgment, and look where it got me." She flung her arm over her forehead and scrunched up her face.

Cady put down her book. "No, you haven't." She paused. "I mean, some of the men were maybe not the greatest, but..."

"Karma, right? All the running around I did, all the men. You think I deserve it."

Cady was offended at this accusation. "I do not think you deserve it! That's not true at all."

Shelby made a sort of *pfft* noise, and Cady stopped to consider it. It wasn't true, was it? She'd honestly had no idea, until she met Reid, how much a man could get under your skin, fuddle your brain, and turn you on. Jeremy had never come close, and before that other guys had come and gone, while she focused on things at home. Whereas Shelby

287

was free as a bird, and willing to throw herself into anything new, leave herself open to all the experiences and sensations she craved. Cady had quietly craved them too, but never had the chance or the courage to pursue it or let it happen. And now she knew what craving *really* was.

Truthfully? Maybe a tiny, envious part of her had sometimes felt that Shelby's fun would come back to bite her on the arse. Ass. Aaass... She sighed, thinking of that last view of Reid as he walked out of her life. That man was walking around with a fine example of that body part, however you pronounced it.

Now Shelby brought her other arm up, covering her face. "I brought it on myself. I know that."

"No. You didn't. And I'm sorry if I've been judgmental. You're braver than me."

Shelby looked at her now. "Except you didn't avoid everything, like I did. I didn't want to deal with the truth."

Cady knew she was referring to their mother's battle with Wodarski-Ebner. She hesitated. "Why did you get tested then?"

"I don't know. To piss you off, probably, and prove that I was different from Mum. She couldn't tell me what to do, and her illness wasn't going to either. I never thought..." Her voice faded, and a few tears crept out, finally breaking through her resistance.

"I'm sorry, Shel. You should have told me. We're in this together, you know."

She rubbed her eyes. "As soon as I knew, I wished to God I didn't. You didn't need to know, when you were in the thick of dealing with Mum."

"Well, I didn't avoid that, but I've avoided the big question. And if you tested positive, I probably will too."

"It's not a certain thing."

"But likely, right?"

"Well...maybe."

There was silence as they each thought about this. Cady knew she should front up and have the test, and face the truth. They were constantly discovering new treatments for all kinds of illnesses—maybe they'd come up with some new thing to help. She told herself this in a soothing kind of inner voice, while completely not believing it.

"I suppose I'd better do something about it when we get home."

She sighed. She could hardly imagine going back now. Despite the drama here, the thought of going back to work and real life in London was totally unappealing. Not to mention being on the other side of the pond from Reid...although it was probably better for Shelby to be a good distance away from Kyle.

"What's the plan, anyway?" she added. "What are we going to do until then?"

"I don't know! I can't think about that." Shelby suddenly veered into sounding angry, as though Cady was being unreasonably demanding. This reaction got her back up, and she felt her patience draining away.

"Well, Holt has been good to us, but we can't just stay here indefinitely, you know."

"Pah," Shelby said, her tone sour. "We're lucky to be here at all. Mrs. G's baby never made it."

"If you feel that way, maybe you shouldn't be staying in his house, eating his food, and using his lawyer." Cady was struggling with the question herself, and Shelby's razor-sharp comment resonated—if it was true. But while it was unproven, and they were here relying on him, the snark was a bit hypocritical. "Maybe we should move on, then."

She huffed, defensive. "Stop pressuring me, okay?"

"I'm not pressuring you! But it'd be fair enough if I did. I need to know what happened. What's the story with Kyle? And what happened with the bus?"

In answer, she rolled over and pulled the covers over her head. Apparently, the conversation was over.

Cady let out an exasperated noise and stood up. "Fine." She knew Shelby must have had a hard time there in the Tenderloin, and that she was still processing the reality of her test results, and hurting over Kyle. She reminded herself how worried she'd been about her sister when she was gone, and how much she'd missed her. God knows why. "I know you've been through a trauma, and you need time to recover," she said, trying to sound sympathetic. "But I'm working in the dark here, and we don't have all the time in the world. I hope you feel better soon."

She waited, but the blanket mound that was her sister remained stubbornly silent. Cady left her to it.

Chapter Thirty-Seven

With Shelby in retreat for an unspecified duration, fussed over by Elva, Cady had time on her hands. Each day, she expected to be summoned for a police interview, but it didn't happen. And each day, she hoped to hear from Reid, but that didn't happen either. After he'd gone, she realized—in an epic face-palm moment—that she hadn't taken his phone number. Talk about fuddled brain.

So, she kept herself occupied while she waited for Shelby to buck the hell up. She borrowed the pickup again, and went into Santa Almendra to get clothes and supplies for her. She was tempted to go and see Mrs. G, but decided in the end that it probably wouldn't help either of them. She phoned to check on their dad, and give him her new number. He was on his way to bed and sounding tired—she'd got the time zones mixed up—so their conversation was short and sweet. She was sorry not to have a proper chat, but relieved that she wasn't obliged to make up some story about where they were. She helped Elva around the house, and learned to make her signature chocolate chunk oatmeal cookies. And she lurked online, waiting to see if anyone from Flashpoint would break the silence. They didn't, although there was plenty of gossip and comment around. She refrained from posting anything, anywhere. What could she possibly say? Even though she knew the Facebook and Twitter logins, it wasn't her place to speak for them—and she didn't want to stir up any (more) trouble. And the whole time, she tried not to think about Wodarski-Ebner, and the truth waiting for her back in London.

Bee came by, riding up to the porch on Rambler as Cady sat with her phone doing some online research into the environmental issues around intensive agriculture. She'd been wondering whether anything could be done around Santa Almendra to lessen the impact of the almond monoculture. It was something to keep her occupied while Shelby was still in seclusion, anyway. Bee jumped down from the horse's back, landing lightly on the ground.

"Hi," Cady said. "It's just us today, and Elva. Holt's down at the office."

"Oh." Her face gave away her disappointment, but she rallied. "Well, I actually came to see you and Shelby, see how you are. I'm so glad she's back safely."

"Thanks, I know. She's sleeping right now." Sleep had been her escape from everything. "But I could use some company. You could help me eat the cookies I made with Elva."

She laughed. "I'm happy to do that." She left Rambler to graze on the lawn, and came up the steps, taking off her cowboy hat. "Did you find out what happened? Elva said Shelby wouldn't talk about it."

"Nope, nothing. It's frustrating, but I'm trying not to feel annoyed about it. She's having a bad time."

"Poor girl. It's great that you can both be here while she recuperates. I know it's been something special for Holt, to have this time with you, even if it hasn't all been ideal."

Cady wondered what to say. There'd been a number of 'not ideal' things lately. The drama of Shelby going missing with Kyle. Her bombshell of the positive test result. And the family drama—discovering their namesakes and the events that happened (or didn't happen) in San Francisco years before. It was hard to begrudge Mrs. G taking to reclusive ways after that. Hopefully Shelby wouldn't go down the same path.

As if reading her mind, Bee started to talk.

"I know you still have doubts about Holt. But you know as much as anyone that family is family, when it counts, and he never had the family he hoped for. Look at this big house." She swept a hand around, taking in the serene beauty of the home and its gardens. "This is a place for a family. You girls could bring it back to life."

"I suppose…" Without a home in England, the idea of this being home was enticing. But loyalty to her dad meant she wouldn't think about throwing her lot in with Holt, even if it was an option. And there was still an unresolved question. While it was just the two of them, Cady decided to lay it on the line. "But what about Mrs. G? She never had her family either. Was that because of Holt?"

"Come on, Cady," she said. "Do you really, truly think the Holt you know would do something like that?"

She hesitated. "I don't know him very well…"

"Well, I do. And I'm telling you, *honestly*, I don't believe it's true." Her voice rose, edged with frustration. "And you shouldn't either. The only person who believes it is Cady Greenwood. I know she must have been heartbroken when she lost the baby. And the guilt, the thinking you should have done something different, must have been unbearable. She paid the heaviest consequences for the wild way all three of us were living. And I'm sorry for her, I really, really am. But other people's lives don't have to be ruined too." She breathed out and shook her hands, throwing off all the emotion. "Now, let's leave it at that."

"Okay." Cady was swayed by that heartfelt testimony, she had to admit. People were complicated, life was complicated, and here she was coming in years after the fact, trying to figure out the truth in the space of days. She could leave it at that, for now. And Bee's steadfast support of Holt was touching. Did he even know what an advocate he had in her? She smiled at the good-hearted woman. "Let's have those cookies then."

The next day, at Holt's insistence, she learned how to shoot a handgun. She was reluctant at first. Where she came from, after all, anyone walking around with a gun would cause a major police alert. But after the events in San Francisco, he was determined, so she gave in and agreed.

He showed her where the gun cupboard was, and where he kept the key, and took out his favorite—a Smith & Wesson .44 Magnum revolver.

"You and Dirty Harry, huh?" Her dad loved those movies.

"Yeah, make my day," he joked. "But it's a serious thing. I want you to learn how to use it safely."

They went out to a field behind the house, where a practice range was set up, and he talked her through it. Holding the gun, she was surprised how natural it felt, weighty in her hands. She really must have watched too many cop shows on TV.

"Remember, keep your finger off the trigger until it's pointed at the target," Holt said as she braced herself for her first shot. "Okay, lean into it...keep a good grip on it."

She grit her teeth, the gun heavy in her grasp, and pulled the trigger. Whoa, baby. There was something in the crack of the shot, the shock of the recoil, the smell of the smoke, that gave her an intoxicating buzz. Something alarmingly thrilling about the sense of power. She looked at him from behind her safety glasses, the Magnum's recoil still stinging her hand.

"I'm ashamed to say how much I liked that." She was pretty sure her voice was over-loud with excitement, even compensating for the earplugs.

He shrugged. "No shame in it. There are people around here who'll talk you to death about the Second Amendment. Sometimes I feel like telling them to just go ahead and shoot me, it'd be more merciful."

She laughed. "But you don't always carry a gun with you."

"No," he said. "And it's illegal to carry a gun in public

in California, unless you have a special license. It's not like we're all running around like bandits. But on private property, here on the farm, I can. And since the Earth Stand people started showing up, I've felt more inclined. Okay, you have five more shots there, go ahead."

So she did. She had no idea she had it in her to enjoy this so much. Turned out she had pretty good aim, too. She was full of surprises for herself lately.

As they walked back to the house, she decided to tell him about an idea she'd had. "Speaking of Earth Stand...has there been more vandalism?"

"There has. We're putting more security in place, but there are a lot of acres to cover."

She paused. "I have an idea to run by you. Something Earth Stand would probably approve of, but something good for the farm too, maybe." With Shelby refusing to make a move, a new project had been taking shape in Cady's mind. Organizing the 'Home' flash mob had whet her appetite for more, and it was better to keep busy than spend her time thinking about certain people...

"Sounds interesting," he said. "Let's put this away, make a coffee, and you can tell me about it."

"Okay. Are you up for something a bit different?"

His blue eyes glittered with good humor. "It's been nothing but, lately."

She nodded. For her, too. Different good, and different bad. Hopefully her idea would be in the good category. She needed the boost, and so did Shelby, and Holt too, even if he didn't know it yet. Whether he deserved it, was another story. Bee would say he did. And apparently the new Cady was the kind of girl who'd give him a chance.

Chapter Thirty-Eight

The town hall was full. Cady sat at the side and watched as the Santa Almendra Resident's Association meeting came to order. She was impressed by how many people were there—the good citizens of Santa Almendra were obviously deeply invested in the effective running of their town.

Shelby had ventured out tonight too, for the first time. A cautious Holt wouldn't leave her home alone, and she didn't want to be there by herself either. They'd caused quite a stir when they came in with him. It seemed like everyone wanted to say hello—whether out of friendliness or plain old nosiness, Cady didn't know. But it was clear from the way people greeted him that Holt was a sort of Santa Almendra royalty, so the girls' arrival was front page, tabloid-worthy news in this small town. Especially given the juicy detail of their names, and the scandalous back-story. She tried to ignore all the glances and whispers as they found seats and settled in.

Bee was there, and Roger the pharmacist, and the librarian from the day they met Cady Greenwood. Cady scanned the hall, but there was no sign of the other Cady herself. She must still not be well enough. Then she

remembered what Roger had said about her reclusiveness—
she probably wouldn't come to something like this anyway.

The chairman banged his gavel, and the meeting was
underway. After the official procedure of apologies and
approving the previous meeting's minutes, they discussed
the possible funding of a second drinking fountain, for the
south end of Main Street. There was much debate over the
location—outside the hardware store, or the post office?—
before a vote decided it. Home handymen and women were
apparently more likely to be thirsty than letter-posters. After
further discussion about a new crosswalk by the
playground, and an oversized sign on the pavement outside
a new café, the chairman announced the next topic.

"Ladies and gentlemen, the next item of business listed
on the agenda is a report from Miss Cady Morrow."

Cady took a deep breath and stood up, and all eyes
turned in her direction. She hadn't been this nervous since
speech day at school. She made her way to the stage, where
the chairman stepped aside from the microphone with a
flourish.

"Thank you for making time for me tonight," she told
him. Then she turned to the residents, sitting row by row.
"It's been a pleasure to meet so many of you. Your lovely
community seems like something very special."

A ripple of approval ran through the hall, and she
continued on with an attentive audience. Obviously, a little
flattery never went astray.

"We're all aware of how important it is to protect our
environment. At the same time, I've learned that the
wellbeing and economic strength of rural communities
depends on cost-effective agricultural practices. With both
of those things in mind, Holt and I have been working on
an idea to tip the scales a little more in nature's favor.
We're going to build a sort of green corridor through the
farm—a bee road, if you like."

She checked her notes. In the last few days, while
Shelby rested, she'd been burning up the internet doing
research, and along with Holt's input she'd formed a plan
she was completely in love with. She'd actually found

herself getting quite fond of Holt too, as they worked together. Behind the silver fox charm, under the ever-present cowboy hat, there did seem to be a genuine kindness.

"Bees in particular have had a tough time in recent years," she continued. "I'd never heard of Colony Collapse Disorder until this week. I've learned—as you probably already know—that beehives are trucked in from out of state every year to pollinate the local almond trees. But it's about more than almonds. They may not register on a company's balance sheet, but bees support whole ecosystems, and without enough of them, the whole cycle of life is compromised. With our bee road project, we're not trying to attract enough bees to replace them in the orchards—too many are needed. But we can make a notable difference by providing suitable environments, and a kind of safe passage through agricultural areas for them and their other insect and animal friends."

Was she explaining it well enough? She wanted to make them all feel as enthusiastic about it as she'd become herself. She caught Holt's eye, and he nodded encouragement, so she carried on.

"So, I'm here to ask for your help, on behalf of the bees and other creatures that make our world work. We're going to start planting this weekend—a working bee for a bee road. It's still a bit hot to put some of the plants in, but it'll be a start, and your help will make all the difference. If this works, it could be the first of many in the area."

She and Shelby would be gone by then, of course, but it was nice to think she was making a positive contribution. Galling though it was, she had to give Earth Stand a little bit of credit for sparking the idea. She wished she could tell Reid about it—he'd probably be happy she wasn't giving someone else all the credit on this one.

"The information sheet should give you all the details you need. But please ask if you have any questions or suggestions. And I hope we'll see you on Saturday."

Roger put up his hand, and Cady nodded. "Hi, Roger. Do you have a question?"

But before he could say anything, the door at the back of the hall opened, and Cady saw Mrs. G come in. Her immediate thought was, *how nice that she's here.* Then she saw the look on her face, and knew that it wasn't so nice after all. She was followed by an older woman, who looked as worried as Cady suddenly felt.

Mrs. G, on the other hand, looked full of fiery indignation as she stood in the aisle and zeroed in on Holt.

"How could you bring them here?" she demanded. "Haven't you done enough, without parading them around town? You always thought you were beyond criticism, but this is disgusting. What kind of sick person names their daughters after their lovers?"

A buzz went around the room as the town realized they had a show on their hands. Cady and Shelby looked at each other, mortified, then at Holt. He stood up, his face set, but then Bee sprang to her feet on the other side of the hall.

"Cady!" she exclaimed. "This is *not* the right time or place."

"Of course," Mrs. G said. "There's never a right time or place to hear the truth. He did away with my baby, but he kept these ones." She looked from Cady to Shelby, her eyes wild. "Why did *you* deserve to live, but not *my* child?"

Up on the podium, Cady hardly knew where to put herself. She knew they were both remembering what Shelby had said a few days ago, about how they were lucky to be here. And they were. Lucky that their mother had formed a secret plan, met Holt, and managed to get pregnant in just a few weekends. It felt wrong to say they were lucky she had cheated on their dad, but that was their own truth. They were, undeniably, wanted. Cady felt terribly sorry for her namesake. She stepped down from the stage, not wanting to be up there for all to see.

"Cady Greenwood, that's enough," Bee told her. "You know the truth, but you've chosen to believe something different all this time. And it hasn't helped you."

"Ha. Really? Well, has your truth helped you? You've pined for him all this time, but you never got him, did you?"

The audience had fallen completely silent, and was listening to this exchange like spectators at a tennis match, back and forth from one side of the argument to the other. At Mrs. G's questioning, Bee flushed bright red, apparently at a loss for words. But then Holt spoke up.

"Cady," he said, in a measured voice. "You're making a scene. Why don't you go home and get some rest? You'll probably feel better in the morning."

Mrs. G snorted and started to reply, but the woman she'd come in with stepped forward and took her hand, shushing her.

"My name is Erin. I'm from San Francisco, and I've been a friend of Cady's for many years, since just before she came home from there. If you can call a place home, when the people there would rather believe a lie than an uncomfortable truth."

Murmuring filled the room as the townspeople took collective umbrage at this comment. But Erin was unmoved. "I'm a nurse. I looked after her when she was in hospital in San Francisco. There were complications after the procedure."

In that moment, Cady could hardly breathe. Holt's expression remained determinedly unchanged, but looking at Bee, Cady could tell she felt the same.

"Complications after the...procedure?" Bee asked.

Erin looked at Mrs. G, questioning. She nodded, so Erin continued. "After the termination. I was working on the ward that Cady was admitted to."

There was silence in the hall as the realization hit. Mrs. G had been telling the truth all along. Holt had lied. To everyone, including Bee. And they'd all believed him—his family, the whole town, even Mrs. G's own husband, it seemed—while regarding her as some kind of crazy person.

Having done what she came for, she turned and left the hall, Erin following behind. The residents burst into a hubbub of voices as the door swung shut. Going down the aisle, Cady could hear *I always thought* and *poor Bee* and *can you believe it?* She didn't want to believe it. Bee was looking at Holt across the room, her face full of confusion. He met her eyes, a laser beam of accusation and questions running between them through the churning noise.

With Shelby close behind, Cady quietly left the hall. As they slipped out the door and into the street, Shelby gave her a look that said, *I told you so.*

"I know," Cady said. "I know."

Mrs. G and Erin were heading down the street. Far from frail, Mrs. G looked in robust good health as she strode along. To Cady, it seemed like there was a certain satisfaction in the set of her shoulders.

"Wait," she called after them. "Mrs. G!"

They stopped and turned, and Cady and Shelby ran to catch up. All the threads of the story were tangling in Cady's mind. First the love triangle, and the abortion. Then her town had turned on her, then she found and lost a husband, and she'd never had another baby. Babies—well, the lack of. The two of them were probably destined to have that in common, as well as their names.

"I'm so sorry," she said. "I really am."

"So am I," she replied, setting off again, unimpressed with Cady's sympathy.

Cady followed. She needed to know more. "Why didn't you tell everyone what really happened? Make them listen?"

"I did, of course!" She stopped in the middle of the pavement, irritated by the question—justifiably, Cady knew. "But I'd been painted as a nut job. I was always kind of eccentric anyway. And yes, okay, we took a lot of drugs in San Francisco. It was just the scene then."

Erin nodded at this. "It's still the scene, depending on where you put yourself."

"Right," said Mrs. G. "But these narrow-minded, small-town people were totally ready to see me according to his story. I was the bad girl in the triangle. And apparently I was so drug-crazed, I recklessly took enough to kill my baby, and to make me completely deluded about what had happened. What was the point in fighting that battle? I could say what I liked, but the town's golden boy would always be the winner."

"I'm sorry," Cady said again, uselessly. What could she possibly do or say at this point?

"Don't be sorry. It was you two who gave me the strength to make a stand. You were the last straw."

Cady and Shelby looked at each other, unsure whether being the last straw was a good thing or a bad thing.

"She's so damn stubborn," Erin said. "I've been telling her for years that I'd come and set these bastards straight." They exchanged a warm look, reflecting years of understanding.

Then, back down the street, people started to emerge from the hall. The meeting must have finished, or been abandoned. Mrs. G saw them and rolled her eyes. Then she turned to Cady.

"Listen. I have some advice for you. You might have my name, but don't be me. If you want to be different, *be* different. You don't always get a second chance."

Cady's breath caught in her throat. Could this woman see right through her? "Okay," she replied.

Then the two women turned and walked away.

Cady and Shelby looked at each other. "Holy *hell*," said Shelby, the drama animating her in a way she hadn't been since her mysterious disappearance in San Francisco. "I knew it. I *knew* it!"

Cady's mind was racing. She'd given Holt a chance. Innocent until proven guilty, right? Until proven guilty. What would they do now?

Chapter Thirty-Nine

They drove home in silence. Holt was grim, and the girls couldn't even begin to think what to say. Mrs. G had said it all. Back at the house, he immediately said goodnight and went up to his room.

Shelby was all for leaving straight away, as usual, but Cady said no. Apart from anything else, the bee road had to go on. It was all organized, the plants were ordered, and—hopefully—people were coming.

Flashpoint's Facebook and Twitter accounts were still sitting inactive, so she'd been cheeky and used them to publicize the first working bee. It would be a big planting, so they needed a big crowd, and if anyone wanted to complain about her hijacking their social media sites, well, they knew how to find her. In the meantime, a little buzz had started to grow online, with people speculating if this was a Flashpoint comeback. Cady let them wonder. After the fun of being with the Flashpointers in Rownville, it felt strange organizing a whole event by herself, and as she worked she wished the others were here too. Especially Reid. But she knew she didn't need them to make it happen. It was a good feeling.

Two days until the planting, and then they could hit

the road again. If they were needed by the police, they could go back to San Francisco. In the meantime, they'd just have to take each day with Holt as it came.

★

The next day, he had already gone when they got up. They sat in the kitchen, going over the plans as they had breakfast. Then they heard Bee's voice, calling a tentative hello from the porch. Cady was more than a little surprised to see her, after the upset of the night before, but she set out another plate and made another coffee.

Bee added two spoons of sugar, then sipped it gratefully. "I didn't get much sleep last night."

"I'm not surprised," Shelby said. "I can't believe you came to see him, after that. He's not here, by the way."

Bee looked disappointed. "I thought I might catch him before he left. How are you girls feeling?"

"Oh, box of birds," Shelby said, the snark heavy in her voice. "Awesome."

"Here we thought our mum was the one who'd done all the lying. I can't believe I'd actually started to feel sorry for him." Cady shook her head.

"Cady, he's not flat-out bad," said Bee. "He's flawed, that's for sure, and he's complex, but he's not wicked. Life is all kinds of complicated, I think you know that now. Please don't write him off."

The girls boggled. "You're defending him already?" Shelby said. "He just showed you up as a fool in public. He showed all of you up."

Bee winced. "Of course I don't like that. But I'm trying to make sense of it. Back then, he had a lot to lose, and he didn't make the right decisions. He'd broken free of his dad, who was so domineering—but as the only child, I think he always knew he'd have to come back and face his responsibilities. On the other hand, he'd had a charmed life, insulated from the world's coldest realities by his money, and by his looks and charm. It was a bad combination. But a lot of water has gone under the bridge, a lot of years of regret." She looked at them, challenging. "What's the statute of limitations on a mistake?"

Cady remembered again what Holt had told them about his trip to London. 'Difficulties at home' hardly began to sum up what it must have meant to the other Cady. He'd said he wasn't young enough to excuse how immature he'd been, and admitted there was no excuse for it then—was Bee really willing to excuse him for it now?

"There's no statute of limitations for Mrs. G, or her baby," she pointed out.

"I know that," Bee replied. "And I don't want to make light of her pain, now that I know the truth. We were friends for a long time, before. But I'm thinking about forgiveness. I need it as much as anyone. And Holt does too."

Forgiveness. Their own mother had died not knowing if her husband and children would forgive her. Cady flopped back in her chair. "I don't know what to think about anything any more. Or anyone."

Their real mother. Their biological father. Bee standing by him despite having every reason not to. Shelby and her plunge from Kyle-induced wildness to broken retreat, and her refusal to say what had happened. Even this new incarnation of Cady herself: half American, part of a whole other family and world. The Cady who was determined to be different, but struggled with the same damn stuff in her head. And then there was Reid, who'd seemed to be one thing, and then...wasn't. And then kind of was again, backward and forward. Along with certain other body parts, he made her head spin in more ways than one. She missed him like crazy, even when she didn't know which version of him she craved.

Maybe Holt was like that for Bee, she suddenly thought. Some people just do that to you. She'd been with him even when she couldn't have him to herself, and after everything, she still believed in him.

Bee watched her as she wrestled with the thoughts in her head. "Holt does want to do the right thing by you."

She paused. "And you know...I'd like to have you in my life too."

Before either of them could reply, she stood up. "Thanks for the coffee. I'll see you on Saturday. Don't see me out, I know the way."

She left them sitting at the table, wondering about forgiveness, family, and who exactly they wanted in their lives, new and old.

Chapter Forty

The morning of Operation Bee Road dawned clear and bright. Cady had no idea whether anyone from town would come, after the fiasco at the meeting. But it seemed like there was enough interest online, so they crossed their fingers and went ahead as planned. Shelby was determined they should leave afterwards, and this time Cady agreed. Forgiveness notwithstanding, it had been an awkward couple of days. No one in the house mentioned Mrs. G or Erin, but they were very much there, as much as if they were sitting in the corner of every room.

The farm workers had put up a marquee the day before, and a hire company had delivered folding tables and chairs, sun umbrellas, a sound system, water coolers, racks full of shovels, and everything else Cady thought they'd need. She hoped she hadn't forgotten anything vital. Holt had insisted on paying, saying it was all good PR for the Santa Almendra brand, and could be covered by their marketing and promotion budget anyway.

Shelby was coming back to herself, so in the morning they both drove out with Holt to set everything up, lay out the information sheets and sign-up forms, and make sure it was all ready and in order for when people started arriving.

It was a beautiful day, and despite the town hall drama, a feeling of camaraderie grew between the three of them as they worked. It felt good to be on the verge of an event they hoped would be something really quite special.

Then a car pulled up, and Shelby looked at her watch. "They're early. They can give us a hand, I suppose."

Then she saw who it was, and her face changed.

Kyle got out of the car, still with the beanie, but looking strangely underdressed without his fur vest. Cady and Holt came out of the marquee and watched as Shelby went toward him, looking uncertain and hopeful and wary all at once.

Wary turned out to be the most appropriate, because once Shelby got close enough, he grabbed her, putting his arm around her neck and holding her in front of him. He'd never struck Cady as a strong person, but it was no contest as Shelby fought to free herself.

Without a moment's hesitation, Holt started toward them, ready to take Kyle on. Irritated by Shelby's resistance, Kyle pulled out a gun. Holt had almost reached them when he saw it, but he didn't stop, just reached out to knock the gun from Kyle's grasp. Kyle raised his hand, then she heard the sickening sound as the butt of the gun struck Holt's head, and saw him fall to the dusty ground, his hat landing alongside.

Shelby let out a scream, which was cut off by Kyle tightening his arm around her neck. Her heart pounding, Cady backed away until she came up against the side of Holt's truck.

"Stand still," Kyle barked at her, and she did exactly that. Shelby looked at her, her eyes wide and desperate as she clung onto his arm, trying to hold it away from her throat.

"All I need is a little help," he said, his tone cool and reasonable as he stepped back from where Holt lay, taking Shelby with him. "It's not much to ask."

Cady stood frozen on the spot, but her mind was racing, trying to think what to do. No one else was due for half an hour at least. Her phone was out of reach in the back seat of the truck, in her bag. She looked around, but there was no sign of anyone. Shit.

"What do you want?" she asked, working to keep her voice steady.

"I just need some cash to see me through," he said. He waved the gun toward Holt, still lying motionless on the ground. "This guy has plenty, but I guess he won't be sharing now. You both have your own money, though."

He gave Shelby a shake, and she whimpered. "I would have had your share the other day, but that asshole Reid got in the way. You were both happy to come along for the ride when things were sweet, and use my networks to push your own event. Now it's your turn to do something for me."

At that moment, Cady knew she would hand over every last bit of their inheritance money to see everyone safe. It didn't feel like theirs, anyway.

Shelby squirmed, her neck twisted the wrong way in Kyle's grip, and he pointed the gun at her head. She gasped and instantly held still. Looking at them, Cady remembered Holt's lesson—keep your finger off the trigger until it's pointed at the target. Kyle's finger was resting against the trigger, just a twitch away from the point of no return.

Then Holt stirred on the ground. As he tried to roll over, Cady could see an open gash on his temple, the blood trickling down the side of his face.

"Oh, for fuck's sake," Kyle said, aiming the gun at him.

"No!" Shelby shouted, trying to pull him away.

Kyle turned to her, telling her to shut the hell up for once, and shoved her so hard she landed heavily in the dirt several feet away. She let out a cry of pain as she hit the ground. At that, Holt began to struggle to his feet. Kyle cursed and kicked him hard in the chest, and he fell to the ground again, winded.

"I don't need you, old man," he said, and lifted his gun.

In that moment, Cady took her chance. There was a clear, cold clarity in her mind. As quickly and quietly as she could, she reached in and took Holt's gun from the glove compartment. Then, as Kyle pointed his gun at Holt, ready to fire, she aimed the Magnum at him. At the sound of her cocking the gun, Kyle looked up, narrowed his eyes, and turned his own gun in her direction. And she pulled the trigger.

Chapter Forty-One

un. Travel. Adventures. A gorgeous man. As Cady sat on the dusty ground in shock, waiting for emergency services to arrive, her mother's words echoed in her head. Yes, her new start had contained all those things. Just not exactly as either of them had imagined.

She cradled Holt's head in her lap, pressing one of the hired tablecloths to his temple. The blood had soaked through the white cloth, but she didn't want to lift it off. He opened his eyes every now and then, but she made him lie still.

"Everything's fine now," she told him. "We've called for help."

Shelby sat with them, holding Kyle's gun, but they left him to writhe on the ground, cursing and clutching his knee, his quiff askew. Cady had tried to aim for his arm, thinking he might drop the gun, but obviously her shooting skills were still not great. Not that she had any intention of touching a gun ever again. For now, though, she kept the Magnum to hand. Better safe than sorry.

"This is insane," Shelby said. "You were *unbelievable*."

"Thanks. I hope I never have to be that unbelievable again."

"No, seriously. That was incredible."

It was kind of nice to have done something to truly impress her sister—just a shame it was something like this. She never would have guessed, in a million years, that she'd go from shooting a water gun the first day she met Kyle at his event, to shooting Kyle himself with a real gun at her own. Thank God she hadn't killed him.

The ambulance and the police turned up at the same time, just as the first volunteers started arriving. Amongst them was Bee and a big gang of Santa Almendra locals. Bee came rushing over.

"Oh my God, are you all okay?" She knelt down and grasped Holt's hand, taking in the guns and his injury. "What happened?"

Where to begin? "We kind of had a showdown," Cady told her. "Holt leaped in to help and got a bash on the head. I think he's okay though."

"Oh, you old fool," she said, but her voice was full of relief. Then she looked over at Kyle, who was being checked by the paramedics. "Who's that?"

"Um...that's my fault," said Cady. "It's Shelby's Kyle."

Bee's eyebrows flew up. "Oh dear."

"He's not *my* Kyle any more," Shelby said emphatically.

Then the paramedics came over to check Holt, and the police were there wanting to interview them. They stood up, leaving Holt in good hands, and Cady got ready to face the music. Never in her life had she expected to answer police questions about shooting someone.

"Could you hold the fort here?" she asked Bee. More and more people were arriving, and someone needed to be at the operations tent to reassure them and coordinate everything. Bee said yes of course, so Cady showed her what to do, and then she and Shelby went with the two policemen.

It was a brief interview. They each told their version of what had happened, and the police officers took their phone numbers.

"We'll be in touch," they promised, as they left for the hospital to question Kyle.

Cady assumed that when they put this incident together with the flash mob riot, they'd come up with a picture that didn't look all that great for him. It seemed so wrong—he had every advantage, yet he'd gotten so far off track. Come to think of it, that could have been a description of Holt, years before. But today, Holt had proven there was something decent at his core, whereas Kyle had revealed the dangerously narcissistic streak that ran deep beneath the hipster charm, and how far desperation and addiction would take him.

When they came back, they found some Flashpointers there too—Gavin and Tino, and Jennifer, but not Alison or Reid. Bee had already made their acquaintance, and now she excused herself, saying she wanted to check on Holt.

"Oh my God, you guys," said Jennifer, as Bee hurried away. "How awful! I'm so glad you're okay. I can't understand how Kyle could do that."

"I know," Cady said, as they hugged. "It was pretty mental for a minute there." She didn't want to say too much, knowing that Shelby had only just started to get back to herself.

"Didn't I say he was a real asshole?" Gavin said loudly. "First time we met you, remember?"

"I remember." Cady stole a look at Shelby. She'd been so hung up on Kyle, and absolutely gutted after the missing night in San Francisco. So much so, she wouldn't even talk about whatever had happened. She seemed to be holding steady now, but Cady purposefully changed the subject. "Is Alison not here?"

"No," Jennifer said. "And I have to apologize to you both on her behalf. I mean, I have to apologize for what she did, because she's not going to. She told Earth Stand about your real dad having all these orchards, because she was pissed that Shelby stole her number one spot with Kyle. And when he made that deal with the agricultural chemical company, she knew that would really provoke them into action. She was mad at you *and* him by then. Oh, and she let go all the balloons at the flash mob. That was just petty. She was so crazy about him, it made *her* crazy."

None of that came as a surprise—Alison had seen them as competition from day one. And Cady remembered seeing the balloons randomly floating away. Well, small things amuse small minds.

Gavin looked at her now. "You'd better be careful. What will she do to you when she finds out you shot him?" As everyone shook their heads, he said, "What? Too early for jokes?"

"Come on, bro," said Tino. "Give it a few more hours at least." He passed Gavin a shovel from the workstation and took one himself, and one for Jennifer.

"This is amazing," she said. "I wish we could've done something like this. It's so cool to really make a difference for the environment. I'm glad you used our accounts to promote it—in a way, Kyle helped you, whether he liked it or not."

"I felt kind of cheeky doing it," Cady replied. "But I'm hoping this planting might start a trend, and maybe get Earth Stand to leave the trees alone here."

"It's all good," Gavin said. "Maybe you'll redeem Flashpoint after all."

"Thanks." She hoped so, although without a leader there wasn't much for Flashpoint to hang its hat on any more. Call it a last hurrah, maybe.

Then Jennifer added, "I have to apologize too. I wasn't very nice to you either, at first. I thought Alison was so cool, being from Hidden Hills and all, and so pretty. But you know what? I found out she's really from Michigan. And I think you're both lovely."

Michigan? Cady actually felt bad for Alison now, if the thought of being ordinary was enough to make her so mean.

"Thank you," she said, smiling back at Jennifer. "You are too."

She allocated them a numbered section of the pegged-out land to work in, and showed them where to collect their plants. There was just one more thing...

"Um…Reid's not with you guys?"

Gavin shook his head. "We thought we'd see him here. He told us we should lie low after the riot, so we didn't say anything online, but then he asked us to come to this. I don't know how he got to be the boss of us," he joked, but Cady could hear the respect in his voice. "Not that we would've missed your event," he added hurriedly.

"Ah, no, that's fine, I just wondered…" Everyone looked a bit sorry for her. Damn, was it that obvious? She shooed them off. "Okay, see you soon," she said. "Work hard! Drink plenty of water!"

Jennifer set off with the guys, but then dashed back for a moment.

"I did like Reid too, you know," she said, making Cady blush. "I mean, what's not to like, right? And Alison had us all set up in her mind, her and Kyle, me and Reid. But I want you to know that we think you're really good with him, and good *for* him. He should open his eyes and see that too."

Then she ran after Gavin and Tino, before Cady could reply. She turned to Shelby, who was looking at her sympathetically.

"What? Don't look at me like that!"

"I thought he might be here too," she said gently. "I know how much you like him."

There was no point in denying it to her sister. She knew her too well. "Yeah, well…we probably won't see him again. And anyway, he's too hot to handle for me."

"What? I don't think so at all. If anything, *you're* out of *his* league. Why do you think he calls you Lady Cady?"

Cady smiled at this staunch defense. "I doubt that, but thank you. And he did prove his knight-in-shining-armor chops when he came and got you out of strife."

"That's true. He's a good one." She sighed. "I'm sorry I didn't tell you what happened. When I realized Kyle was doing drugs like that, I should've stepped away, but I wanted him to be my escape, so badly. And, shame on me, I still *wanted* him. I knew I shouldn't, but I couldn't help it. And when that flash mob went wrong, I was just...everything was doing my head in." She circled a hand on each side of her head, demonstrating her inner state.

"You're only human," Cady said. Now she understood the wanting herself.

"I suppose so," Shelby went on. "But then when we were being held captive, and Kyle was trying to talk me into giving him money, I felt like such a freaking idiot. How could I have got everything so wrong? Those new guys, the bastards—they were dealing, and Kyle was hooked. Apparently he's up to his eyeballs in debt to them, but without his dad's money, he's got nothing to give them."

"Well, he just added to his problems today." She didn't have much sympathy for him. "But how did Reid get you out?"

Shelby leaned against the trestle table. "When he came, the head honcho guy wasn't there, it was just the three of them. He seemed really matey with them, but not like one of them, exactly."

"The weasels." She screwed up her nose.

Shelby laughed. "Yeah, dirty weasel polecat bastards. I guess he timed it that way."

Cady nodded, remembering the phone call at Reid's cottage.

"He talked them into letting me go. Said they'd cause an international incident. He put the fear of Interpol and the entire royal family into them, and I don't know, probably Jason Statham and Daniel Craig combined too. I didn't hear everything, because they had us sitting back to back in the corner like in some clichéd mob movie—but whatever he said, it worked."

"Wow. A smooth talker." So he wasn't one of them after all...but still a mystery. Who was the real Reid?

Shelby nodded. "It was epic. He just walked out with me, and left Kyle behind. No wonder he was pissed off. He must have talked them into giving him one more chance to get their money."

"And we know how that turned out," Cady said.

A late arrival ran up to the tent, and she got him equipped and on his way. Then she turned back to Shelby.

"What about you now—are you okay?" she asked. "I didn't think of it then, but maybe you could've gone with Kyle in the ambulance."

"Are you kidding?" Shelby shook her head. "I wanted to bloody well shoot him myself. But I would've aimed higher. Just high enough…if you know what I mean."

"I know." She laughed, glad to see Shelby feisty again. Her Kyle slump was clearly over. "Sorry my aim was off."

"Maybe you need Holt to give you some more lessons."

"Lessons in what?" The man himself came up behind them, a big white bandage on his temple.

"Holt! You should have gone home," Cady told him.

"No, I'm all stitched up. You can't keep a…" he faltered on the last words, perhaps remembering their reaction to Mrs. G's dramatic appearance at the meeting.

"Good man down," she finished for him. "That's true." In the face of danger, his instant reaction was to step forward and protect them. No one could argue the goodness of that.

"Or a good woman." He smiled at her. "That was some shot."

"It was a complete fluke. I had no idea what I was doing."

The last people arrived to collect tools and instructions, and Cady thanked them as they set off to do their planting, laughing and chatting. When they were gone, Holt said, "Can we talk?"

They each found a folding chair, and sat in the shade of the marquee. He rubbed the back of his neck as the girls looked at him, waiting.

"About Cady Greenwood," he said. "I was wrong. I freaked out and did something terrible. Then I lied to my parents, because I was weak, and afraid of losing everything. I never thought I wanted what they had for me, until I thought I'd lose it. And once the lie was begun, it had to be carried on. I was never strong enough to speak out, so I let it continue. I was the lucky one—people believed me because they wanted to. I owe Cady

317

Greenwood an apology the size of Texas."

When he finished, there was a moment of silence. Then Shelby got up, went over, and gave him a hug. Coming from her—the toughest nut to crack—that one gesture said it all. He passed a hand across his blue eyes, shining with emotion below the bandage.

"Now that Cady has shot someone, do you think we'll need that lawyer of yours again?" Shelby asked him. "He was pretty cute."

He and Cady laughed, and Shelby shrugged. In all the craziness, something was back to normal. It was a good sign.

Then Bee came over, and tentatively lay a hand on his shoulder. He reached up and covered it with his own, a wordless gesture that spoke volumes. The girls left them together on duty, and maybe on the mend, and went off together to make a difference.

Chapter Forty-Two

By the time everyone came back from planting, dinner had arrived. Burgers, tacos and burritos, Thai and Korean, Pacific fusion—Cady had been lucky to find a world's worth of food trucks willing to make the trip from San Francisco. The dusty, thirsty volunteers thronged to get their food, and then sat at the tables or on picnic blankets enjoying the atmosphere and the music. As Shelby had started to come out of her self-imposed bedroom retreat, she'd taken charge of making a compilation, and now she watched with satisfaction as people chilled out to her selection. As well as lots of Santa Almendra locals, Marian had turned up with her man, relieved to see Shelby safely back. Cady had forgotten to phone and tell her, but she'd seen the Operation Bee Road event updates on the Flashpoint Twitter feed, and figured it out.

As the sun started to go down, Cady took the microphone.

"Thank you all so much for being here today. You've worked so hard. We promise to take good care of your plants, so that when you come back next time you'll see a growing, thriving little ecosystem."

As applause rang out in the evening air, she felt a

sudden sadness. She wouldn't be the one looking after these plants. She'd be back in grey old London, probably at the bank. Still, it was nice to think that this would be here, a legacy of their visit. And maybe they'd be back one day to visit. They had a way to go, but things were different now, with Holt. They had Kyle to thank for that, at least.

She'd thought hard about how to end the night in a beautiful but eco-friendly way. After the flash mob riot debacle, she didn't want there to be a single thing for the online critics to pick on. So they'd set big battery-operated bubble machines in the center of the picnicking volunteers, asking the nearest people to turn them on when they got the word. Then, while everyone was eating and hanging out, she and the other Flashpointers handed out bubble mixture in little recyclable containers. Now, as the expectant crowd waited to see what would happen, she continued.

"We hope the flight of the bumblebees, and the honeybees, will be made a little easier by what we've done today. Every great journey starts with a single step, and we've made one here together—thank you for that. Now let's send up a little magic."

She nodded to the volunteers, who switched on the bubble machines, sending hundreds, and then thousands, of bubbles into the air. At the same time, Shelby threw a switch in the tent, and 'The Flight of the Bumblebee' immediately burst into the evening air, the music casting a dramatic, whimsical spell. Lights set around the edge of the picnic area shone into the sky, flashing multicolored beams that caught and reflected the shining bubbles as they ascended ever higher.

The crowd got to its feet, unable to resist the racing, soaring music and the temptation to blow—and pop—bubbles. Some little ones were dancing wildly, waving their arms and running like crazy on the spot, keeping up with the frenetic pace of the music. The unbridled enjoyment in their shining faces was infectious, and Cady laughed too, her heart singing with the joy of creating such an uplifting moment. She'd come a long way from watching the world on her laptop in her tiny bedroom. As the bubbles glided heavenwards with the music, shimmering with kaleidoscopic colors into the dusky sky, she thought again of her mum. She would've loved this—and hopefully been proud. She opened her bubble mix and blew a string of bubbles into the air, sending up love and thanks along with the little globes of sparkly magic. As they rose, she let herself imagine Anne looking down, approving.

Amongst it all, she spotted Bee sharing a tender moment with Holt, and felt glad for them. They probably had a way to go, to sort things out, but maybe it was a new start for them too.

Then she saw someone else, coming toward her through the happy commotion. Reid. He was smiling, and she couldn't stop the answering smile that completely overtook her face, along with the heart-pumping rush of seeing him again when she'd been convincing herself to give up. In the last few steps he took, their eyes said everything their words never had, and she knew the game had changed.

As the swirling, intoxicating music came to an end, and the volunteer army cheered and applauded, he gathered her up. She dropped her bubble mix and put her arms around his shoulders as he lifted her off her feet, crushing her close. He was warm and tall and strong and, oh God, he felt better than anything, ever. She pressed into the side of his neck and breathed him in as he squeezed her tight. Then he set her back on the ground and they looked at each other, their faces millimeters apart.

"You're okay," he said.

"I am now," she replied.

And, as she knew he would, he kissed her.

She flared with pure lust in the kiss, hot and hungry and bad and oh so good. But the feeling between them now was the lust-plus-more she'd yearned for in his car that day. All the teasing, the banter, the wondering, the holding back and the letting go of the last weeks tangled in her mind as his fingers tangled in her hair. She let herself sink into the blurry-hot bliss of lips and tongues, her breasts pressed against his chest, exhilarating in the almost painful drive to thrust her hips up and against his, as close as they could meld in public without getting her arrested again. As she'd done that night on the bus, a hundred years ago, she lay her hand on the curve of his neck, and felt the racing of his heart in the pulse point at his jaw. It matched her own, and this time she knew there would be no pulling away, no *I just can't.*

Then, from somewhere far away, back there in reality, she heard Shelby calling her name. She reluctantly drew back, only letting her lips part slowly from his, leaving him with a last tease of her tongue that drew a small, satisfying groan. Oh, the power. After all this time, it was mind-blowing to realize he was feeling everything she'd been trying to hide.

Then she turned as Shelby yelled out to her again. "What?" she called back, trying not to break the spell. Seriously, that girl was so self-absorbed sometimes. There were some things you just didn't interrupt.

"Come here," Shelby called, her phone in her hand. "It's Dad! Come *on*."

"Oh, for...okay." She looked apologetically at Reid, gratified to see his eyes still hazy with desire too. "Sorry, I'd better do it. I haven't had a proper talk to him in a while, with everything that's gone on."

He nodded, and she snuck in one more kiss for good measure, pressing her lips to his as though there might not be a chance for another, ever again. Now he was here, she didn't want to stop. But they went over to the tent, popping bubbles as they went, and she held out her hand for the phone.

When Shelby didn't pass it to her, she said, "Hey, I do want to talk to him."

Then she took in Shelby's shell-shocked expression.

"You can't talk to him," she said, her face pale. "He's dead."

Chapter Forty-Three

S ummer was waning, and it was much cooler in England than in California. In the little attic room at Aunt Netta's house in Broadstairs, Cady tugged on skinny jeans and a t-shirt, a bit crumpled from her suitcase. For a moment she looked at herself in the mirror, the black tee making her think of Reid's endless wardrobe of black band t-shirts, printed with The Ramones, or Social Distortion, or The Black Keys. He was seriously hot in them. Seriously hot for someone else to appreciate now, unfortunately. Yet again, she closed her eyes and relived the bee road kiss, that short-lived moment of bliss when what she'd craved was hers.

The trip back had been a long, torturous blur. After the phone call with news of their father's heart attack, Holt had told them not to worry about a thing, just do what they had to do. So they'd said hurried farewells to everyone, and left the fun behind. They went back to the house and booked flights, leaving for New York at six the next morning, then on to England. Shelby insisted on going immediately and waiting at the airport, so Reid drove them down to San Francisco. He kissed her goodbye, but she was so knocked sideways by her dad's death, coming on top of the day's

Kyle drama, that their connection seemed broken, and he'd said nothing about seeing each other again. Well, why would they?

As the plane took off, leaving American soil behind, the irresistible g-force that pushed her back in her seat also pushed the last reserves of strength out of her. Finally, inconsolably, she cried for everything—for the loss of her mother and father, the confusion of figuring out her 'new' family, Shelby's diagnosis and the illness lurking in her own future, delayed shock from the violent showdown with Kyle, and goodbye to the man she desperately wanted as part of her new start. When they'd gone back to the bus for her 'Home' flash mob idea, she'd cautioned herself against falling hard enough for someone that goodbye would be a painful wrench...but it had happened anyway.

She would've been grateful for his steady company at the funeral yesterday. It had been unreal to go through it all over again so soon—the same people saying the same kind things, but this time about their father instead of their mother. And in every respect, just as much as ever to Cady, he *was* their father. He always would be.

It had been strange not going back to the Peckham Rye house after the funeral. Instead, she and Shelby had taken a late train back to Broadstairs with Aunt Netta, grabbing a dinner of coffee and slightly aged-looking paninis at Victoria Station. On their first night back, after a long, uncomfortable plane trip made longer with delays, they'd been too exhausted to talk properly, instead falling into bed and mercifully dreamless sleeps. So last night, after the funeral—sitting up late with a jug of Pimm's and lemonade for old times' sake, a small dog nestled on Aunt Netta's lap—they'd caught up, telling her about everything that had happened in the States over the last few weeks. When they'd talked about it on the plane, Shelby had asked Cady not to mention her test results yet—having only just admitted the truth to herself, she was still getting used to it—so they left that part out for now. Then Aunt Netta told them what she knew about Anne's time in London.

"I was very surprised to see the detective," she said,

"but I knew it was time. If she'd already told you part of the story, Cady, she must have known you'd ferret out all the details eventually. I think she wanted you to, really. It weighed on her terribly, from the day you were born."

The facts Aunt Netta had weren't any more than they already knew from the private investigator—but somehow hearing that their mother had struggled with guilt made Cady feel better. She'd struggled with it herself, keeping the secret first from Shelby, and then from their dad. And along with her grief, she was wrestling with the guilt of not being there for her dad's last weeks.

"I was so busy chasing around after Lawson Holt, I missed my last days with him." She felt sick with the regret.

"You couldn't have known that," Aunt Netta said gently. "And you know, he wanted you to have an adventure."

"I know. But it's such a slap in the face for him that I was secretly running around with my other father."

She dropped a slice of orange into another Pimm's and lemonade, and handed it to Cady. "Really? Running around?"

"Well, you know..." The sentence petered out. "He was just always there for me. And in his last few weeks, I wasn't there for him."

"You were *always* there for him. You were his everything, both you girls. His best thing."

At this, Shelby burst into tears, the burden of the last days, weeks and years too much all over again. Cady took her hand. That was exactly what Reid had said about Lily—his best thing. Not having her own best thing was maybe something she'd just have to get used to. She squeezed Shelby's hand. They might be chalk and cheese, but for all their differences, they'd been through so much together. They *knew*. And they'd be okay, whatever happened, as long as they stuck together.

Aunt Netta got up then, tipping the dog off her lap, and took an envelope from the oversized French dresser in the corner of the room.

"Last week, your dad asked me to go and see him at

325

Ingleside. I think he must have known that he wasn't well. He gave me this—he wanted to be sure I was the one to give it to you."

As Cady took the envelope, she remembered how tired he'd sounded on the phone. "We should have been here."

Aunt Netta held out an old-fashioned letter opener. "Just open it."

She carefully slit open the top of the envelope, took out the letter, and started reading...and could hardly believe the words on the page. As she absorbed what her dad had written, she was overtaken with a wave of emotion—disbelief, amazement, gratitude, and wonder. She handed it to Shelby, who read it with eyes wide.

"He knew," Cady told Aunt Netta. "He knew all this time, and he never said anything."

Aunt Netta nodded. "I did have my suspicions."

Cady put her hand to her forehead. "I can't even...he let her think she'd kept the secret, that whole time."

"He really loved her," Aunt Netta said. "And you."

"Wow." For once, Shelby was lost for words.

Cady took the letter back and quoted from the last paragraph, the slightly formal language doing nothing to lessen the feeling in what he'd written. "However we define 'fatherhood', I want you to know that I will always love you, and I always have. Of course we've had ups and downs, just like any fathers and daughters do. No matter what, you are my girls, and nothing could have changed that. And now you are free to discover who you really are."

On the last sentence, her voice broke, and she shook her head. "I can't believe it."

"I wonder if he guessed that we knew," Shelby said. "And how did he find out himself?"

Aunt Netta held up her hands. "I never said a word, I promise you."

They talked and talked, trying to figure out how he could have known. Cady wondered if blood types might have been a clue—they both had the more unusual B blood type. But however he found out, they were stunned by the way their mother's secret had somehow turned back on itself, and become not secret after all. They tried to imagine what he must have gone through as he processed the knowledge, and came to the decision not to say anything. Amongst all the secret keeping, they never would have guessed there was one more—their dad keeping his own secret, of knowing their mother's.

"It says a lot about the kind of man he was," Aunt Netta commented, and they had to agree.

Later, all talked out and sleepy with Pimm's, they lay in the attic beds like they had as children. After the huge beds in spacious rooms at Santa Almendra, Cady felt like they were sleeping in a dollhouse. With the sash window pushed up slightly she could smell salt on the air, the sea-tang of happy childhood memories. It was comforting. In the quiet, her mind wandered back across the Atlantic, and she wondered what was happening now in San Francisco.

"Do you miss him?" she asked quietly.

She heard Shelby turn over. "Dad?"

"No, I know you miss *him*. I do too. And I'm still completely blown away by everything. But I meant Kyle."

Shelby hesitated. "Yes. I shouldn't, but I do." She sighed. "Or really, I miss the person I thought he was."

"I'm sorry I shot him."

"Oh God, I'm sorry too. But let's face it, he deserved it." She laughed. "Bet you never thought you'd be saying those words to me."

"No, never." She had to laugh too. "I suppose it helped get us back on better terms with Holt, anyway."

"True."

For the price of Kyle's ruined kneecap, they'd left the States on steadier ground with Holt. Shared disaster had a way of bringing people together. Maybe they'd never be really close, in distance or emotions, but they were family. He and Aunt Netta were pretty much it now.

"What about you?" Shelby asked. "Are you missing Reid?"

She looked toward the narrow window, where the moonlight shone in. It would be hours before he got into his big bed in the cottage. When he looked out his own bedroom window, would he think of her too? Or would he sensibly move on, instead of wasting time thinking about someone a continent and an ocean away? Probably.

"I am missing him," she admitted. "Quite a lot."

He'd believed in her, and wanted her to have credit for her ideas. And he made her realize that she should give herself credit too. She knew now that even though life has countless contradictions and complications, and people are compelled to layer all kinds of different adornments and disguises and secrets on top, the truth of anyone lies beneath all that. The real person. And having been around the world, organized two big events, lost a father and a mother, discovered a new family, shot a man (heaven help her), and survived it all, now she agreed with Reid: she was a person worth giving credit to. What started out as 'fake it 'til you make it' had become her reality.

So now it was the day after the funeral, the day after her dad's belated bombshell, and she was new Cady, in old Cady's territory. She looked at herself in the mirror again, smoothing her t-shirt over her waist. Reid would probably be in bed now, *not* wearing a black t-shirt. She smiled at the thought. Then she pulled the tee over her head and threw it back in her suitcase. Instead, she put on a dusky pink top, then slid her feet into gold flats. She had to move on, even though she wanted so badly to be in that bed with him, getting up to no good in the cottage under the hill. Snuggling on the couch in the cozy living room, making pancakes in the big kitchen, bouncing with Lily and Violet on the trampoline...

Well, she'd hold on to the good stuff, take it with her, and use it as fuel. After all, her new start didn't end when they took off from San Francisco. Whatever this phase of her life held, she was strong enough to face it. Medical tests, a job that wasn't at the bank, a parentless life with unknown challenges ahead—fear and doubt could kiss her aaass. Learning her father's secret-inside-a-secret had set her free a little more too—the guilt of not telling him was gone, and it was a huge relief. She shook out her hair, put on some of Shelby's lip gloss, and went downstairs.

"Sorry I slept in," she said to Aunt Netta, who was washing her little dog in the kitchen sink. "Jet lag and Pimm's. Where's Shelby?"

"Ergo! Keep still." She wiped dog shampoo from her nose with the back of her hand. "Sorry, my dear. She went out earlier, for a walk."

"Oh, okay." A walk? Shelby wasn't the walking kind....but maybe she was taking some time to think about everything herself. She helped herself to tea from the pot, and dropped two slices of bread into the toaster. Aunt Netta turned her attention back to the wet and scraggly dog, and Cady turned hers to breakfast. Well, brunch really, seeing as it was just hitting eleven o'clock.

Just as she was finishing her toast and tea, a text came from Shelby.

> *Down at Viking Bay being a kid again. Feel like Mum and Dad are here somehow. Come and meet me?*

Oh, nice idea. Sweet Viking Bay, lying like a postcard beach below Broadstairs town, was the scene of her favorite childhood reminiscences. She texted back yes, put her mug and plate in the dishwasher, and said goodbye to Aunt Netta, who was busy attempting to dry the squirming dog with a hairdryer.

It was only a short walk down to the coast. She crossed the promenade at the top of the cliff and went down the steps to the sand, breathing deeply, letting the sea air flood her lungs and fill her spirits. At the bottom, she slipped off her shoes and dug her toes into the sand, looking around for Shelby. It was quieter than their childhood visits in the height of summer, but there were kids playing, and people walking dogs, and a few swimmers braving the cold sea. The curve of the bay, the row of huts, the stripy beach shelters, all overlooked by the town sitting high above, were just the same as they'd always been. No garish beach developments marred the quaint British scene, and she was glad that it wasn't being ruined. It was the perfect place to remember her parents, letting echoes of their happy family wash over her like waves. And it *was* happy, despite the underlying untruth. No one could take that away from them.

Then, further along the beach, something caught her eye. Someone had built a creation in the sand. A classic castle, but way bigger than the usual bucket and spade variety, with turrets and a moat and charming shell-and-feather decoration. Her heart squinched in her chest, and she sighed. That was just the kind of thing Reid would build, probably. Damn. There was half a world between them, but she had the feeling she was going to keep being reminded of him for a long time to come.

Shelby came up beside her, making her jump. "Cute, isn't it? A castle fit for a princess. Or a *Lady*."

There was an emphasis on the last word that made Cady look at her more closely. She laughed and said, "My work is done here—Lady Cady." Then she pointed to where a man was sitting higher up the beach, on the soft sand.

Cady held up her hand to shade her eyes from the sun as she looked. No...

"Go, for God's sake," Shelby said. "Jeez, he came all this way."

"Shut up," Cady told her, but the rush of adrenaline at seeing him made it impossible to copy her sister's faux-tetchy tone.

"You shut up," Shelby replied, smiling too. "Shut up and get over there, you lucky cow." She gave Cady a rib-crunching hug, then turned to make her way back up to the town, leaving them to it.

Chapter Forty-Four

C ady started toward him, her chest full to bursting, and he stood up, brushing the sand off his jeans. He had short hair, not spiky but kind of rumpled upwards, and he was clean-shaven. His t-shirt was blue, not black, without a logo, but it fit his body snugly, showing familiar broad shoulders and tanned, muscular arms. As she reached him he took off his sunglasses, and the warmth in his golden-brown eyes just about undid her. She swallowed, gathering her composure. It had been an emotional time lately.

"Hi," she said, cautiously, hopefully.

"Hi." There was that old tease in his voice, the tone that got her every time...including this time.

For a moment they stood, smiling at each other as though they'd lost the power of speech. It was strange seeing him here, so changed, and completely out of context.

"You look so different," she said, stating the glaringly obvious.

He ran his hand through his hair, mussing it even more. Was he nervous? "Yeah...it's the same old me though."

She had to know. If he couldn't tell her now, he might as well get right back on the plane. "Who *is* the same old you, anyway? Come on, surely you can tell me now."

He nodded, and she held her breath. What was she going to find out, finally?

"Okay...you waited long enough, that's for sure. I'm Reid, but I'm Daniel Reid. I work for the San Francisco Police Department. I was undercover with Flashpoint, using Kyle's involvement with the drug ring to gather info for a bust."

She stared at him. So many things made sense now. "So *that's* why you had cred with the weasels. I thought it was just a sign of extremely poor taste in mates."

"No. I think I have pretty good taste." He looked meaningfully at her, and she felt herself blush. "Gavin aside," he added, making her laugh.

"So that Crusty Demons meeting with Gavin wasn't a coincidence then. You weren't really friends."

"No, and yes. I couldn't help liking that doofus in the end." He grinned.

"I figured." You couldn't not like Gavin—for all his flaws, he was a really decent guy. She thought back to the flash mob riot, remembering how he'd urged them to get out of trouble's way. It reminded her of the shocking moment when she saw Reid heave the kid through the store window. "And the kid at the flash mob? In the window?"

"Yeah, not really a kid. He was in a rival operation, and just felt like taking on anyone associated with your weasels. Tensions run high in that world. Gavin happened to be in the firing line, so I stepped in. I didn't actually mean for it to be quite so dramatic, but..." He shrugged.

She thought about the implications of what he'd told her. "You must have been putting all your undercover work at risk to get Shelby out, when they took her and Kyle. Why did you do that?"

"Because, Lady Cady, you totally cloud my good judgment. You might have noticed that I can't help myself when you're around. And because there are a lot of things I'd do for you, and getting your sister back was one of them."

"Oh..." After all the days of wishing, it was hard to

believe he was actually saying these things, about her. She thought back to all the teasing and flirting, the almost and not-quite moments, the interrupted kisses that had driven her mad. "Yes, you were absolutely disgraceful. But...thank you."

"And you don't have to wonder about all the various things the police might want to talk to you about," he added. "It's sorted out. By the way, I'm glad that was his kneecap, and not mine. Nice shot, 99." He grinned.

"Oh, no." She grimaced. "That was terrible. Thank you for getting me off the hook." Then she looked at the Disney-worthy sandcastle. "So...you weren't a sand sculptor after all."

"Actually, I kind of was. It was ridiculous how that fake job took on a life of its own. I made quite a lot of money at it, but I couldn't keep it."

"Well, you're good at it." She held out a hand to the sandcastle, as proof. "So...what are you now? A regular police officer again?"

"Nope. I'm unemployed. Kyle was my last assignment. I've finished with all that—it's no good with Lily needing me, especially now she'll be with us full time."

She nodded. In any version of Reid, there was the good father. She liked that so much. At the same time, it made her nervous, because what if he wanted to be a father again? She probably couldn't go there, and that was something she didn't want to burden him with, let alone the whole getting sick thing. Not that she was assuming he was here with an eye on forever. Hoping, maybe. Assuming, no.

"But," he added, oblivious to her thoughts, "there is a kind of beach art I do. That pewter table you admired at my parents' house was mine."

"You *made* that?" She was genuinely impressed. "So you're the local artist your mum talked about. It was amazing."

He shrugged, carefully modest, but she could see he was pleased. "Thanks. It's fun. And it earns a bit of money too. They seem to have gotten popular."

"I bet." She regarded him, processing all this new

information, reconciling this new, neatly trimmed Daniel Reid, undercover cop, artist, with the Reid of her last few weeks.

"You okay?" he asked. "That's kind of a lot to lay on you."

"I don't think any surprise can throw me now," she said. "It's been a crazy few weeks. Big highs, and lows I never saw coming. One surprise after another, good and bad. You know, when I left for the States, I really wanted to change myself, be someone different. But it seemed like everything around me changed faster than I could."

"You don't have to be anyone other than yourself," he said. "That's the version of you I like."

"Oh..."

He ran a thumb gently across her lips, and they parted slightly. Then he leaned down and lay a whisper of a kiss on her mouth, sending a thrum of desire through her body.

"You know," she said in a slightly husky voice, "all the things I thought were the new Cady, were actually just the bits of regular me that I never set free before."

"Is that right?" he said, his tone teasing. "Which bits did you set free? Any bits I might be interested in?"

She laughed, feeling shy all of a sudden. "I think you already know."

"Humor me."

She took a breath. "Okay...the talking dirty on the phone bit. The fooling around in the back of a bus bit. Oh, and the pressing up against you until I feel you pressing against me bit."

He laughed. "That's one of my favorites."

"I kind of like it too." She stepped closer, still not touching him, but only a breath away.

"I think you need some practice though." His voice was low, gravelly.

She loved the new knowledge of her power over him. "I might have already forgotten how it goes," she teased.

"I haven't."

He leaned down and pulled her against him, pressing in a very convincing way, and kissed her—without hesitation, without any space between them, without secrets. The sea breeze caught her hair, the sand was warm under her toes, and the kiss was like the breath of life, every breath she wanted to take from here on. Life was short, but he was here, and she clung on, feeling her body warm and her heart fill again.

Then a seagull swooped over their heads with a whooshing kerfuffle, making them jump, and landed on the sandcastle tower. He sprang into motion to shoo it away.

"Can't have seagull poop on your castle, Lady Cady," he called back to her as he waved the bird off.

"That's for me?" she said, even though she knew it was.

"If it pleases you." He swept an arm out and bent at the waist, a parody of a bow.

"Oh, it pleases me very much." She put a finger to her lips, still tingly from the kiss. "You know how to please me."

He came back and reached for her again, drawing her close, and she dropped her shoes in the sand so she could hold him properly in return.

"Come back with me," he said. "I can't give you a real castle, but I'll try to give you the fairytale."

There was no joking in his tone, just the simple wanting of a man who knew what he needed, and was willing to risk asking for it. It was exactly what she wanted to hear, but alongside the joy was a doubt. She hesitated, then the words came tumbling out.

"What about the...you know, I have to be tested. You love Lily so much. I know we're not at that place, maybe we never will be, I'm not saying we will, but what if you want more and I can't give it to you? Or I get sick?" Heaven help her, she knew she was saying too much, but she couldn't stop herself. "I don't want to be a burden on you."

He shook his head. "And I might get Alzheimer's, or be run over by a bus, or go bald." She laughed at this, and he smiled, but then went back to serious. "You can only cross bridges as you come to them."

She thought of Jeremy, and how he'd bailed out. "It's

easy to say that now, but I think that bridge could be ahead. I'm not sure."

He shrugged. "There's no point in what-ifs. You have to give things a try, or you'd never do anything."

After her adventures in the last while, this resonated. "I've definitely been giving things a try lately. New starts are my specialty."

"Exactly. And we can't be sure of anything until it's right in front of us." He stepped back and took her hands in his, holding her steady in front of him. "And what I have in front of me right now is you, Cady. I don't know what the future will bring. But what I do know—what I'm sure of—is that I want you. The question is, what do you want?"

She looked into his eyes, the tiger eyes that got her every time, sparking her desire and distraction and longing even as they teased her, or watched her with an unreadable expression. He waited, holding his ground as she looked back at him, thinking about what she already knew to be true. All the crazy events of the last weeks, good and bad, were part and parcel of bringing her here. And even the events long before that—her mother's desperate decision, and her chance meeting in London twenty-five years ago with a young Holt, instead of some other man, was the start of Cady's own path from England to California and back to this beach, with this man, wanting her. How could she be second-guessing any of it?

"You," she said, finally letting her heart override her last fear. "I want you."

And she tiptoed in the sand to kiss him, sure that this was the new start she'd been waiting for.

Epilogue

S tinson Beach at this time of year was wild and rugged, the Pacific Ocean stretching into a cold grey infinity off the coast. Cady sat in a camp chair, rugged up in a thick jacket, with a blanket around her shoulders and ugg boots on her feet. Down in the hard sand, Reid was working, pouring molten metal into the mold he'd carefully dug out for another table. Alongside him were several burners, keeping pots of metal hot. Every now and then she caught the metallic smell as the breeze veered in her direction.

Lily was engrossed in digging too, a series of ditches around Cady's chair, filled with shells and sticks. Then she looked up, suddenly intent on something urgent.

"Can I have my ears pierced for my birthday?" she asked. "Please? I'm going to be seven, you know. And Violet can get her ears pierced too."

Cady looked at her earnest face, remembering how badly she'd wanted real earrings herself when she was little. "I know, chicken. Your dad and I will talk about it."

Even though she knew his real name, he'd always be Reid to her. And with Jody permanently in Canada now, all the day-to-day decisions were falling to him and Cady. She was pretty sure the answer to this question would be a yes.

Lily clambered up onto her knee and snuggled in, trying to get comfortable. "The baby gets in the way now," she complained.

"Sorry about that," Cady said. "He'll be out soon, though." She shifted Lily a little more sideways on her lap, making it snug for all three of them in the chair, and the little girl leaned in, keeping warm under the blanket too.

Reid came up, his heavy work pants and shirt covered in sand and flecks of metal. He pressed his arm to his forehead, hot from working with the scalding liquid.

"Okay, now we wait for it to cool." He bent down and kissed Cady, laying his fingertips on her belly. Then he pinched Lily's nose, making her giggle.

"Is the man in the gallery going to take this one too?" Lily asked.

"He is. He wants so many I can't keep up."

"You need to work harder," she said, making him laugh.

"You keep me too busy, Lily-Pilly."

She smiled up at him. "I like coming to the beach with you."

"Me too," said Cady. He was extra sexy here in his element, working up a sheen of sweat as he toiled on the sand, digging the delicate mold and handling the scorching liquid metal. The fact that the end result was exquisitely artistic only added to the attraction. And she wasn't surprised that his art was in demand, enough to earn a very decent living.

She'd put her freelance event management work on hold for now, but they'd be okay in the cottage under the hill, until they found a house for all four of them. Holt was excited to be a granddad, and wanted them to move closer, but they were staying in San Francisco. They liked being near Lily's grandparents and the other Flashpointers (even though Flashpoint itself was over, with Kyle having joined the weasels in jail for the next while), and being near the beach, where Reid's art took shape.

"Good things happen to us on the beach," he said now, his expression wicked as he looked pointedly at Cady's belly.

"You must *never* tell the baby," she instructed him sternly, but he just grinned, and she shook her head in mock despair. The hidden meaning went over Lily's head, as they knew it would.

"We should get married here," he added, making her heart ping with happiness. It wasn't totally out of the blue—even pre-baby, it was obvious they were heading that way—but he'd never mentioned anything in front of Lily. Now they smiled at each other, no need to spell it out. Her days of faking it were long past, and there was no mystery any more, only the sure truth of the simple, good thing they had together.

Then he bent down and picked up the plastic spade Lily had abandoned by her earthworks.

"Come on, Lily," he said. "Let's build another castle for Lady Cady. Remember we were talking about a double moat, to keep the dragons out?"

He started down the beach, but Lily hesitated. "Are you really going to marry Dad?" she asked, putting a finger on Cady's cheek.

"It seems like it, maybe," she said, watching closely to see her reaction. She would never take this little cherub for granted. Not this one on her knee, or the one growing safely in her belly. Safely, without any fear of growing up to suffer from Wodarski-Ebner. She'd been tested when she came back to the States with Reid, and the result came back negative. She should have had the test years before, of course, and saved herself a lot of doubt and heartache—heartache that was well and truly behind her now. It seemed monumentally unfair that she was in the clear, and not Shelby too. She was back in London working, living healthily now, and researching all kinds of alternative therapies. One good thing had come of all the drama since their mum died—despite being far away in miles, they were closer than they'd ever been.

Now Cady waited for Lily's response to the getting married idea. "Would that be okay with you?"

"He already asked me that," she said, winding a strand of Cady's hair around and around her finger. "It'd be different, I guess."

She nodded, elated to hear that he'd already checked in with Lily, but anxious that she should be okay with it. "Yes, a bit different. But mostly the same, really."

"That's good," she said. "'Cause I like it this way." She jumped down and dashed off to join Reid, waiting where the soft sand became firm.

"Me too," Cady said to herself, as she watched them start on the castle's foundations. "I like it this way too."

Thanks for reading *The Same But Different!*
For more information about Serena and her other books,
visit www.serenaclarke.com. While you're there, sign up
for her VIP newsletter to receive new book news, special
offers, and exclusive extras.

*Reviews help other readers find the kind of books they love. If you
enjoyed The Same But Different, please do consider leaving a
rating and comment at your favorite online retailer or review site.
Your review is greatly appreciated!*

Acknowledgements

Heartfelt thanks…

To my friends and family, at home and around the world—for all the encouragement and support, for leaping in to help with research, and for telling your own friends and family about my books.

To Adam, Nate, and Zach, for putting up with a wife/mother permanently glued to her laptop, and being proud of me all the while.

To the amazing Beta Babes—Alison, Carla, Dee, Julianne, Lauren, LaVerne, Liz, Maxine, Nicky, Paula, and Suzanne—for beta reading the first draft of the story.

To Vanessa, for proofreading the book, and for the happy geeky proofreader discussions.

And to the incomparable Unicorn girls: sweethearts, badasses, life changers. It wouldn't be the same without you.

Also by Serena Clarke

A North So True
All Over the Place
One Distant Summer

About the Author

Serena Clarke writes escapist romantic fiction set all over the world. Readers have described her books as engaging page-turners, with sigh-worthy happy endings that will leave you smiling.

Her own story? She's lived in thirty-nine houses, in seven cities, in four countries. She's been a riding instructor, edited a medical journal, worked at a London law firm, and taught English as a second language to wayward teenagers. And now she's found her own happy ending—living near the beach in beautiful New Zealand with her family, writing the kind of feel-good books she loves to read. She hopes you'll love them too!

Find her online at www.serenaclarke.com.

www.ingramcontent.com/pod-product-compliance
Lightning Source LLC
Chambersburg PA
CBHW032137190626
46814CB00005BA/1733